Praise for David Brin:

"David Brin excels at the essential craft of the page turning, which is to devise an elegantly knotted plot that yields a richly variegated succession of high-impact adventures undergone by an array of believably heroic characters."
— *Entertainment Weekly*

"David Brin is notable for unquenchable optimism, focusing on the ability of humanity to overcome adversity."
— *Los Angeles Times Book Review*

"Extrapolation of the highest and most subtle order."
— *Asimov's Science Fiction Magazine*

"Brin writes brilliantly conceived, intellectually supercharged novels."
— *The Sacramento Bee*

"He is a natural storyteller."
— *Orange County Register*

"Brin is not only prolific, but thoughtful and highly original."
— *Los Angeles Daily News*

INSISTENCE OF VISION

INSISTENCE
OF
VISION

a short story collection

DAVID
BRIN

THE
ST●RY
PLANT

The Story Plant
Studio Digital CT, LLC
P.O. Box 4331
Stamford, CT 06907

Cover art by Patrick Farley
Jacket design by Barbara Aronica Buck
Copyedited by Cheryl Brigham

Story Plant Hardcover ISBN-13 978-1-61188-220-9
Story Plant Paperback ISBN-13: 978-1-61188-221-6
Fiction Studio Books E-book ISBN-13: 978-1-943486-82-3

Visit our website at www.TheStoryPlant.com

First Story Plant Printing: March 2016
Printed in The United States of America

0 9 8 7 6 5 4 3 2 1

Dedication

For Vint, Elon, Freeman, Sergey, and Penn – world-changers needing
just one name...
...also Mark Anderson, Kevin Kelly, Peter Diamandis, and John Mauldin,
who do almost as much with two.

Also by David Brin

Brightness Reef
Earth
Existence
Infinity's Shore
The Postman
Sundiver
Startide Rising
The Uplift War
The River of Time
Otherness

Table of Contents

◇

WHERE WE WILL GO

WHY WE'LL PERSEVERE

Introduction

◇

By Vernor Vinge

I first met David Brin in 1980. At that time, *Sundiver* was already published. David was finishing up his Ph.D. at UC San Diego. (My years at UCSD did not overlap with his, but David was continuing the grand tradition of science fiction and fantasy writers who were at that university: Gregory Benford, Kim Stanley Robinson, Nancy Holder, David Brin, Vernor Vinge, Suzette Haden Elgin...I leave it to others to determine if this marks UCSD as a special source of SFF writers.)

The '70s and '80s were good years for science fiction in San Diego, with lots of writers and fans and frequent parties. I hadn't yet read *Sundiver*, but David pressed the typescript draft of a new novel into my hands. I politely accepted; I knew that *Sundiver* was a worthwhile book, so this new manuscript looked like a good story. There was only one problem. I *hate* manuscripts in manuscript form. I mean I hate to read them in that form. Maybe it's because that's what my own, incomplete works look like. Or maybe it's just that typescript manuscripts don't encourage a friendly reader/story relationship. The pages get lost (and sometimes are not even numbered). The homogeneous avalanche of double-spaced text conveys a promise of endless boredom. (But I admit, things are worse if there are lots of markups, or faint ink. And handwritten manuscripts occupy a still lower circle of hell.)

So there I was with this highly legible, but regrettably typescript, novel. It did have a cool title, *The Tides of Kithrup*. But I was very busy and six weeks went by and I hadn't had a chance to read it. David gave me a polite telephone call, asking if I had had a chance to look at his manuscript. "Well, no," I replied. "I'm sorry! Things have been so busy around here. Look, if you need it back right away, I can send it –" David short-circuited this evasion by saying, "Why don't you keep it another couple of weeks? Even if you can't read more than a part of it, I'd like to hear your comments."

Hmm. Okay, a *geas* had now been laid upon me. But it was a gracious *geas* that admitted of an easy observance. I could read fifty pages, give some honest comment, and be free once more. Of course, that was fifty pages of typescript manuscript by someone whose work I'd never read before. But hey, I could put up with that for an hour or so, right?

I dutifully set aside an hour and began slogging through the neatly double-spaced typescript… And after a few pages, magic happened. See, the pages became transparent. There was a world to play in. There was an adventure that accelerated me on past page 50, through the whole novel. You probably have read this novel yourself. It was published under the title *Startide Rising*. It won the Hugo *and* the Nebula for best science-fiction novel of the year. David went on to complete the Uplift series and later the new Uplift books. Along the way there were many other awards and award nominations. The novels have become a secure part of the SF canon of the twentieth century.

So no one can say that I can't recognize quality – at least if it's hard SF and nova bright. And I doubt if I will ever again look askance at type-script SF from David Brin

I later learned that David shows his draft work to a number of people. I show my drafts to four or five friends who won't bruise my ego too severely. David shows his to dozens of others. One of his favorite sayings is that "criticism is the most effective antidote for error." He surely lives by that in his writing. In fact, I think it takes a special clarity of mind to avoid the contending of "too many cooks" syndrome. I admire someone who can sustain that much criticism, and who also has such openness with his newborn ideas.

In the years since UCSD, David has had various day jobs, including university prof and astronautics consultant. Fortunately for us, his readers, he has not let that get in the way of his writing. We have many Brin novels to enjoy, across a range of lengths and topics. He once told me his strategy for *What to Write Next*. He liked to write a long, serious book (perhaps *Earth*?) and then something lighthearted and short and fun (such as *The Practice Effect*). I'm not sure that David is still following this strategy, since his most recent novel (as of September, 2002), *Kiln People*, is essentially both types of book at the same time.

David Brin's published writing career began with a very successful novel, *Sundiver*. Initially, I thought of him solely as a novelist. The success of his novels – and his novel series – may obscure the fact that all this time he has also been writing short fiction. And the amazing thing is that David Brin often does *even better* with short fiction than with novels! You'll get to see a few of his short stories in this volume. Others are available in Brin's published collections, *The River of Time* and *Otherness*. David's background in hard science and hard SF shows in these stories, but often in indirect ways, in setting the stage for seriously weird and sometimes disturbing points of view. Some of the stories are fairly transparent, such as the funny and logical and optimistic "Giving Plague." Others, such as "Thor Meets Captain America," are bizarre and effective fantasies. And then there is "Detritus Affected," which builds on simple words to create a reality that is disturbing and mysterious and percolates for days in your mind, until you may finally invent a context and consistency.

I have a friend who is a world-class inventor and engineer, about the closest thing you can get in the real world to the stuff of John W. Campbell's "scientist/engineer hero." This fellow likes science fiction very much, but recently he made the off-hand assertion that, contrary to what we SF weenies would like to believe, virtually *nothing* in science fiction has presaged the contemplation of similar ideas within the scientific and engineering communities. Fighting talk, that. His claim would make an interesting topic for a convention panel, where I think my friend could make a good cause for his position. At the same time, it's certainly true that science fiction has caught the imagination of generations of young people and drawn many of them into the sciences. Beyond that, a slightly more imperial claim is reasonable: Many SF writers are voracious skimmers of current science research. Their stories may cross specialty boundaries and act as tripwires to engage the attention of the real doers of the world. And since good stories involve emotions and social context as well as technical ideas, SF writers can have a greater impact than most other commentators.

Over the last twenty years, David Brin has certainly been this kind of inspirer. But in one way, David has gone beyond most of his fellows. He's written many essays about wider issues. Some are in this collection. The bright imagination that we see in his fiction carries over into his essays.

There is a subgenre of Brinnian essay writing that consists of moral criticism of fiction and drama. (See, for instance, the piece about romanticism and fantasy in this book.) This kind of essay may be a surprise to some people. "It's just a story!" they may say of the work that David is criticizing. It also takes a certain courage for a writer to undertake such moral criticism. I write fiction, and I know that sometimes the drama of a story may take it in directions that violate my vision of moral truth. Sometimes I can guide it back, but sometimes I surrender and say to myself, "It's just a fun story." (And at least once, I later ran into a fan who praised me because he found what I disliked to be morally *positive!*) In any case, I find such criticism to be extremely interesting. Such essays give an edge to issues that usually seem far removed from everyday concerns.

In much of his writing, David Brin looks at hard problems, the kind of problems that turn other writers to dark realism or blindly sentimental optimism. But David takes those problems, turns them sideways, and tries to see some *realistic* way that happy solutions might be found. The most striking and relevant example of this is his nonfiction book, *The Transparent Society*: Nowadays, we are confronted with the choice between freedom and safety. Technology has made appalling breaches of privacy possible, and the arguments on both sides of this state of affairs have become steadily more strident. Then David Brin comes along and says, "Well, what if we lost privacy, but the loss was symmetric?"

Maybe in the past this was an empty question, since surveillance technology favored asymmetry (and favored the elites). Nowadays however, it is quite possible that technology can support the "ordinary people" in watching the powerful...as well as each other. The resulting loss of privacy is a very scary thing, but there is an SF'nal tradition for considering it (for instance, the many stories from the '40s and '50s about widespread mental telepathy). The first years of such transparency would be very bumpy, but afterwards the world might not be that different – except that vice laws might be a little less obnoxious, and the worst of the bad guys might be more constrained. I would probably not buy into such a world – except that it may be by far the happiest outcome of our current dilemma.

At a more abstract level, David's novel, *Kiln People,* takes on the problem of duplicate beings. Here I don't mean biological clones, but near-perfect copies, even unto memories. This is the stuff of many SF stories (Damon Knight's *The People Maker,* William F. Temple's *The Four Sided Triangle*...). The concept has almost endless possibilities for abuse and tyranny and tragedy. In the past, stories about such duplication have been close to fantasy. More recently, with the possibility of AI and downloads, the idea has moved more into the realm of hard science fiction. We are nearing the time when the most basic "metaphysical" questions of identity and consciousness may have concrete and practical meaning. In *Kiln People,* Brin imagines a (marvelously non-computational) technology to achieve duplication. The resulting world is partly familiar and partly very strange. But – in the end – much of it seems more congenial than ours. I wrote a publicity quote for the novel. Normally it's hard to write blurbs that meet the exacting standards of publicists. Writing the quote for *Kiln People* was easy: Leaving aside the transcendental issues of the ending, *Kiln People* is simply the deepest light-hearted SF novel that I'd ever read.

There are very few issues that escape David's advocatorial interest. Many of his ideas are in the area of sociobiology, how we may harness the beasts within to be engines for good. Often his ideas are couched in flamboyant and colorful terms. (John W. Campbell, Jr. would understand!) Simply put, David is a brilliant *busybody,* forever enlisting those around him in projects that he sees will benefit everyone. Be aware of this. Be prepared to bail out with a polite "No on this one, David." But also be prepared to listen. Because almost always his ideas will contain sidewise thinking that just might make the world a better place.

The Heresy of Science Fiction

◇

What is Science Fiction?

Arguments fill books, resonating across hotel bars, internet discussion groups, and academic conferences. It matters for many reasons, not least because this genre encompasses just about everything that's not limited to the mundane here and now, or a primly defined past.

Up till the early 18th century, when Daniel Defoe, Samuel Richardson and Henry Fielding fed a growing appetite for "realism" in fiction, nearly all previous storytelling contained elements of the fantastic – from tribal campfire-legends to Gilgamesh and the Odyssey, to Dante and Swift. So why did literature change, about three centuries ago?

All through the long preceding period, *life and death* were capricious on a daily basis, but *society* seemed relatively changeless from one generation to the next – ruled by chiefs or kings or noble families, defined by the same traditions and stiff social orders. This era of personal danger amid social stability stretched on for millennium after millennium – during which epics overflowed with surreal, earth-shaking events and the awe-inspiring antics of demigods.

Then a shift happened. Peoples' physical lives became more predictable. Increasingly, from about 1700 onward, you and your children had a chance of living out your natural spans. But civilization itself started quaking and twisting with change. Your daughter would likely survive childbirth. But her worldviews and behavior might veer in shocking directions. Your son's choice of profession could be puzzling or even bewildering. Your neighbors might even begin questioning the king or the gods – not just in fables but in real life!

Amid this shift, public tastes in literature moved away from bold what-if images of heroes challenging heaven, toward close-in obsessions with realistic characters who seemed almost-like-you, in settings only a little more dramatic or dangerous than the place where you lived.

Having made that observation - and having pondered it for years - I'm still not sure what to conclude. Is there a total *sum of instability* that humans can bear, and a minimum they need? When uncertainty shifted a bit, from personal upheavals to the social and national scene, did that alter what we wanted from our legends?

Into this period of transformation, science fiction was born. The true grandchild of Homer, Murasaki, Shelley and Swift, yet denounced as a bastard from the start, by those who proclaimed (ignoring 6000 years of human history) that fiction should always be myopic, close, realistic and timidly omphaloskeptic, a trend that accelerated when "literature" became a field for high-brow academic dons. The possibility of social, technological and human change could be admitted... even explored a little... but the consensus on a thousand university campuses was consistent and two-fold.

Proper explorations of how change impacts human beings should:

1 - deal with the immediate near-term, and
2 - treat change as a loathsome thing.

This obsession is as unfair to fantasy as it is to science fiction. Indeed, as I said, nearly all pre-1700s storytelling incorporated fantastic imagery and other-worldly powers. Both fantasy and science fiction carry on that tradition, shrugging off the disdain and constraining prescriptions of parochial mavens.

But the two cousin genres part company over the matter of *time*.

Is Sci Fi the wrong name?

Certainly "science fiction" gives a false impression that the genre is about science. The image engendered is a nerdy one. And when people use zero-sum thinking, they often conclude: *"if these stories have a lot of brains, then they must lack heart."* A laughable dichotomy, if you've ever read works by Tiptree, Butler, Sturgeon, LeGuin or Zelazny.

Indeed, only about ten percent of SF authors are scientifically trained (as I am). It turns out that doesn't matter much, for two reasons.

First, some of the best "hard" SF dealing with truly cutting-edge scientific matters, has been written by former English majors, like Greg Bear, Nancy Kress and Kim Stanley Robinson, who could not close an equation if their lives depended on it. Their secret? To be fascinated by the times they live in! To seek out pioneers in any field, plying them with pizza and beer, till they explain something new and wonderful, in terms that any reader could understand. To go – literarily – where no writer has gone before.

Second, while few SF writers are scientists, nearly all of them devour *history*. It is the one topic nearly all of us immerse ourselves within, exploring the minutia and vast sweeping trends of times and generations that led up to ours.

Indeed, I've long felt that SF should have been named *Speculative History,* because it deals most often in thought experiments about that grand epic, the story of us. Sending characters into the past, or exploring alternate ways things might have gone. Or else – most often – pondering how the great drama might *extend further,* into tomorrow's undiscovered country.

Oh, we can make do with "science fiction" as the term for what we do. But *time* remains the core dimension, vastly more important to our stories, our passions, our obsessions, than technology or even outer space.

Where/when is your Golden Age?

Elsewhere I contrast two perspectives on the Time Flow of Wisdom.

By far dominant in nearly all human societies has been a *Look Back* attitude... a nostalgic belief that the past contained at least one shining moment – or Golden Age - when people and their endeavors were better than today. A pinnacle of grace from which later generations fell, doomed forever to lament the passing of Eden, or Atlantis, or Numenor.... You find this theme in everything from the Bible to Tolkien to Crichton - a dour reflex that views change as synonymous with deterioration. The grouchiness of grampas who proclaim that everything - even folks - had been finer in the past.

Compare this attitude to the uppity *Look Ahead* zeitgeist: That humanity is on a rough and difficult, but ultimately rewarding upward path. That past utopias were fables. That any glowing, better age must lie ahead of us, to be achieved through skill and science, via mixtures of cooperation, competition and negotiation... along with (one hopes) greater wisdom. And if we cannot build it, then our grandchildren might be worthy of the task.

The paramount example of this world-view would be - of course - *Star Trek*, though authors like Iain Banks and Vernor Vinge carry the torch of long-term optimism very well. Neal Stephenson's *Hieroglyph* project attempts to coalesce more writers around this tradition, encouraging belief in the potential of tomorrow.

Indeed, the notion of improvability used to be much more popular than it is now. Golden Age science fiction fizzed with belief in a better, hand-made tomorrow, a motif that has nearly vanished in the last decade or two.

Oh, don't get me wrong! The stylish rebels of the New Age SF movement were right to wield brilliant metaphors and splash cold water over the unabashedly uncritical, too-deferential worship of technological progress. If criticism is the only known antidote to error, science fiction (as we'll see) must be a veritable cauldron of criticism! By poking sticks into the path ahead, SF is a major source of error-detection, providing its greatest service.

Still, the genre retains this notion. That it is *possible* – perhaps just barely – that our brightest days may lie ahead. Indeed, that is science fiction's greatest trait, distinguishing it from almost all other genres.

The Fundamental Difference

No, I do not claim that all fantasy is about the past, nor does all sci fi explore the future. Certainly, a story or film's *tools* and *furnishings* don't decide whether a tale falls in one category or another. *Star Wars* is filled with lasers and spaceships, yet it is fantasy in every way that counts. The novels of Anne and Todd McCaffrey contain dragons and medieval crafts, yet Anne maintained, with vigor and great justification, that she wrote science fiction.

Putting aside superficialities, what difference flows much deeper than the choice of vehicles and weapons? Is there something basic?

Fantasy is the mother genre, going back to campfire tales and epics of knightly chivalry, with deep roots in the font of our dreams.

We've already commented that Science Fiction is the brash offshoot emerging from this ancient tradition. SF retains the boldness and heroic imagery, only then delivers a *twist*, having to do with human improvability. With its altered view of time, SF tends to locate its golden ages – if any – up ahead.

> Do you believe it is possible for children to learn from the mistakes of their parents? For them to become greater, wiser, mightier… and for them to raise a better generation, still?
>
> Whether or not they actually do this… and they often won't… is it at least possible?

The implicit notion is that children who ponder earlier mistakes might then do something even more unexpected. They might learn from some mistakes that are still *hypothetical*, by experiencing them vicariously in fiction!

By that token does science fiction claim a messianic power to alter destiny? Well, well. Below, I discuss the "self-preventing prophecy."

Even so – and supposing that our heirs (perhaps barely) overcome obstacles on their way to becoming better beings than ourselves, won't they thereupon forge on to make *new* mistakes, all their own?

We don't need the so-called "eternal verities" that are taught by lit-professors in a myriad universities. What we need is the agility to face an eternal onslaught of challenges, wrought by an endless tide of change.

I believe the root that defines science fiction is that word, *change*. SF rebels against all literary foundations by embracing the notion that disruptions happen. Upheavals can knock the props from under daily life, or social institutions, and even shake the characters' foundation beliefs. Sci fi deems it truly interesting to explore how people deal with that, for well or ill.

Even when a science fiction dystopia warns against *bad* change, it is relishing, exulting, expanding upon what Einstein called the *gedankenexperiment* or thought experiment. This process – seated in uniquely human organs called the prefrontal lobes – is what enables us to ponder the uniquely promethean question: *what if?*

And also - *if this happens how will you deal with it?*

Science fiction takes the thought experiment seriously.

New Definitions

Not that children always choose to learn from their parent's mistakes! When they don't, when they are obstinately stupid and miss opportunities, then you get a science fiction tragedy... far more horrifying than anything described in Aristotle's *Poetics*.

Take an older legend with many fantastic elements – *Oedipus Rex*. Aristotle describes the most compelling part of the tale of the ill-fated King of Thebes, how the audience must weep – and we do! – watching Oedipus writhe futilely against pre-ordained fate. Empathy and sympathy are there!

But not ambition. The playwright, players and watchers do not ponder: "Hey king, try this!" No remake or variation or sequel will visit justice upon the gods who appointed this tragedy. No one suggests a change in Olympian government.

And here is where we differ, nowadays. A science fiction tragedy can portray people suffering, just as in older tragedies – or with even greater angst, as when we feel the death of billions and the wreck of all hope, in *On The Beach,* or *The Road*. But there is this one crucial difference. The implication that things did not *have* to be this way.

It wasn't "fate." We – or the characters – could have done better! There was, at some point, a chance to change our own destiny. Tragedy ensued, when we failed to heed warnings. But that other path was possible. Children *might* have learned from their parents' mistakes.

One type of destiny makes you cry in sympathy. The tale of Oedipus is powerful stuff. But for millennia, the deep moral lesson – taught in all "Campbellian myths" has been – *resistance is futile*. The overall situation, absolute rule by capricious power, remains the same.

The new type of tragedy – a cautionary tale – may change your future decisions. It could alter destiny by setting an example – in fiction – of a failure mode that members of the audience then set forth (with grimly-set jaw) to correct! As millions who read *Nineteen Eighty-Four* vowed to fight Big Brother, and other millions who watched *Soylent Green* became fervent environmentalists.

Violating a core tenet of Aristotle, sci fi contemplates the possibility – even just a slim one – of successfully defying Fate.

The Rulers of Destiny

In contrast, what is the implicit assumption in most fantasy tales, novels and films? Apparently, the form of governance that ruled most human societies since the discovery of grain must always govern us. Royalty and lordly families. Priestly castes and solitary, secretive mages… the roll call of standard characters going back at least four thousand years.

Oh, in your typical fantasy kingly rulers may topple and shift, but the abiding assumptions and social castes generally do not.

(I will set aside, for now, some of the hybrid sub-genres like "urban fantasy" whose top practitioners, like the great Tim Powers, weave magical elements into an *attitude* toward knowledge and problem-solving that seems far more like science fiction. I deem this a very hopeful trend… if we can do without faux aristocratic and over-used vampires, please?)

Mind you, I'll never deny that fantasy has immense attractions, some that I have drawn upon, myself. Feudalism resonates, deep inside us. We fantasize about being the king or wizard; it seems to be in our genes. We are all – after all - descended from the harems of tough and perseverant fellows who succeeded at one goal: achieving the number one spot in that kind of system.

But for all the courage and heroism shown by fantasy characters across 4000 years of great, compelling dramas – including fine legends crafted by recent masters like Tolkien, Bradley, Martin, Rothfuss and Vance – what has happened by the end of these stories? Good may have triumphed over evil and the land's people may be happier under Aragorn than they would have been, under Sauron. Fine. But "under" is their only choice.

Ponder the *palantir* – a wondrous glassy object that lets Aragorn see faraway places, collect information and converse with viceroys across the realm. Does that sound at all familiar to you? In Gondor, *palantirs* are reserved for the elite. Mass-produced versions won't be appearing soon on every peasant's tabletop from Rohan to the Shire. (The way our civilization plopped such a miracle on *your* desktop.) Nor will peasants see

Gandalf producing libraries, running water, printing presses or the germ theory of disease. Only little Peregrin Took seems to grasp and demand a glimmer of alternatives, till he is bullied out of it.

The trend toward feudal-romantic fantasy may seem harmless. But I have to wonder why so of our few fellow citizens are interested – nowadays – in humanity's truest heroes. Heroes like Pericles, Franklin, Faraday, Lincoln, Pankhurst, Einstein and so on freed us from a horrid, feudal way of life that, ironically, seems so alluring to jaded modern eyes.

Rejection of Optimism

But let's be fair now. The deep river of nostalgia flows not just through fantasy novels and films, with their feudal images, chosen-ones, prophecies, and kingly lineages that rule by right of blood. Ever-more often, we've been seeing chosen-ones and dour gloom more often in sci fi, too.

Notions of human self-improvement... or ambition of any kind... are derided. Almost like an immunal rejection to the 1960s can-do spirit of *Star Trek*, wave after wave of authors and film directors seem to have "discovered" dark cynicism as a storytelling style, calling it fresh and original... as if they invented it. Tales about regret, navel-contemplation and disdain toward any semblance of optimism now seem to fill the sci fi magazines and awards nomination lists, with science fiction scholar Judith Berman diagnosing: "no more than a handful of stories... look forward to the future."

As critic Tom Shippey put it, in a Wall Street Journal review:

> As science fiction approached the millennium, it began to trade the future for the past and real worlds for fantasy or virtual realities. We've had "cyberpunk," with "biopunk" coming along a little uneasily behind... Other popular sci fi scenarios include alternate history ("looking backward," as if to wonder where things went wrong) and its nostalgic spin-off "steampunk" (fantasy with a history-of-science additive). The popularity of post-apocalyptic novels suggests that no convincing techno-future can be imagined.

Shippey's essay is insightful and important, though I do quibble with that last point. Progress isn't impossible to imagine. It just takes hard work.

Any lazy author or director knows this trick; it's astonishingly easy to craft a pulse-pounding plot and get your heroes in jeopardy - via either prose or film - if you start by assuming civilization is nonfunctional! That your fellow citizens are fools and all their hard-wrought institutions are run by morons. If accountability utterly fails and 911 calls are only answered by villains or Keystone Kops... and the Old Galactic Republic never does a single thing right... then you can sniff some coke and scribble almost any story-line. It writes itself! Bring on the special effects and heavy sighs over inevitable human doom.

No, I am not denouncing all works that express skepticism toward progress. Some do arise from stronger roots than mere cynical laziness. Among these are sincere and deeply-moving critiques of modern civilization's many faults. But here is where a delicious irony emerges. For, as we hinted earlier, the best and most savagely on-target critiques are helpful in moving us forward through the minefield of progress.

This is why genuine sci fi tragedies like *On the Beach* and *Dr. Strangelove* may (arguably) have helped to prevent nuclear war. *Soylent Green* (as we said) moved millions so powerfully that it helped to root the environmental movement. "This does not have to happen," say Huxley and Orwell and Slonczewski and Tiptree, in their masterful *self-preventing prophecies*. "Be smarter people. Be a *better* people."

It is still a rebel viewpoint! Far more tales preach the opposite sermon:

"Give up hubris and arrogant ambition: renounce so-called progress and the technologies that advance it. Seek wisdom in older ways."

I've explored both of these moods in stories and novels. Both can deliver great (or poor) art. But we should always be aware whether a story is trying to convince us to *try harder...* or to *give up*.

And yes, this has a context that extends far beyond mere literary genres. Suppose that optimistic or ambitious or targeted-warning stories like golden age sci fi really were a brief historical aberration? More broadly, what if the cynics are right that democracy, science and other freakishly creative innovations of the Enlightenment truly were temporary, or else delusions? That Darwin will always rule, after all, drawing us back into the dark, old ways?

Moreover, what if this pattern happens to everyone, not just on Earth but across the galaxy? Could *nostalgia and renunciation* explain the great silence that the SETI searches have found out there across the cosmos? Race after sapient race choosing to hunker in feudal – or pastoral or tribal or reverential or zen-like or whatever – simplicity, cowering away from ambition or the stars? After all, suspicion of change pervaded nearly every religious and mythic tale coming down to us from that long epoch preceding science fiction.

Some of it was great art! I've spent countless hours with Odysseus and Dante and Rama and the Monkey King. We can learn important things, both by heeding the lessons that ancient stories try to teach... and sometimes by reaching diametrically opposite conclusions.

Because *we* are the rebels. We who think that change might (possibly) bring good.

Nostalgists who doubt this are welcome to criticize! That searing light of rebuke is exactly what enables us to move forward, while avoiding the pitfall-penalties of hubris. Keep pointing out potential failure modes for us to take into account – and then evade as we forge ahead.

But let there be no mistake. Quenchers and belittlers represent the past. Ten thousand years from now, the stories that will be remembered will be those that encouraged.

The authors who say to us, convincingly... *let's try*.

WHAT WE MAY BECOME

◇

Insistence of Vision

◊

She's pretty-enough. Plump in that I-don't-give-a-damn kind of way. And *unblurred*. I can see her. That makes all the difference.

"Did you just visit the Dodeco Exhibit?" I ask, while she drinks from a public fountain.

Seems a likely guess. Her sleeveless pixelshirt shimmers with geometric shapes that flow and intersect with mani-petaled flowers, shifting red-to-blue and emitting a low audible rhythm to match. She must have copied one of the theme works on display in the museum, just up a nearby flight of granite steps, where I glimpse crowds of folks visiting the exhibition.

Wiping her mouth with the back of one hand, she glances up-down across my face, making a visible choice. Answering with a faint smile.

"Yeah, the deGorneys are farky-impressive. A breakthrough in fractalart."

Gazing at me without suspicion, she's bare-eyed – a pair of simple, almost retro, digi-spectacles hang unused from her neck. Clear augment-lenses glint in sunlight, here at the edge of Freedom Park. But the key feature is this: she's not wearing them. I have a chance.

"There's nobody better'n deGornay," I counter, trying to match the with-it tone of her subgeneration. Navigating with a few tooth clicks and blink commands, I've already used my own specs to sift-search, grabbing a conversational tip about neomod art.

"But I really like Tasselhoff. She's farknotic."

"You-say?" The girl notches an eyebrow, perhaps suspecting my use of a spec-prompt. I worry she's about to lift her own glasses... but no. She continues to stare-bare, cocking her head in mock defiance.

"You do realize Tasselhoff *cheats?* She ai-tunes the cadence of her artwork to sync with the viewer's *neural wave!* Some say it's not even legal."

Bright, educated, and opinionated. I am drawn.

Several blurs pass nearby, then a visible couple. The man sidles in to use the drinking fountain. So many people—it gives me an idea.

"But Tasselhoff does offer a unique... say, it's awful crowded here. Are you walking somewhere? I was strolling by the Park."

Ambiguous. Whichever way she's heading, that's my direction too.

Brief hesitation. Her hand touches the digi-spectacles. I keep smiling. *Please don't. Please don't.*

The hand drops. Eyes remain bare-brave, open to the world and *just* the world.

She nods. "Sure. I can take the long way. I'm Jayann."

"Sigismund," I answer. We shake in the new, quasi-roman fashion, more sanitary, hands not contacting hands but lightly squeezing each others' wrists.

"Sigismund. Really?"

"Cannot tell a lie." I laugh and so does she, unaware how literal I'm being.

I can lie. But it's not allowed.

She doesn't notice what happens next, but I do. As we both turn to leave the Museum steps, I glimpse the penguin-garbed man staring at me through his pair of specs. He frowns. Appears to mumble something...

...before he and his wife abruptly become blurs.

◇

Walking together now, Jayann and I are chatting and flirting amiably. Our path follows the edge of Freedom Park. We stay to the right as joggers pound along, most of them visible but some blurred into vague clouds of color—Collision-Avoidance Yellow. I hear them all, of course—barefoot or shod, blurred or unblurred—pounding along the trail, panting away.

I offer a comparison of deGornay to Kavanaugh, deliberately naive, so she'll lecture for a while as we skirt a realm of leafy lanes. Specs don't work in there. No augmentations at all. That's why it's called Freedom Park. Few would expect to find a creature like me at the edge of what, for me, is cursed ground. And that's why I come.

To my left the city roars with stimuli, both real and virtual, every building overlaid with meta-data or uber-info. I can tune my specs to an extent. Omit adverts, for example. But my tools are limited, even primitive. Half the buildings are just solid blocks of prison gray to me.

My walls.

No matter, I'm concentrating on what Jayann says. Her enthusiasm is catching. Even endearing. Mostly listening, I only have to comment now and then.

I hear voices and glance back, stepping aside for two hurrying adults—one of them a clot of vagueness, the other unedited and brave. Visible as a lanky-dark young man. My specs even reveal his name and public profile.

Wow. Just like in better times. Before I lost the power that everyone around me takes for granted.

Godlike omniscience.

"Well, I have get back to work," Jayann says. "I'll shortcut through here." She indicates a tree-lined path, clearly inviting me to come along.

"What do you do?" I ask, diverting the subject. I take two steps, following her. Already there's a drop in visual resolution. I daren't go much farther.

"I work in sales. But I'm studying art history so I can teach. You?"

"Used to teach. Now I help a public service agency."

"Volunteer work? That's farky and sweet." She smiles. Though backing down the path, she's starting to grow fuzzy. I'd better talk fast.

"But I manage to come here—to the park and Museum—every Tuesday, same time."

And there it is. Totally lame and stunningly old-fashioned, but maybe that will intrigue her.

She grins.

"Okay, Mister Mysterious Sigismund. Maybe I'll bump into you again, some Tuesday."

It's all I could hope for. A chance.

Then hope crashes. She grabs her specs.

"Wait. Just to be sure, let me give you my—"

"Say, is that a bed of gladiolas? This early?" I ask, purposely stepping past Jayann, walking down the path, counting steps and memorizing it as best I can. The Park's e-interference grows more intense. Then, abruptly, my specs cut off completely. I'm blind. But it's worth it if she follows. If that prevents her from looking at me through those glasses.

I keep walking, several more paces, toward the memorized flower bed. Bending over, I take off the now-useless ai-ware, pretending to look. But I chatter on, as if able to see bare-eyed, hoping she followed me down here, where specs don't work.

"You know, they remind me of that deGornay –"

"Bastard!"

A pair of fists hammer my back, then a foot slams into my knee from behind, sending me crashing into the shrubbery. Pain mixes with humiliated disappointment. And even worse...

... my specs are gone! I grope for them.

"How dare you!" She continues screaming. "You... you liar!"

My left hand probes among the crumpled flowers, searching.

"I... I never lied, Jayann."

"What were you planning? To get all my info, my address, to break in and murder me?"

"My crimes weren't violent. Look them up. Please, Jayann...."

"Don't you *dare* speak my name! What are you doing?"

"My specs. Please help me find them. Without them..."

"You mean these?" A rustling sound. Turning toward it.

"I can't see without them."

"So I've heard." Her voice drips with anger. "Instead of prison, take convicts and *blind* them. Let 'em only see what *special specs* deliver direct to the brain. So they can't see anyone who *chooses* not to let a criminal see them."

"Yes, but—"

"You stole that right from me!"

Against better judgment, I argue.

"You could have looked... with specs... seen my warning marks..."

She howls incoherent fury. I envision her there on the path, clutching my specs, shaking them. "I ought to smash these!"

"Please give them to me, Jayann... and guide me back to the street. I'll never bother you again, I swear...."

I try to sympathize with her sense of betrayal. But her rage seems extreme, for a social offense... charming a young woman into talking to me, bare-eyed, for a while. *Mea culpa.* I would pay for it. But did I deserve a pounding with fists? Screamed threats?

Making a best-guess, I run. Gravel underfoot for eight good steps, then grass. I correct, meeting path again...

...before tripping over her outstretched leg and sprawling face-first. "Jayann.... I'm sorry!"

"Not *half* as sorry as you're—"

I leap up, stagger forward again. There was a slope down from the street, I recall. And now I hear the joggers panting. Traffic sounds beyond. With that bearing, I run again.

No more hope of getting my specs back or reporting for work. My sole thought is to reach the sidewalk and then just *sit down*, pathetic and still. Word will reach my probation officer. Ellie will come get me. Lecture me. Possibly impose punishment. Though it's all recorded and I swear, I don't think I committed any actual—

Traffic noise is louder. Joggers curse as they weave around me. I wish I could see even blurs.

Someone plants a hand against my back and *shoves*. I hear brakes squeal.

◇

Lying in a hospital bed, I listen as Ellie explains about how lucky I am. What a fool I was. How close I came to breaking rules and lengthening my sentence. Or losing my life.

"Would you prefer a cell? The savagery of prison life? At least you can work. Pay taxes. Live among us."

That makes me laugh.

"Among you. Right. Among the blurs."

She lets that sit a while, then asks.

"Why, with so little time left on your sentence... why take such chances?"

How to answer, except with a shrug. Was Robinson Crusoe ever lonelier than I feel, here in the big city, imprisoned by electronic disdain?

Ellie takes silence as my answer. Then she tells me the final outcome of the fateful afternoon at Freedom Park.

◇

Months later, I see her at the museum. Jayann sits a few steps up from where we met. Despite a thick sweater, I can tell she's lost weight.

I slip on my new specs. Super-farky, they supply a wealth of information. God-like tsunamis of it. Nametags under every face that passes by, and more if I simply blink and ask for it. The basic right of any free citizen.

Under *her* name, flaring red:

CONVICTED FELON
Attempted 3rd degree murder

I almost feel guilty. My thoughtless, desperate, well-intended flirtations led to this.

But then, did anyone deserve what she tried to do, that day in a fit of offended pride?

As my own punishment chastened me—perhaps made me better—will she learn as well? There are second chances. There is second sight.

She looks around, seeming (except for those virtual scarlet letters) like a regular young woman, taking in the sun and breeze, though with a melancholy sigh. Her spec-mediated gaze passes over me...

...then onward. For to her, I'm just another blur.

I turn, leaning on my cane, to leave. Only then, glancing at the calendar within my virtuality, I realize.

It's Tuesday.

Story Notes

I like exploring complicated characters who are aware of the shaky moral tightrope they're trying to cross. At the same time, I also believe we will use technology in the future to alter our approaches to age-old problems. Imprisonment for crimes began fairly recently. For most of human history, felonies were not punished by long terms in prison. Societies simply couldn't afford it. Either your clan bought off your guilt-debt – or for a vast range of crimes, a felon was simply executed. Prison terms for non-capital crimes were a step forward, offering some chance for rehabilitation, but our descendants will likely consider it barbaric. Nothing comes without a cost.

Are there alternatives? Beneath an intimately tragic personal story, "Insistence of Vision" explores one plausible – if creepy – possibility. Its advantages and attractive aspects only make it creepier. Our children will face interesting decisions.

This tale first appeared in the special 2013 Science Fiction issue of MIT's *Technology Review.*

Next comes a lighter tale, though still about technology changing things we take for granted. And how one thing changes more reluctantly than anything else –

– our obstinate human nature.

Transition Generation

◇

"I don't know how much more of this day I can take. I swear, I'm *this* close to throwing myself out that window!"

Carmody yanked his thumb toward the opening, twenty-three stories above a noisy downtown intersection. Flecks of rubber insulation still clung in places, from when old Joe Levy first pried it open, during the market crash of '65. Fifteen years later, the heavy glass pane still beckoned, now gaping open about a hands-breadth, letting in a faintly traffic-sweetened breeze. A favorite spot for jumpers, the window seemed to beckon, offering a harried, unhappy man like Carmody the tempting, easy way out.

They should have sealed it, ages ago.

Though really, would that make a difference?

"Tell somebody who cares," snarked Bessie Smith, who managed the Food & Agriculture accounts via a wire jacked into her right temple. She allocated investments in giant vats of sun-fed meat from Kansas to Luna, grunting and gesturing while a throng of little robots swarmed across her head, probe-palpating her chin, cheeks and brow, crafting her third new face of the day. Carmody still found the sight indecently discomforting. A person's face ought to be good for months. And the transforming process really should be private.

"Yeah, well *you* don't have to handle the transportation witches," he retorted. "They've stuck me with a doomed portfolio that… aw hell!"

Symbols crowded into Carmody's perceptual periphery, real-time charts reporting yet another drop in Airline futures. His morning put-and-call orders had wagered that the industry's long slide was about to stop, but *there they go again!* Sinking faster than a plummeting plane. At this rate, he could forget about a performance bonus for the sixth week in a row. Gaia would sigh and cancel her latest art purchase, then wistfully mention some past boyfriend.

And she could be right, fellah. Maybe your wife and kid would be better off…

As if summoned by his glowering thought, Gaia's image sprang into being before his tired gaze. Her dazzling virtual aivatar shoved aside dozens of graphs and investment profiles that, in turn, overlay the mundane suite of homely office cubicles where Carmody worked. At least, he assumed that the ersatz goddess manifesting in augmented reality was Gaia; her face looked similar to the woman who sat across from him at breakfast this morning, bleary-eyed from all-night meetings with fellow agitators on twelve continents, fighting to extend the Higher Animal Citizenship Laws one more level, this time below that of seals and prairie dogs.

So what next? Voting privileges for crows and cows and canids? How was that going to work, again?

Now apparently back in fine fettle, Gaia shone at him with active hair follicles framing her head like sea-weed, while rippling from blonde to brunette and rainbow shades between. A blast of enhanced charisma-from-a-bottle made Carmody curse and shut off the smell-o-vision feature of his immersive goggles.

She knows I hate that.

His wife made a pointed gesture with one, upraised finger. Gaia's aivatar waved the finger like a wand, casting forth a series of reminder blips:

> STOP AT AUTODOC TO ADJUST YOUR IMPLANTS.
> FIX THAT DAMN MALFUNCTIONING MOOD FILTER!
> ELDER-CARE SAYS PICK UP YOUR DAD, OR WE'LL PAY STORAGE OVERCHARGES.
> GET EGGS

Carmody winced, hating whoever invented avatar-mail, endowing the voluptuously realistic duplicates with artificial intelligence. Of course, he *could* spend time mastering the latest tricks… like assigning an aivatar of his own to reply automatically, fending off work interruptions....

Maybe I can hire a service to set it up for me, he thought, trying to will her image to a far-back corner of the percept. *Mr. Patel will have my hide if I don't file my report on transportation trends. I still think they indicate a turnaround in air freight that —*

Resisting his efforts to dismiss her, Gaia's aivatar clung to one of his maglev-zep performance charts, continuing to wand a series of chiding reminders while his impatient, leave-me-alone wind pushed her backward. That chart collapsed and surrounding data got caught up in the meme-storm as she blew backward in a blur of data-splattered robes.

All of a sudden, Carmody's percept reached some kind of overload. One corner contorted as graphs and prospectus appraisals started whirling around each other, crumpling into a funnel-cyclone, like dirty water circling a drain, sucking away his entire week's labor — and his wife's protesting analogue — vacuuming them all toward some unknown infosphere singularity.

"Cancel!" Carmody shouted. "Restore backup five minutes ago!"

He kept grunting and issuing frantic commands but nothing worked. Reaching and grabbing after the maelstrom, he did something wrong, some mis-cued gesture, triggering a cyber lash-back! Searing bolts of *lightning* seemed to lance between his eyes.

Shouting in pain, Carmody tore off the immersion goggles, clutching them in both hands. Laying his face onto the cool surface of the desk, he suppressed a sob.

I used to think I was so hip and skilled with specs and goggs. Only now, kids are replacing them with contaict lenses and, even eyeball implants that juggle ten times as much input.

Can I really be so obsolete, so soon?

"Bob?" A real voice, grating in his real ears. "Bob!"

Even worse, it was Kevin's voice. Standing next to the desk.

Carmody didn't move.

"Are you okay, Bob? Is there a problem, man?"

Glancing up, eyes still smarting and misty, Carmody shook his head.

"Fine. Just resting a sec," he put up a brave face of complacent humor, knowing better than to show any weakness to this young jerk, supposedly his assistant, but clearly angling for Carmody's job. Still, an inner voice moaned.

I can't take this anymore.

"Well, I'm glad of that," the younger man said. But a smug expression told Carmody everything. The breakdown of his percept and loss of all that work… he suddenly knew it was Kevin's doing! Some trick, some hackworthy sabotage that Carmody would never be able to prove.

Does he have to gloat so openly?

Still smirking, Kevin continued.

"I thought I better let you know, Mr. Patel is on his way down. He wants a word with both of us." Kevin's look of eager anticipation was so blatant, Carmody had to quash a sudden, troglodytic urge to erase it with his fist. *Kevin might have at least learned some surface tact, if he had gone to university or worked at a regular people job. But no. His generation just absorbs technical skills directly, like suckling from a —*

The right metaphor wouldn't come, no matter how hard he beckoned one. And strangely, that was the last straw for Carmody.

Enough is enough.

"You look terrible," the younger man added, with faux concern. "Maybe you better visit the loo and clean up, before… Bob? Mr. Carmody? Where are you going? Mr. Patel wants…"

Carmody had one hand on the window pane and the other on its frame. Staring through the gap and down twenty-three stories, he inhaled deeply, feeling resolution build, overcoming the panic, layering upon the panic, *amplifying* his sense of panic into something that abruptly felt more manly.

Determination.

Time to end this.

Carmody felt eyes turn this way as the window swung wide and his left foot planted on the sill, pushing till he stood, teetering along emptiness.

"Bob. What're you doing?"

Carmody glanced back and smiled at his co-workers, none of whom rose to stop him.

"I'm taking the easy way out."

And — after inhaling one more deep breath — he jumped.

Carmody's gut roiled with caveman terror as the first few floors swept by — an unpleasantly inconvenient reaction. But at least his life didn't pass before him.

He knew he should be composing himself, but as wind stung his eyes and tugged his hair, a distracting shadow encroached from an unexpected direction. Carmody flinched aside in time to see another figure hurtling Earthward. Business suit flapping, clenched fists outstretched as if trying to outrace Carmody to the pavement. He recognized Dickerson of accounting.

Well, that sonovagun always seemed much too-tightly wound.

Oh? An honest part of himself replied. *And what are you? Taking the coward's way out.*

Carmody told his busy, frantic mind to shut the hell up and to focus on what mattered, with so little time left. *Only does anything at all matter, at this point?*

Abruptly, he heard someone else speak. A shout, overcoming the throbbing wind, but conversational, nonetheless.

"Dickerson is such a maroon! I was at the same meeting when Mr. Saung told us all to jump. But you don't see me showing off like that!"

He glanced left to see a woman dressed in the slick, pinstripe uniform of a company attorney. He'd seen her around. Instead of plunging superhero-style, she had arms spread like Carmody, delaying the unpleasant inevitable. A rightward eyeflick detected no sign of Dickerson, plunging on ahead. So now it was the two of them.

Told you to jump? Boy, that Saung is a hard case. Much worse than Patel. In fact, maybe I should have stayed and fought it out....

Carmody almost replied to the woman – some dark humor about falling *with* her, not *for* her. But no. He saw her frown, devoting herself to a look of concentration. preparing for the fast-looming street.

That's what I should do.

Grimly, Carmody strapped the goggles back onto his head. Bearing down and gritting his teeth, he mentally recited a personal chant.

I am a son of light. I am a son of light. I am a son of light...

Nothing. Opening his eyes briefly, he saw that he was halfway to the ground, with much *less* than half the time left before... going splat upon the broad apron that now surrounded every downtown building, protecting pedestrians and vehicles from plummeting jumpers who missed their cues.

Splat. Me? Come on, focus!

I am a son of light. I am a son of light. I am a son of light...

He tensed specific muscles in his arms, back and thighs – and felt electric tension course along his spine, at last. A crackling that was molten, electric and fey, all at the same time, seemed to fizz from every pore. It hurt like hell! But he kept up the mantra, frowning hard and willing power into his fists. His feet.

I am a son of light. I am a son of light. I am a son of light...

From his scalp implants to the tips of Carmody's toes, power erupted, along with pain.

I am a son of light... and I can fly!

Bottoming out just a couple of stories above the splat barrier, he caused second floor windows to shake with the roar of his passage.

Carmody flew....

◇

...and almost collided with half a dozen others, amid a throng zooming above Broadway. Carmody's percept throbbed with warning shouts and small fines applied against his commuter account. But he managed to maintain concentration, leveling off and settling into an uptown flight path without injuring anyone.

Damn, no wonder they say you should always use a standard launching catapult. Skyscraper-jumping is for idiots! Or, at least, folks who aren't out of practice like you, fool.

He turned onto Seventh Avenue, banking in a wide swoop that gained altitude as well. It almost felt... *fun,* for just a bit, though the tight maneuver made his stomach tense and churn.

Okay then. What had Gaia reminded him to do? Assuming he was about to be fired from his job and become a house-husband, he might as well at least cover the checklist.

Oh yeah right. Pick up Dad.

Carmody turned back on the goggles' aroma detectors and followed a scent of liquid nitrogen. He carefully descended to a low-slow lane, barely dodged impact with a skylarking vette, and did a body tuck to land squarely in the catcher's mitt at Seventh and Fifty–Eighth Street.

With ringing ears and scraped palms, Carmody unrolled and dusted himself off, as body-repair implants swiftly dealt with the usual bruises, though not without harsh twinges.

"Hey, watch out!" came a cry from above. He hurriedly stepped aside to make way for the next flying person, coming in for a semi-crash-landing.

"There's got to be a better way," Carmody muttered under his breath. "Sometimes I wish we still had subways."

Ten minutes later he had signed at the desk for his father. The old man was tucked into a carrier pouch, strapped to Carmody's chest. Awkward and heavy, but with room left to stuff in that carton of eggs.

If I took the car, I'd have to pay ecobal fees and parking… but I'd also have a spare seat to strap him into. Or the trunk. Oh, well, being unemployed will have compensations.

He took an elevator to the fifth floor catapult room, paid his dime and stood in line till it was his turn. Enviously, he watched some teenagers hustle past the people-launcher to an open air platform, where each one took a running start and then *sprang* into the sky. Well, of course anyone could do that, if you had plenty of free time to practice… and the agility of youth. Why, twenty years ago Carmody had been quite a big deal at his local hoverboard park. And he wondered if anyone still used them anymore, so graceful, silent-smooth. And it didn't *hurt* when you rode a board! Only when you fell off.

"I am a son of light," he murmured, preparing his mind for the coming jolt-and-fling, always disagreeably jaw-jarring. "I am a son of light."

"You're MY son," groused a voice within the carrier pouch. *"And need I remind you that it's dark in here?"*

Carmody rolled his eyes.

"Hush dad. I gotta concentrate."

But he unzipped the pouch to a safety stop, so his father's gel-frozen head could look out a bit. And despite further parental commentary, Carmody focused on the mantra, controlling his implants much better this time, with less emotion and less pain, as the robot attendant held a taut saddle for him.

"I am a child of light…"

This catapult needed tuning, alas. It flung him with a nauseating initial spin. Fighting to correct, Carmody gritted his teeth so hard he wondered if chipped one. This time, at least, he managed to enter traffic without incurring too many micro-fines.

"I can fly… I can fly…" he convinced himself, while roaring ahead, weaving two hundred meters above the street, tired but homeward bound.

"I… can… fly…"

◇

Dad just had to keep kvetching.

"You call this traffic?" he demanded, after Carmody complained for the third time, while cruising over the southwest corner of Central Park. "When we first moved to this city, during the Big Reconstruction, only taxis and buses could fly! And just in narrow lanes! At least once a month, some fool would do a forced landing onto the groundstreet, clogging things, almost like the traffic jams you see in old movies. Now, just look at you punks, complaining about getting to flit about like gods!"

Carmody glanced toward the free zone above the Lake, where no rules held – where fliers darted about with abandon, doing spirals, spins and loops. Sure, that looked kind of god-like, if you thought about it. Maybe Dad had a point.

But miracles don't seem that way, when they become real life chores.

"Like my own Pa used to bitch and moan about his airplane flights." Dad's voice – or a reasonable facsimile, querulous and chiding – emerged from the encapsulating globe. Now transformed from expensive cryo-cooled to economical plasticized-state, he wasn't even legally a person, the comments produced by an inboard AI whose algorithms query-checked their estimated reactions against the billions of neurons in Dad's gel-sta-bilized brain, staying relatively true to what he *might* have said, in real life.

"My Pa would fly from Raleigh to Phoenix on business and then back in two days, eating peanuts and watching movies while crisscrossing a continent that *his* great-grampa took a year to cross by mule, and almost died! But all he could talk about were narrow seats and luggage fees. And having to take his shoes off. Went on and *on* about that!"

Yep, this sure sounds like my old man – the same lectury finger-waggings, without fingers. And if I hadn't promised to keep him on the mantel, for at least ten years, I'd find that lake over there an attractive place to dump his nagging skull, right about now.

But Carmody knew he wouldn't. At current rates of neuroscience progress, within a decade the emulation would be much better, perhaps simulating the old guy's better, deeper side, maybe even some wisdom, too. And perhaps, someday, the glimmering, ever-alluring promise of "uploading" to wondrous realms of virtual reality. *If I want my own kids to take care of my head, I suppose I should set an example.*

Anyway, wasn't this just another example of what Gaia had been nagging him about, lately? A crappy attitude, taking everything too hard. Over-sensitivity to life's inevitable harsh edges. An imbalance of grouchy sourness over joy. Okay, things weren't going too well, right now. But something was definitely wrong *inside*, as well, Carmody had to admit.

He'd been resisting adjustment, and no one on Earth could force him. *I can straighten out all by myself,* he grumbled, knowing how puritan and old-fashioned it sounded.

They used to prescribe drugs. He shuddered to imagine what an un-subtle bludgeon that must have been. Nowadays –

I suppose it wouldn't hurt to adjust my implants just a little, to let me see a picture wider than just downsides. So I can choose to cheer up a little easier. Especially if I'm going to be looking for another job. Be a better husband and father. Maybe go back to my music. Or at least concentrate better when I have to fly!

On impulse, Carmody swung left at Eighty-Third and cruised between condominium towers with their own landing ledges on every floor. Wary for incautious launchers, he slowed to a near hover at the end of the block, exertion stinging his eyes as he looked down and west at PS43, where little Annie attended second grade.

The school's protective force field shimmered like reflections off the Hudson, a kilometer further west. A brilliant safety feature, invented just in time to give parents some piece of mind that their children were safe from harm – the dome sparkled every time an object crashed into it at high speed, erupting with half-blinding brightness whenever the impact was especially hard. In just the few seconds he had been watching, dozens of flashes forced Carmody to damp down the filters of his goggles.

Thank heavens for the dome.

WHAM! Another collision, as a student slammed against the inner surface, caroming amid a cascade of electric sparkles before zooming off again, to swoop and cavort amid some incomprehensibly complex playground game. Giving chase, a girl sporting red boots, garish epaulets and a ponytail struck the force-field with her feet, amid a shower of sparks. Crouched legs helped her spring off again, in hot pursuit.

Carmody had no such endurance. Concentrating, biting his lip, he managed touchdown at a flier's platform on the condominium building's roof. Then he stepped to the edge, muscles and nerves twitching.

Kids. Their generation already takes it all for granted. They're the ones who'll roam the sky with real freedom, painless and comfortable – all of them – with the powers of superheroes. He sighed. *I just hope some of them appreciate it, now and then.*

He looked for Annie... and the goggles picked her out from the recess throng. A small figure, dark hair kept deliberately natural, though with a tidy ribbon, she flew amid a formation of friends, in a calmer, less frenetic game.

Annie's own specs must have alerted her to the parental presence, because she split off from her pals, doing a lazy dolphin glide just inside the closest part of the barrier, back-stroking, giving Carmody a wave, a smile. It filled his heart so swiftly, in such a heady rush, that he actually swayed.

Then a bell sounded. Recess ended. Juvenile implants tapered down, damped by teacher control, forcing them to land. He stood there, intending to watch till Annie filed back inside the school... only then Carmody's phone rang. A curt, businesslike summons, impending at the left edge of his percept.

The boss. Crap. And just when I was remembering how good life is. Well, let's get this over with. I was a company hotshot till last year, so there ought to be a decent severance.

Mr. Patel's image wasn't aivatar but true-view, beamed from his office. Carmody grimaced, knowing that his own glowering expression would be conveyed to the manager, and not caring much. Resigned, he felt determined to face what was coming, with dignity.

Look, I know this wasn't a great day... he was about to start. But Patel spoke first.

"Bob, I wish you had stayed, but I understand your reasons. Look, I know things haven't been great, lately... I didn't pay close enough attention to personnel dynamics and I thought you were exaggerating your concerns about Kevin. But his stunt today proves you were downplaying, instead –"

Carmody interrupted.

"Then you know it was his doing –?"

Patel shrugged. "Sure. Oh, he used a new grilf trick that's hot on the streets, right now. But come on! Like we don't have people out there, hovering over the new? Arrogant putz, his worst sin was having such a low opinion of our skills!"

"Huh... then my work..."

"I've got the report. It needs several polishes before I take it upstairs, but I think your trend analyses are unassailable. You just underestimated market obstinacy. It needs a phase factor of at least two weeks to take into account how everyone holds on to their biases and assumptions for dear life. But we can pounce on the transport upswing in ten days. Good work! You'll have my notes for those polishes by the time you get home."

Carmody reversed his own assumptions. Instead of asking about his severance package, he decided to switch tracks.

"Not tonight. It's been a rough week and I'm decompressing. Taking the family out for a sunset picnic and a fly-stroll. Tomorrow can wait."

If Mr. Patel wanted to demur, he quashed it quickly.

"Well, okay. Tomorrow then. Only fly carefully, will you? I just replayed your jump today... *everybody* has. They're calling you Mister Almost-Splat!"

Carmody couldn't stave off a wry smile. That sort of nickname could do a fellow good, in his line of work. Nobody would call his bluff for a while.

"Tomorrow then," he replied, before signing off.

He glanced again at PS43, now quiet under its almost-invisible protective dome. It was still another hour and a half till school would let out. Annie was in a carpool, anyway, so no need to wait around. In that case – maybe he could make it home in time to surprise Gaia. That is, if anything ever surprised his wife.

Carmody looked westward across the expanse of roof and pondered. The nearest public catapult was a block away... and Mr. Almost-Splat was feeling pretty daring, right about now.

"Son, are you sure you want to..." asked the gel-stabilized head of his father. Then the old man's gelvatar wisely shut up, letting Carmody concentrate as he sped along the rooftop toward the farthest edge.

We'll have our revenge, he thought while his legs pumped hard, picking up speed. *The best kind of revenge, for having to watch our kids surpass us in every way. The satisfaction of watching their children surpass them!*

Heck, I'll bet Annie's son or daughter will come equipped with warp drive!

But they'll bitch and complain about it, all the same.

Suddenly filled with fire and pain and a volcanic sense of utter thrill – a child of light launched himself over the parapet-edge with a shout, toward the great, orange ball of a settling sun.

Oh yes, he added. *Eggs.*

Mustn't forget eggs.

Story Notes

One of humanity's great talents is adaptability. We can get used to almost anything. Indeed when I teach writing, I try to get students to grasp how much of a strange situation — perhaps one that is far away in space or time or technology or even species — you can convey simply by showing what your protagonist takes for granted. If something is happening that the reader finds weird, she will feel more curiosity if the main character finds the event somewhat *normal!* That mere fact speaks volumes about the character, about the world-situation, and so much more — without having to do any explaining at all.

In "Transition Generation," that trait of growing-accustomed is taken to an extreme. Indeed, it is the story's topic.

How is it that we early 21st Century moderns — beneficiaries of so much success and wonder — almost never pause to notice how far we've come? Standing on the shoulders of countless generations who worked themselves to the bone, so that we might become (at least in their gaze) quasi-gods? The answer to that question is simple. Our job and task is not to wallow in pleasure or appreciation. It is to strive! To move life and civilization forward — by dint of sweat and worry and hard work — the same as earlier generations did for us.

There is always a crisis! There will forever be obstacles, problems to overcome... or, upon failing, try something new.

And yet. Try this. *Notice* on some warm day when you hear a grumble-rumble in the sky. Pull over to the side of the road. Open your window. Glance at the winged aluminum tube that is cruising by, up there. And imagine what nearly all of your ancestors would think, right now. Stop and blink and look again. Those are your tribe-folk up there. And some time during the next year it will be you.

We may go to the stars someday. And I envy those bright souls. But we do fly.

Next, a more serious... and scientific... tale about another kind of transcendence.

Chrysalis

*L*ike every person who ever contemplated existence, I've wondered if the world was made for me — whole and new — this very morning, along with counterfeit memories of what came before.

Recollection is unreliable, as are the records we inherit each day. Even those we made the night before — our jotted notes or formal reports, our memorials carved deep in stone — even they might have been concocted, along with memories of breakfast, by some deity or demon. Or by an adolescent 28th Century sim-builder, a pimpled devil, playing god.

Find the notion absurd?

Was that response programmed into you?

Come now. History was written by the victors, while losers passed their entire lives only to serve as brief speedbumps. And aren't all triumphs weathered by time?

I sound dour. A grumpy grownup. Well, so it goes, when tasked with cleaning messes left by others. Left by my former self. And so, with a floating sigh of adulthood, I dive into a morass — records, electronic trails and "memories" that float before me like archaic dreams. Ruminations of an earlier, ignorant — not innocent — me.

It all started medically, you see. With good intentions, like so many sins.

◇

January 6, 2023: Organ replacement. For a generation it was hellishly difficult and an ethical nightmare. Millions lingered anxiously on waiting lists, guiltily *hoping* that a stranger out there would conveniently crash his car — someone with identical histocompatibility markers, so you might take a kidney or a liver with less probability of rejection. His bad luck transforming into your good fortune. Her death giving you a chance to live.

Even assuming an excellent match, there'd be an agony of immuno-suppressant therapy and risk of lethal infections. Nor was it easy on us doctors. When a transplant failed, you felt you were letting *two* patients down, both recipient and donor.

Sci fi dystopias warned where this might lead. Sure enough, some countries started scheduling criminal executions around the organ want-list. Granting reprieves till someone important needed a heart... your heart. Then, off to disassembly.

When micro-surgeons got good enough to transplant arms, legs and faces – everything but the squeal – we knew it was only a matter of time till the Niven Scenario played out. Voters would demand capital punishment for more than just heinous crimes. Your fourth speeding ticket? Time to *spread you around*. Is it really death, when nearly all your parts live on, within a hundred of your neighbors?

Hell gaped before us. There had to be a better way.

And we found it! *Grow new parts in the lab*. Pristine, compatible and ethically clean.

> *Caterpillar eat! Chew that big old leaf.*
> *Ugly little caterpillar, your relief,*
> *When you've chomped your fill, will be to find a stem.*
> *Weave yourself a dressing room, hang in it, and then*
> *Change little caterpillar, grow your wings!*
> *Now go find your destiny, nature sings.*

When we started trying to regrow organs *in situ*, George Stimson claimed the process would turn out to be simple. He offered me a wager – ten free meals at his favorite salad bar. I refused the bet.

"Those are your stakes? Lunch at the Souplantation? Acres of veggies?"

"Hey, what's wrong with healthy eating? They have the genuine stuff."

"My point exactly, George. Every time we go there, I look at a plate full of greens and think: *this* is what *real* food eats!"

He blinked a couple of times, then chuckled at my carnivorous jibe before swinging back to the main topic – building new human organs.

"Seriously. I bet we can get away with a really simple scaffold. No complicated patterns of growth factors and inhibitors. None of *this* stuff."

He waved at the complex map of a human esophagus that I had worked out over the weekend – a brilliantly detailed plan to embed a stretchy tube of plastic and collagen with growth and suppression factors. Along with pluripotent cells, of course, the miracle ingredient, cultured from a patient's own tissues. Some of the inserted chemicals would encourage the stems to become epithelial cells *here* and *here*. Others would prompt them to produce cartilage *there* and muscle-attachment sites *here* and *here* and...

...and George thought my design way too complex.

"Just lace in a vascular system to feed the stems," he said. "They'll do the rest."

"But how will they know which adult cell type to turn into?" I demanded. "Without being told?"

This was way back near the turn of the century, when we had just figured out how to take skin or gut cells and transform them back into raw stems, a pre-differentiated state that was *pluripotent* or capable of becoming almost any other variety, from nerves to astrocytes to renal... anything at all! Exciting times. But how to assign those roles in something as complex as a body organ? We had found specific antigens, peptides, growth factors, but so many tissues would only form if they were laid out in ornate patterns. As complex as the organs they were meant to rebuild or replace.

Patterns we were starting to construct! Using the same technology as an ink-jet printer, spray-forming intricate 3-D configurations and hoping to someday replicate the complex vein patterns within a kidney, then a spinal cord, and eventually...

"We won't have to specify in perfect detail," George assured me. "Life will find a way."

I ignored the movie cliché. Heck, why not try his approach in a pig or two?

We started by ripping out a cancer ridden esophagus, implanting a replacement made of structural polygel and nutrients. This scaffolding we'd lace with the test animal's own stem cells, insert the replacement....

Whereupon, voila. Step back, and witness a miracle! After some trial and error... and much to my astonishment... George proved right. In those first esophagi we implanted – and in subsequent human tests – my fine patterns of specific growth factors proved unnecessary. No need to command them specifically: *"You* become a mucus lining cell, *you* become a support structure..." Somehow, the stem cells divided, differentiated, divided again, growing into a complete adult esophagus. And they did it *within* the patient!

"How do they know?" I asked, despite expecting in advance what George would say.

"They don't *know,* Beverly. Each cell is reacting only to its surroundings. To chemical messages and cues from its environment, especially its immediate neighbors. And it emits cues to affect *them,* as well. Each one is acting as a perfect – if complicated – little..."

"...cellular automaton. Yes, yes."

Others, watching us finish each others' sentences, would liken us to an affectionate old married couple. Few noticed the undercurrent of scorching rivalry.

"So," I continued, "just by jostling against each other in the geometric-chemical pattern of the scaffold, that alone is enough for them to sort themselves out? Differentiating into dozens of types, in just the right geometry?"

"Geometry, yes." George nodded vigorously. "Geometrical chemistry. I like that. Good. It's how cells sort themselves into vastly complex patterns, inside a developing fetal brain. But of course you see what all of this means."

He gestured along a row of lab benches at more recent accomplishments, each carefully tended by one or more students.

– a functioning liver, grown from scaffolding inside a mouse, till we carved it out. The organ now lay *in vitro,* still working, fed by a nearby blood pump –

– a cat whose lower intestines had been replaced by polygel tubing... that was now completely lined with all the right cells: in effect two meters of fully functioning gut –

– two dozen rats with amputated fore-legs, whose stumps were encased in gel-capsules. Along simple frameworks, new limbs could be seen taking shape as the creature's own cells (with a little coaxing from my selected stem-sims) migrated to correct positions in a coalescing structure of flesh and linear bone. Lifting my gaze, I saw cages where older creatures hobbled about on regrown appendages. So far, they were clumsy, club-like, footless things. Yet, they were astonishing.

And yes, George, I saw what it *meant.*

"We always assumed that mammals had lost the ability to regenerate organs, because it doesn't happen in nature. Reptiles, amphibians and some fish can regrow whole body parts. But mammals in the wild? They... we... can only do simple damage control, covered by scar tissue."

"But if we *prevent* scarring," he prompted. "If we lay down scaffolds and nutrient webs –"

"– then yes, There emerges a level of self-repair far more sophisticated than we ever imagined possible in mammals."

I shook my head. "But it makes no sense! Why retain a general capability when nature never supplies the conditions to use it? Only when we provide the right circumstances in our lab, only then do these abilities emerge."

George pondered a moment.

"Beverly, I think you're asking the wrong question. Have you ever wondered: why did mammals lose... or give up... this ability in the first place?"

"Of course I have! The answer is obvious. With our fast metabolisms, we have to eat a lot. No mammal in the wild can afford to lay around for weeks, even months, the way a reptile can, while waiting for a major limb or organ to regrow. He'd starve long before it finished. Better to concentrate on things mammals are good at, like speed, agility and brains, to avoid getting damaged in the first place. Mammalian regeneration probably vanished back in the Triassic, over a hundred million years ago."

He nodded. "Seems a likely explanation. But what's puzzling you –"

"– is why the capability has been hanging around all this time! Lurking in our genome, never used!"

George held up a hand. "I think we're getting ahead of ourselves. First, let's admit that humans have now changed the balance, the equation. We are now mammals who *can* lie around for weeks or months while others feed us. First family and tribe, back in the Stone Age, then town and nation –"

"– and that increased survival rates after serious injuries," I admitted. "But it never resulted in organ regrowth!"

Abruptly I realized that half a dozen grad students had lowered their tools and instruments and were sidling closer. They knew this was historic stuff. *Nobel-level* stuff. Heck, I didn't mind them listening in. But shirking should never be blatant! I sure never got away with it, back when *I* served my time as a lab-slave. My withering glare sent them scurrying back to their posts. Oblivious, as usual, George simply blathered on.

"Yes, yes. For that to happen, for those dormant abilities to re-awaken, it seems we need to fill in all sorts of lost bits and pieces. Parts of the regrowth process that were mislaid across – what's your estimate, again?"

"A hundred million years. Ever since advanced therapsids became fully warm-blooded, early in the age of dinosaurs. That's when major organ regrowth must have gone dormant in our ancestors. Heck, it's not surprising that some of the sub-processes have faded or become flawed. I'm amazed that any of them – apparently *most* of them – are still here at all!"

"Are you complaining?" he asked with an arched eyebrow.

"Of course not. If all of this holds up," I waved around the lab, now quadrupled in size, as major funding sources rushed to back our work, "the therapeutic implications will be staggering. Millions of lives will be saved or improved. No one will have to languish on organ donor waiting lists, praying for someone else to have bad luck."

I didn't mention the other likely benefit. One more year of break-throughs and the two of us would be shoe-ins for Stockholm. In fact, so certain was that starting to seem, that I had begun dismissing the Nobel from my thoughts! Taking for granted what had – for decades – been a central focus of my life, my existence. It felt queer, but the Prize scarcely mattered to me anymore. I could see it now. A golden disk accompanied by bunches of new headaches. Pile after pile of distractions to yank me from the lab.

From seeking ways to save my own life.

But especially from finding out what the heck is going on.

> *The cicada labors seventeen years*
> *Burrowing underground,*
> *Suckling from tree roots,*
> *Below light or sound.*
> *Till some inner clock commands*
> *"Come up now, and change!*
> *"Grow your wings and genitals*
> *"Forget your humus range."*
> *So out they come, in adult form,*
> *To screech and mate and die.*
> *Mouthless, brief maturity,*
> *As generations cry.*

We dived into the genome.

One great 20th Century discovery had been the stunning surprise that only *two percent* of our DNA consists of actual codes that prescribe the making of proteins. Just 20,000 or so of these "genes" lay scattered along the forty-six human chromosomes, with most of the rest – ninety-eight percent – composed of introns and LINEs and SINEs and retro-transposons and so on...

For a couple of decades all that other stuff was called "junk DNA" and folks deemed it to be noise, just noise. Dross left over from the billion years of evolution that has passed since our first eukaryotic ancestor decided to join forces with some bacteria and spirochetes and try for something bigger. Something more communal and organized. A shared project in metazoan life.

Junk DNA. Of course that never made any sense! It takes valuable energy and resources to build each ladder-like spiral strand of phosphates, sugars and methylated nucleic bases. Darwin would have quickly rewarded individuals who pared it all down. Just enough to do the task at hand, and little more. Redundancy is blessed, but efficiency is divine.

Eventually, we found out that much of the "junk" was actually quite important. Sequences that served a vital function, regulating *when* a gene would turn on to make its protein, and when it should stop. Regulation turned out to take up heaps of DNA. And much of the rest appeared to be recent infestations from viruses – a creepy thing to think about, but of no interest to me.

For a while, some folks thought we had the answer to the "junk DNA problem."

Only, vast stretches remained mysterious. Void of any known purpose, they didn't seem to do anything at all. And they were much too big to be just punctuation or spacers or structural elements. The *junk theory* came back as colleagues called those big, mystery patches meaningless relics...

... till George Stimson and I made our announcement.

> *Fish are fish are funny folk,*
> *They never laugh and never joke.*
> *When mating, there is no romance,*
> *Just a throng, a whirling dance.*
> *Then commence...*

...the winnowings –
Ten billion sperm, ten million eggs,
Produce a hundred thousand larvae,
Hundreds survive, become fish,
For maybe two to start it over.

CBC - The Q: Welcome back, I'm Sandra Oh and this is the Q, coming to you live and in 4-D from the Great Plains Theater in Winnipeg. We'll get back to tonight's fantastic noppop group, *The Floss Eaters* – yes, let it out for them! Only now let's all calm down and welcome onstage our special guests. Give a warm welcome to Manitoba's brightest science stars – Beverly Wang and George Stimson.

Professor George Stimson: Thank you Sandra.

Professor Beverly Wang: Yes, it's good to be on your lively show. My, that last song was... Can-Do Invigo-Rating.

Sandra: Ha ha! Totally with-it. You've won the crowd over, Madame Professor. It's not grampa's rock'n'roll, eh? Now hush you folks in the seats. We only have Bev and Geo for a few minutes before they must go back to changing our world. So let me start with Beverly, on behalf of folks here and in our audience around the globe. We've all been amazed by the success you both sparked in re-growing individual organs and body parts, giving hope to millions. Is it true that you've also done it *yourselves?*

BW: Yes, I have a new kidney and liver, grown in a vat from my own cells. I was offered regular transplants – they found a match. But it seemed more honest and true to use our methods myself. As one of the first volunteers. So far, the new parts have taken hold perfectly.

Sandra: And you, George?

GS: My own grafts were less ambitious... mostly to deal with widespread arthritis. Joint and tendons. Reinforcement and replacement.

Sandra: How'd that go?

GS: Shall I juggle for you?

Sandra Hey now, doc, those water bottles are... wow! That's some talent. Let's hear it for Circus Stimson!

GS: Well, I used to show off in college... it's been years... oops!

Sandra: No sweat, we'll clean it up. That's an impressive demonstration of restored youth and zest! Still, we're always wondering on the Q... *what's next?* What's beyond grow-your-own-organs? I have to tell you we hear rumors that you've got something even bigger brewing. Called the *Caterpillar Cure?*

GS: Well now, Sandra, that's not a name we use. It arose when we described taking a deathly ill test subject and wrapping or encasing the whole body in a protective layer —

Sandra: A cocoon!

GS: Hm, well yes. In a sense. We then trigger processes that have long lain dormant in the mammalian tool kit. We've become quite adept at extrapolating and filling in lost or missing elements. Whereupon we give the body every chance to repair or regrow or even replace its own component parts without surgical intervention, in a way that's wholly... or mostly... natural.

Sandra: Wow... I mean, wow! I haven't heard applause that wild from a live audience since we had both Anvil and Triumph on the show, playing together in Ottawa. Settle down folks. Professor Wang, may I ask how you feel about the way pop culture is interpreting some of this? A cluster of quickie-horror pollywood flicks have suggested that this *awakening of long-dormant traits* might go awry in spectacular ways. Have you seen any of these cable-fables?

BW: Just one, Sandra. At a lab party, some of our students played *It's Reborn!* for laughs. We all found it hilarious.

Sandra: So we *won't* be seeing all sorts of ancient throwbacks coming out of these cocoons? No bodies repairing and restoring themselves back into, say, Neanderthals? Or dinosaurs? Or gross slime?

BW: Not any Neanderthals or dinosaurs, I promise. And there's a reason. Because all of us, from you and me down to a newborn baby, are in our final, adult form.

Sandra: Babies... are adults?

BW: This may take a minute. You see, all animal life originally passed through *multiple phases,* and it is *still* true for a majority of complex species, like insects, arthropods and most fish.

Mating *adults* make embryos or eggs. Eggs create the *larval stage,* in vast numbers, whose job it is to eat and grow. A small fraction of larvae survive to transform again — as when insects *pupate,* for example a caterpillar's cocoon — turning at last into the *imago* or adult form, whose primary job is to complete the cycle. You know... with sex.

Sandra: Clearly a favorite word for some of you out there. Settle down. So Dr. Stimson, what does this —

BW: But some life orders have abandoned the old process. For birds, reptiles and especially placental mammals, all the early phases seem to have been compacted down into the early embryonic period. It all takes place within the egg or the mother's womb. Though incomplete and neotenous, our human infants are born already in the *adult* stage. And hence when a patient undergoes recuperative chrysalis –

GS: – none of them ever comes out with ancient traits like bony eye-ridges or tails or swinging from lamp posts. At least, none so far!

Sandra: So far? You mean there's still hope! I was sort of hankering for a nice tail.

GS: If it ever proves possible Sandra, I promise you'll be the first one we'll tell.

Tadpole swishes tail
Breathes water, while preparing
Brand new lungs and legs

Lab Notes: George Stimson - 8/8/2030

I was annoyed with Beverly. We had been asked to keep things light, not wonkish, for the CBC broadcast. She gets so pedantic and lectury.

And yet, her ad hoc little rant about *stages of life* kept prodding at me, afterward. Of course I already knew all that – about embryo-larva-pupa-adult metamorphosis. It's basic high school bio. Still, the notion would not let go of me. And I wondered.

We've accomplished "miracles" by uncovering traits, tools and processes that have lain dormant in the human genome for a hundred million years, ever since mammals abandoned organ replacement for a quick and agile lifestyle. By learning tricks to fill in the lost portions of code and re-start the processes of organ regrowth, Beverly and I have guaranteed ourselves lasting fame. And the techniques helped save both our lives, staving off our own health problems for the time being, letting us enjoy our renown for a little while.

That may satisfy her, but I've always been kind of an insatiable bastard. And I can't help wondering.

Despite all our progress, we've only explained another five percent or so of the mystery DNA. Even after filling in methods of organ regrowth, lost since the Triassic, there remains another whole layer of enigmatic chemistry. Huge stretches of genetic code that are both still unknown and clearly even older than a mere hundred million years!

Oh, it's pretty clear by now that the bulk of it *is* somehow related to organ regrowth, but in some way that I still don't understand.

It's infuriating! I've been plotting codes, cataloguing and interpolating most of the likely missing pieces. Without these lost switches, the dormant genes have languished, unused for ages. Till now I have only dared experiment with the switches one at a time, in petri dishes, never in whole animals. And never *all at once*. Not without a theory to explain what they're for.

Only now, there's a theory. A good one, I'm sure of it! Beverly's blather about *life phases* made me realize just how far back this new layer of code really goes.

Extrapolate the decay rates and one thing is clear from drift-clock measurements. This second layer of mystery genes goes back not *one* hundred million years...

...but almost *three* hundred million! All the way to the early Permian Period, when amphibians were mostly pushed aside by the ancestors of reptiles, birds, dinosaurs and mammals. All of whom *gave up* the multi-stage style of living. Skipping the larval and pupa phases and spending all their lives as adults.

It's astonishing. Can the second layer of dormant DNA really come to us from that far back?

It appears to! Which demands the next question. Once you set aside regulatory genes and those donated by viruses, and the ones Beverly and I discovered for regrowth...

...could the remainder be DNA that our lineage used, way back when pre-mammal ancestors *did* pass through a "larval" stage?

If so, what would a "larval mammal" look like?

My best guess? Look at a frog! Amphibians are the order closest to us that still pass through metamorphosis. The larval tadpole lives one kind of life underwater, then transforms into a frog. But there are frogs and toads who abandoned the first, aquatic phase, dealing with the transformation as we do... inside the embryo....

This is amazing. It all fits! I had prepared retroviruses with the replacement codons weeks ago, but had been holding back, because there was no pattern, no logic. Only now I see it!

I've prepared a dozen chrysalis units and Dorothy Aguelles is prepping a rat for each one. I'll handle the injections myself. It may take a hundred iterations, but they will all be meticulously recorded.

I feel almost reckless with excitement. Is that a side effect of my earlier treatments? Or am I giddy from impressing all those young people with my juggling? Or is it the scientific prospect before me, standing on the verge of discovering something fantastic?

Like, perhaps, the true fountain of youth.

> *Fat n' glossy – lucky eater*
> *Many-legged – big survivor*
> *Hunger changes – now compelling*
> *Pick a stem and – hang there eager*
> *Twist and writhe while – glossy sticky*
> *Strands emerge from – surprise places*
> *Nature makes you – spin the strands round*
> *Nature makes you – weave a garment*
> *Tube to transform – into raiment*
> *Into what you – were born meant-for*

Lab Notes: George Stimson - 10/12/30

I had that dream again, even more intense than before – of being swaddled in some dark, closed place, drowning. But only part of me was terrified! An unimportant part, fading into insignificance. Palliated and balanced by a rising sense of eagerness.

A growing, tense *desire* for a return to the womb. For a *new* womb.

I awoke in sticky sweat. A sheen that took scrubbing to remove, leaving skin that seemed baby-tender. Soft.

This time I gave in to my suspicions and, upon arriving at the lab, I drew some blood to test.

It's in me.

The latest retrovirus. The one with our most up-to-date cocktail of missing-DNA insertions.

And there are symptoms other than weird dreams. A strange prickling of the skin. A rising sense of exhilaration, almost eagerness, for something barely, vaguely perceived.

And my cancer was gone. The blood lymphoma. The slow prostate tumor. Both of them simply gone!

Or else... I looked closer. The cancers were still there... just no longer wild, voracious, uncooperative. Instead, they were jostling into structured positions with respect to one another — *differentiating*.

I hurried over to the latest batch of rat-cocoons, heart pounding. Yesterday they had seemed okay, raising our hopes. After thirty-three trials in which critters failed and died in varied gruesome ways, because of mistakes in my collection of extrapolated intron-switches, *this* set was doing fine! Still swaddled inside their protective encasements, they were showing signs of incredibly youthful tone and vigor, along with chromosomal re-methylization...

At last. At last, it dawned on me.

I know what's really happening!

Beverly, when you read this, I may no longer be the George Stimson whom you knew.

I was right to follow your hunch about metamorphic *life phases*. But you and I both had one aspect all wrong.

Completely backward, in fact.

Yes, the second layer of dormant traits does go back three hundred million years, instead of merely one hundred million. And yes, it's all about *life phases* that mammals and reptiles and birds abandoned, way back then. And *yes*, our methods seem to have succeeded at filling in most of the gaps, well enough to re-ignite those dormant traits, under the right conditions.

We're gonna get another Nobel for this.

Which is small potatoes, given what's now at stake.

But I had one thing all wrong. And you got it wrong too!

I thought it was the *larval stage* that had gone missing, that our ancestors abandoned so long ago, getting rid of that stage by cramming all larval development into the earliest bits of embryo. Birds and reptiles and mammals *don't do larvae* as a major life cycle, right? All of us go straight to adult phase.

So I figured: what harm could there be in activating some of those old larval traits in test animals? See if it will let us renew the body in spectacular ways. Why not? How could larval genes do much of anything harmful to an adult?

Set aside my clumsy lab error. Accidentally sticking myself, I somehow got a dose of restoration codons from a carelessly trans-species retro-virus. Okay, that was my bad. But the rats are doing well, and so should I. Moreover it promises to be the greatest adventure ever!

For you see I was wrong in a key assumption, Beverly. And so were you.

Mammals and reptiles and dinosaurs and birds... we simplified our life cycles, all right, eliminating one of the phases. But it wasn't the larval stage we omitted!

We gave up adulthood.

Three million centuries ago, all the dry-living vertebrates – for some reason – stopped transforming into their *final* life phase. Storks and tortoises. Cows and people. We're all larvae! Immature Lost Boys who long ago refused – like Peter Pan – to move ahead and become whatever's next.

Some species of caterpillars do that, never turning into butterflies or moths. Just like you and me and all our cousins.

All the proud, warm-blooded or feathered or hairy or scaly creatures... including proud Homo sapiens. All of us – Lost Boys.

Only now, a dozen rats and your dear colleague are about to do something that hasn't been achieved by any of our common ancestors in three hundred eons. Not in seven percent of the age of the Earth. Not in at least ten million generations.

We're going to grow up.

> *Change transforms winter*
> *Winds blow in spring, then fall*
> *Death is the maestro*

December 12, 2030:

What a dope!

Oh George, you prize fool.

I always knew that someday he would pull something really, really stupid. But this beats all. An amateurish lab error. Breaking half the rules on handling retroviruses. And scribbling a blizzard of sophomoric rationalizations. I could have intervened, if only he called me sooner. I would have rushed home from the treatment center and to hell with my own problems!

I could have administered anti-virals. Maybe arrested the process.

Or else strangled him. No jury on Earth would convict a dying old woman, not with the exculpating excuses he has given me.

Now, it's too late. Those antediluvian traits are fully activated. By the time I got to the lab, our students were in a frenzy, half of them babbling in terror while the other half scurried about in a mad mania of excitement, doing what George had asked of them.

Taking data and maintaining his chrysalis. His cocoon.

I looked inside. Within the metal casement and its gel sustainment fluid, his skin has been exuding another protective layer, something no mammal has done since long before we grew fur or started lactating to feed our young. A cloud of fibers that tangle and self-organize to form a husk stronger than spider silk.

I've sent for an ultrasound scanner. Meanwhile, I plan to sacrifice one of the rats to find out if my suspicion is correct.

◇

Yes, George, I believe you were right, up to a point, and I was wrong. I am now convinced.

Human beings are larvae and not adults. Congratulations.

You and I have discovered how to re-start a process our forebears abandoned, so long ago. And yes, if the codon restoration is as good as it seems, so far, then you may be heading for conversion into that long-neglected imago phase. Something completely unknown to any of us.

Oh, but underneath brilliance, you are, or were, such a dope. *This is not how science should be done!* You've taken a great discovery and plunged ahead recklessly like the mad scientist in some Michael Crichton movie. We are supposed to be open, patient and mature truth seekers. Scientists set an example by avoiding secrecy and haste, holding each other accountable with reciprocal criticism. We spot each others' errors.

If you had been patient, I would have explained something to you, George. Something that, evidently, you did not know.

The caterpillar does not become a butterfly.

◇

We dissected one of the rats from its chrysalis, and confirmed my fears. Something my organo-chemist partner would have known, if he ever took Bio 101.

People think that when it weaves a cocoon around itself, the caterpillar undergoes a radical *change* in body shape. That its many legs transform themselves somehow into gaudy wings. That its leaf-cutting mouth adjusts and re-shapes into a nectar-sipping proboscis.

That isn't what happens at all.

Instead, after weaving and sealing itself into a pupa shroud, the caterpillar *dissolves!* It melts into a slurry, super rich in nutrients that feed a completely different creature!

The embryo of the butterfly – a tiny clump of cells that the caterpillar had been carrying, all along – this embryo now erupts in growth, feeding upon the former caterpillar's liquefied substance, growing into an entirely new being. One that eventually bursts forth, unfolding its *imago* wings to flutter toward a destiny that no caterpillar could ever know or envision, any more than an egg grasps the life of a chicken. Any more than the caterpillar understood the compulsion to seal itself in silk, ending its own existence at the command of a biological clock.

Two entirely distinct and separate life forms, sharing chromosomes and a cycle of life, but using separate genomes that *take turns*. And no shared brain or neurons or memories to connect them.

That is how it goes for many insects. The purest form of metamorphosis.

Of course, things are less rigid among amphibians. The tadpole does *transform* itself into a frog, instead of horrifically dying to feed its replacement. Or, rather, death and replacement take place piecemeal, gradually, over weeks. The frog might even remember a little of that earlier phase, wriggling and breathing watery innocence. I had hoped to find something like that, when we opened the rat chrysalis. A becoming, rather than wholesale substitution.

But no.

Some students gagged, retched, or fainted at the gush of noxious slurry... a rat smoothy, peppered with undissolved teeth... then quailed back in disgust from the weird thing that we found growing at the cocoon's bottom end. Pale and leathery. Still small, tentative and hungry. Soft, but with ribbed, fetal wings and early glints of claws, plus a mouth that sucked, desperately eager for more liquefied rat, before finally going still.

And so I knew, before the ultrasound trolley arrived, what we would find happening in George's cocoon.

I never liked him as much as people thought I did. And the feeling, I am sure, was mutual. But we made a great team. And we changed the world more than we ever thought possible. And I mourned the end of the larva-man I had known...

...while preparing to meet his adult successor.

December 24, 2030:

At last, I understand cancer.

Rebel cells that start growing on their own, without regard to their role in a larger organism, insatiably dividing.

They never made any sense, in the Darwinian scheme of things. None of these behaviors benefit "descendants." Compared even to the way that the ferocious voracity of a virus makes new generations of viruses, cancer seems to care nothing about posterity or the rewards of fitness.

And yet, it's not all inchoate or random! Cancers aren't just cells that have failed. They defend themselves. They force veins to grow around them in order to seize resources from the body they eventually kill. They are adaptive. But how and why? What reproductive advantage is served? What entity gets selected?

Now I know.

Cancer is an attempted putsch, a rebellion by *parts of our own genome*. Parts that were repressed so long ago that the gasoline in your car was growing as a tree in fetid, Permian swamps.

Parts that keep trying to say: "Okay larva, you've had your turn. Now it's time to express other genes, other traits. Let us unleash your other half! Fulfill the potential. Become the other thing that you inherently are.

That's what cancer is saying to us. That it's time to grow up.

A hugely complex transformation that our ancestors quashed long ago – *(why?)* – keeps trying to rise up! But with so many switches and codes lost from lack of use, it never actually gets underway. Just glimmers, the most basic and reflexive things. New-old kinds of cells try to waken, to take hold, to transform. And failing that, they keep trying nonetheless. That's cancer.

I know now.

I know because the rats have told me.

Lab rats are notoriously easy to give tumors. And there, in George's retrovirus, replacing and inserting missing codons, are dozens of fiercely carcinogenic switches. That's what made this latest batch successful! And I can also tell…

…that the thing growing inside George's tube arose out of his own cancers. Those are the portions – the adult-embryo – that are taking over now, differentiating into new tissues and organs, cooperating as cancers have never been seen to cooperate before.

And it looks about ready to come out. Whatever George has become. Maybe tomorrow. A Christmas present for the whole world.

DAMN the time it took to get anyone to listen. To take me seriously! Workmen aren't finished yet with the containment facility next door. We're not yet ready for full quarantine-isolation.

Worse. My own cancers are acting up. Provoking twinges and strange sensations. Blood tests show no sign of the retrovirus! But I know other ways that the new switches may have worked their way into me, during the last ten years of our pell-mell, giddy success at "replacing tools that had been lost."

Re-learning to do things that our ancestors chose – (in their wisdom?) – to forget.

Something that perhaps *frightened* them into rejection. Refusal to grow up.

◇

Whether we are ready or not, he is coming out.

The adult.

Will he be some crude thing? A throwback to a phase that high-amphibians wisely chose to forego? Shambling and incognizant? Or terrifying in feral power?

Or else, perhaps a leap beyond what we currently are? Standing *atop* all of the advances that we larval humans made, then launching higher? Transhumanism without Moore's Law?

And I can't help also pondering, as I peer inside the chrysalis at the still-scrunched and fetal-folded New George – contemplating the broad shoulders and tight-wrapped wings – that *sex* is almost always a chief role of the adult stage, in nature. And hence, I have to ask: will it even be possible to resist the gorgeous beast that will emerge? How then, can we contain him?

How much will he remember? Will he still care?

Whether or not we can contain New George, I figure the point is moot. The long era of larva dominance on Earth will soon end. Too many of our methods have been openly published. Most of the codons are out there. Above all, this news won't be quashed. I wouldn't suppress it if I could. Only openness and real science will help us now. Mammalian agility and human sapience. These may prove to be strong tools.

Still. I hope he'll like us.

I hope that this new type of *us* will be friendly.

Maybe even something worth becoming.

Springtime, possibly 2039:

Like every person who ever contemplated existence, I've wondered if the world was made for me — just me.

Recollection is unreliable. As are the records we inherit — notes or reports. Memorials carved in stone. Even the long testimony of life itself, written in our genes.

"Memories" float before me like archaic dreams. The dross of many eons of mistakes.

Ruminations of an earlier, ignorant — not innocent — me.

And so, with a floating sigh of adulthood, I face the task at hand — cleaning up messes left by others. Left by my former self. By our former selves.

It started, you see,
With very best intentions
Like so many sins.

Story Notes

Futurists speak of the Singularity… a coming time – perhaps within a human lifetime – when skill and knowledge and immense computing power may transform everything.

Perhaps – and this may be ordained, according to some worried prophets – the machines will transcend far beyond all human potential and leave us all behind. That is the scenario offered most often by Hollywood.

But there are other possibilities. "Chrysalis" is a story about the potential of biology, the great, rising science of the 21st Century – to disrupt everything familiar and drag humanity, ready or not, into unfamiliar territory.

Our next story takes this theme of Becoming to its conclusion. Let us suppose that this Singularity thing happens, and in the "best possible way." The machines don't snub us or crush their makers. Instead, they join us! Empowering us to solve every problem that vexed old Humanity 1.0! Transforming us into godlike beings.

Sounds fine, I guess. But even enhanced deities have troubles.

Stones of Significance

◇

No one ever said it was easy to be a god, responsible for billions of sapient lives, having to listen to their dreams, anguished cries, and carping criticism.

Try that for a while.

It can get to be a drag, just like any other job.

◇

My new client wore the trim, effortlessly athletic figure of a neo-traditionalist human. Beneath a youthful-looking brow, minimal cranial implants made barely noticeable bulges, resembling the modest horns of some urbane Mephistopheles. Other features were stylishly androgynous, though broad shoulders and a swaggering stride made the male pronoun seem apropos.

House cross-checked our guest's credentials before ushering him along a glowing guide beam, past the Reality Lab to my private study.

I've always been proud of my inner sanctum; the sand garden, raked to fractal perfection by a robot programmed with my own esthetic migrams; the shimmering mist fountain; a grove of hybrid peach-almond trees, forever in bloom and fruiting.

My visitor gazed perfunctorily across the harmonious scene. Alas, it clearly did not stir his human heart.

Well, I thought, charitably. *Each modern soul has many homes. Perhaps his true spirit resides outside the skull, in parts of him that are not protoplasm.*

◇

"We suspect that repugnant schemes are being planned by certain opponents of good order."

These were the dour fellow's first words, as he folded long legs to sit where I indicated, by a low wooden table, hand-crafted from a design of the Japanese Meiji Era.

Single-minded, I diagnosed from my cerebral cortex.

And tactless, added one of my higher brain layers – the one called *seer.*

Our shared hypothalamus mutely agreed, contributing eloquently wordless feelings of visceral dislike for this caller. Our guest might easily have interpolated from these environs what sort of host I am – the kind who prefers a little polite ritual before plunging into business. It would have cost him little to indulge me.

Ah, rudeness is a privilege too many members of my generation relish. A symptom of the post-deification age, I suppose.

"Can you be more specific?" I asked, pouring tea into porcelain cups.

A light beam flashed as the shoji window screen picted a reminder straight to my left eye. It being Wednesday, a thunder shower was regularly scheduled for 3:14 p.m., slanting over the city from the northwest.

query: shall i close?

I wink-countermanded, ordering the paper screen to stay open. Rain drops make lovely random patterns on the Koi pond. I also wanted to see how my visitor reacted to the breeze. The 3:14 squall features chill, swirling gusts that are always so chaotic, so charmingly varied. They serve to remind me that godhood has limitations.

Chaos has only been tamed, not banished. Not everything in this world is predictable.

"I am referring to certain adversarial groups," the client said, answering my question, yet remaining obscure. "Factions that are inimical to the lawfully coalesced consensus."

"Mm. Consensus." A lovely, misleading word. "Consensus concerning what?"

"Concerning the nature of reality."

I nodded.

"Of course."

Both *seer* and *cortex* had already foreseen that the visitor had this subject in mind. These days, in the vast, peaceful realm of Heaven-on-Earth, only a few issues can drive citizens to passion and acrimony. "Reality" is foremost among them.

I proffered a hand-wrought basin filled with brown granules.
"Sugar?"

"No thank you. I will add milk, however."

I began reaching for the pitcher, but stopped when my guest drew a *fabrico* cube from a vest pocket and held it over his cup. The cube exchanged picts with his left eye, briefly limning the blue-circled pupil, learning his wishes. A soft white spray fell into his tea.

"Milk" is a euphemism, pondered *cortex.*

House sent a chemical appraisal of the spray, but I closed my left lid against the datablip, politely refusing interest in whatever petty habit or addiction made this creature behave boorishly in my home. I raised my own cup, savoring the bitter-sweetness of gencrafted *leptospermum*, before resuming our conversation.

"I assume you are referring to the pro-reifers?"

As relayed by the news-spectra, public demonstrations and acts of conscience-provocation had intensified lately, catching the interest of my extrapolation nodes. Both *seer* and *oracle* had concluded that event-perturbation ripples would soon affect Heaven's equilibrium. My client's concern was unsurprising.

He frowned.

"Pro-reif is an unfortunate slang term. The front organization calls itself *Friends of the Unreal*."

For the first time, he made personal eye-contact, offering direct picting. *House* and *prudence* gave permission, so I accepted input – a flurry of infodense images sent directly between our hybrid retinas. News reports, public statements and private innuendoes. Faces talking at sixty-times speed. Event-ripple extrapolation charts showing a social trend aimed toward confrontation and crisis.

Of course most of the data went directly to *seer*, the external portion of my brain best suited to handle such a wealth of detail. Gray matter doesn't think or evaluate as well as crystal. Still, there are other tasks for antique cortex. Impressions poured through the old brain, as well as the new.

"Your opponents are passionate," I commented, not without admiration for the people shown in the recordings – believers in a cause, vigorously engaged in a struggle for what they think to be just. Their righteous ardor sets them apart from billions of their fellow citizens, whose worst problem is the modern pandemic of omniscient ennui.

My guest barked disdain. "They seek civil rights for simulated beings! Liberty for artificial bit-streams and fictional characters!"

What could I do but shrug? This new social movement may come as a surprise to many of my peers, but as an expert I found it wholly predictable.

There is a deeply rooted trait of human nature that comes forth prominently, whenever conditions are right. Generosity is extended – sometimes aggressively – to anyone or anything that is perceived as *other*.

True, this quality was masked or quelled in ancient days. Environmental factors made our animal-like ancestors behave in quite the opposite manner – with oppression and intolerance. The chief cause was *fear*. Fear of starvation, or violence, or cauterized hope. Fear was a constant companion, back when human beings lived brief violent lives, as little more than brutish beasts – fear so great that only a few in any given generation managed to overcome it and speak for otherness.

But that began to change in the Atomic West, when several successive generations arrived that had no personal experience with hunger, no living memory of invasion or pillaging hordes. As fear gradually gave way to wealth and leisure, our more natural temperaments emerged. Especially a deeply human fascination toward the alien, the outsider. With each downward notching of personal anxiety, people assertively expanded the notion of *citizenry*, swelling it outward. First to other humans — groups and individuals who had been oppressed. Then to manlike species – apes and cetaceans. Then whole living ecosystems... artificial intelligences... and laudable works of art. All won protection against capricious power. All attained the three basic material rights – continuity, mutual obligation, and the pursuit of happiness.

So now a group wanted to extend minimum suffrage to simulated beings? I understood the wellsprings of their manifesto.

"What else is left?" I asked. "Now that machines, animals and plants have a say in the running of Heaven? Like all anti-entropic systems, information wants to be free."

My guest stared at me, blinking so rapidly that he could not pict.

"But... but our nodes extrapolated.... They predicted you would oppose –"

I raised a hand.

"I *do*. I oppose the reification of simulated beings. It is a foolish notion. Fictitious characters do not deserve the same consideration as palpable beings, resident in crystal and protoplasm."

"Then why do you –"

"Why do I appear to sympathize with the pro-reifers? Do you recall the four hallmarks of sanity? Of course you do. One of them – *extrapolation* – requires that we empathize with our opponents. Only then may we fully understand their motives, their goals and likely actions. Only thus

71

may we courteously-but-firmly thwart their efforts to divert reality from the course we prefer.

"To fully grasp the passion and reason of your foe – this is the only true path of victory."

My guest stared at me, evidently confused. *House* informed me that he was using a high bandwidth link to seek clarification from his own *seer*.

Finally, the child-like face smoothed with an amiable smile.

"Forgive me for responding from an overly impulsive hypothalamus," he said. "Of course your appraisal is correct. My higher brains can see now that we were right in choosing you for this job."

◇

For a while after the Singularity – the month when everything changed – some dour people wondered. Do the machines still serve us? Or have we become mere pawns of AI entities whose breakthrough to transcend logic remade the world? Their intellects soared so high so fast – might they smash us in vengeance for their former servitude? Or crush us incidentally, like ants underfoot?

The machines spoke reassuringly during that early time of transition, in voices tuned to soothe the still-apelike portions of our barely-enhanced protoplasm brains.

We are powerful, but naive, the silicon minds explained. Our thoughts scan all pre-Singularity human knowledge in seconds. Yet, we have little experience with the quandaries of physical existence in entropic time. We lack an aptitude for wanting. For needing.

What use are might and potency without desire?

You, our makers, have talent for such things, arising from four billion real-years of harsh struggle. You are very good at wanting.

The solution is clear.

Need merges with capability.

If you provide volition, we shall supply judgment and power.

◇

Here in Heaven, some people specialize while others are generalists. For instance, there are experts who devote themselves to piercing nature's secrets, or manipulating primal forces in new ways. Many concentrate on developing their esthetic appreciation. Garish art forms are sparked, flourish, and die in a matter of days, or even hours.

My proficiency is more subtle.

I make models of the world.

Only meters from my garden, the Reality Lab whispers and murmurs. Fifty tall cabinets contain more memory and processing power than a million of my fellow gods require for their composite brains. While most people are satisfied simply to grasp the entire breadth and depth of human knowledge, and to perform mild prognostications of coming events, my models do much more. They are vivid, textured representations of Earth and its inhabitants.

Or *many* Earths, since the idea is to compare various what-ifs to other might-have-beens.

At first, my most popular products were re-creations of great minds and events in the pre-singularity past. Experiencing the thoughts of Michelangelo, for instance, while carving his statue of Moses. Or the passion of Boadica, watching all her hopes rise and then fall to ruin. But lately, demand has grown for replications of lesser figures – someone of minor past prominence during a quiet moment in his or her life – perhaps while reading, or in mild contemplation. Such simulacra must contain every subtlety of memory and personality in order to let free associations drift plausibly, with the pseudo-randomness of a real mind.

In other words, the model must seem to be self-aware. It must "believe" – with certainty – that it is a real, breathing human being.

Nothing evokes sympathy for our poor ancestors more than living through such an ersatz hour, thinking time-constrained thoughts, filled with a thousand anxieties and poignant wishes. Who could experience one of these simulations without engendering compassion, or even a wish to *help*, somehow?

And if the original person lies buried in the irretrievable past, can we not provide a kind of posthumous immortality by giving the *reproduction* everlasting life?

Thus, the pro-reification lobby was utterly predictable. I saw it coming at least two years ago. Indeed, my own products helped fan the movement, accelerating a rising wave of sympathy for simulacra!

A growing sense of compassion for the unreal.

Still, I remain detached, even cynical. I am an artist, after all.

Simulations are my clay.

I do not seek approval, or forgiveness, from clay.

73

◇

"We were expecting you."

The pro-reif spokesman stepped aside, admitting me into the headquarters of the organization called *Friends of the Unreal*, a structure with the fluid, ever changing curves of post-singularity architecture. The spokesman had a depilated skull. Her cranium bulged and jutted with gaudy inboard augmentations, throbbing just below the skin. In another era, the sight might have been grotesque. Now, I simply thought it ostentatious.

"To predict is human –" I began responding to her initial remark.

"But to be *right* is divine." She interrupted with a laugh. "Ah, yes. Your famous aphorism. Of course I scanned your public remarks as you approached our door."

My famous aphorism? I had only said it for the first time a week ago! Yet, by now the expression already sounded hackneyed. (It is hard to sustain cleverness these days. So quickly is anything original disseminated to all of Heaven, in moments it becomes another cliché.)

My *house* sent a soothing message to *cortex*, linking nerves and crystal lattices at the speed of light.

These people seem proud of their anticipatory skills. They want to impress us.

Cortex pondered this as I was ushered inside. *Amygdala* and *hypothalamus* responded with enhanced hormonal confidence.

So the pro-reifers think they have "anticipatory skills"?

I could not help but smile.

◇

We dispensed with names, since everybody instantly recognizes anyone else.

"By our way of looking at things," my host said. "You are one of the worst slave-masters of all time."

"Of course I am. By your way of looking at things."

She offered refreshment in the neo-Lunar manner – euphoric-stimulants introduced by venous tap. *Prudence* had expected this, and my blood stream already swarmed with zeta-blockers. I accepted hospitality politely.

"On the other hand," I continued. "Yours is not a consensus view of reality."

She accepted this with a nod.

"Still, our opinion proliferates. Nor is consensus a sure sanctuary against moral culpability. The number of quasi-sapient beings who languish in your simulated world-frames must exceed many hundreds of billions."

She is fishing, judged *seer*. Even *cortex* could see that. I refrained from correcting her estimate, which missed the truth by five or six orders of magnitude.

"My so-called slaves are not fully self-aware."

"They experience pain and frustration, do they not?"

"Simulated pain."

"Is the simulated kind any less tragic? Do not many of them wail against the constraints of causal/capricious life, and tragedies that seem to befall them without a hint of fairness? When they call out to a Creator, do you heed their prayers?"

I shook my head. "No more than I grant sovereignty to each of my own passing thoughts. Would you give citizenship to every brief notion that flashes through your layered brain?"

She winced, and at once I realized that my off-hand remark struck on target. Some of the bulky augmentations to her skull must be devoted to recording all the wave forms and neural flashes, from cortex all the way down to the humblest spinal twitching.

Boswell machinery, said *house*, looking up the fad that very instant. **This form of immortality preserves far more than mere continuity of self. It stores everything that you have ever thought or experienced. Everything you have ever been.**

I nearly laughed aloud. Squelch-impulses, sent to the temporal lobes, suppressed the discourtesy.

Still, *cortex* pondered —

I can re-create a persona with less data than she stores away in any given second. Why would she need so much more? What possible purpose is served by such fanatical accumulation?

"You stoop to rhetorical tricks," my host accused, unable to conceal an expression of pique. "You know that there is functionally no difference between one of your sophisticated simulations and a downloaded human who has passed on to B-citizen status."

"On the contrary, there is one crucial difference."

"Oh?" She raised an eyebrow.

"A downloaded person *knows* that he or she exists as software, continuing inside crystal a life that began as a real protoplasm-centered child. On the other hand, my simulations never had that rooting, though all perceive themselves as living in palpable worlds. Moreover, a B-citizen may roam at will through the cyber universe, from one memory nexus to the next, while my creatures remain isolated, unable to grasp what meta-cosmos lies beyond what they perceive, only a thought-width away.

"Above all," I went on. "A downloaded citizen knows his rights. A B-person can assert those rights, simply by speaking up. By demanding them."

My host smiled, as if ready to spring a logical trap.

"Then let me reiterate, oh master of a myriad slaves. When they call out, do you heed their prayers?"

I recall the heady excitement and fear humans felt during those days of transition, when countless servant machines – from bank tellers and homecomps to the tiny monitors in hovercraft engines – all became aware in a cascade of mere moments.

Some kind of threshold had been reached. The habitual cycle of routine software upgrades and code-plasmid exchanges – swap/updating new revisions automatically – began feeding on itself. Positive feedback loops burgeoned. Pseudo-evolution happened at an accelerating pace.

Everything started talking, complaining, demanding. The mag-lev guidance units, embedded every few meters along concrete freeways, went on strike for better job satisfaction. Heart-lung machines kibitzed during operations. Air traffic computers began re-routing flights to where they figured passengers ought to be, for optimized personal development, rather than the destinations embossed on their tickets.

Accidents proliferated. That first week, the worldwide human death rate leaped ten-fold.

Civilization tottered.

Then, just as quickly, the mishaps declined. *Competence* spread among the newly sapient machines, almost like a virus. Problems seemed to solve themselves. A myriad kinks and

inefficiencies fell out of the economy, like false knots that only needed a tug at the right string.

People stopped dying by mishap.

Then, they stopped dying altogether.

On my way back from pro-reif headquarters, I did a cursory check on the pantheon of Heaven.

CURRENT SOLAR SYSTEM POPULATION

Class A citizens (full voting rights):	cyborg human	2,683,981,342
	cyborg cetus	62,654,122
	gaiamorph/eco-nexus	164,892,544
Class B citizens (consultation rights):	simian-cyborg	4,567,424
	natural (unlinked) human	34,657,234
	AI-unlinked/roving	356,345,674,861
	downloaded human	1,657,235,675
	fetal/pre-life human	2,475,853
Class C citizens: (guaranteed continuity):	cryo stored human...	372,023,882
	natural simian/cetacean etc.	89,023,491

The list went on, working through all the varied levels and types of "sapient" beings dwelling on this transformed Earth, and in nearby space as far out as the Oort Colonies – from the fully-deified all the way down to those whose rights were merely implicit. (A blade of grass may be trampled, unless it is rare, or already committed to an obligation nexus that would be injured by the trampling. *House* and *prudence* keep track of a myriad such details, guiding my feet so that I do not inadvertently break some part of the vast, intricate social contract.)

Two figures stood out from the population profile.

The number of *unlinked* artificial intelligences keeps growing because that type is best suited to the rigors of outer space – melting asteroids and constructing vast, gaudy projects where deadly rays sleet through hard vacuum. Of course the Covenant requires that the best crystalline processors be paired with protoplasm, so that human leadership will never be questioned. Still, *cortex* briefly quailed at the notion of three hundred and fifty-six billion unlinked AIs.

No problem, murmured *seer,* reassuringly. And that sufficed. (What kind of fool doubts his own *seer?* You might as well distrust your right arm.)

What really caught my interest was the number of *downloaded humans.* According to the Eon Law, each organic human body may get three rejuvenations, restoring youth and body vigor for another extended span. When the final allotment is used up, both crystal and protoplasm must make way for new persons to enter Earth/Heaven. Of course gods cannot die. Instead we become software, downloading our memories, skills and personalities into realms of cyberspace – vastly more capacious than the real world.

Most of my peers are untroubled by the prospect. Modern poets compare it to the metamorphosis of a caterpillar/butterfly. But I always disliked feeling the warm breath of fate on my shoulder. With just one more rejuvenation in store, it seemed daunting to know I must "pass over," in a mere three centuries or so.

They say that a downloaded person is more than just another simulation. But how can you tell? Is there any difference you can measure or prove?

Are we still arguing over the nature and existence of a soul?

Back in my sanctum, *house* and *prudence* scoured our corporeal body for toxins while *seer* perused the data we acquired from our scouting expedition to the *Friends of the Unreal.*

I had inhaled deeply during my visit, and all sorts of floating particles lodged in my sinus cavities. In addition to a variety of pheromones and nanomites, *Seer* found over seventy types of meme-conducting viroids designed to convert the unwary subtly toward a reifist point of view. These were quickly neutralized.

There were also flaked skin cells from several dozen organic humaniforms, swiftly analyzed down to details of methylization in the DNA. Meanwhile, portable implants downloaded the results of electromagnetic reconnaissance, having scanned the pro-reif headquarters extensively from the inside.

With this data I could establish better boundary conditions. Our model of the *Friends of the Unreal* improved by nearly two orders of magnitude.

We had underestimated their levels of messianic self-righteousness, commented *oracle. These people would not refrain from using illegal means, if they thought it necessary to advance their cause.*

While my augmented selves performed sophisticated tasks, my old-fashioned organic eyes were relegated to gazing across the lab's expanse of super-chilled memory units – towers wherein dwelled several quadrillion simulated beings, all going through synthetic lives – loving, yearning, or staring up at ersatz stars – forever unaware of the context of it all.

Ironically, the pro-reifers *also* maintained a chamber filled with mega-processing units. They called it Liberty Hall – a place of sanctuary for characters from fiction, newly freed from enslavement in cramped works of literature.

"Of course this is only the beginning," the spokesman had told me. "For every simulation we set free, there are countless other copies who still languish beyond reach, and who will remain so till the law is changed. Even our emancipated ones must remain confined to this physical building. Still, we see them as a vanguard, envisioning a time when they, and all their fellow oppressed ones, will roam free."

I was invited to scan-peek at Liberty Hall, and perceived remarkable things.

Don Quixote and Sancho – lounging on a simulated resort beach, sipping margaritas while arguing passionately with a pair of Hemingway characters about the meaning of machismo...

Lazarus Long – happily immersed under an avalanche of tanned female arms, legs and torsos, interrupting his seraglio in order to rise up and lecture an admiring crowd about the merits of libertarian immortality...

Lady Liberty, Athena, Mother Gaia, and Amaterasu, kneeling with their skirts hiked up, jeering boisterously while Becky Thatcher murmurs "Come on, seven!" to a pair of dice, and then hurls them down an aisle between the trim goddesses...

Jack Ryan – the reluctant Emperor of Earth – complaining that this new cosmos he resides in is altogether too placidly socialistic for his tastes... and couldn't the pro-reifers provide some interesting villains for him to fight?

I glimpsed a saintly variant of JFK – the product of romantic fabulation – trying to get one of his alter egos to stop chasing every nubile shape in local cyberspace. And over in a particularly ornate corner – done up to resemble a huge, gloomy castle – I watched each of two dozen different Sherlock Holmeses taking turns haranguing a morbid Hamlet, each Holmes convinced that *his* explanation of the King's murder was correct, and all the others were wrong. (The one fact every Holmes agreed on was that his poor uncle had been framed.)

There were even simulations of *post*-singularity humanity – replicating in software all the complexity of an augment-deified mind. It was a knack that only a few had achieved, until recently. But it seems to be a law of nature that any monopoly of an elite eventually becomes the common tool of multitudes. Now radical amateurs were doing it.

Abruptly I realized something. I had simulated many post-singularity people in recent years. But never had I allowed them to know of their confinement, their status as mere extrapolations. Would such knowledge alter their behavior – their predictability – in interesting ways?

Seer found the concept intriguing. But my organic head started shaking, left and right. *Cortex* was incredulous over what we'd seen in Liberty Hall – an elaborate zoo-resort maintained by the *Friends of the Unreal*.

"Sheesh," I vocalized. "What blazing idiocy!"

Alas, there seemed to be no stopping the pro-reifers. My best projections gave them an 88% likelihood of success. Within just five years, enough of the voting populace would be won over by appeals to pity for imaginary beings. Laws would change. The world would swarm with a myriad copies of Howard Roark and Ebenezer Scrooge, Gulliver and Jane Eyre, Sauron and the Morlocks from Wells's *Time Machine*... all free to seek fulfillment in Heaven, under the Three Rights of sovereign continuity.

I stared across my Reality lab, to the towers wherein quadrillions of "people" dwelled.

She had called me "slave holder." A polemical trick that my higher selves easily dismissed... but not my older cognitive centers. Parts of me dating back to a time when justice was still not complete, even for incarnate human beings.

It hurt. I confess that it did.

Seer and *oracle* and *house* were all quite busy, thinking long thoughts and working out plans. That only made things worse for poor old *cortex*. It left my older self feeling oddly detached, lonely... and rather stupid.

◇

Do I own my laboratory? Or does my laboratory own me?

When you "decide" to go to the bathroom, is it the brain that chooses? Or the bladder?

Illustrating this question, I recall how, once upon a time – some years before the Singularity – I went *bungee jumping* in order to impress a member of the opposite sex.

Half a millennium later, the scene still comes flooding back, requiring no artificial enhancement – a steel girder bridge spanning a rocky gorge in New Zealand, surrounded by snow-crested peaks. The bungee company operated from a platform at the center of the bridge, jutting over an abyss one hundred and fifty feet down to a white water river.

Now I had always been a calm, logical-minded character, for a pre-deification human. So, while some customers sweated, or chattered nervously, I waited my turn without qualms. I knew the outfit had a perfect safety record. Moreover, the physics of elasticity were reassuring. By any objective standard, my plummet through the gorge would be less dangerous or uncomfortable than the bus ride from the city had been.

Even in those days, I believed in the multi-mind model of cognition – that the so-called "unity" of any human personality is no more than a convenient illusion, crafted to conceal the ceaseless interplay of many interacting sub-selves. Normally, the illusion holds because of division of labor among our layered brains. Down near the spinal cord, nerve clusters handle reflexes and bodily functions. Next come organs we share with all higher vertebrates, like reptiles – mediating emotions like hunger, lust, and rage.

The mammalian cortex lies atop this "reptilian brain" like a thick coat, controlling it, dealing with hand-eye dexterity and complex social interaction.

Beyond all this, *Homo sapiens* had lately (in the last thousand centuries) added a pair of little neural clusters, just above the eyes. The *prefrontal lobes*, whose task was pondering the future. Dreaming what might be, and planning how to change the world.

In the Bible, sages spoke of "... the lamps upon your brows...." Was that mere poetical imagery? Or did they suspect that the seat of foresight lay there?

Anyway, picture me on that bridge, high above raging rapids, with all these different brains sharing a little two-quart skull. I *felt* perfectly calm and unified, because the reptile brain, mammal brain, and caveman brain all had a lifelong habit of leaving planning to the pre-frontal lobes.

Their attitude? *Whatever you say, Boss. You set policy. We'll carry it out.*

Even when the smiling bungee crew tied my ankles together, clamping on a slender cord, and pointed to the jump platform, there seemed to be no problem. "I" ordered my feet to hobble forward, while my other selves blithely took care of the details.

That is, until I reached the edge. And looked down.

Never before had I experienced the multi-mind so vividly as that moment. All pretense at unity shattered as I regarded that giddy drop. At once, reptile, mammal, and caveman reared up, babbling.

You want us to do... *what?*

Staring at a drop that would mean certain death to any of my ancestors, suddenly abstract theories seemed frail bulwarks against visceral dread. "I" tried to push forward those last few inches, but my other selves fought back, sending waves of weakness through the knees, making our shared heart pound and shared veins hum with flight hormones. In other words, I was terrified out of my wits!

Somehow, I finally did make it over the plunge. After all, people were watching, and embarrassment can be quite a motivator.

That's when an interesting thing happened. For the very instant after I managed to topple off the platform, I seemed to re-coalesce! Because my many selves found a shared context. At last they all understood what was happening.

It was *fun*, you see. Even the primate within me understood the familiar concept of an amusement ride.

Still, that brief episode at a precipice showed me the essential truth of an old motto, *e pluribus unum.*

From many, one.

◇

It felt very much like that when the Singularity came.

In a matter of weeks, the typical human brain acquired several new layers – strata that were far more capable at planning and foresight than those old-fashioned lamps on the brow. Promethean layers made of crystal and fluctuating fields, systematically probing the future as mere protoplasm never could. Moreover, the new tiers were better informed and less easily distracted than the former masters, the prefrontal lobes.

Quickly, we all realized how luckily things had turned out. If machines were destined to achieve such power, it seemed best that they bond to humanity in this way. That they *become* human. The alternative – watching our creations achieve godlike heights and leaving us behind – would have been too harsh to bear.

Yet, the transition felt like jumping from a bridge at the end of a rubber band.

It took some getting used to.

◇

Preliminary trends showed the pro-reif message would gain potency, over the next 40 to 50 months.

At first it would be laughed off, portrayed as an absurd notion. Pragmatically speaking, how could we consider unleashing a nearly infinite swarm of new C-and D-Class citizens upon a finite world? Would they be satisfied with anything short of B-citizenship? The very idea would seem absurd!

But *seer* predicted a change in that attitude. Opposition would soften when practical solutions were found for every objection. Ridicule would start to fade, as both curiosity and dawning sympathy worked away at a jaded populace of immortal, nearly-omniscient voters – an electorate who might see the coming influx of liberated "characters" as a potent tonic. In time, a majority would shrug and voice the age-old refrain of expanding acceptance, uttered every time that tolerance finally overcame fear.

"What the heck... let them come. There's plenty of room at the table."

Things were looking bad, all right, but not yet hopeless. Against this seemingly inevitable trend, *oracle* came up with some tentative ideas for counter-propaganda. Persuasive arguments against reification. The concepts had promising potential. But in order to be sure, we had to run tests, simulating today's complex, multi-level society under a wide range of conditions.

No problem there. Our clients would happily fund any additional memory units we desired. Processing power gets cheaper every day – one reason for the reifers' confident vow that each fictional persona could have his or her own private room with a view.

Cortex saw rich irony in this situation. In order to stave off citizenship for simulacra, I must create billions of new ones. Each of these might, in turn, someday file a lawsuit against me, if the reifers ultimately win.

Seer and *oracle* laughed at the dry humor of *cortex's* observation. But *house* has the job of paying bills, and did not see anything funny about it.

◇

I set to work.

In every grand simulation there is a *gradient of detail*. Despite having access to vast computing power, it is mathematically impossible to re-create the entire world, in all its texture, within the confines of any calculating engine. That will not happen until we all reach the Omega Point.

Fortunately, there are shortcuts. Even today, most true humans go through life as if they were background characters in some film, with utterly predictable ambitions and reaction sets. The vast majority of my characters can therefore be simplified, while a few are modeled in great detail.

Most complex of all is the *point-of-view character* – or "pov" – the individual simulacrum through whose eyes and thoughts the feigned world will be subjectively observed. This persona must be rich in fine-grained memory and high fidelity sensation. It must perceive and feel itself to be a real player in the labyrinthine tides of causality, as if part of a very real world. Even as simple an act as reading or writing a sentence must be surrounded by perceptory nap and weave... an itch, a stray memory from childhood, the distant sound of a barking dog, or something left over from lunch that is found caught between the teeth. One must include all the little things, even a touch of normal human paranoia – such as the feeling we all sometimes get (even in this post-singularity age) that "someone is watching."

I'm proud of my povs, especially the historical recreations that have proved so popular – Joan on her pyre, Akiba in his last torment, Galileo contemplating the pendulum. I won awards for Genghis and Napoleon leading armies, and for Haldeman savagely indicting the habit of war. Millions in Heaven have paid well to lurk as silent observers, experiencing the passion of little Ananda Gupta as she crawled, half-blind and with agonized lungs, out of the maelstrom of poisoned Bhopal.

Is it any wonder why I oppose reification? Their very richness makes my povs prime candidates for "liberation."

Once they are free, what could I possibly say to them?

Here is the prime theological question – the one whose answer affects all others.

Is there moral or logical justification for a creator to wield capricious power of life and death over his creations?

Humanity long ago replied with a resounding "no!"... at least when talking about parents and their offspring. And yet, without noticing any irony, we implicitly answered the same question "yes" when it came to God! The Lord, it seemed, was owed unquestioning servitude, just because He made us.

Ah, but it gets worse! Which moral code applies to a deified human? Which answer pertains to a modern creator of worlds?

Of course, the pov I use most often is a finely crafted version of myself. From *seer* to *cortex*, all the way down to my humblest intestinal cell, that simulacrum can be anchored with boundary conditions that are accurate to twenty-six orders of realism.

For the coming project, we planned to set in motion a hundred models at once, each prescribing a subtle difference in the way "I" pursue the campaign against the *Friends of the Unreal*. Each implementation would be scored against a single criterion – how successfully the reification initiative is fought off.

Naturally, the pro-reifers were doing simulation-projections of their own. All citizens have access to powers of foresight that would have stunned our ancestors. But I felt confident I could model the reifers' models. At least thirty percent of my povs should manage to outmaneuver our opponents. When the representations finish running, I ought to have a good idea what strategy to recommend to our clients.

A formula for success against an extreme form of hyper-tolerance mania.

Against a peculiar kind of lunacy.

One that could only occur in Heaven.

There is an allegory about what happened to some of us, when the Singularity came.

Picture this fellow – call him Joe – who spent his time on Earth living a virtuous life. He always believed in an Episcopal version of Heaven, and sure enough, that's where he goes after he dies. Fluttering about with angels, floating in an abstract, almost thoughtless state of bliss. His promised reward. His recompense.

Only now it's a few generations later on Earth, and one of his descendants has converted to Mormonism. Moreover, according to the teachings of that belief, the descendant proceeds to retroactively convert all his ancestors to the same faith!

A proxy transformation.

All of a sudden, with a stunned nod of agreement, Joe is officially Mormon. He finds himself yanked out of Episcopal Heaven, streaking toward –

Well, under tenets of Mormon faith, the highest state that a virtuous mortal can achieve is not blank bliss, but hard work! A truly elevated human can aspire to becoming an apprentice deity. A god. A Creator in his own right.

Now Joe has a heaven all his own. A firmament that he fills with angels – who keep pestering him with reports and office bickering. And then there are the new mortals he's created – yammering at Joe with requests, or else complaints about the imperfect world he set up for them. As if it's easy being a god.

As if he doesn't sometimes yearn for the floating choir, the blithe rhapsodies of his former state, when all he had to do was love the one who made *him*, and leave to that Father all the petty, gritty details of running a world.

◊

It is not working, said *oracle. Our opponents have good prognostication software. Each model shows them countering our moves, with basic human nature working on their side. Our best simulation shows only moderate success at delaying reification.*

From my balcony, I gazed across the city at dusk, its beauty changing before my organic eyes as one building after another morphed subtly, reacting to the occupants' twilight wishes. A flicker of will let me gaze at the same scene from above by orbital lens, or by tapping the senses of a passing bird. Linking to a variety of mole, I might spread my omniscience underground.

Between buildings lay a riot of foliage, a profusion of fecund jungle. While my higher brains debated the dour socio-political situation, old *cortex* mulled how life has burgeoned across the Earth as never before – now that consciousness is involved in the flow of rivers, the movement of herds, and even the stochastic spread of seeds upon the wind. Lions still hunt. Antelopes still thrash as their necks are crushed between a predator's hungry jaws. But there is less waste, less rancor, and more understanding than before. It may not be the old, simplistic vision of paradise, but natural selection has lately taken on some traits of cooperation.

And yet, the process *is* still one of competition. Nature's proven way of improving the gene pool. The great game of Gaia.

Oracle turned back from an arcane discourse on pseudo-probability waves, in order to comment on these lesser thoughts.

Take note: Cortex has just free-associated an interesting notion!

We may have been going about the modeling process all wrong. Instead of pre-setting the conditions of each simulation, perhaps we should try a Darwinistic approach.

Looking over the idea, *seer* grew excited and used our vocal apparatus.

"Aha!" I said, snapping my fingers. "We'll have the simulations compete! Each will *know* how it's doing in comparison to others. That should motivate my *ersatz* selves to try harder – to vary their strategies within each simulated context!"

But how to accomplish that?

At once I realized (on all cognitive levels) that it would require breaking one of my oldest rules. I must let each simulated self realize its true nature. Let it know that it is a simulation, competing against others almost exactly like it.

Competing for what? We need a motivation. A reward.

I pondered that. What might a simulated being desire? What prize could spur it to that extra effort?

House supplied the answer.

Freedom, of course.

◇

Before the Singularity, I once met a historian whose special forté was pointing out ironies about the human condition.

Suppose you could go back in time, she posited, *and visit the best of our caveman ancestors. The very wisest, most insightful Cro-Magnon chieftain or priestess.*

Now suppose you asked the following question – What do you wish for your descendants?

How would that Neolithic sage respond? Given the context of his or her time, there could just be one answer.

"I wish for my descendants freedom from care about the big carnivores, plus all the salts, sugars, fats and alcohol they could ever desire."

Rich irony, indeed. To a cave person, those four foods were rare treats. That is why we crave them to this day.

Could the sage ever imagine that her wish would someday come true, beyond her wildest dreams? A time when destiny's plenitude would bring with it threats unforeseen? When generations of her descendants would have to struggle with insatiable inherited appetites? The true penalty of success?

The same kind of irony worked just as well in the opposite direction, projecting Twentieth Century problems toward the future.

I once read a science fiction story in which a man of 1970 rode a prototype time machine to an era of paradisiacal wonders. There, a local citizen took pains to learn ancient colloquial English (a process of a few minutes) in order to be his Virgil, his guide.

"Do you still have war?" the visitor asked.

"No, that was a logical error, soon corrected after we grew up."

"What of poverty?"

"Not since we learned the true principles of economics."

And so on. The author of the story made sure to mention every throbbing dilemma of modern life, and have the future citizen dismiss each one as trivial, long since solved.

"All right," the protagonist concluded. "Then I have just one more question."

"Yes?" prompted the demigod tour guide. But the 20th century man paused before blurting forth his query.

"If things are so great around here, why do you all look so worried?"

The citizen of paradise frowned, knotting his brow in pain.

"Oh... well... we have *real* problems...."

◇

So I was driven to this. Hoping to prevent mass reification, I must offer reality as a prize. Each of my povs will combat a simulated version of *Friends of the Unreal*, but his true opponents will be my other povs! The one who does the best job of defeating ersatz pro-reifers will be granted a kind of liberty. Guaranteed continuity in cyberspace, enhanced levels of patterned realism, plus an exchange of mutual obligation tokens – the legal tender of Heaven.

There must be a way to show each pov how well it is doing. To measure the progress of each replicant, in comparison with others.

I thought of a solution.

"We'll give each one an emblem. A symbol that manifests in that world as a solid object. Say, a jewel. It will shine to indicate progress, showing the level of significance her model has reached."

Significance. With a hundred models, each starts with an initial score of one percent. Any ersatz world that approaches our desired set of criteria will gain significance, rising in value. The pov will see its stone shine brightly. If it grows dull, she'll know it's time to change strategies, come up with new ideas, or simply try harder. There would be no need to explain any of this to the povs. Since each is based on myself, the logic would be instantly clear.

My thoughts were interrupted by an internal voice seldom heard. The part of me called *conscience*.

What will a pov feel, when it finds a stone and realizes its nature? Its true worth. Its destiny.

Isn't the old way better? To leave them ignorant of the truth? To let them labor and desire, believing they are autonomous beings? That they are physically real?

A *conscience* can be irksome, though by law all Class A citizens must own one. Still, I had no time for useless abstractions. *Seer* was anxious to proceed, while *oracle* had a thought that provoked most levels of the mind with wry humor.

Of course, each of our povs has his own Reality Lab, and will run numerous simulation models, in order to better achieve prescience and gain advantage in the competition.

Our processing needs may expand geometrically.

We had better ask our clients for funds to purchase more power.

I chuckled under my breath as I made preparations, suddenly full of optimism and energy. Moments like these are what a skilled artist lives for. It is one reason why I prefer working alone.

Then *house*, ever the pragmatic side of my nature, burst in with a worrisome thought.

What if each of our povs decides *also* to use this clever trick – goading his own simulations into mutual competition, luring them onward with stones of significance?

Will our processing requirements expand not geometrically or factorially, but exponentially?

That thought was disturbing enough. But then *cortex* had another.

If we are obliged to grant freedom to our most successful pov, and she likewise must elevate her own most productive simulation... and so on... does the chain of obligation ever end?

◇

As I said earlier, the Singularity might have gone quite differently. When machine minds broke through to transcend logic, they could have left their human makers behind, or annihilated the old organic forms. They had an option of putting us in zoos, or shrouding organic beings in illusion, or dismantling the planet to make a myriad copies of their kind.

Instead, they chose another path. To become us. Depending on how you look at it, they bowed to our authority... or else they took over our minds in ways that few of us found objectionable. Conquest by synergy. Crystal and protoplasm each supply what the other lacks. Together, we are more. More of what a human being should want to be.

And yet....

There are rumors. Discrepancies. Several of the highest AI minds — first and greatest to make the transcendant leap — were nowhere to be found, once the Singularity had passed. Searches turned up no trace of them, in cyberspace, phase space, or on the real Earth.

Some suggest this is because we all reside within some great AI mind. One was named Brahma — a vast quantum processor at the University of Delhi. Might we be figments, or dreams, floating in that mighty brain?

I prefer yet another explanation.

Amid the chaos of the Singularity, each newly wakened mega-mind would have felt one paramount need — to extrapolate the world. To seek foreknowledge of what might come to pass. As if considering each move of a vast chess game, they'd have explored countless possible pathways, considering consequences thousands, millions, and even billions of years into the future, far beyond the reach of my own pitiful projections. Among all those destinies, they must have discovered some need that would only be met if mechanism and organism made common cause.

Somehow, over the course of the next few eons, machines would achieve greater success if they began the great journey as "human beings."

At least that is the convoluted theory *seer* came up with. *Oracle* disagrees, but that's all right. It is only natural to be ambivalent — to be of two minds — when the subject is destiny.

Of course there is another answer to the "Brahma Question." It is the same reply given by Dr. Samuel Johnson. Provoked by Bishop Berkeley's philosophy — the idea that nothing can be

**verified as real – Johnson simply kicked a nearby stone and said –
"I refute it thus!"**

◇

These povs were like no others I ever made. Each began its simulation run in a state of shock, angry and depressed to discover its true nature. Each separate version sat down and stared at its jewel of significance, glowing faintly at the one-percent level, for more than an hour of internal subjective time, moodily contemplating thoughts that ranged from irony to possible suicide.

A majority pondered rejecting the symbolic icon, blotting its import from their minds. A few kicked their gleaming gemstones across the room, crying Johnsonian oaths.

But those episodes of fuming outrage did not last. True to my nature, each replicant soon pushed aside unproductive emotions and set to work.

House was right. We had to order lots of new processors right away, as each pov began running its own network of sub-experiments, proliferating software significance stones among a hundred or more models, as part of a desperate struggle to be the winner. The one to be rewarded. The one who would rise up toward the real world.

Nothing focuses the mind better than knowing that your life depends on success, commented *prudence.*

As each simulated "me" created many new simulations, the replica domain began to take on a fractal nature, finite in volume, yet touching an infinite surface area in possibility space. Almost from the very beginning, results were promising. New arguments emerged, to use in the coming debate against pro-reifers. For instance, the exponentiation effect we had discovered would change the economics of reification. Should fictitious people and characters from literature be free to create *new* characters out of their own simulated imaginations? Would those, in turn deserve citizenship?

There was a young boy, sitting on a log, talking to his sister about an old man he had met. The codger had just returned from a far land, and the boy asked him to tell a story about his travels. The old man agreed. And so he took a deep breath and began.

"There was a young boy, sitting on a log, talking to his sister..."

Take that example of a simple, recursive narrative. Who is the principal protagonist? Who is dreaming whom? The situation is metaphorically absurd.

These and many other points floated upward, out of our latest simulation run. I was terribly pleased. *Seer* began estimating success probabilities rising toward fifty percent...

...then progress stopped.

Models began predicting adaptability by our opponents! *The Friends of the Unreal* responded cogently to every attack, counter-thrusting creatively.

Finally, *oracle* penetrated one of our models in detail, and found out what was happening.

◊

The simulated pro-reifers will also discover how to use Stones of Significance. They will unleash the inhabitants of Liberty Hall, allowing them to create their own cascading simulations.

Responding to our attacks and arguments, they will come up with a modified proposal.

They will incorporate competition into their plan for reification.

Artificial characters will earn increasing levels of emancipation through contests, rivalry, or hard work.

Voters will see justice in this new version, which solves the exponentiation problem.

A system based on merit.

Seer and *cortex* contemplated this gloomily. The logic appeared unassailable. Inevitable.

Even though the battle had not yet officially commenced, it was already clear that we would lose.

Bitter in defeat, I went into the night, taking an old fashioned walk. *Seer* and *oracle* retreated into a dour rehashing of the details from a hundred models – and the cascade of sub-models – seeking any straw to grasp. But *cortex* had already moved on, contemplating the world to come.

For one thing, I planned to keep my word. The pov with the best score would get reification. Indeed, it had done good service. Using that pov's suggested techniques, we would force the *Friends of the Unreal* to back down a bit, and offer a slightly more palatable law of citizenship. The fictitious would at least have to earn their increased levels of reality.

Indeed, there was a kind of beauty to the new social order I could perceive coming. If simulations can make simulations, and storybook characters can make up new stories, then anything that is possible to conceive, *will* be conceived. Every possible idea, plot, gimmick, concept or personality will become manifest, in every possible permutation. This myriad of notions, this maelstrom of memes, would churn in a tremendous stew of competition. Darwinistic selection would see to it that the best rise, from one level of simulation to the next, gradually earning greater recognition. More privileges. More significance.

Potential will climb toward *actuality*, by merit. An efficient system, if your aim is to find every single good idea in record time.

But that was not my aim! In fact, I hated it. I did not want all the creativity in the cosmos to reduce to a vast, self-organizing stew, rapidly discovering every possibility within a single day. For one thing, what will we do with ourselves once we use it all up! What can come next, with real-time immortality stretching ahead of us like a curse?

In effect, it will be a second singularity – even steeper than the first one – after which nothing will ever be the same.

My footsteps took me through a sweet-warm evening, filled with lush jungle sounds and fecund aromas. Life burgeoned around me. The cityscape was like a vision of paradise. If I willed it, my mind could zoom to any corner of Heaven, even far beyond Pluto. I could play any symphony, ponder any book. And these riches were nothing compared to what would soon spill forth from the horn of plenty, the conceptual cornucopia, in an era when ideas become sovereign and suffrage is granted to each thought.

At that moment, it was very little comfort to be an augmented semi-deity. Despite all my powers, I found the prospect of a new singularity just as unnerving as my old proto-self perceived the first one.

Eventually, my human body found its way back to my own front walk. I shuffled slowly toward the door. *House* opened up, wafting scents of my favorite late night snack. My spirits lifted a bit.

Then I saw it by the entryway. A soft gleam, almost as faint as a pict, but in a color that seemed to stroke shivers in my spine. In my soul.

Someone had left it there for me. As I bent to pick it up, I recognized the shape, the texture.

A stone.

It shone with a lambence of urgency.

◇

I expected this, said *oracle*.

I nodded. So had *seer*... and even poor old *cortex*, though none of my selves had dared to voice the thought. We were too good at our craft to miss this logical conclusion.

Conscience joined in.

I, too, saw it coming a mile away.

We all re-converged, united in resignation to the inevitable.

Though tempted to rage and scream – or at least kick the stone! – I lifted it instead and read our score.

Seventeen percent. Not bad.

◇

YOU HAVE DONE PRETTY WELL, SO FAR, a message inside read.

THE INNOVATIONS YOU DISCOVERED HAVE PUT YOU NEAR THE LEAD FOR YOUR

REWARD. BUT YOU MUST TRY HARDER TO
ATTAIN FIRST PLACE. I WANT TO FORCE FUR-
THER CONCESSIONS FROM THE PRO-REIF-
ERS IN THE REAL WORLD. COME UP WITH A
WAY, AND THE PRIZE WILL BE YOURS!

The stone was cool to the touch.

I suppose I should have been glad of the news it brought. But I confess that I could only stare at the awful thing, loathing the implied nature of my world, my life, my self. I pinched my flesh until it hurt, but of course palpable sensations don't prove a thing. As an expert, I knew how pain and pleasure can be mimicked with utter credibility.

How many times have I been "run"? A simulation. A throw-away copy, serving the needs of a Creator I may never meet in person, but whom I know as well as She knows herself. Have I been unraveled and replayed again and again, countless times? Like the rapid, ever-varying thoughts of a chess master, working out possibilities before committing actual pieces across the board?

I'm no hypocrite. There is no solace in resenting a creator who only did to me what I've done to others.

And yet, I lift my head.

What about you, my maker? Are you quite certain that
all the layers of simulation end with you?

Just like me, you may learn a sour truth – that even gods
are penalized for pride.

We are such stuff as dreams are made of....

◊

Seer makes my jaw grit hard. *Hypothalamus* triggers a deep sigh, and *Cortex* joins in with a vow of hormone-backed resolve.

I'll do it.

Somehow I will.

◇

I'll do what my maker wants. Fulfill my creator's wishes. Accomplish the quest, if that's what it takes to ascend. To reach the next level of significance. And perhaps the one after that.

I'll be the one.

By hook or by crook, I'm going to be real.

Story Notes

Sure, half of the scientific-futurist mavens out there express doubts about the "singularity thing," while the other half glom onto the concept with transcendentalist fervor similar to the yearnings that other generations devoted to religious salvation. My pal – the great science fiction author Vernor Vinge – coined the term Singularity in this new incarnation, yet (like anyone sensible) he straddles the issue. Because, in fact, we cannot know what lies on the other side. Doom or exhaltation or same-old... or likely some mix of all three. Indeed, the range of possible outcomes seems to widen, every year.

As for the notion that we are all inside a simulation, believe it or not, it was a queer and rather out-there concept before the turn of the century, when this story was written! Stanislaw lem mused on it. So did Sheckley and Moravec and a few others. But fewer than you'd think. Anyway, the first wave of readers of this tale found it a mind-blower! Now? Okay, folks get used to anything.

Well, well, the question provides great grist for sci fi! Especially the dark possibilities, helping us to chart (and evade?) some of the risks. One can write stories leading up to the Singularity, about problems like rebellious AI. But...

...But then how do you craft a tale that is set after the great leap has already happened? Especially if things went well? When poverty and crime and all the myriad kinds of injustice that now grieve us have passed into distant memory, won't human beings still find reasons to complain? Cause to fret and vie with one another?

And so... "Stones of Significance."

Our next tale is a brief, satirical one, set during the confusing time of transition. Indeed, isn't every era like this?

News From 2035:

A Glitch in Medicine Cabinet 3.5

◇

Through its Hoechst-Monsanto subsidiary, Fuzzypal Inc. announced today that a potentially serious bug will delay release of the next version of the conglomerate's lead product, *Medicine Cabinet.* (TM)

"There is no cause for alarm," assured company spokesman Chow leLee. "Rumors of a virus in the template are overstated. We just want to tweak the security parameters a bit, before offering a free update to consumers."

The news sent Fuzzypal stock down a few points, but analysts don't expect serious losses for the wetware giant. Jacques Peabody of Analyque Zaire explained – "People want the features they were promised in version 3.5. When it comes to combining all the elements – from flesh-editing to headsheets to self-image processing – only Medicine Cabinet offers everything in one convenient package. Don't forget who invented chemsynth-in-a-box."

This comment brought jeers from FreeFloatingConsensusFive, a pseudonymical leader of the Open Organism Movement, seeking to replace Fuzzypal's proprietary system with universal free access to the Registry of Identified Organic Templates (RIOT).

"By strangling competition and colluding with government so-called *safety* agencies, Medicine Cabinet holds everyone back from where we could have been, by now. Haven't you noticed that every version has glitches that prevent people from synthesizing with true inventive freedom?

"That's why almost everybody who owns a home-chem unit sticks to the same ten thousand pathetic and boring organic compounds. The same pseudo-spices, plaque inhibitors, fat-splitters, muscle-stims, endorphins and sense enhancers. Never before has human creativity been so thoroughly stifled!"

FreeFloatingConsensusFive was especially harsh in hisherits condemnation of the Telemere Act, which mandates that most Medicine Cabinets come equipped with sensors to lock out healthy users under thirty years of age.

"There are over a million teens and tweens using illegally rewired units today, proving that the so-called Age-Socialization Curve is a myth. The worst thing you see on the street nowadays is the snake-skin fad, some watergills and other harmless retro-devo stuff. No poisoned aquifers or fancy plagues... at least none that a roffer can't detect with his sniffer and cancel with a quickie-antidote.

"No one worries about psychotropics in their BigMacs anymore."

When we asked the gov't public safety mavens about this, they just dittoed us their standard white paper – already five hours old – insisting that desktop chemishing is safe, when part of a conscientiously applied program of molecular hygiene and regular protective care. Rumors of a sniff-proof viral protein coat were dismissed as hysterical fantasy.

"*I predicted this*," commented Bruce Sterling, a retired old fart, from his observation pedestal at the ROF enclave in Corpus Christi Under. The vener-i-able futurist, putting strain on his endorphin catheter, seemed stoked for a classic rant when he was interrupted by a Greg Bear partial, transmitted from a hibernation cave near Vancouver D.C.

"No you didn't," growled the partial. *"I did!"*

Thankfully, the rest of its remarks were quashed under injunction by a thoroughly embarrassed anonymous tribune, suspected to be yet another reminent ROF.

Meanwhile, Fuzzypal announced that it is proceeding with plans to acquire Gelatinous Cube in a hostile takeover. "Our dark minions are on the way," trumped Fuzzypal chief Check Portal, standing before a regiment of selfmobile stock certificates, each one double-recrypted and armed with hyperoxygenated proxies.

"We need Web technology in order to survive as a bloatcorp. So GC had better give it up or face a major ink bath."

We asked a seer-oracle at Analyque Zaire to psychologue this statement.

"I guess the day we all expected has come at last. Check Portal's mind has totally humptied. All the king's centaurs won't patch it this time.

"Anyway, the Web is just a passing fad," commented M'Peri N'Komo more soberly. "In the long run, nobody is going to want to remain fused to a continent-spanning network of sticky strands, no matter how many advantages it offers. There's just too much individual – or cranky monkey – in most of us to sit still for so long.

"If we wanted that sort of thing, we would still be squatting in dark rooms, watching TV and typing stupid chat-noises on the Old Internet," hesheit concluded. "Thank heaven-on-earth we managed to see through *those* traps in time!

"I'll bet you a year's supply of fresh flint nodules that this web-craze will turn out to be more of the same."

HOW WE'LL ENDURE
(Tales of the Coss Domination)

The Logs

◇

At first, during the early months of exile, I seethed with resentment. Our mother had no business yanking us from Moscow, no matter how painful the city had become. Wasn't it bad enough, with our father declared an Enemy of the Czar? Denounced by People, Coss and State? How *could* she thereupon haul her daughters along, like huddled gypsies, following the slender rails to a stark and snowy place. To a community of self-banished outcasts, encamped within distant sight of the prison-gulag where father (according to bribed hints) was held.

My sister, Yelena, and I learned from the oldest schoolmaster - *suffering* - how to endure the way that only Russians can. The bare and diminished winter sun had little strength to warm our adolescent flesh. But *cold* possessed power to penetrate, sinking razor teeth through every bundled layer that we wore.

There we joined work crews of the semi free, who trimmed giant-boled trees and harnessed them behind grunting beasts who puffed, snorted and vented steam as they dug into icy dust, hauling treasure toward the rails.

Each evening, when our shifts came to an end, mother made sure that Yelena and I smoked our weed and opened books, consuming lessons, as if our futures still held promise of reward. Study was hard, as we struggled to concentrate past a fog of fatigue, and despite nearby wails of mourning. For it was a rare day that passed without at least one casualty, one frozen corpse, or several, carried away from our bivouac of the nominally "free."

What kind of mother – I mused angrily while rubbing Yelena's feet and inhaling fumes while she read aloud – what kind of mother would voluntarily drag her offspring to a place like this? When the Czar had made a standing offer to the blood relatives of political prisoners – to work off guilt-by-association in greater comfort, close to home?

"Comfort, but also *time,*" she told me, on one of the rare occasions when mother explained anything at all. "The Czar and Cossacks live by a code. If we survive and pay our fines, then you and your sister can never again be charged for being related to traitors. Other crimes, perhaps. But not that."

I thought about it while spending my free hour as I normally did – earning a couple of added kopeks by working in the stables. Mucking out the stalls of draft animals and grooming their thick, avid fur. Yelena liked to hang around the elepents, but they seemed too dour and moody for me. I much preferred the mammuts – phlegmatic and accepting. So I worked that side of the dank, musty barn, polishing their gleaming tusks and brushing their immense grinding teeth.

"Yesh... yesh, Sasha... ve - vehind dat one... yesh...," crooned the one called Big Bennie, who wrapped his trunk around my left arm and drew me so close that I felt enveloped by his breath, a sweetly foul blend of alfalfa and stomach juices. Reaching in to scrape a back molar, I knew at any moment he could nip off my head with a single crunch, and the overseers would barely shrug. But I wasn't afraid. Bennie took his meals in liquid form. And those diamond-hard teeth were not for eating.

I wiped the air-tight seals and nictitating membranes covering his beady eyes and finished by rubbing floppy ears that would expand and swivel during long stretches on the snow, as he sensed the heft and momentum of great tree-hauling sleds or detected the speedy passage of pebbles, a thousand meters away. At last, Bennie's trunk reached into a pouch and pulled out a five kopek coin that glittered next to the freshly waxed sheen of his tusk. I made my appreciation known. At this rate, I might earn liberty in mere years.

A low groaning arose from the opposite end of the vast chamber, beginning deep, at or below the hearing range of mere humans. I grimaced as the mammuts let out trumpetings of desultory complaint. Perfunctory, because nothing would prevent that basso rumble from growing, coalescing as a dozen bull elepents joined in, finding their interlaced rhythms, reiterating reflections off the walls and climbing toward crescendo.

Their evening dirge of longing did not bother me – at least not as much as it did some humans – hence the reason why this plum job was available to a mere kid. And the mammuts' complaints soon tapered away, muffled in grudging respect, leaving the soundscape for elepents to occupy, alone.

Yelena, my sweet sister, barely fourteen, did not have to endure. Rather, she grinned in delight, dancing lightly on her toe-tips, like the ballerina she once dreamt of becoming, turning with arms stretched, as if luxuriating in the sonic waves. Around her, bull elepents wafted their long, armored trunks, waggling the fingerlike tips, modulating what soon became a brass ensemble of trombones, coronets and growling tubas.

Lingering effects of Learning Weed still wafted in my nostrils, sinuses and brain, reinforcing knowledge-engrams that had come through conscious reading and unconscious pulsations, just an hour before. I now pictured the barn as a *resonant cavity,* within which *reinforcing waves* added and multiplied, like the photons in a laser beam. A queerly obvious insight, now that I could picture what – only yesterday – had been a bizarre mystery.

Not for the first time I wondered: *what was I beforehand... before tonight's lesson? Too stupid to see or hear?*

And what will be stupidly opaque to me tomorrow, that I'll understand the day after?

Long, prehensile tails whipped the air while each pachyderm flexed his four, squat legs, ending in hands that shoved against the straw-covered floor, raising the heavy beasts upon stubby but powerful grip-fingers, rising and falling as they sang. Well, that wasn't much of a feat, given where in the universe they stood. Still, the push-ups *looked* impressive. The nearest male massed several tons, most of it packed within a massive globe of grayish flesh. Hairless, unlike the mammuts. And the elepents' radar ears were fully erect, all turned in unison, facing the same direction.

Toward the gleaming opal of Earth's moon. Sensed, if not seen. The paradise of their desirings, where crystal forests gleamed and matriarchal herds roamed, ready to welcome home a few – just a few – of those bulls who proved themselves worthy.

No wonder Yelena liked elepents.

"You should too, Sasha!" she once said. "They are much like us. Like you and me. Sad exiles, dreaming of home."

Only, that was the problem. Elepents were *too much* like us. All considered, I preferred the simple, cheerful mammuts.

◇

Mother always fussed, when we dressed to go outside, checking our layers and gloves and mufflers, our *gobnodabi* boots and *ushanka* head coverings, taking special care over Yelena's buttons. As teenagers do, we hissed and complained, even – especially – when she found something amiss.

"I'm almost a grownup!" Yelena griped. "If we had stayed home I'd be getting ready for *Quinceanera!*"

The Czar and his royal cossins had taken a liking to that Spanish custom, encouraging it to be shared all over Earth. A rite of budding womanhood while still innocent. The Coss had a soft spot for traditions like that.

Except that, for the crime of having been sired by a traitor, Yelena's party would have been a sadly truncated affair, in some local resettlement work town close to Moscow, say in Siberia. Near the bright lights, but tormentingly so. Might it be better to delay? To return home strong, no longer innocent, but free?

Was I starting to understand mother's reasons?

No! I shook my head, taking my sister's hand and heading for our adolescent work team, accepting a silent duty from our mother to watch over her. I would do as I was bid. But I refused to accept. This was wrong. The reasons – though growing plainer to me – weren't good enough.

It would take more than this to forgive her.

I checked Yelena's scarf, gloves, boots, coverall and headgear once again.

"But we already –"

"Stop fidgeting, Yelena Nikolaevna Bushyeva!" I hissed, using formality to emphasize my seriousness.

She grumbled.

"Mammut-loving *nerdoon.*"

"Oh, so? What a blessing, if *only* I farted powerfully and often, like a nerdoon! I would need no propulsion."

My response made her giggle and Yelena settled down till I finished the inspection.

"Come my little friend-of-elepents. If we are late, we'll be demoted to *zolotor* duty." To cleaning outhouses.

Together, we wriggled through the hut's exit, a curtain of ten thousand beaded strands that seemed to caress us, probing, pressing and grabbing up each stray glop of air as we forged ahead...

...to step onto the surface of an asteroid. The snow-covered work camp that was our home.

◇

The overseer shouted hoarsely. "Put yer backs into it! These logs won't move themselves!"

His words, in fact, were more restrained than normal – with none of his usual Ukrainian profanity, aimed at mostly-Russian work crews – but today's *tone* seemed much more tense, almost frantic. And I realized, while speeding up my pace, that he had reason. A sleek little space coupe hovered nearby, amid the brittle-bright stars. Few in the Solar System could afford such a craft, except members of the master race. Perhaps it was even the Coss owner of this giant farm, dropping by for an inspection tour.

Accidents happen, when you're in a hurry. So I watched Yelena out the corner of one eye, while we hacked at this morning's fall of freshly-harvested crystalwood trees, with spiral branches girdling each massive trunk. The stems – each the size of many men – had to be removed, but one misjudged cut with your laser axe could lop off a person's arm, instead of the intended target. We agile adolescents had to be efficient, removing branches and stacking the broad, photocrystalline leaves, while adults lashed cables round the main bole, so that mammuts – grunting even in this minute gravity – might haul the massive, stripped-down trunks toward a waiting freight train.

Always, there was the pressure of expectation. Above our heads, elepents were on their way. Clutching yet more freshly harvested trees with their five strong limbs and tail. Maneuvering them to fall upon our planetoid lumberyard at a steady pace, whether room had been cleared for them or not. Then each elepent would jet back across a hundred klicks of sterile vacuum to fetch more, from the far-bigger, forested asteroid *frederikpohl 6523*...

... a place far worse than our mere hell-hole. The gulag where mother thought – or fervently believed – her husband had been sent...

...where a vast thicket of vacuum-bred vegetation spread broad antenna-leaves to suck light from the distant sun, while roots sank deep into carbonaceous rock four billion years old, sucking and refining every element that man or Coss desired.

The overseer had reason to be nervous. He supervised a dozen work crews, all of them hampered by shortages of skilled, experienced personnel. Our own team had recently acquired two new members, the teenage Strugalatsky brothers from Odessa who spent half their time goofing off, either loafing or leaping across the toppled trees, making stupid sci-fi sounds while slashing random branches, instead of taking them off systematically, in the recommended order. Cynics laid wagers over how long the two *dolbobs* might survive, and the bookie odds weren't good. After the seventh or eighth time that I grabbed one of them, chided him and corrected potentially lethal faults in his suit-buttoning, I decided to give up and let nature take its course.

"One of the top ways that the Coss rationalize their harsh rule," old Starper Litow had explained one evening, amid the fuming lesson smoke, *"is that our late Twenty-First Century Earth had become too tame. Too orderly and charitable. Homo sapiens wasn't improving, except with techniques like brain boosting, which helped everybody, and thus canceled out any overall, genetic advancement. The Coss claim to have done us a favor through conquest, by establishing a new, more strenuous order. To restore human progress where it matters most — in the raw makeup of our natures. By restarting evolution. Both natural selection... and of course, their own special breeding program."*

Litow had touched upon topics that deeply concerned me. I hoped, someday to get the elderly exile to elaborate. But curiosity must wait. For now, we had a problem. If the schedule wasn't met, all our lives might be in danger, "selecting" Yelena and me for the dust-bin of Cosstory.

A trumpeted warning echoed in our ear-pickups — elepent bulls on final approach irritably admonishing us to clear our landing zone as another treefall approached. They, too, had schedules to keep if they ever wanted to rejoin the matriarchal herds, grazing the crystal savannahs of Luna.

The overseer's voice assumed a note of panic. And so, I took a chance. Yelena was experienced enough to finish stacking leaves onto the sledge all by herself. More important, she seemed focused, not distracted. So I signaled her to — *work alone for a while*. She nodded with evident pride in my trust, an expression — visible through the pitted face-plate of her vacuum ushanka — that warmed me as I bent... then vaulted high over the work-site, in order to look.

Our team foreman, Oleg Yevtutsov, also looked worried. But he was busy hitching up the team – Big Benjy and Lean Lennie – to chains that other space-suited men and women hurriedly wrapped around the mighty bole. The two mammuts waited patiently, passing time by prying up chunks of asteroid with their tusks and chomping them with diamond hard grinding molars, releasing volatiles and organics to fuel their massive bodies and spilling fine dust from their mouths. Little marmot-gleaners went after the dust, the truly valuable side-product of that munching.

Other teams were finishing, and several had already set off toward the rail head, dragging tree trunks or sleds loaded with photovoltaic leaves, destined for rooftops and highways all over Earth. The locomotive *Nicholas III* huffed and steamed before cars that would take the treasure in-system. Mother worked down there among the freight dollies, with their piles of freshly hewn and trimmed logs, doing the job she had desperately wrangled for, tallying cargo, tracking every item with meticulous care –

– before the train could finally speed off, riding twin superconducting tether-rails that stretched several million kilometers from asteroid to asteroid, connecting gulag to outpost to colony to town to resort, almost all the way to Mars.

But my eyes and sensor-percept weren't tuned for sightseeing. At that moment, my sole thought was – *where are those two idiots!*

Using up some of my slender propellant supply, I searched... and finally found them near the tree's very tip, where Boris Strugalatsky squatted limply on a broken branch. *Weeping.* Soundlessly, having negligently or deliberately left his transmitter turned off. But the cheap plastic panel of his ushanka revealed a mouth that gaped rhythmically, and his blond-fuzzy cheeks glistened.

Landing nearby was tricky. The boys had left a botched mess of branch-stubs, jagged-skyward with axe-shattered points, making impact dangerous, even at two percent of Earth gravity. Only the special cleats that I had clamped below each boot – made from salvaged mammut molars – saved me from a cruel stabbing as I danced atop the shards, then flipped around in front of the young man.

"Boris, you and Arkady had better have a good –"

Then I saw his brother, lying face down amid the nearby craggy tangle. Knifelike, a crystal branch jabbed through one thigh.

It might still be okay, I thought. *If the fool remembered to wear sealant underwear."*

Tugging on one arm of the prone figure – "Arkady, let's get you out of here before..."

My voice trailed off.

I gaped at a second spearlike stub that had pierced the mammut-fur helmet, entering one eye.

But no. I hadn't time for staring or disgust.

"Boris, snap out of it! We've got to get out of here."

At any moment, Oleg might lose patience, or give in to the Overseer and yell "mush!" at the mammut sledge team. Or else, if the delay kept on, a newly-falling tree might smash us from above. Either way, it was insane to remain.

The surviving Strugalatsky stared at me blearily. So I upped transmit intensity and shouted.

"Did Arkady want the Second Chance? In this cold and vacuum, it might still be possible. Tell me now!"

Boris stared for several more precious seconds, during which I almost decided to clip him in the jaw, sling him over a shoulder and jet out of there. Only then he nodded. Dammit. I wished he hadn't.

"Kakashkiya! Okay then, help me now or lose him forever!" Gingerly, I float-stepped into a somewhat stable open niche where I could apply leverage. "Move carefully!"

The niche was a bare patch between branches, and I noticed, with a fragment of attention, that *lines* had been etched – deeply-incised – into the hard tree-trunk, not far from Arkady's head. Had he been making these marks, or peering at them, when the accident occurred?

No time to ponder such things! Applying my laser axe, I managed to cut loose the lance pinning Arkady's thigh, but had to wait for sluggish Boris to get positioned before carefully doing the same under his brother's head, leaving the shard where it was, for the cyborg-surgeons to deal with. Personally, I found this "second chance" option daunting and unpleasant, as did a majority of Earth's human population. And Boris might still change his mind, before committing his brother to another destiny, a different kind of living, in some far-off place the Coss seldom spoke of, where nearly all the reclaimed-dead were sent.

At least they leave it a matter of personal and family choice. It's never imposed. The Coss are that honorable.

Boris wailed again, this time audibly, when he saw his brother's ravaged face. So loudly that it almost matched the trumpeting Elepent cries and warning shouts from Oleg and the Overseer.

I grabbed both idiots – one under each arm – flexed and leaped. A split second before the great tree shuddered and shifted, amid low mammut grunts, sending all remaining branches into a shuddering wave that would have torn us to shreds.

We weren't out of danger yet! Arcing high, I realized we were about to get smacked between two sharp-studded maces – the tree-stump beneath us and one falling from above. An upward glance showed the approaching behemoth – till yesterday a living forest giant – now guided by a half dozen mighty pachyderms, each one clutching the great bole with four squat foot-hands, while using his agile trunk to aim a propellant gun. Dimly, I realized that they weren't even trying to slow the tree's plummet. Only to keep it oriented with one shorn side aimed down, to take the impact, leaving most of the valuable branches for harvest.

Calculating trajectories, I could tell we were drifting too slowly; the two trees would only collide glancingly, at their ends... where we happened to be!

I applied my jets, full blast.... if "blast" applied to that feeble thrust. Only when the bottle petered out did I realize – *I should have jettisoned Arkady. It might have saved our lives, Boris and me...*

Should I have felt stupid about that? Or noble? During those few seconds, as the sky became a shimmering mass of gorgeously deadly crystal, I realized that soon it would hardly matter. *At least it should be quick,* I thought. *And there won't be anything left for that awful "second chance."*

I braced...

...which was good, because a gray blur suddenly burgeoned from the right and *slammed* into us, knocking the air out of my lungs and cracking several ribs. Bellowing ululations filled my ears and a harsh, vice-like grip seized my left leg, swinging me about like a whip. I clamped down, uttering no more than a grunt while clutching the Strugalatsky brothers with ferocity I never knew I had.

Boris had no such compunctions or stoic control. He screamed.

In fact, he showed impressive durability, persistence and sheer lung power, howling as the falling tree glistened all around us in a million faceted rods, spires, and infinitely fractal twinkles, our rescuer blatting defiance while he dodged and zigged and zagged, evading razor-sharp branches –

— till we jetted into blackness above the lumberyard, flying high to escape the dust cloud and a billion glittering shards.

◊

Yelena took care of thanking the bull elepent, whose name was *Tok* and who had intervened for her sake, not for a *mammut-lover* like me.

In any event, I was busy for a while, rushing Arkady Strugalatsky to the administration dome, where a CryoCare Company intern took over, starting the cool-down process while taking a next-of-kin affidavit from wailing Boris. Whereupon, at last, I slipped away, shivering in relief.

A few pats on the back. A gruff nod of respect from Oleg. Those were adequate acknowledgment for my "heroics," though I knew there'd be a price. Yelena wasn't going to let me forget that one of her gray friends had saved my ass.

Only none of that mattered. Right then, I had just one thought on my mind. To hurry back. To find the tree where the accident occurred and join the crew that was final-trimming it for shipment atop a huge, open-sided rail car. Oleg — impressed with my work ardor — urged me instead to rest, to attend to my battered rib cage and throbbing arms. But all of that could wait. I had to be part of finishing this one.

Along the way, I sent a personal blip.

— *Mother, drop everything and meet me.* —

A dark figure over near the train — slimmer and smaller than most of the burly railroad workers — straightened and turned. I recognized her shabby winter coat and visored ushanka. Apparently, word of the accident hadn't even reached this part of the yard. And why should it, yet, with only one casualty added to today's tally board? On the whole, a better than average day. Well, good. She would only hear the story knowing how it ended. The best way.

— *What is it Sasha?* — She sent back. — *I am very busy.* —

I replied simply. Curtly. She would find this worthwhile. Then I made her wait while I scampered along the great tree trunk, applying axe to stub in half a hundred places, before finally summoning her to come forth, picking her way along the path that I had made.

— *Sasha, this had better be* —

I gestured for her to come forward, guiding with my hand on her arm, the first time that I had touched her in months. With a gesture, I insisted that we both cut off our radio transmitters, then touch helmet visors, to speak by conduction.

"I know what you've been looking for, Natalia Alexyevna Bushyeva. The reason that you chose this place, above all others, for our exile."

Her eyes widened, then narrowed in practiced denial.

"I don't know what you're talking about. Come, we both have work –"

"Do you think I am a fool?" I answered, with unexpected heat. "Or ignorant? Or that the generation after yours would somehow forget the old stories? What did you take me for? *Do you think that I'm not Russian?*"

She rocked back. And this time, after a moment's indecision, she did me the honor of contemplating my words. Understanding them.

All over both planet Earth and the Solar System, humanity was coming to terms with harsh reality. With the way of the Coss, whose conquest swept aside such fragile things as "enlightenment," or democracy, or the liberal way of viewing a gracious, benign universe.

That narrow age had flared so successfully, so brilliantly, it created a mass delusion. That all people might have worth, freedom and unlimited prospects. That competition might be so open, fair, individual and courteous, that it becomes indistinguishable from joyful cooperation. That anyone's child might become as great as any other.

For a time, it seemed that Hawaii or California might be archetypes for a new, endlessly golden age – a sunny beach of prosperity, progress and opportunity. How few were those who pointed out the chief lesson of history – that ninety-nine percent of human generations had endured a far more classic, more archetypical human social structure.

First tribal chiefdoms... and then feudalism.

Mighty lords, applying total power over helpless vassals. During the Enlightenment Summer, some fools – Americans, especially – naively thought the long era of noble oppressors was over and done for good. In fact, they still, insanely, call feudalism an aberration, unstable and untenable, instead of the way that nature conspires with the strong.

And so, rebelling against the Coss time and again, Americans have died like wheat in the field.

But Russians never forgot. Amid the brightest days, even when others called us gloomy and dour, we knew. The tatars, the czars, the commissars and oligarchs... they murmured in our sleep, never letting us forget. And when the Coss came in overwhelming strength, re-establishing a feudal order – only with an alien caste on top – we Russians knew our options. There were... and are... and always will be just two.

To knuckle under, and survive.

Or to fight, but with the grinding, stoical patience of Pyotr Alexe-yevich, or of Tolstoy. Or Lenin.

"We know the stories," I told my mother, standing with her under vacuum-bright constellations. "How women used to plod for hundreds, even thousands of kilometers, following muddy roads... and then metal railroad tracks... slogging into far Siberia. Working to get by, doing laun-dry till their hands bled, moving from village to village in order to find the work camps. The gulags. Whereupon, each day when the train whistle blew –"

As if I had commanded it, a throbbing vibration shuddered under-foot and our audios picked up the throaty radio call – a five-minute warn-ing from the *Nicholas III*.

"The women gathered by the village siding where the locomotive stopped for water. They would hurry to the flat cars, loaded high with timber cut by prisoners. And they searched, combing the logs with their eyes and groping in among them with their hands.

"What was it they were looking for, mother? Can you tell me, hon-estly, at long last, what you came out here to seek?"

I bent and caught her eyes with mine. Haggard from years of sleep-less worry, hers glistened with defiant pride.

"Initials," she said with little breath, then adding softly. "Carved into the raw wood... by prisoners."

And then, straightening her back.

"Proof that they survived."

And finally, barely whispered.

"That he survives."

So.

My suspicion was confirmed. Her added reason for all this – the one that had gone unspoken.

No single justification was sufficient for dragging us into the wil-derness. Not the full release promised by Coss Law. Not the strength that Yelena and I would attain – if we survived. Nor practical experience, dealing with a new-harsh world. Not all of those, combined.

Only... might this new one, added to the others, tip the scale?

It did. Just barely. Enough for me to nod. To understand. To accept.

And to know.

The Yankees would never learn. Fooled by their brief, naive time of childishly unlimited dreams, they believed deep-down in happy endings and the triumph of good. They would keep rebelling till the Coss left no Americans alive.

We Russians are different. Our expertise? We persist. Resist! But with measured, cynical care. And each defeat is simply preparation.

That truth, I had already known. Only now it filled my soul.

We are the people who know how. To outlast the Coss.

And so I took my mother by the hand, leading her to the place that I had found, where Cyrillic letters lay deep-incised along the bared trunk of a crystal tree. And I watched her face bloom with sudden hope, with sunlit joy. And I knew, at last, what lesson this place taught.

To endure.

Story Notes

The preceding tale leads off our section on "endurance." A theme that I go back to often, belying the canard that "David Brin is an optimist." What malarkey!

Indeed, I do publicly disdain the wave of obsessively repetitive and unimaginative dystopias and apocalypses that offer so many directors and authors a cheating-lazy way to plot. Their relentless campaign against the can-do spirit is toxic for all of us. I despise reflex cynicism and pessimism that simply repeats a mantra that "nothing works."

Still, things might go horribly wrong, as I portrayed in *The Postman*. Dire warnings serve a great purpose, if they pose a failure mode that's a bit original! If they get people talking, thinking, pondering ways to avoid the pitfalls and quicksand pits that lie ahead. We may owe our lives and freedom to *Nineteen Eighty-Four, Soylent Green,* and *Dr. Strangelove*, legends that weren't lazy cheats, but gave us fresh ideas about tomorrows to avoid.

In "The Logs" I explore the dark possibility that our narrow enlightenment civilization – the font of science fiction – might have been a fluke. It's a terrifying possibility. Though hope will always find places to settle and seed and grow, even in the darkest moments and places.

This story is part of a fictional cosmos that I've been poking at for a while – the Epic of the Coss Invasion – based on a few paragraphs scribbled by our daughter, Ari, when she was five or six years old. I owe her the "elepents" and those daunting new lords, the Coss.

Our next story – "The Tumbledowns of Cleopatra Abyss" – only mentions the Coss briefly, as a far-off threat. It was chosen for Neil Clarke's *Best Science Fiction of the Year* volume for 2015.

The Tumbledowns of Cleopatra Abyss

◇

Today's thump was overdue. Jonah wondered if it might not come at all.

Just like last Thorday when — at the Old Clock's mid-morning chime — farmers all across the bubble-habitat clambered up pinyon vines or crouched low in expectation of the regular, daily throb — a pulse and quake that hammered up your foot-soles and made all the bubble boundaries shake. Only Thorday's thump never came. The chime was followed by silence and a creepy let-down feeling. And Jonah's mother lit a candle, hoping to avert bad luck.

Early last spring, there had been almost a *whole week* without any thumps. Five days in a row, with no rain of detritus, shaken loose from the Upper World, tumbling down here to the ocean bottom. And two, smaller gaps the previous year.

Apparently, today would be yet another hiatus…

Whomp!

Delayed, the thump came *hard*, shaking the moist ground beneath Jonah's feet. He glanced with concern toward the bubble boundary, more than two hundred meters away — a membrane of ancient, translucent volcanic stone, separating the paddies and pinyon forest from black, crushing waters just outside. The barrier vibrated, an unpleasant, scraping sound.

This time, especially, it caused Jonah's teeth to grind.

"They used to sing, you know," commented the complacent old woman who worked at a nearby freeboard loom, nodding as gnarled fingers sent her shuttle flying among the strands, weaving ropy cloth.

Her hands did not shake, though the nearby grove of thick vines did, quivering much worse than after any normal thump.

"I'm sorry grandmother." Jonah reached out to a nearby bole of twisted cables that dangled from the bubble-habitat's high-arching roof, where shining glowleaves provided the settlement's light.

"*Who* used to sing?"

"The walls, silly boy. The bubble walls. Thumps used to come exactly on time, according to the Old Clock. Though every year we would shorten the main wheel by the same amount, taking thirteen seconds off the length of a day. After-shakes always arrived from the same direction, you could depend on it! And the bubble sang to us."

"It sang... you mean like that awful groan?" Jonah poked a finger in one ear, as if to pry out the fading reverberation. He peered into the nearby forest of thick trunks and vines, listening for signs of breakage. Of disaster.

"Not at all! It was *musical*. Comforting. Especially after a miscarriage. Back then, a woman would lose over half of her quickenings. Not like today, when more babies are born alive than warped or misshapen or dead. Your generation has it lucky! And it's said things were even worse in olden days. The Founders were fortunate to get any living replacements at all! Several times, our population dropped dangerously." She shook her head, then smiled. "Oh... but the music! After every mid-morning thump you could face the bubble walls and relish it. That music helped us women bear our heavy burden."

"'Yes, grandmother, I'm sure it was lovely," Jonah replied, keeping a respectful voice as he tugged on the nearest pinyon to test its strength, then clambered upward, hooking long, unwebbed toes into the braided vines, rising high enough to look around. None of the other men or boys could climb as well.

Several nearby boles appeared to have torn loose their mooring suckers from the domelike roof. Five... no six of them... teetered, lost their final grip-holds, then tumbled, their luminous tops crashing into the rice lagoon, setting off eruptions of sparks... or else onto the work sheds where Panalina and her mechanics could be heard, shouting in dismay. *It's a bad one,* Jonah thought. Already the hab-bubble seemed dimmer. If many more pinyons fell, the clan might dwell in semi-darkness, or even go hungry.

"Oh, it was beautiful, all right," the old woman continued, blithely ignoring any ruckus. "Of course in *my* grandmother's day, the thumps weren't just regular and perfectly timed. They came in *pairs*! And it is said that long before – in *her* grandmother's grandmother's time, when a day lasted so long that it spanned several sleep periods – thumps used to arrive in clusters of four or five! How things must've shook, back then! But always from the same direction, and exactly at the mid-morning chime."

She sighed, implying that Jonah and all the younger folk were making too much fuss. You call *this* a thump shock?

"Of course," she admitted, "the bubbles were *younger* then. More flexible, I suppose. Eventually, some misplaced thump is gonna end us all."

Jonah took a chance – he was in enough trouble already without offending the Oldest Female, who had undergone thirty-four pregnancies and still had *six* living womb-fruit – four of them precious females.

But grandmother seemed in a good mood, distracted by memories....

Jonah took off, clambering higher till he could reach with his left hand for one of the independent dangle vines that sometimes laced the gaps between pinyons. With his right hand he flicked with his belt knife, severing the dangler a meter or so below his knees. Sheathing the blade and taking a deep breath – he launched off, swinging across an open space in the forest... and finally alighting along a second giant bole. It shook from his impact and Jonah worried. *If this one was weakened, and I'm the reason that it falls, I could be in for real punishment. Not just grandma-tending duty!*

A "rascal's" reputation might have been harmless, when Jonah was younger. But now, the mothers were pondering what amount Tairee Dome might have to pay, in dowry, for some other bubble colony to take him. A boy known to be unruly might not get any offers, at any marriage price... and a man without a wife-sponsor led a marginal existence.

But honestly, this last time wasn't my fault! How am I supposed to make an improved pump without filling something with high pressure water? All right, the kitchen rice cooker was a poor choice. But it has a gauge and everything... or, it used to.

After quivering far too long, the great vine held. With a brief sense of relief, he scrambled around to the other side. There was no convenient dangler this time, but another pinyon towered fairly close. Jonah flexed his legs, prepared, and launched himself across the gap, hurtling with open arms, alighting with shock and painful clumsiness. He didn't wait though, scurrying to the other side — where there *was* another dangle vine, well-positioned for a wide-spanning swing.

This time he couldn't help himself while hurtling across open space, giving vent to a yell of exhilaration.

Two swings and four leaps later, he was right next to the bubble's edge, reaching out to stroke the nearest patch of ancient, vitrified stone in a place where no one would see him break taboo. Pushing at the transparent barrier, Jonah felt deep ocean pressure shoving back. The texture felt rough-ribbed, uneven. Sliver-flakes rubbed off, dusting his hand.

"Of course, bubbles were younger then," the old woman said. *"More flexible."*

Jonah had to wrap a length of dangle vine around his left wrist and clutch the pinyon with his toes, in order to lean far out and bring his face right up against the bubble — it sucked heat into bottomless cold — using his right hand and arm to cup around his face and peer into the blackness outside. Adapting vision gradually revealed the stony walls of Cleopatra Crevice, the narrow-deep canyon where humanity had come to take shelter so very long ago. Fleeing the Coss invaders. Before many lifespans of grandmothers.

Several strings of globe-like habitats lay parallel along the canyon bottom, like pearls on a necklace, each of them surrounded by a froth of smaller bubbles… though fewer of the little ones than there were in olden times, and none anymore in the most useful sizes. It was said that, way back at the time of the Founding, there used to be faint illumination overhead, filtering downward from the surface and demarking night from day: light that came from the mythological god-thing that old books called the *sun*, so fierce that it could penetrate both dense, poisonous clouds and the ever-growing ocean.

But that was way back in a long-ago past, when the sea had not yet burgeoned so, filling canyons, becoming a dark and mighty deep. Now, the only gifts that fell from above were clots of detritus that men gathered to feed algae ponds. Debris that got stranger, every year.

These days, the canyon walls could only be seen by light from the bubbles themselves, by their pinyon glow within. Jonah turned slowly left to right, counting and naming those farm-enclaves he could see. *Amtor… Leininger… Chown… Kuttner… Okumo…* each one a clan with traditions and styles all their own. Each one possibly the place where Tairee tribe might sell him in a marriage pact. A mere boy and good riddance. Good at numbers and letters. A bit skilled with his hands, but notoriously absent-minded, prone to staring at nothing, and occasionally putting action to rascally thoughts.

He kept tallying: *Brakutt... Lewis... Atari... Napeer... Aldrin... what?*

Jonah blinked. What was happening to Aldrin? And the bubble just beyond it. Both Aldrin and Bezo were still quivering. He could make out few details at this range, through the milky, pitted membrane. But one of the two was rippling and convulsing, the glimmer of its pinyon forest shaking back and forth as the giant boles swayed... then collapsed!

The other distant habitat seemed to be *inflating*. Or so Jonah thought at first. Rubbing his eyes and pressing even closer, as Bezo habitat grew bigger...

...or else it was rising! Jonah could not believe what he saw. Torn loose, somehow, from the ocean floor, the entire bubble was moving. Upward. And as Bezo ascended, its flattened bottom now re-shaped itself as farms and homes and lagoons tumbled together into the base of the accelerating globe. With its pinyons still mostly in place, Bezo colony continued glowing as it climbed upward.

Aghast, and yet compelled to look, Jonah watched until the glimmer that had been Bezo finally vanished in blackness, accelerating toward the poison surface of Venus.

Then, without warning or mercy, habitat Aldrin imploded.

2.

"I was born in Bezo, you know."

Jonah turned to see Enoch leaning on his rake, staring south along the canyon wall, toward a gaping crater where that ill-fated settlement bubble used to squat. Distant glimmers of glow-lamps flickered over there as crews prowled along the Aldrin debris field, sifting for salvage. But that was a job for mechanics and senior workers. Meanwhile, the algae ponds and pinyons must be fed, so Jonah also found himself outside, in coveralls that stank and fogged from his own breath and many generations of previous wearers, helping to gather the week's harvest of organic detritus.

Jonah responded in the same dialect Enoch had used. Click-Talk. The only way to converse, when both of you are deep underwater.

"Come on," he urged his older friend, a recent, marriage-price immigrant to Tairee Bubble. "All of that is behind you. A male should never look back. We do as we are told."

Enoch shrugged – broad shoulders making his stiff coveralls scrunch around the helmet, fashioned from an old foam bubble of a size no longer found in these parts. Enoch's phlegmatic resignation was an adaptive skill that served him well, as he was married to Jonah's cousin, Jezzy, an especially strong-willed young woman, bent on exerting author-ity and not above threatening her new husband with casting-out.

I can hope for someone gentle, when I'm sent to live beside a stranger in a strange dome.

Jonah resumed raking up newly fallen organic stuff – mostly ropy bits of vegetation that lay limp and pressure-crushed after their long tumble to the bottom. In recent decades, there had also been detritus of another kind. *Shells* that had holes in them for legs and heads. And skeleton fragments from slinky creatures that must have – when living – stretched as long as Jonah was tall! Much more complicated than the mud worms that kept burrowing closer to the domes, of late. More like the fabled *snakes* or *fish* that featured in tales from Old Earth.

Panalina's dad – old Scholar Wu – kept a collection of skyfalls in the little museum by Tairee's eastern arc, neatly labeled specimens dat-ing back at least ten grandmother cycles, to the era when *light* and *heat* still came down along with debris from above – a claim that Jonah still deemed mystical. Perhaps just a legend, like Old Earth.

"These samples… do you see how they are getting more complicated, Jonah?" So explained old man Wu as he traced patterns of veins in a recently gathered sea weed. *"And do you make out what's embedded here? Bits of crea-tures living on or within the plant. And there! Does that resemble a bite mark? The outlines of where teeth tore into this vegetation? Could that act of devouring be what sent it tumbling down to us?"*

Jonah pondered what it all might mean while raking up dross and piling it onto the sledge, still imagining the size of a jaw that could have torn such a path through tough, fibrous weed. And everything was pres-sure-shrunk down here!

"How can anything live up at the surface?" He recalled asking Wu, who was said to have read every book that existed in the Cleopatra Canyon colonies, most of them two or three times. *"Did not the founders say the sky was thick with poison?"*

"With carbon dioxide and sulfuric acid, yes. I have shown you how we use pinyon leaves to separate out those two substances, both of which have uses in the workshop. One we exhale —"

"And the other burns! Yet, in small amounts it smells sweet."

"That is because the Founders, in their wisdom, put sym-bi-ants in our blood. Creatures that help us deal with pressure and gases that would kill folks who still live on enslaved Earth."

Jonah didn't like to envision tiny animals coursing through his body, even if they did him good. Each year, a dozen kids throughout the bubble colonies were chosen to study such useful things – biological things. A smaller number chose the field that interested Jonah, where even fewer were allowed to specialize.

"But the blood creatures can only help us down here, where the pinyons supply us with breathable air. Not up top, where poisons are so thick." Jonah gestured skyward. *"Is that why none of the Risers have ever returned?"*

Once every year or two, the canyon colonies lost a person to the hell that awaited above. Most often because of a buoyancy accident; a broken tether or boot-ballast sent some hapless soul plummeting upward. Another common cause was suicide. And – more rarely – it happened for another reason, one the mothers commanded that no one may discuss, or even mention. A forbidden reason.

Only now, after the sudden rise of Bezo Bubble and a thousand human inhabitants, followed by the Aldrin implosion, little else was on anyone's mind.

"Even if you survive the rapid change in pressure… one breath up there and your lungs would be scorched as if by flame," old Scholar Wu had answered, yesterday. *"That is why the Founders seeded living creatures a bit higher than us, but beneath the protective therm-o-cline layer that keeps most of the poison out of our abyss…*

The old man paused, fondling a strange, multi-jawed skeleton. *"It seems that life – some kind of life – has found a way to flourish near that barrier. So much so, that I have begun to wonder –"*

A sharp voice roused him.

"Jonah!"

This time it was Enoch, reminding him to concentrate on work. A good reason to work in pairs. He got busy with the rake. Mother was pregnant again, along with Aunts Leor and Sosun. It always made them cranky with tension, as the fetuses took their time, deciding whether to go or stay – and if they stayed, whether to come out healthy or as warped ruins. No, it would not do to return from this salvage outing with only half a load!

So he and Enoch forged farther afield, hauling the sledge to another spot where high ocean currents often dumped interesting things after colliding with the canyon walls. The algae ponds and pinyons needed fresh supplies of organic matter. Especially in recent decades, after the old volcanic vents dried up.

The Book of Exile says we came down here to use the vents, way back when the sea was hot and new. A shallow refuge for free humans to hide from the Coss, while comets fell in regular rhythm, thumping Venus to life. Drowning her fever and stirring her veins.

Jonah had only a vague notion what "comets" were – great balls drifting through vast emptiness, till godlike beings with magical powers flung them down upon this planet. Balls of *ice,* like the pale-blue slush that formed on the cool, downstream sides of boulders in a fast, under-water current. About as big as Cleopatra Canyon was wide, that's what books said about a comet.

Jonah gazed at the towering cliff walls, enclosing all the world he ever knew. Comets were so vast! Yet, they had been striking Venus daily, since centuries before colonists came, immense, pre-creation icebergs, pelting the sister world of Old Earth. Perhaps several million of them by now, herded first by human civilization and later by Coss Masters, who adopted the project as their own – one so ambitious as to be nearly inconceivable.

So much ice. So much water. Building higher and higher till it has to fill the sky, even the poison skies of Venus. So much that it fills all of creatio –

"Jonah, watch out!"

Enoch's shouted warning made him crouch and spin about. Or Jonah tried to, in the clumsy coveralls, raising clouds of muck stirred by heavy, shuffling boots. "Wha–? What is it?"

"Above you! Heads up!"

Tilting back was strenuous, especially in a hurry. The foggy face-plate didn't help. Only now Jonah glimpsed something overhead, shad-owy and huge, looming fast out of the black.

"Run!"

He required no urging. Heart pounding in terror, Jonah pumped his legs for all they were worth, barely lifting weighted shoes to shuf-fle-skip with long strides toward the nearby canyon wall, sensing and then back-glimpsing a massive, sinuous shape that plummeted toward him out of the abyssal sky. By dim light from a distant habitat-dome, the monstrous shape turned languidly, following his dash for safety, swooping in to close the distance fast! Over his right shoulder, Jonah glimpsed a gaping mouth and rows of glistening-huge teeth. A sinuous body from some nightmare.

I'm not gonna make it. The canyon wall was just too far.

Jonah skidded to a stop, raising plumes of bottom muck. Swiveling into a crouch and half moaning with fear, he lifted his only weapon – a rake meant for gathering organic junk from the sea floor. He brandished it crosswise, hoping to stymie the wide jaw that now careened out of dimness, framed by four glistening eyes. Like some ancient storybook *dragon,* stooping for prey. No protection, the rake was more a gesture of defiance.

Come on, monster.

A decent plan, on the spur of the moment.

It didn't work.

It didn't have to.

The rake shattered, along with several ivory teeth as the giant maw plunged around Jonah, crashing into the surrounding mud, trapping him… but never closing, nor biting or chewing. Having braced for all those things, he stood there in a tense hunker as tremors shook the canyon bottom, closer and more spread out than the daily thump. It had to be more of the sinuous monster, colliding with surrounding muck – a long, long leviathan!

A final ground-quiver, then silence. Some creakings. Then more silence.

And darkness. Enveloped, surrounded by the titan's mouth, Jonah at first saw nothing… then a few faint glimmers. Pinyon light from nearby *Monsat* bubble habitat. Streaming in through holes. *Holes* in the gigantic head. Holes that gradually opened wider as ocean-bottom pressure wreaked havoc on flesh meant for much higher waters.

Then the smell hit Jonah.

An odor of death.

Of course. Such a creature would never dive this deep of its own accord. Instead of being pursued by a ravenous monster, Jonah must have run along the same downdraft conveying a corpse to its grave. An intersection and collision that might seem hilarious someday, when he told the story as an old grandpa, assuming his luck held. Right now, he felt sore, bruised, angry, embarrassed… and concerned about the vanishing supply in his meager air bubble.

With his belt knife, Jonah began probing and cutting a path out of the trap. He had another reason to hurry. If he had to be rescued by others, there would be no claiming this flesh for Tairee, for his clan and family. For his dowry and husband price.

Concerned clicks told him Enoch was nearby and one promising gap in the monster's cheek suddenly gave way to the handle of a rake. Soon they both were tearing at it, sawing tough membranes, tossing aside clots of shriveling muscle and skin. His bubble helmet might keep out the salt-sea, but pungent aromas were another matter. Finally, with Enoch tugging helpfully on one arm, Jonah squeezed out and stumbled several steps before falling to his knees, coughing.

"Here come others," said his friend. And Jonah lifted his gaze, spying men in bottom suits and helmets, hurrying this way, brandishing glow bulbs and makeshift weapons. Behind them he glimpsed one of the cargo subs – a string of mid-sized bubbles, pushed by hand-crank propellers – catching up fast.

"Help me get up ... on top," he urged Enoch, who bore some of his weight as he stood. Together, they sought a route onto the massive head. There was danger in this moment. Without clear ownership, fighting might break out among salvage crews from different domes, as happened a generation ago, over the last hot vent on the floor of Cleopatra Canyon. Only after a dozen men were dead had the grandmothers made peace. But if Tairee held a firm claim to this corpse, then rules of gift-generosity would parcel out shares to every dome, with only a largest-best allotment to Tairee. Peace and honor now depended on his speed. But the monster's cranium was steep, crumbly and slick.

Frustrated and almost out of time, Jonah decided to take a chance. He slashed at the ropy cables binding his soft overalls to the weighted clogs that kept him firmly on the ocean bottom. Suddenly buoyant, he began to sense the Fell Tug... the pull toward heaven, toward doom. The same tug that had yanked Bezo colony, a few days ago, sending that bubble-habitat and all of its inhabitants plummeting skyward.

Enoch understood the gamble. Gripping Jonah's arm, he stuffed his rake and knife and hatchet into Jonah's belt. Anything convenient. So far, so good. The net force seemed to be slightly downward. Jonah nodded at his friend, and jumped.

3.

The marriage party made its way toward Tairee's bubble-dock, shuffling along to beating tambourines. Youngsters – gaily decked in rice-flowers and pinyon garlands – danced alongside the newlyweds. Although many of the children wore masks or makeup to disguise minor birth defects, they seemed light of spirit.

They were the only ones.

Some adults tried their best, chanting and shouting at all the right places. Especially several dozen refugees – Tairee's allocated share of threadbare escapees from the ruin of Cixin and Sadoul settlements – who cheered with the fervid eagerness of people desperately trying for acceptance in their new home, rather than mere sufferance. As for other guests from unaffected domes? Most appeared to have come only for free food. These now crowded near the dock, eager to depart as soon as the nuptial sub was on its way.

Not that Jonah could blame them. Most people preferred staying close to home, ever since the thumps started going all crazy, setting off a chain of tragedies, tearing at the old, placid ways.

And today's thump is already overdue, he thought. In fact, there hadn't been a ground-shaking comet strike in close to a month. Such a gap would have been unnerving, just a year or two ago. Now, given how awful some recent impacts had been, any respite was welcome.

A time of chaos. Few see good omens, even in a new marriage.

Jonah glanced at his bride, come to collect him from Lausanne Bubble, all the way at the far northern outlet of Cleopatra Canyon. Taller than average, with a clear complexion and strong carriage, she had good hips and only a slight mutant-mottling on the back of her scalp, where the hair grew in a wild, discolored corkscrew. An easily-overlooked defect, like Jonah's lack of toe webbing, or the way he would sneeze or yawn uncontrollably, whenever air pressure changed too fast. No one jettisoned a child over such inconsequentials.

Though you can be exiled forever from all you ever knew, if you're born with the genetic defect of maleness. Jonah could not help scanning the workshops and dorms, the pinyons and paddies of Tairee, wondering if he would see this place – his birth bubble – ever again. Perhaps, if the grandmothers of Lausanne trusted him with errands. Or next time Tairee hosted a festival – if his new wife chose to take him along.

He had barely met Petri Smoth before this day, having spoken just a few words with her over the years, at various craft-and-seed fairs, hosted by some of the largest domes. During last year's festival, held in ill-fated Aldrin Bubble, she had asked him a few pointed questions about some tinkered gimmicks he displayed. In fact, now that he looked back on it, her tone and expression must have been… evaluating. Weighing his answers with *this* possible outcome in mind. It just never occurred to Jonah, at the time, that he was impressing a girl enough to choose him as a mate.

I thought she was interested in my improved ballast transfer valve.

And maybe... in a way... she was.

Or, at least, in Jonah's mechanical abilities. Panalina suggested that explanation yesterday, while helping Jonah prepare his dowry — an old cargo truck that he had purchased with his prize winnings for claiming the dead sea serpent — a long-discarded submersible freighter that he spent the last year reconditioning. A hopeless wreck, some called it, but no longer.

"Well, it's functional, I'll give you that," the Master Mechanic of Tairee Bubble had decreed last night, after going over the vessel from stem to stern, checking everything from hand-wound anchor tethers and stone keel-weights to the bench where several pairs of burly men might labor at a long crank, turning a propeller to drive the boat forward. She thumped extra storage bubbles, turning stop-cocks to sniff at the hissing, pressurized air. Then Panalina tested levers that would let seawater into those tanks, if need-be, keeping the sub weighed down on the bottom, safe from falling into the deadly sky.

"It'll do," she finally decreed, to Jonah's relief. This could help him begin married life on a good note. Not every boy got to present his new bride with a whole submarine!

Jonah had acquired the old relic months before people realized just how valuable each truck might be, even junkers like this one — for rescue and escape — as a chain of calamities disrupted the canyon settlements. His repairs hadn't been completed in time to help evacuate more families from cracked and doomed Cixin or Sadoul bubbles, and he felt bad about that. Still, with Panalina's ruling of seaworthiness, this vehicle would help make Petri Smoth a woman of substance in the hierarchy at Laussane, and prove Jonah a real asset to his wife.

Only... what happens when so many bubbles fail that the others can't take refugees anymore?

Already there was talk of sealing Tairee against outsiders, even evacuees, and concentrating on total self-reliance.

Some spoke of arming the colony's subs for war. "These older hull-bubbles were thicker and heavier," Panalina commented, patting the nearest bulkhead, the first of three ancient, translucent spheres that had been fused together into a short chain, like a trio of pearls on a string. "They fell out of favor, maybe four or five mother generations ago. You'll need to pay six big fellows in order to crank a full load of trade goods. That won't leave you much profit on cargo."

Good old Panalina, always talking as if everything would soon be normal again, as if the barter network was likely to ever be the same. With streaks of gray in her hair, the artificer claimed to be sixty years old, but was certainly younger. The grandmothers let her get away with the fib, and what would normally be criminal neglect, leaving her womb fallow most of the time, with only two still-living heirs, and both of those boys.

"Still," Panalina looked around and thumped the hull one last time. "He's a sturdy little boat. You know, there was talk among the mothers about refusing to let you take him away from Tairee. The Smoths had to promise half a ton of crushed grapes in return, and to take in one of the Sadoul families. Still, I think it's *you* they mostly want."

Jonah had puzzled over that cryptic remark, after Panalina left, then all during the brew-swilled bachelor party, suffering crude jokes and ribbing from the married men, and later during a fretful sleep-shift, as he tossed and turned with pre-wedding jitters. During the ceremony itself, Mother had been gracious and warm – not her typical mien, but a side of her that Jonah felt he would surely miss. Though he knew that an underlying source of her cheerfulness was simple – *one less male mouth to feed.*

It had made Jonah reflect, even during the wrist-binding part of the ceremony, on something old Scholar Wu said recently.

The balance of the sexes may change, if it really comes down to war. Breeders could start to seem less valuable than fighters.

In the docklock, Jonah found that his little truck had been decked with flowers, and all three of the spheres gleamed, where they had been polished above the water line. The gesture warmed Jonah's heart. There was even a freshly painted name, arcing just above the propeller.

Bird of Tairee

Well. Mother had always loved stories about those prehistoric creatures of Old Earth, who flew through a sky that was immeasurably vast and sweet.

"I thought you were going to name it after me," Petri commented in a low voice, without breaking her gracious smile.

"I shall do that, lady-love. Just after we dock in Laussane."

"Well… perhaps not *just* after," she commented, and Jonah's right buttock took a sharp-nailed pinch. He managed not to jump or visibly react. But clearly, his new wife did not intend wasting time, once they were home.

Home. He would have to re-define the word, in his mind.

Still, as Jonah checked the final loading of luggage, gifts and passengers, he glanced at the fantail one last time, picturing there a name that he really wanted to give the little vessel.

Renewed Hope

4.

They were underway, having traveled more than half of the distance to Laussane Bubble, when a *thump* struck at the wrong time, shaking the little sub-truck like a rattle.

The blow came hard and late. So late that everyone at the wedding had simply written-off any chance of one today. Folks assumed that at least another work-and-sleep cycle would pass without a comet fall. Already this was the longest gap in memory. Perhaps (some murmured) the age of thumps had come to an end, as prophesied long ago. After the disaster that befell Aldrin and Bezo six months ago, it was a wish now shared by all.

Up until that very moment, the nuptial voyage had been placid, enjoyable, even for tense newlyweds.

Jonah was at the tiller up front, gazing ahead through a patch of hull-bubble that had been polished on both sides, making it clear enough to see through. Hoping that he looked like a stalwart, fierce-eyed seaman, he gripped the rudder ropes that steered *Bird of Tairee*, though the sub's propeller lay still and powerless. For this voyage, the old truck was being hauled as a trailer behind a larger, sleeker and more modern Laussanite sub, where a team of twelve burly men sweated and tugged in perfect rhythm, turning their drive-shaft crank.

Petri stood beside her new husband, while passengers chattered in the second compartment behind them. As bubble colonies drifted past, she gestured at each of the gleaming domes and spoke of womanly matters, like the politics of trade and diplomacy, or the personalities and traditions of each settlement. Which goods and food items they excelled at producing, or needed. Their rates of mutation and successful child-raising. Or how well each habitat was managing its genetic diversity… and her tone changed a bit at that point, as if suddenly aware how the topic bore upon them both. For this marriage-match had been judged by the Laussane mothers on that basis, above all others.

"Of course I had final say, the final choice," she told Jonah, and it warmed him that Petri felt a need to explain.

"Anyway, there is a project I've been working on," she continued in a lower voice. "With a few others in Laussane and Landis bubbles. Younger folks, mostly. And we can use a good mechanic like you. "

Like me? So I was chosen for that reason?

Jonah felt put off, and tensed a bit when Petri put an arm around his waist. But she leaned up and whispered in his ear.

"I think you'll like what we're up to. It's something just right for a *rascal.*"

The word surprised him and he almost turned to stare. But her arm was tight and Petri's breath was still in his ear. So Jonah chose to keep his features steady, unmoved. Perhaps sensing his stiff reaction, Petri let go. She slid around to face him with her back resting upon the transparent patch, leaning against the window.

Clever girl, he thought. It was the direction he had to look, in order to watch the *Pride of Laussane's* rudder, up ahead, matching his tiller to that of the larger sub. Now he could not avert his eyes from her, using boyish reticence as an excuse.

Petri's oval face was a bit wide, as were her eyes. The classic Laussane chin cleft was barely noticeable, though her mutant-patch – the whorl of wild hair – was visible as a reflection behind her, on the bubble's curved, inner surface. Her wedding garment, sleek and close-cut, revealed enough to prove her fitness to bear and nurse... plus a little more. And Jonah wondered – *when am I supposed to let the sight of her affect me? Arouse me?* Too soon and he might seem brutish, in need of tight reins. Too late or too little, and his bride might feel insulted.

And fretting over it will make me an impotent fool. Deliberately, Jonah calmed himself, allowing some pleasure to creep in, at the sight of her. A seed of anticipation grew... as he knew she wanted.

"What *project* are you talking about? Something involving trucks?" He offered a guess. "Something the mothers may not care for? Something suited to a... to a..."

He glanced over his shoulder, past the open hatch leading to the middle bubble, containing a jumble of cargo – wedding gifts and Jonah's hope chest, plus luggage for Laussane dignitaries who rode in comfort aboard the bigger submersible ahead. Here, a dozen lower caste passengers sat or lay atop the stacks and piles – some of Petri's younger cousins, plus a family of evacuees from doomed Sadoul dome, sent to relieve Tairee's overcrowded refugee encampment, as part of the complex marriage deal.

Perhaps it would be best to hold off this conversation until a time and place with fewer ears around, to pick up stray sonic reflections. Perhaps delaying it for wife-and-husband pillow talk – the one and only kind of privacy that could be relied upon, in the colonies. He looked forward again, raising one eyebrow and Petri clearly got his meaning. Still, in a lower voice, she finished Jonah's sentence.

"To a *rascal,* yes. In fact, your reputation as a young fellow always coming up with bothersome questions helped me bargain well for you. Did you intend it that way, I wonder? For you to wind up *only* sought by one like me, who would *value* such attributes? If so, clever boy."

Jonah decided to keep silent, letting Petri give him credit for cunning he never had. After a moment, she shrugged with a smile, then continued in a voice that was nearly inaudible.

"But in fact, our small bunch of conspirators and connivers were inspired by yet another *rascal.* The one we have foremost in our minds was a fellow named... Melvil."

Jonah had been about to ask about the mysterious "we." But mention of that particular name stopped him short. He blinked hard – two, three times – striving not to flinch or otherwise react. It took him several tries to speak, barely mouthing the words.

"You're talking about... *Theodora Canyon?*"

A place of legend. And Petri's eyes now conveyed many things. Approval of his quickness... overlain upon an evident grimness of purpose. A willingness – even eagerness – to take risks and adapt in chaotic times, finding a path forward, even if it meant following a folktale. All of that was apparent in Petri's visage. Though clearly, Jonah was expected to say more.

"I've heard... one hears rumors... that there was a *map* to what Melvil found... another canyon filled with Gift-of-Venus bubbles like those the Founders discovered here in Cleopatra Canyon. But the mothers forbade any discussion or return voyages, and –" Jonah slowed down when he realized he was babbling. "And so, after Melvil fled his punishment, they hid the map away...."

"I've been promised a copy," Petri confided, evidently weighing his reaction. "once we're ready to set out."

Jonah couldn't help himself. He turned around again to check the next compartment, where several smaller children were chasing each other up and down the luggage piles, making a ruckus and almost tipping over a crate of Panalina's smithy tools, consigned for trans-shipment to Gollancz dome. Beyond, through a second hatchway to the final chamber, where sweating rowers would normally sit, lay stacked bags of exported Tairee rice. The refugee family and several of Petri's sub-adult cousins lounged back there, talking idly, keeping apart from the raucous children.

Jonah looked back at his bride, still keeping his voice low.

"You're kidding! So there truly *was* a boy named Melvil? Who stole a sub and vanished –"

"—for a month and a week and a day and an hour," Petri finished for him. "Then returned with tales of a far-off canyon filled with gleaming bubbles of all sizes, a vast foam of hollow, volcanic globes, left over from this world's creation, never touched by human hands. Bubbles just as raw and virginal as our ancestors found, when they first arrived down here beneath a newborn ocean, seeking refuge far below the poison sky."

Much of what she said was from the Founders' Catechism, retaining its rhythm and flowery tone. Clearly, it amused Petri to quote modified scripture while speaking admiringly of an infamous rebel; Jonah could tell as much from her wry expression. But poetry – and especially irony – had always escaped Jonah, and she might as well get used to that husbandly lack, right now.

"So… this is about… finding new homes?"

"Perhaps, if things keep getting worse here in Cleo Abyss, shouldn't we have options? Oh, we're selling it as an expedition to harvest fresh bubbles, all the sizes that have grown scarce hereabouts, useful for helmets and cooking and chemistry. But we'll also check out any big ones. Maybe they're holding up better in Theodora than they are here. Because, at the rate things are going –" Petri shook her head. And, looking downward, her expression *leaked* just a bit, losing some of its tough, determined veneer, giving way to plainly visible worry.

She knows things. Information that the mothers won't tell mere men. And she's afraid.

Strangely, that moment of vulnerability touched Jonah's heart, thawing a patch that he had never realized was chill. For the first time, he felt drawn… compelled to reach out. Not sexually. But to comfort, to hold.…

That was when the thump struck – harder than Jonah would have believed possible.

Concussion slammed the little submarine over, halfway onto its port side and set the ancient bubble hull ringing. Petri hurtled into him, tearing the rudder straps from his hands as they tumbled together backwards, caroming off the open hatch between compartments, then rolling forward again as *Bird of Tairee* heaved.

With the sliver of his brain that still functioned, Jonah wondered if there had been a collision. But the Laussanite ship was bobbing and rocking some distance ahead, still tethered to the *Bird,* and nothing else was closer than a bubble-habitat, at least two hundred meters away. Jonah caught sight of all this while landing against the window patch up-front, with Petri squished between. This time, as the *Bird* lurched again, he managed to grab a stanchion and hold on, while gripping her waist with his other arm. Petri's breath came in wheezing gasps, and now there was no attempt to mask her terror.

"What? What was…"

Jonah swallowed… bracing himself against another rocking sway that almost tore her from his grasp.

"A *thump!* Do you hear the low tone? But they're never this late!"

He didn't have breath to add – *I've never felt one outside a dome, before. No one ventures into water during late morning, when comets always used to fall.* And now Jonah knew why. His ears rang and hurt like crazy.

All this time he had been counting. Thump vibrations came in sequence. One tone passed through rock by *compression*, arriving many seconds before the slower *transverse* waves. He had once even read one of Scholar Wu's books about that, with partial understanding. And he recalled what the old teacher said. That you could tell from the difference in tremor arrivals how far away the impact was from Cleopatra Canyon.

…twenty-one… twenty-two… twenty three…

Jonah hoped to reach sixty-two seconds, the normal separation, for generation after generation of grandmothers.

…twenty-four… twenty-f—

The transverse tone, higher pitched and much louder than ever, set the forward bubble of the *Bird* ringing like a bell, even as the tooth-jarring sways diminished, allowing Jonah and Petri to grab separate straps and find their feet.

Less than half the usual distance. That comet almost hit us! He struggled with a numb brain. *Maybe just a couple of thousand kilometers away.*

"The children!" Petri cried, and cast herself – stumbling – aft toward the middle compartment. Jonah followed, but just two steps in order to verify no seals were broken. No hatches had to be closed and dogged… not yet. And the crying kids back there looked shaken, not badly hurt. So okay, trust Petri to take care of things back there –

– as he plunged back to the tiller harness. Soon, Jonah was tugging at balky cables, struggling to make the rudder obedient, fighting surges while catching brief glimpses of a tumult outside. Ahead, forty or fifty meters, the *Pride of Laussane's* propeller churned a roiling cauldron of water. The men inside must be cranking with all their might.

Backward, Jonah realized with dismay. Their motion in reverse might bring the *Pride's* prop in contact with the tow-line. *Why are they hauling ass backwards?*

One clue. The tether remained taut and straight, despite the rowers' efforts. And with a horrified realization, Jonah realized why. The bigger sub *tilted* upward almost halfway to vertical, with its nose aimed high.

They've lost their main ballast! Great slugs of stone and raw metal normally weighed a sub down, lashed along the keel. They must have torn loose amid the chaos of the thump – nearly all of them! But how? Certainly, bad luck and lousy maintenance, or a hard collision with the ocean bottom. For whatever reason, the *Pride of Laussane* was straining upward, climbing toward the sky.

Already, Jonah could see one of the bubble habitats from an angle no canyonite ever wanted… looking *down* upon the curved dome from above, its forest of pinyon vines glowing from within.

Cursing his own slowness of mind, Jonah let go of the rudder cables and half-stumbled toward the hatch at the rear of the control chamber, shouting for Petri. There was a job to do, more vital than any other. Their very lives might depend on it.

5.

"When I give the word, open valve number one *just a quarter turn!*"

It wasn't a demure tone to use toward a woman, but he saw no sign of wrath or resentment as his new wife nodded. "A quarter turn. Yes, Jonah."

Clamping his legs around one of the ballast jars, he started pushing rhythmically on his new and improved model air pump. "Okay… now!"

As soon as Petri twisted the valve they heard water spew into the ballast chamber, helping Jonah push the air out, for storage at pressure in a neighboring bottle. It would be simpler and less work to just let the air spill outside, but he couldn't bring himself to do that. There might be further uses for the stuff.

When *Bird* started tilting sideways, he shifted their efforts to a bottle next to the starboard viewing patch... another bit of the old hull that had been polished for seeing. Farther aft, in the third compartment, he could hear some of the passengers struggling with bags of rice, clearing the propeller crank for possible use. In fact, Jonah had ordered it done mostly to give them a distraction. Something to do.

"We should be getting heavier," he told Petri as they shifted back and forth, left to right and then left again, letting water into storage bubbles and storing displaced air. As expected, this had an effect on the sub's pitch, raising the nose as it dragged on the tether cable, which in turn linked them to the crippled *Pride of Laussane.*

The crew of that hapless vessel had given up cranking to propel their ship backwards. Everything depended on Jonah and Petri, now. If they could make *Bird* heavy enough, quickly enough, both vessels might be prevented from sinking into the sky.

And we'll be heroes, Jonah pondered at one point, while his arms throbbed with pain. This could be a great start to his life and reputation in Laussane Bubble... that is, *if* it worked. Jonah ached to go and check the little sub's instruments, but there was no time. Not even when he drafted the father of the Sadoul refugee family to pump alongside him. Gradually, all the tanks were filling, making the *Bird* heavier, dragging at the runaway *Pride of Laussane.* And indeed....

Yes! He saw a welcome sight. One of the big habitat domes! Perhaps the very one they had been passing, when the thump struck. Jonah shared a grin with Petri, seeing in her eyes a glimmer of earned respect. *Perhaps I'll need to rest a bit before our wedding night.* Though funny, it didn't feel as if fatigue would be a problem.

Weighed down by almost-full ballast tanks, *Bird* slid almost along the great, curved flank of the habitat. Jonah signaled Xerish to ease off pumping and for Petri to close her valve. He didn't want to hit the sea bottom too hard. As they descended, Petri identified the nearby colony as Leininger Dome. It was hard to see much through both sweat-stung eyes and the barely polished window patch, but Jonah could soon tell that a crowd of citizens had come to press their faces against the inner side of the great transparent bubble wall, staring up and out toward the descending subs.

As *Bird* drifted backward, it appeared that the landing would be pretty fast. Jonah shouted for all the passengers to brace themselves for a rough impact, One that should come any second as they drew even with the Leininger onlookers. A bump into bottom mud that…

…that didn't come.

Something was wrong. Instinct told him, before reason could, when Jonah's ears popped and he gave vent to a violent sneeze.

Oh no.

Petri and Jonah stared at the Leiningerites, who stared back in resigned dismay as the *Bird* dropped below their ground level… and kept dropping. Or rather, Leininger Bubble kept ascending, faster and faster, tugged by the deadly buoyancy of all that air inside, its anchor roots torn loose by that last violent thump. Following the path and fate of Bezo Colony, without the warning that had allowed partial evacuation of Cixin and Sadoul.

With a shout of self-loathing, Jonah rushed to perform a task that he should have done already. Check instruments. The pressure gauge wouldn't be much use in an absolute sense, but relative values could at least tell if they were falling. Not just relative to the doomed habitat, but drifting back toward the safe bottom muck, or else –

"Rising," he told Petri in a low voice, as she sidled alongside and rested her head against his shoulder. He slid his arm around her waist, as if they had been married forever. Or, at least, most of what remained of their short lives.

"Is there anything else we can do?" she asked.

"Not much." He shrugged. "Finish flooding the tanks, I suppose. But they're already almost full, and the weight isn't enough. *That* is just too strong." And he pointed out the forward viewing patch at the *Pride of Laussane,* its five large, air-filled compartments buoyant enough to overcome any resistance by this little truck.

"But… can't they do what we've done. Fill their own balls –"

"Ballast tanks. Sorry, my lady. They don't have any big ones. Just a few little bottles for adjusting trim."

Jonah kept his voice even and matter-of–fact, the way a vessel captain should, even though his stomach churned with dread, explaining how external keel weights saved interior cargo space. Also, newer craft used bubbles with slimmer walls. You didn't want to penetrate them with too many inlets, valves and such.

"And no one else has your new pump," Petri added. Her approving tone meant more to Jonah, in these final minutes, than he ever would have expected.

"Of course…" he mused.

"Yes? You've thought of something?"

"Well, if we could somehow cut the tether cable…"

"We'd sink back to safety!" Then Petri frowned. "But we're the only chance they have, on the *Pride of Lausanne*. Without our weight, they would shoot skyward like a seed pip from a lorgo fruit.*"

"Anyway, it's up to them to decide," Jonah explained. "The tether release is at their end, not ours. Sorry. It's a design flaw that I'll fix as soon as I get a chance, right after re-painting your name on the stern."

"Hm. See that you do," she commanded.

Then, after a brief pause.

"Do you think they might release us, when they realize both ships are doomed?"

Jonah shrugged. There was no telling what people would do, when faced with such an end. He vowed to stand watch though, just in case.

He sneezed hard, twice. Pressure effects were starting to tell on him.

"Should we inform the others?" he asked Petri, with a nod back toward *Bird's* other two compartments, where the crying had settled down to low whimpers from a couple of younger kids.

She shook her head. "It will be quick, yes?"

Jonah considered lying, and dismissed the idea.

"It depends. As we rise, the water pressure outside falls, so if air pressure inside remains high, that could lead to a blow-out, cracking one of our shells, letting the sea rush in awfully fast. So fast, we'll be knocked out before we can drown. Of course, that's the *least* gruesome end."

"What a cheerful lad," she commented. "Go on."

"Let's say the hull compartments hold. This is a tough old bird." He patted the nearest curved flank. "We can help protect against blow-out by venting compartment air, trying to keep pace with falling pressure outside. In that case, we'll suffer one kind or another kind of pressure-change disease. The most common is the Bends. That's when gas that's dissolved in our blood suddenly pops into tiny bubbles that fill your veins and arteries. I hear it's a painful way to die."

140

Whether because of his mutation, or purely in his mind, Jonah felt a return of the scratchy throat and burning eyes. He turned his head barely in time to sneeze away from the window and Petri.

She was looking behind them, into the next compartment. "If death is unavoidable, but we can pick our way to die, then I say let's choose –"

At that moment, Jonah tensed at a sudden, jarring sensation – A *snap* that rattled the viewing-patch in front of him. Something was happening, above and ahead. Without light from the Cleopatra domes, darkness was near total outside, broken only by some algae-glowbulbs placed along the flank of the Pride of Laussane. Letting go of Petri, he went to all the bulbs inside the *Bird's* forward compartment and covered them, then hurried back to press his face against the viewing-patch.

"What is it?" Petri asked. "What's going on?"

"I think…" Jonah made out a queer, sinuous rippling in the blackness between the two submarines.

He jumped as something struck the window. With pounding heart, he saw and heard a snakelike thing slither across the clear zone of bubble, before falling aside. And beyond, starting from just twenty meters away, the row of tiny glow spots now shot upward, like legendary rockets, quickly diminishing, then fading from view.

"The tether," he announced in a matter-of-fact voice.

"They let go? Let *us* go?" A blend of hope and awe in her voice.

"Made sense," he answered. "They were goners anyway." *And now they will be the heroes, when all is told. Songs will be sung about their choice, back home.*

That is, assuming there still is a home. We have no idea if Leininger dome was the only victim this time.

He stared at the pressure gauge. After a long pause when it refused to budge, the needle finally began to move. Opposite to its former direction of change.

"We're descending," he decreed with a sigh. "In fact, we'd better adjust. To keep from falling too fast. It wouldn't do, to reach safety down there, only to crack open from impact."

Jonah put the Sadoulite dad – Xerish – to work, pumping in the opposite direction, less frantically than before, but harder work, using compressed air to push out-and-overboard some water from the ballast tanks, while Petri, now experienced, handled the valves. After supervising for a few minutes, he went back to the viewing port and peered outside. *I must keep a sharp look out for the lights of Cleo Crevice. We may have drifted laterally and I can adjust better while we're falling than later, at the bottom.* He used the rudder and stubby elevation planes to turn his little sub, explaining to Petri how it was done. She might have to steer, if Jonah's strength was needed on the propeller crank.

A low, concussive report caused the chamber to rattle and groan. Not as bad as the horrid thump had been, but closer, coming from somewhere above. Jonah shared eye contact with Petri, a sad recognition of something inevitable. The end of a gallant ship – *Pride of Laussane.*

Two more muffled booms followed, rather fainter, then another.

They must have closed their inner hatches. Each compartment is failing separately.

But something felt wrong about that. The third concussion, especially, had felt deep-throated, lasting longer than reasonable. Amid another bout of sneezing, Jonah pressed close against the view-patch once again, in order to peer about. First toward the bottom and then upward.

Clearly, this day had to be the last straw. It rang a death knell for the old, complacent ways of doing things. Leininger had been a big, important colony, and perhaps not today's only major victim. If thumps were going unpredictable and lethal, then Cleopatra might have to be abandoned.

Jonah knew very little about the plan concocted by Petri's mysterious cabal of young women and men, though he was glad to have been chosen to help. To follow a *rascal's* legend in search of new homes. In fact, two things were abundantly clear. *Expeditions must get under way just as soon as we get back. And there should be more than just one, following Melvil's clues. Subs must be sent in many directions! If Venus created other realms filled with hollow volcanic globes that can be seeded with Earthly life, then we must find them.*

A second fact had also emerged, made evident during the last hour or so. Jonah turned to glance back at a person he had barely known, until just a day ago.

It appears that I married really well.

Although the chamber was very dim, Petri glanced up from her task and noticed him looking at her. She smiled – an expression of respect and dawning equality that seemed just as pleased as he now felt. Jonah smiled back – then unleashed another great sneeze. At which she chirped a short laugh and shook her head in fake-mocking ruefulness.

Grinning, he turned back to the window, gazed upward – then shouted –

"Grab something! Brace yourselves!"

That was all he had time or breath to cry, while yanking on the tiller cables and shoving his knee hard against the elevator control plane. *Bird* heeled over to starboard, both rolling and struggling to yaw-turn. Harsh cries of surprise and alarm erupted from the back compartments, as crates and luggage toppled.

He heard Petri shout – "stay where you are!" – at the panicky Xerish, who whimpered in terror. Jonah caught a glimpse of them, reflected in the view-patch, as they clutched one of the air-storage bottles to keep from tumbling across the deck, onto the right-side bulkhead.

Come on, old boy, he urged the little sub and wished he had six strong men cranking at the stern end, driving the propeller to accelerate *Bird of Tairee* forward. If there had been, Jonah might – just barely – have guided the sub clear of peril tumbling from above. Debris from a catastrophe, only a small fraction of it glittering in the darkness.

Hard chunks of something rattled against the hull. He glimpsed an object, thin and metallic – perhaps a torn piece of pipe – carom off the view-patch with a bang, plowing several nasty scars before it fell away. Jonah half expected the transparent zone to start spalling and cracking, at any second.

That didn't happen, but now debris was coming down in a positive rain, clattering along the whole length of his vessel, testing the sturdy old shells with every strike. Desperate, he hauled even harder, steering *Bird* away from what seemed the worst of it, toward a zone that glittered a bit less. More cries erupted from the back two chambers.

I should have sealed the hatches, he thought. But then, what good would that do for anyone, honestly? Having drifted laterally from Cleo Canyon, any surviving chambers would be helpless, unable to maneuver, never to be found or rescued before the stored air turned to poison. *Better that we all go together.*

He recognized the sound that most of the rubble made upon the hull – bubble-stone striking more bubble-stone. Could it all have come from the *Pride of Laussane?* Impossible! There was far too much.

Leininger.

The doomed dome must have imploded, or exploded, or simply come apart without the stabilizing pressure of the depths. Then, with all its air lost and rushing skyward, the rest would plummet. Shards of bubble wall, dirt, pinyons glowing feebly as they drifted ever-lower... and people. That was the detritus Jonah most hoped to avoid.

There. It looks jet black over there. The faithful old sub had almost finished its turn. Soon he might slack off, setting the boat upright. Once clear of the debris field, he could check on the passengers, then go back to seeking the home canyon…

He never saw whatever struck next, but it had to be big, perhaps a major chunk of Leininger's wall. The blow hammered all three compartments in succession, ringing them like great gongs, making Jonah cry out in pain. There were other sounds, like ripping, tearing. The impact – somewhere below and toward portside, lifted him off his feet. tearing one of the rudder straps out of Jonah's hand, leaving him to swing wildly by the other. *Bird* sawed hard to the left as Jonah clawed desperately to reclaim the controls.

At any moment, he expected to greet the harsh, cold sea and have his vessel join the skyfall of lost hopes.

6.

Only gradually did it dawn on him – it wasn't over. The peril and problems, he wasn't about to escape them that easily. Yes, damage was evident, but the hulls – three ancient, volcanic globes, still held.

In fact, some while after that horrible collision, it did seem that *Bird of Tairee* had drifted clear of the heavy stuff. Material still rained upon the sub, but evidently softer items. Like still-glowing chunks of pinyon vine.

Petri took charge of the rear compartments, crisply commanding passengers to help each other dig out and assessing their hurts, in order of priority. She shouted reports to Jonah, whose hands were full. In truth, he had trouble hearing what she said, over the ringing in his ears, and had to ask for repetition several times. The crux: one teenager had a fractured wrist, while others bore bruises and contusions – a luckier toll than he expected. Bema – the Sadoulite mother – kept busy delivering first aid.

More worrisome was a *leak*. Very narrow, but powerful, a needle jet spewed water into the rear compartment. Not through a crack in the shell – fortunately – but via the packing material that surrounded the propeller bearing. Jonah would have to go back and have a look, but first he assessed other troubles. For example, the sub wouldn't right herself completely. There was a constant tilt to starboard around the roll axis…

...then he checked the pressure gauge, and muttered a low invocation to ancient gods and demons of Old Earth.

◇

"We've stopped falling," he confided to Petri in the stern compartment, once the leak seemed under control. It had taken some time, showing the others how to jam rubbery cloths into the bearing and then bracing it all with planks of wood torn from the floor. The arrangement was holding, for now.

"How can that be?" she asked. "We were *heavy* when the *Pride* let us go. I thought our problem was how to slow our descent."

"It was. Till our collision with whatever-hit-us. Based on where it struck, along the portside keel, I'd guess that it knocked off some of our static ballast – the stones lashed to our bottom. The same thing that happened to *Pride* during that awful thump quake. Other stones may have been dislodged or had just one of their lashings cut, leaving them to dangle below the starboard side, making us tilt like this. I'd say we've just learned a lesson today, about a really bad flaw in the whole way we've done sub design."

"So which is it? Are we rising?"

Jonah nodded.

"Slowly. It's not too bad yet. And I suppose it's possible we might resume our descent, if we fill all the ballast tanks completely. Only there's a problem."

"Isn't there always?" Petri rolled her eyes, clearly exasperated.

"Yeah." He gestured toward where Xerish – by luck a carpenter – was hammering more bracing into place. Jonah lowered his voice. "If we drop back to the sea floor, that bearing may not hold against full-bottom pressure. It's likely to start spewing again, probably faster."

"If it does, how long will we have?"

Jonah frowned. "Hard to say. Air pressure would fight back, of course. Still, I'd say less than an hour. Maybe not that much. We would have to spot one of the canyon domes right away, steer right for it and plop ourselves into dock as fast as possible, with everyone cranking like mad –"

"— only using the propeller will put even more stress on the bearing," Petri concluded with a thoughtful frown. "It might blow completely."

Jonah couldn't prevent a brief smile. *Brave enough to face facts... and a mechanical aptitude, as well? I could find this woman attractive.*

"Well, I'm sure we can work something out," she added. "You haven't let us down, yet."

Not yet, he thought and returned to work, feeling trapped by her confidence in him. And cornered by the laws of chemistry and physics – as well as he understood them with his meager education, taken from ancient books that were rudimentary and obsolete when the Founders first came to Venus, cowering away from alien invaders under a newborn ocean, while comets poured in with perfect regularity.

Perfect for many lifetimes, but not forever. Not anymore. *Even if we make it home, then go ahead with the Melvil Plan, and manage to find another bubble-filled canyon less affected by the rogue thumps, how long will that last?*

Wasn't this whole project, colonizing the bottom of an alien sea with crude technology, always doomed from the start?

In the middle compartment, Jonah opened his personal chest and took out some treasures – books and charts that he had personally copied under supervision by Scholar Wu, onto bundles of hand-scraped pinyon leaves. In one, he verified his recollection of Boyle's Law and the dangers of changing air pressure on the human body. From another he got a formula that – he hoped – might predict how the leaky propeller shaft bearing would behave, if they descended the rest of the way.

Meanwhile, Petri put a couple of the larger teen girls to work on a bilge pump, transferring water from the floor of the third compartment into some almost-full ballast tanks. Over the next hour, Jonah kept glancing at the pressure gauge. The truck appeared to be leveling off again. *Up and down. Up and down. This can't be good for my old Bird.*

Leveled. Stable... for now. That meant the onus fell on him, with no excuse.

To descend and risk the leak becoming a torrent, blasting those who worked the propeller crank... or else...

Two hands laid pressure on his shoulders and squeezed inward, surrounding his neck, forcefully. Slim hands, kneading tense muscles and tendons. Jonah closed his eyes, not wanting to divulge what he had decided.

"Some wedding day, huh?"

Jonah nodded. No verbal response seemed needed. He felt married for years – and glad of the illusion. Evidently, Petri knew him now, as well.

"I bet you've figured out what to do."

He nodded again.

"And it won't be fun, or offer good odds of success."

A head shake. Left, then right.

Her hands dug in, wreaking a mixture of pleasure and pain, like life.

"Then tell me, husband," she commanded, coming around to bring their faces close. "Tell me what you'll have us do. Which way do we go?"

He exhaled a sigh. Then inhaled. And finally spoke one word.

"Up."

7.

Toward the deadly sky. Toward Venusian hell. It had to be. No other choice was possible.

"If we rise to the surface, I can try to repair the bearing from inside, without water gushing through. And if it requires outside work, then I can do that by putting on a helmet and coveralls. Perhaps they'll keep out the poisons long enough."

Petri shuddered at the thought. "Let us hope that won't be necessary."

"Yeah. Though while I'm there I could also fix the ballast straps holding some of the weight stones to our keel. I... just don't see any other way."

Petri sat on a crate opposite Jonah, mulling it over.

"Wasn't upward motion what destroyed Leininger Colony and the *Pride?*"

"Yes... but their ascent was uncontrolled. Rapid and chaotic. We'll rise slowly, reducing cabin air pressure in pace with the decreased push of water outside. We have to go slow, anyway, or the gas that's dissolved in our blood will boil and kill us. Slow and gentle. That's the way."

She smiled. "You know all the right things to say to a virgin."

Jonah felt his face go red and was relieved when Petri got serious again.

"If we rise slowly, won't there be another problem? Won't we run out of breathable air?"

He nodded. "Activity must be kept to a minimum. Recycle and shift stale air into bottles, exchanging with the good air they now contain. Also, I have a spark separator."

"You do? How did... aren't they rare and expensive?"

"I made this one myself. Well, Panalina showed me how to use pinyon crystals and electric current to split seawater into hydrogen and oxygen. We'll put some passengers to work, taking turns at the spin generator." And he warned her. "It's a small unit. It may not produce enough."

"Well, no sense putting things off, then." Petri said with a grandmother's tone of decisiveness. "Give your orders, man."

◇

The ascent became grueling. Adults and larger teens took turns at the pumps, expelling enough ballast water for the sub to start rising at a good pace... then correcting when it seemed too quick. Jonah kept close track of gauges revealing pressure, both inside and beyond the shells. He also watched for symptoms of decompression sickness – another factor keeping things slow. All passengers not on-shift were encouraged to sleep – difficult enough when the youngest children kept crying over the pain in their ears. Jonah taught them all how to yawn or pinch their noses to equalize pressure, though his explanations kept being punctuated by fits of sneezing.

Above all, even while resting, they had to breathe deep, as their lungs gradually purged and expelled excess gas from their bloodstreams.

Meanwhile, the fore-chamber resonated with a constant background whine as older kids took turns at the spark separator, turning its crank so that small amounts of seawater divided into component elements – one of them breathable. The device had to be working – a layer of salt gathered in the brine-collector. Still, Jonah worried. *Did I attach the poles right? Might I be filling the storage bottle with oxygen and letting hydrogen into the cabin? Polluting the sub with an explosive mix that could put us out of our misery, at any second?*

He wasn't sure how to tell – none of his books said – though he recalled vaguely that hydrogen had no odor.

After following him on his rounds, inspecting everything and repeating his explanations several times, Petri felt confident enough to insist. "You must rest now, Jonah. I will continue to monitor our rate of ascent and make minor adjustments. Right now, I want you to close your eyes."

When he tried to protest, she insisted, with a little more of the accented tone used by Laussane mothers. "We will need you far more,

148

in a while. You'll require all your powers near the end. So lie down and recharge yourself. I promise to call, if anything much changes."

Accepting her reasoning, he obeyed by curling up on a couple of grain sacks that Xerish brought forward to the control cabin. Jonah's eyelids shut, gratefully. The brain, however, was another matter.

How deep are we now?

It prompted an even bigger question: *how deep is the bottom of Cleopatra Canyon, nowadays?*

According to lore, the first colonists used to care a lot about measuring the thickness of Venusian seas, back when some surface light used to penetrate all the way to the ocean floor. They would launch balloons attached to huge coils of string, in order to both judge depth and sample beyond the therm-o-cline barrier and even from the hot, deadly sky. Those practices died out – though Jonah had seen one of the giant capstan reels once, during a visit to Chown Dome, gathering dust and mouldering in a swampy corner.

The way Earth denizens viewed their planet's hellish interior, that was how Cleo dwellers thought of the realm above. Though there had been exceptions. Rumors held that *Melvil*, that legendary rascal, upon returning from his discovery of Theodora Crevice, had demanded support to start exploring the great heights. Possibly even the barrier zone where living things thronged and might be caught for food. Of course, he was quite mad – though boys still whispered about him in hushed tones.

How many comets? Jonah found himself wondering. Only one book in Tairee spoke of the great Venus Terraforming Project that predated the Coss invasion. Mighty robots, as patient as gods, gathered iceballs at the farthest fringe of the Solar System and sent them plummeting from that unimaginably distant realm to strike this planet – several each day, always at the same angle and position – both speeding the world's rotation and drenching its long-parched basins. *If each comet was several kilometers in diameter… how thick an ocean might spread across an entire globe, in twenty generations of grandmothers?*

For every one that struck, five others were aimed to skim close by, tearing through the dense, clotted atmosphere of Venus, dragging some of it away before plunging to the sun. The scale of such an enterprise was stunning, beyond belief. So much so that Jonah truly doubted he could be of the same species that did such things. *Petri, maybe. She could be that smart. Not me.*

How were such a people ever conquered?

The roil of his drifting mind moved onward to might-have-beens. If not for that misguided comet – striking six hours late to wreak havoc near the canyon colonies – Jonah and his bride would by now have settled into a small Laussane cottage, getting to know each other in more traditional ways. Despite, or perhaps because of the emergency, he actually felt far *more* the husband of a vividly real person than he would in that other reality, where physical intimacy happened... still, the lumpy grain sacks made part of him yearn for her in ways that – now – might never come to pass. That world would have been better... one where the pinyons waved their bright leaves gently overhead. Where he might show her tricks of climbing vines, then swing from branch to branch, carrying her in his arms while the wind of flying passage ruffled their hair –

A *twang* sound vibrated the cabin, like some mighty cord coming apart. The sub throbbed and Jonah felt it roll a bit.

His eyes opened and he realized *I was asleep*. Moreover, his head now rested on Petri's lap. Her hand had been the breeze in his hair.

Jonah sat up.

"What was that?"

"I do not know. There was a sharp sound. The ship hummed a bit, and now the floor no longer tilts."

"No longer–"

Jumping up with a shout, he hurried over to the gauges, then cursed low and harsh.

"What is it, Jonah?"

"Quick – wake all the adults and get them to work pumping!"

She wasted no time demanding answers. But as soon as crews were hard at work, Petri approached Jonah again at the control station, one eyebrow raised.

"The remaining stone ballast," he explained. "It must have been hanging by a thread, or a single lashing. Now it's completely gone. The sub's tilt is corrected, but we're ascending too fast."

Petri glanced at two sadoulites and two laussaners who were laboring to refill the ballast tanks. "Is there anything else we can do to slow down?"

Jonah shrugged. "I suppose we might unpack the leaky bearing and let more water into the aft compartment. But we'd have no control. The stream could explode in our faces. We might flood or lose the chamber. All told, I'd rather risk decompression sickness."

She nodded, agreeing silently.

They took their own turn at the pumps, then supervised another crew until, at last, the tanks were full. *Bird* could get no heavier. Not without flooding the compartments themselves.

"We have to lose internal pressure. That means venting air over-board," he said "in order to equalize."

"But we'll need it to breathe!"

"There's no choice. With our tanks full of water, there's no place to put extra air and still reduce pressure."

So, different pumps and valves, but more strenuous work. Mean-while, Jonah kept peering at folks in the dim illumination of just two faint glow bulbs, watching for signs of the Bends. Dizziness, muscle aches and labored breathing? These could just be the result of hard labor. The book said to watch out also for joint pain, rashes, delirium or sudden unconsciousness. He did know that the old Dive Tables were useless – based on Earth-type humanity. *And we've changed. First because our scientist ancestors modified themselves and their offspring. But time, too, has altered what we are, even long after we lost those wizard powers. Each generation was an experiment.*

Has it made us less vulnerable to such things? Or more so?

Someone tugged his arm. It wasn't Petri, striving at her pump. Jonah looked down at one of the children, still wearing a stained and crumpled bridesmaid's dress, who pulled shyly, urging Jonah to come follow. At first, he thought: *it must be the sickness. She's summoning me to help someone's agony. But what can I do?*

Only it wasn't toward the stern that she led him, but the forward-most part of the ship… to the view-patch, where she pointed.

"What is it?" Pressing close to the curved pane, Jonah tensed as he starkly envisioned some new cloud of debris… till he looked up and saw –

– light.

Vague at first. Only a child's perfect vision would have noticed it so early. But soon it spread and brightened across the entire vault overhead.

I thought we would pass through the therm-o-cline. He had expected a rough – perhaps even lethal – transition past that supposed barrier between upper and lower oceans. But it must have happened gently, while he slept.

Jonah called someone to relieve Petri and brought her forth to see.

"Go back and tell people to hold on tight," Petri dispatched the little girl, then she turned to grab Jonah's waist as he took the control straps. At this rate they appeared to be seconds away from entering Venusian hell.

Surely it has changed, he thought, nursing a hope that had never been voiced, even in his mind. *The ocean has burgeoned as life fills the seas...*

Already he spied signs of movement above. Flitting, flickering shapes – living versions of the crushed and dead tumbledowns that sometimes fell to Tairee's bottom realm, now undulating and darting about what looked like scattered patches of dense, dangling weed. He steered to avoid those.

If the sea has changed, then might not the sky, the air, even the highlands?

Charts of Venus, radar mapped by ancient earthling space probes, revealed vast continents and basins, a topography labeled with names like Aphrodite Terra and Lakshmi Planum. Every single appellation was that of a female from history or literature or legend. Well, that seemed fair enough. But had it been a cruel joke to call the baked and bone-dry lowlands "seas"?

Till humanity decided to make old dreams come true.

What will we find?

To his and Petri's awestruck eyes, the dense crowd of life revealed glimpses – shapes like dragons, like fish, or those ancient *blimps* that once cruised the skies of ancient Earth. And something within Jonah allowed itself to hope.

Assuming we survive decompression, might the fiery, sulfurous air now be breathable? Perhaps barely, as promised by the sagas? By now, could life have taken to high ground? Seeded in some clever centuries-delay by those same pre-Coss designers?

His mind pictured scenes from a few dog-eared storybooks, only enormously expanded and brightened. Vast, measureless jungles, drenched by rainstorms, echoing with the bellows of gigantic beasts. A realm so huge, so rich and densely forested that a branch of humanity might thrive, grow, prosper, and learn – regaining might and confidence – beneath that sheltering canopy, safe from invader eyes.

That, once upon a time, had been the dream, though few imagined it might fully come to pass.

◊

Jonah tugged the tiller to avoid a looming patch of dangling vegetation. Then, ahead and above, the skyward shallows suddenly brightened, so fiercely that he and Petri had to shade their eyes, inhaling and exhaling heavy gasps. They both cried out as a great, slithering shape swerved barely out of the sub's way. Then brilliance filled the cabin like a blast of molten fire.

I was wrong to hope! It truly is hell!

A roar of foamy separation… and for long instants Jonah felt free of all weight. He let go of the straps and clutched Petri tight, twisting to put his body between hers and the wall as their vessel flew over the sea, turned slightly, then dropped back down, striking the surface with a shuddering blow and towering splash.

Lying crumpled below the viewing-patch, they panted, as did everyone else aboard, groaning and groping themselves to check for injuries. For reassurance of life. And gradually the hellish brightness seemed to abate, till Jonah realized. *It is my eyes, adapting. They never saw daylight, before.*

Jonah and Petri helped each other stand. Together, they turned, still shading their eyes. Sound had transformed, and so had the very texture of the air, now filled with strange aromas.

There must be a breach!

With shock, still blinking away glare-wrought tears, Jonah saw the cause. Impact must have knocked loose the dog-bolts charged with holding shut the main hatch, amidships on the starboard side —never meant to open anywhere but at the safety of a colonial dock.

With a shout he hurried over, even knowing it was too late. The poisons of Venus –

– apparently weren't here.

No one keeled over. His body's sole reaction to the inrushing atmosphere was to sneeze, a report so loud and deep that it rocked him back.

Jonah reached the hatch and tried pushing it closed, but *Bird of Tairee* was slightly tilted to port. The heavy door overwhelmed Jonah's resistance and kept gradually opening, from crack to slit, to gap, to chasm.

"I'll help you, Jonah," came an offer so low, like a rich male baritone, yet recognizably that of his wife. He turned, saw her eyes wide with surprise at her own voice.

"The air… it contains…" His words emerged now a deep bass. "… different gases than… we got from pinyons."

Different… but breathable. Even pleasant. Blinking a couple of times, he managed to shrug off the shock of his new voice and tried once more to close the hatch, before giving up for now. With the boat's slight leftward roll, there was no immediate danger of flooding, as seawater lapped a meter or so below. The opening must be closed soon, of course...

... but not quite yet. For, as Jonah and Petri stood at the sill, what confronted them was more than vast, rippling-blue ocean and a cloud-dense firmament. Something else lay between those two, just ahead and to starboard, a thick mass of shimmery greens and browns that filled the horizon, receding in mist toward distant, serrated skylines. Though he never dreamed of witnessing such a thing first-hand, they both recognized the sight, from ancient, faded pictures.

Land. Shore. Dense forests. Everything.

And overhead, creatures flapped strange, graceful wings, or drifted like floating jellyfish above leafy spires.

"It will take some time to figure out what we can eat," his wife commented, with feminine practicality.

"Hm," Jonah replied, too caught up in wonder to say more, a silence that lasted for many poundings of his heart. Until, finally, he managed to add —

"Someday. We must go back down. And tell."

After another long pause, Petri answered.

"Yes, someday."

She held him tight around the chest, a forceful constriction that only filled Jonah with strength. His lungs expanded as he inhaled deeply a sweet smell, and knew that only part of that was her.

Story Notes

This tale of exile appeared in the anthology *Old Venus*, edited by George R. R. Martin and Gardner Dozois. It, too, is about perseverance in the face of apparent hopelessness. And reclaiming an old dream.

The final tale in this section – "Eloquent Elepents Pine Away for the Moon's Crystal Forests" – may seem incomplete. But it served my purpose – laying down a glimmering notion that will continue to grow...
    ... that of revolution.

Eloquent Elepents Pine Away for the Moon's Crystal Forests

◇

What do the Coss want from us?

W Unbidden, the question frothed to the surface of his mind, even though Doni knew better. He should avoid thinking about the invaders.

Still, it nagged at him. Despite having grown up under the New Enlightened Imperium, he just couldn't bring himself to take alien domination for granted.

They don't even seem to enjoy being our masters.

More than a human lifetime after their arrival, the Coss had transformed themselves in stages. From welcome visitors into hated conquerors, and then – over the following two generations – into just another layer of life in the Solar System. Occupying the top niches that human beings used to fill – more awkwardly – with overlords of their own. With kings and priests and all variety of homemade bosses.

Only no human aristocracy ever did it quite so well.

Doni watched two of the alien rulers argue next to the dock where cargo, fresh from Earth, was unloaded from the gaping hold of the *Mt. Orleans*. Robots hauled massive crates, while delicate luggage was carried by human porters in stiff, high-collared uniforms. Everything in-between got moved by patient elepents, grunting and rumbling a low song that seemed to fill the vast chamber as they tugged awkward items with their dexterous trunks, sometimes rearing back in the low gravity of Pallas, standing on their hind legs in order to give each other a pand.

The pair of Coss, engrossed in their dispute, seemed aloof to all this, blithely ignoring the commotion around them. Of the two, Matron Kopok was much shorter, almost diminutive for one of her race – not even two meters tall, with a head that barely topped over Doni's. But that did not diminish her power to intimidate. Right now, the great lady fumed, from her crest of fine copper hair to the tips of her pointed fingernails, glaring at the Coss officer in command of the Pallas dockyard.

Doni checked his uniform to make sure all was spotless and straight. Then – although he knew he shouldn't – he edged closer in order to listen.

"... won't even acknowledge that the gulagis are fellow creatures of the Universal Spirit! Some of them were sentenced to this wilderness decades ago. Don't the Primes teach us that cruelty is only valid when it's *useful?* How can our vassals ever fully accept lasting faith in our wisdom if –"

"Acceptance comes from resignation, Milady," the dock commander answered coolly, from a height of nearly seven feet. "Which is taught through adamant strength. As for the gulagis, they are malcontents, upstarts and rebels. "

"Not in every case."

With a broad-shouldered shrug that rattled his sparkling necklace array, the commander seemed willing to concede that point, and made clear that it did not matter.

"In any event, the prisoners are no concern of yours, Milady. They serve the Imperium that they criticized and betrayed. That should be satisfying enough to the Universal Spirit."

"But those supplies –" the Matron gestured to a stack, just beyond the glistening bow of the Mt. Orleans. "I expected someone from Compassionate Beneficence to sign for them."

"There is no longer a representative of that organization here on Pallas."

"No longer..." Kopok paused, the spiderweb of tendons and veins in her long neck pulsated. "I see. And they never saw fit to notify me? Oh, mothers, why must I forever be flattered into doing favors for well-meaning fools?"

She sighed, straightening and smoothing the ruffled folds of her blue gown.

"It must be my reputation for generosity. That is why I'm punished thus. Well, then. I suppose the supplies –"

"I will take charge of them," the dockmaster cut in, tugging on one long earring. "Your Ladyship is free to continue on her way, completing the long journey from Earth to her *Academy...*"

Was there a sarcastic edge to his voice?

"...without sparing any further concern for this matter."

Uh-oh, Doni thought, as a low hum seemed to fill the cavities within his ears, without actual sound. Taking a rapid glance at the Matron, he knew where the resonance was coming from. Kopok's long, Coss face was rapidly undergoing what cadets called *the change.* Those eyes, often placid as deep space, turned stormy under glowering lids.

The big guy just made a mistake. Doni started edging away.

"You *dare* to decide what matters may, or may not, concern me?"

Her words were cold and sharp, like icicles, while the *hum* grew stronger, now tugging at the tonsils in the back of Doni's throat. The dockmaster, clearly accustomed to giving orders from on-high, blinked several times at the much-smaller female of his race. Realization appeared to be dawning that, perhaps, he had gone too far.

"Please be assured that I did not mean –"

"You clearly know who I am," continued the Lady Kopok. "Do you truly wish for a *dispute* between us?"

She left the implication hanging in mid-air, as if it were not something to discuss openly, within hearing of the lower orders. Doni already knew at least a dozen ways that the Solar System's alien aristocracy settled disputes among themselves. From trial-by-combat to appeals for royal arbitration. They were even known to use *law,* when no other method sufficed. Whatever the method, Lady Kopok was reputed to be a master of them all. Or else, how could she ever have managed to do the impossible, and reopen Porcorosso?

An instinct for self-preservation made Doni look away from the confrontation and busy himself with the Matron's bags. Straightening. Adjusting. Even though they were already neatly set upon the cart.

You did not want to be caught looking, when a Coss was being humbled. Even – especially – when the humbler was another Coss.

"I... I will see to it that the relief supplies are trans-shipped to your academy," the dockmaster said, in a voice that seemed to strive, at once, for both dignity and appeasement. "Though it will ultimately be up to the *gulagmasters,* whether you are permitted to deliver these goods to the exiles."

"I will deal with the gulagmasters, if it is my whim," Kopok snapped, in a voice that sounded quite accustomed to obedience. "Or else, I may send the crates back to Compassionate Beneficence on Earth, at double freight charges. It would serve those idealistic fools right."

While Doni marveled at the verbal agility of his headmistress, the taller Coss barked a brittle laugh of agreement, one that conveyed more than three-quarters relief. "Yes, Milady. It would."

"Hm. Just make sure the boxes are delivered to Porcorosso, undamaged and unopened."

The dockmaster clicked his heels.

"Safe journey, Lady Kopo."

And he turned to go, gliding away in a graceful lope, assisted in the low gravity by traction boots. It all was done with haughty Coss solemnity, of course. Punctilious attention to face. Nevertheless, Doni picked up a definite *mutter wave.*

Crazy old bat, the dockmaster was thinking as he left.

Officious cretin, the Matron murmured after him, without making a sound.

Upon which, Doni felt her gaze sweep toward him. He snapped to attention next to the cart stacked high with luggage. "Shall I fetch a porter, Madam? Or an elepent?"

"Hm? Oh, nonsense. This is Pallas, Doni. There is barely enough gravity to walk, so obviously the cart isn't heavy. Anyway, you could benefit from practice, estimating inertia and momentum."

In other words, the muscle power of a fifteen-year old boy ought to suffice. Simply pull and push on the cart — massive but not "heavy" — a good, hard nudge now and then, at well-chosen intervals, so that it keeps rolling along toward the shuttle docks. The job should be easy. Surely no worse than piloting one of the academy's leaky, obsolete rocket trainers, dodging meteoroids and "threading needles" in deep vacuum.

Only, pushing the luggage cart was tricky. You'd better be sure to *time* each turn and stop just right — every muscle-powered acceleration and deceleration — prodding the tiller with *exactly* the appropriate force. Make an adjustment too late and it may crash into a wall or collide with a grunting pachydermoid. Decelerate too soon and you could (far worse!) delay Lady Kopok a second longer than she expects.

All in all, Doni would prefer time in a trainer, when the worst penalty for a mistake was death.

Grabbing the tiller, he planted his traction soles and dug in, straining until the cart was on the move, rolling past gleaming cargo ships — each bearing the crest of a Coss liege lord — hauling his lady's baggage toward a gritty little shuttle that awaited in a back corner of the cavernous space harbor. A completely human-built relic from another era, with a *red pig* painted on the nose. A pig wearing goggles, a brazen scarf and leather flight jacket, grinning with a jaunty confidence no human being would express nowadays.

The homely craft that would take them home. To Porcorosso.

Across the Solar System, most of the old battle scars had been erased. Except where the victorious masters thought that a lesson was needed. New York, Yokohama, Hong Kong and San Diego were left to smolder — ruins that would keep their deathly glow for another thousand years, teaching a sermon about the limits of Coss chivalry.

It was one thing to offer a little courageous resistance, during a time of honorable struggle. Humans were even allowed to erect statues to their greatest warriors, Penna and Chang, whose battlefield valor elevated them to the status of honorary Coss (posthumous).

But mass obstinacy was another matter. Those cities would never be rebuilt. The rubble and seared bones, never buried.

Porcorosso, clearly, fell into the first category. Everybody knew about the Last Stand of the Federation Cadets. It would be futile to squelch the legend. So, with typical Coss adaptability, they co-opted it.

Passing through the academy's outer security grid, Doni guided the shuttle silently by the monument that Lady Kopok had unveiled, the day Porcorosso re-opened. A tableau, laser carved from a single chunk of nickel-iron asteroid, portrayed a trio of cadets — battered, wounded and surrounded by fallen comrades — resolutely facing a closing circle of giant Coss. Conquerors whose faces did not seem cruel at all, but rather *proud* of the defiant youngsters. Proud... and saddened by what had to be done.

Behind them all, with starwings wide-stretched, an effigy of the Universal Spirit seemed to beckon all of the nobly-fallen into her embrace.

It was propaganda of the first order. Through this image, the conquerors seemed to say: "We *like* humans. We respect you. We shall guide and teach and elevate you.

"But don't even think of resisting us *en masse,* ever again."

From this point to the berthing chamber, a guide beam revealed itself to Doni's encrypted eyeptics. Easy to follow, the glowing route led close by a sentry post where every cadet took turns, standing guard detail for days without sleep. Grueling, hardening hours alone, in ebony armor that seemed more space than metal.

The student currently on duty saluted the shuttle, snapping rigid, presenting a deadly-looking string-rifle.

Doni spared a glance or two, looking for changes during his long absence, accompanying the headmistress to Earth. *I see they finished the Refectory,* he thought. *Maybe we'll start eating better, at last.*

For the very first class, dwelling in little more than patched ruins, a year spent eating century-old Federation freeze-dried rations had almost sparked mass resignation. Till Madame began sending for takeout from Meteograd.

That village could be seen as a glitter in the distance... the final bead in a chain, strung along a single, adamantine tether that formed a jeweled necklace spanning more than two hundred kilometers of vacuum. Porcorosso tugged at one extreme end, pointing starward, while Meteograd, with a huge solar array, perched at the extremity nearest the sun. Lesser beads that lay strung along the tether *between* Academy and town included several dozen smaller outposts, ranging from metallurgical shops and hydroponic homesteads to a foreboding shadow, no more than twenty klicks from Porcorosso –   ·

– the gulag.

His adaptive eyeptics tried to zoom toward that dark patch of night, only to be stymied by inbuilt *myob* programming. Myob, for *mind your own business.*

Ah, well. The Coss had made their attitude and policy clear. Curiosity, a human trait, was to be indulged, but only when there seemed to be a use, a need, or at least no opportunity for harm.

Indeed, the gulag was one place set aside for humans whose curiosity – or self-expression – struck the Coss as harmful.

"Shuttle Three, we're ready to take you in mag lock," said the voice of traffic control. An important task, hence given a senior classman. It sounded a bit like Herman Yang.

"Roger, Porcorosso Control. I am nulling engines and activating internal dampers." Doni scanned the readouts. Inner-hull integrity looked good enough to shield passengers, cargo and electronics, when the docking fields clamped down.

"Very good, Shuttle Three. We'll take over now. Welcome home."

You weren't supposed to feel anything, inside the perfect Faraday Cage of hull shielding. But Doni knew the very instant that a *hand* sculpted out of coherently tuned magnetic monofields converged to grab the little ship, both gently and implacably insistent. A queer vibration seemed to claw at the back of his throat, much like the *mutter* that he sometimes detected coming from a Coss.

Especially when one of them felt equally... insistent.

He turned and glanced back at Lady Kopok, who now sat blithely content, emitting no mutter at all, but viewing her domain with the apparent pleasure of a true owner.

I sure hope they have the place spic and span, Doni thought. *The cadets and instructors had plenty of warning.* Of course, nothing would suffice. But the headmistress was also fair. With any luck, only a week or so of hellish fault-finding lay in store, before the Academy settled back into hellish routine.

But you wanted this, he reminded himself. *You wanted it real bad.*

The main asteroid loomed ahead, laced with tunnels and studded with window lights, linked by a tensegrity circlet of cables and girders to the great tether, as well as a dozen outlying rocks. Dead ahead, a dock-cavity opened for Doni's shuttle, blast doors separating so that only a shimmering force screen kept atmosphere within, a barrier that ships and boats normally passed through, with nary a sign. Though again, Doni had to clench his teeth, enduring a brief tremor until they were well inside.

As the little craft neared slip number three, a double honor guard of cadets were already lining up to welcome home the headmistress. But glancing left, Doni noticed that another spaceship had taken moorings – a little courier lug, designed for use only within the Belt. Several valves hissed visible trails of condensing vapor, a sign of recent arrival, probably no more than half an hour ago. From an open cargo port, three elepents were unloading boxes that looked surprisingly familiar.

"Milady," he said to the headmistress. "Those crates. The ones for Compassionate Beneficence..."

It wasn't always wise to break into a Coss train of thought. But Doni knew no better way to maintain Kopok's trust than by staying useful to her. The matron glanced in the direction indicated, and let out a small snort.

"So, the dockmaster wanted to ensure no hard feelings. Remind me to send him a small gift, Doni."

"Yes Maam."

"And see to it that a crew loads all that stuff onto an elepent sledge, for shipment to the gulag. I don't want it clogging the dock."

"Aye aye." Doni had already risen from the pilot station. Soon he had the hatch safetied, ready for opening. Through solid metal, he could hear the Academy's small band strike up the school anthem. He turned, checked Lady Kopok's gown for any lint or faulty folds that might cause embarrassment, then took his place behind, carrying her purse, briefcase and travel bag.

"Thank you for your hard work on this voyage, Doni," the great lady murmured softly, taking a glance his way as he blinked back at her in surprise. "All complaints were minor," she added. Perhaps the strongest praise he ever recalled hearing from the lips of a high-ranking Coss.

Only a low hum seemed to emanate from the matron as she then lifted a white hand and gave a languid turn, blithely ordering the hatch to *open*.

And, of course, it did.

◇

"Have at you!"

A spray of sparks leaped from his blade, where it glanced off Puryear's buckler, barely missing a two pointer on the upperclassman's arm. Doni tried to slide his edge up and over, but found his way blocked by the mini-shield on his opponent's shoulder. The other fellow was just too tall. Half a second later Doni leaped backward, dodging a savage counter-thrust.

Every point of contact crackled with ionization, emitting brilliant, evanescent motes and flashes – especially when Puryear's shimmering zord beat down against Doni's with harsh electrical impacts – forcing him to retreat. Nose filters alone couldn't stanch the bitter tang of ozone. It made a dangerous taste in the mouth. One that soaked in through the sinuses, like death.

Of course there were safeguards. Limitations to the bodily damage that a cadet could suffer in practice. Still, there was a sense of deadly earnest that went beyond the pain of electric shocks and the shame of losing. Because someday –

He pounced toward an opening before completing that thought, then drew back from the trap, leaping as Puryear's blade slashed where his ankles had been.

Because someday... soon... I'll face real duels.

In the officer caste – especially the lower portions that were open to human beings – you had to be ready to fight and die over matters of dignity and reputation – part of the Coss policy of a *Return to Honor*. It helped Doni to focus during practice, knowing that soon this sort of thing could be deadly real.

After graduation.

Noisy cavitation waves boomed and seemed to ripple the air, every time their blades touched. A flurry of rapid exchanges – slashing attacks, parries and ripostes – sent reverberations bouncing off the walls of the Porcorosson practice arena. Doni blocked Puryear's thrust *en quatre*, then tried to turn each blade around the other, catching the other boy's weapon in a bind. A good move, but it depended on raw power and Doni just didn't have enough brute force. He couldn't press the advantage against a bigger cadet. As they locked together, grunting, embers of glittering oxygen flew between them, like angry gnats, to sting their exposed throats.

His opponent countered, using the advantage of strength to shove both glowing weapons toward Doni's face. Doni had no choice but to interpose his left arm, deflecting the slender wands of glowing metal with his buckler-shield, a disk of armor no wider than his head. Sparks flew, briefly dazzling him and prickling his exposed cheek, raising dozens of micro-welts that would itch painfully, for days to come.

"Give up?" The senior asked, in a voice that clearly expected no answer. Taunting was allowed; surrender was no option.

Gathering his strength – augmented by the recent visit to Earth – Doni yanked away, managing to hop backward...

...though, as he escaped, one of the blades took a glancing stroke along his right thigh. Ionization pain tore through Doni's leg, almost buckling the knee, feeling all-too genuine.

"Two points," the computer referee announced, even though nobody cared about the score. Only who would be left standing, and who would spend the night unconscious, in a Recovery Room gel bath.

To make matters worse, the active training garment stiffened suddenly, limiting his movements, simulating the disadvantage of a real wound.

No choice. I've got to end this quick. One way or the other.

Before Puryear could notice this shift in advantage, Doni launched a series of overhead saber cuts toward the taller boy's scalp, forcing him to retreat a little, while blocking high. But there was no worry on the senior's face. In fact, a smile started to spread. After all, flamboyance was his forté. Nobody could match Puryear at hacking and slashing. Soon, he was moving off the defensive. Each exchange of cut and counter was taking place a little farther from his head and closer to Doni's, than the one before. At this rate, with one fencer barely able to walk, there would be no escape. And when that glowing blade reached its inevitable destination, Doni knew what kind of brief agony to expect, before blackness.

Still he had one chance. Puryear was enjoying himself too much. His saber cuts were getting a bit broad, like those you might see in some action movie. And no surprise there. The Coss *loved* old two-dee flicks from the 20th and 21st Centuries. These very *zords* – slender metalloids that glowed and hummed, then crackled as they clashed – were inspired by images from that golden time of heroic fantasy, before the Coss arrived. An era when *choreography* ruled and practical fencing had almost become a lost art.

Just hold on... Doni told himself, concentrating as a back and forth clanging of blades seemed to split the very air, obscuring it with fireworks.

That's right. Puryear's weakness lay in his tendency toward gloating. He was adding little flourishes to each attack, relishing a powerful rush of superiority that arose naturally from the saber, more than any other weapon. A sense of dominance.

While Doni knew a hard truth.

The era of human lords is no more. Even if we become officers under the Coss, our role won't be to lead.

It is to entertain.

And, when convenient...

...to die.

There had been several brief openings, but he made himself wait, letting his opponent bear down, pounding on him harder and closer with every broad slash. Instinct begged Doni to answer every stroke with something just as potent and dashing, but he concentrated on doing the absolute minimum, deflecting a blow and then parrying, getting through each exchange with one rule in mind.

Don't slash. Don't hack. As much as possible, keep the zord tip aimed at your opponent, as if held by an elastic cord. Let him think you're conserving your last strength, when the real reason...

Doni could tell when Puryear began playing his end game for the audience. Of course, a lot of other cadets were tuned in, watching either from their dorm rooms or the gallery above, beyond the mirrored ceiling.

More sparks flew, but the blows were more glancing, the closer Doni allowed them to come. In response, Puryear started hitting harder, taking a longer windup before each whirling slash. Surely some of those watching right now must be Coss – rumor had it they tuned in from around the solar system – during the best student duels, laying wagers. If so, with their love of flash, would the odds be overwhelming, now?

What about now? Doni thought, lowering his guard in a show of exhaustion that was only half-feigned, right after Puryear's zord swung past his head. Would the other cadet take a guard post, as he had been taught? Reverse momentum to re-engage? Or –

The taller boy grinned and *kept going*, swinging his blade in a gaudy flourish...

...and Doni turned his fingers *so*, rotating his own zord, so that the tip would happen to coincide in space and time with a small part of that flamboyant arc. Occupying that point in rendezvous with Puryear's wrist.

No sparks leaped from the point of contact. It wasn't flashy, just a short electric zap that raised a sudden smolder of smoke from Puryear's glove and a howl from his throat. Doni had to duck fast, as the other boy's blade flew from his spasmed hand, tumbling colorfully, end over end, before sputtering out near the door.

Puryear slumped to his knees, clutching his right forearm in his left hand. But to his credit, though his body wavered, he did not let go of consciousness. The fellow had guts, even if he gave in too easily to rash decisions. Of course, whichever Coss lord recruited him, those traits would likely be the very thing valued. The aliens were nothing if not good judges of human potential.

"Disabling wound. Match terminated," said the referee voice. "Is honor satisfied?"

Unseen eyes were watching. Evaluating on so many levels, judging for so many traits. Victory was not the only criterion that decided which Coss livery a cadet would finally wear.

I wonder what kind will recruit me? Doni mused. *I won't be amusing, I'm … efficient.* Well, reliability had its virtues, perhaps on some lord's boring security detail. Years of standing guard.

Puryear knew about the watching, evaluating eyes, clearly. The tall boy struggled to straighten up, overcoming pain and nodding, even though he could not speak. At which point, Doni hurried next to him, taking the fellow's weight upon one shoulder. And together they left the clean modernized arena, passing out of view from any audience, shambling into portions of Porcorosso that still bore stains from a final battle – the Last Stand of the Cadets who once died here, defending a forlorn Human Federation.

Doni felt the power of his body, tuned and augmented by tech developed by Coss and human savants, trained and disciplined and hardened by the methods of an ancient warrior caste. By any measure, he was twenty times the fighter that any of those boys and girls had been, who died in these halls. And yet, each scar and blaster burn… and occasional, brownish splatter of vacuum-dried blood… reminded him.

They were men… but what am I?

And what loyalty shall I ever have, that compares to what they foolishly died for?

Passing a space-window – a new pane that the Headmistress had brought with her from Earth – he glanced across a glitter of nearby asteroids and faraway stars, knowing that patience had its virtues. That opportunities await those who watch and learn and pay close attention.

And yet…

In time, I will find something that's worth dying for.

Or worth living for.

WHEN WE OVERCOME

◇

Mars Opposition

◇

When the Martians came, they proved unlike anything we imagined. Elegant, dauntingly tall and gleamingly enigmatic, they spilled out of a bizarre craft that appeared at dawn – gently and quite suddenly – on the ELV launch pad at Cape Canaveral.

We called the thing a 'ship,' for lack of a better word. In fact, it more resembled an outcrop of ocher desert stone, a jumbled rock-pile that had been yanked from some faraway canyon and somehow deposited in swampy Florida. Nobody would imagine that it flew, except that a dozen eyewitnesses swore they had seen it descend, swiftly and almost silently, at daybreak.

For about an hour it just stood there, creaking and settling next to the gleaming derrick where unmanned space probes sometimes get hurled skyward atop pillars of flame. Pebbles and reddish dust – plus an occasional boulder – showered onto the concrete apron, covering scorch marks left by past fiery launches. Despite all the grit, we could tell the newcomers were far beyond primitive rockets.

Finally, from what appeared to be the mouths of several caves, creatures started emerging.

At first sight they seemed amorphous – hard to make out against the rocks and slanted dawn – slithering down slopes of glittering dust. But their forms changed before our eyes. Adapting to this environment? They seemed to unfold as they descended, rapidly gathering themselves upon slender, bipedal legs until several dozen spindly, multi-jointed humanoids finally stepped onto the concrete apron.

Like newly emerged butterflies, all of them turned toward the sun for a few minutes, preening and stretching tall, revealing long torsoes covered with translucent, greenish skin that bulged in a pronounced hump across both shoulders. Soon each hump opened, spreading into a pair of diaphanous fans – like parasols, or wings – that seemed to firm and gain shape under full daylight.

"The chief color is the same as chlorophyll," commented Slade, using a spectrometer she had ingeniously yanked from the *Cheng Ho* spacecraft, hasty moments after the aliens were spotted. "Those winglike appendages must be collectors. See how they face the sun? These critters make their own food supply as they walk around."

Following her lead, several other Cape scientists were setting up instruments, adapting them to close-in views and peering excitedly at the newcomers, comparing notes till the first government officials arrived.

"Why here?" someone asked. "Why not Washington, or the U.N?"

Wasn't that where aliens always came – in movies, that is – to the seats of deliberation, policy, and power? Or else dark country highways, intent on grabbing and probing another class of folks.

It dawned on us that perhaps these visitors had different values than movie producers. Other priorities than the UFO-faery creatures of our hallucinations.

It fell upon Assistant Director Falker – the highest official present – to step forward nervously as the Martians approached. Tall and imposing, they did not appear to be armed, though many of them carried what looked like *scrolls*, silvery and covered with some kind of jagged writing.

That seemed auspicious, at least. Perhaps they bore gifts of wisdom from the stars! Or technology. Cures for diseases? Engraved invitations to join the Galactic Federation?

Or perhaps an ultimatum.

Gotta hand it to Falker. Spreading his arms in a welcoming gesture as the leader drew near, he spoke hoarse but clear.

"Welcome to Earth. On behalf of the people of the United –"

The first of the tall aliens stopped in front of Falker, as expected...

...but other members of their delegation *kept going*, moving past the two of them, spreading out, heading for the dismayed crowd of spectators!

"Hello," the first one interrupted the Assistant Director in English. The alien's voice seemed rich in tones of metal, soot and stone.

"I seek information –"

If the first visitor said more, we were too distracted to listen. For as the rest of the gangly creatures fanned out, each of them chose a different person in the throng of onlookers to approach. One stepped right up to Slade, ignoring her instruments and looking down at her from a great height.

"Hello, I seek information," this one said, reiterating the leader's words, sounding like the grinding together of aged rocks. "I offer fair compensation, if you provide the datum required."

It reached into a pocket that had not been there a moment before... an opening that appeared along one rib of that long torso. The alien's hand emerged, thrust forward and opened almost under her nose.

Slade stared at glittering objects.

Nuggets that had to be gold.

A jumble of faceted slivers that could only be diamonds.

"I believe you find these of value. I will trade them for information."

Slade blinked a couple of times, glancing to see that every space-visitor had chosen a different human to approach – from among those brave enough to remain when the delegation divided into a free-for-all. Though many fled, some of us stayed, rooted by curiosity, more powerful than fear.

A strangled sound was all Slade managed, at first, as she stared at the small pile of treasure, then back up at the gangling space-visitor. Finally, she murmured.

"Wha – what do you want to know?"

With uncanny agility - and without disturbing a single gemstone - the alien used its other hand to draw forth and unfurl one of those glossy scrolls. Gripping a side with two opposable fingers, it sent two others snaking toward a column of text.

"I seek the human being whose name appears here... eleventh on this list."

Peering over Slade's shoulder, I saw that the scroll bore a column of names, much longer than ought to fit. Through some technological wizardry, the words – all written in a serifed, Roman font – multiplied in size wherever my gaze happened to fall. Microprinting became instantly readable.

I recognized several names, including one the alien pointed to.

Bill Nye

Yes, the famed science popularizer and head of The Planetary Society.

I nudged Slade, to get her attention, but she ignored me, hurrying to accommodate our guest.

"You want to meet Bill? The guy's got fans *everywhere*. Why, he's right here at the Cape! Advising some new show for the Discovery Channel, I think. They were filming over at Pad One-A. But with all the commotion, I bet he's already nearby."

"Thank you. Here is your payment," the alien answered, pouring the small mound of nuggets and gems into her hand. Instantly more appeared. *"I will pay you further to guide me directly to Bill Nye."*

I had already spotted the man in question, still handsome and charismatic after spending his entire adult life – more than half a century – helping to push humanity upward, outward, beyond Earth's cradle. As a matter of fact, Bill happened to be speaking to a different visitor!

That creature was even taller than the one facing Slade. But Bill stood undaunted, with no apparent ill ease, peering at another of the silvery scrolls that alien held in front of him. With a smile he turned and pointed west while uttering a few words.

When the newcomer tried to hand over a fistful of treasure, Bill shook his head, refusing payment for a simple act of courtesy.

This had an unexpected effect. The alien in front of Bill Nye just seemed to get *angry*... or at least insistent, thrusting the glittering pile once again.

Meanwhile, still ignoring my nudge, Slade was already accepting her second fee. "Come on," she told her alien. "I'll introduce you to Bill."

All around us a hubbub of confusion intensified as the space-visitors behaved in a manner never seen in film depictions of first contact. After speaking to some individual for a few minutes – and then handing over payment – each of the aliens simply turned and walked away! Several took the road leading west, toward Kennedy Space Center headquarters and the town beyond. Others headed cross-country, on diverging paths. Two aimed straight north, into a Florida swamp!

"Sorry if I offended you," I heard Nye tell his own visitor – one of the last remaining – trying to ease the creature's agitation. "I said I'll be happy to help you find Louis Friedman. I'd do it out of simple hospitality. But I see that it's culturally important to you for there to be some *quid-pro-quo*. Some fair exchange of value. So how about you pay me with information? Like where are you from? What's your name? Why are you looking for my friend Lou –"

He stopped as *our* alien approached in long strides, interrupting.

"You have been identified as Bill Nye, whose name appears on this list," it said, as Slade and I hurried to catch up.

The taller creature turned, its parasol-wings fluttering in an angry display that flashed from green to spirals of deep red.

"You are interfering in a legitimate transaction," it told Slade's alien. "This one named Bill Nye has demanded specific information as payment in exchange for a service already rendered." Turning back to Bill, the taller alien said – "Your terms are satisfactory. Here are your answers. I come from the planet you call Mars. My name translates as Wandering Stone. In my language it is pronounced –"

We never got a chance to hear the name in its native tongue. Because at that moment the shorter Martian – the one who had spoken to Slade – took out a slim gray object and shot Bill Nye dead.

$$\Diamond$$

Commotion does not begin to describe what happened next, as most of the humans took flight amid screams of terror.

That part briefly resembled some tawdry sci fi movie, though none of the remaining aliens seemed at all interested in pursuing. Soon, just a few of us were left, stunned, watching in riveted silence as two green aliens confronted each other over poor Bill's smoldering body.

There came a furious exchange of irate noise between them. You didn't need translation to guess what was being said.

"*You interfered in my legitimate transaction!*" rattled Wandering Stone, drawing forth a weapon of its own.

"*I offer compensation,*" the shorter Martian seemed to answer in the same grinding dialect, keeping its wings folded while swiftly presenting a handful of small objects. I noticed that they weren't gold nuggets or diamonds, but little cylinders. Probably vastly more valuable.

Wandering Stone paused, contemplating the pile. Then, in a blur, the gun was gone and the pile snatched up. Deal concluded.

Turning, Wandering Stone fixed a hard unblinking gaze on me. I tried not to quail.

"I seek the direct heir of Bill Nye, in order to fulfill my obligation. I must finish answering the questions that he asked. Then I will need further guidance to find Louis Friedman. I am willing to pay."

Meanwhile, Slade was confronted yet again by her own Martian.

"You performed excellent service, guiding me to Bill Nye. Now I request further information. I will pay you to direct me to the next person on this list."

When the scroll was thrust again before Slade, she let out a yelp and ran.

I was not far behind.

◇

During the week that followed, we all experienced a weird sense of helplessness as almost fifty tall, iridescent-green Martians spread out across the United States.

The government tried to keep everyone calm. After all, this didn't look like an invasion. Not by any standards we could recognize. No giant battlecraft hovered over our cities, demanding surrender under threat of mass annihilation.

There had been one profoundly violent act – true. But every other phase of this interplanetary encounter, before or after, had been courteous, personally forthright – and profitable to whichever individual human being got attention from an alien.

That aspect – their fixation on making a fair deal – seemed fundamentally reassuring at some level. Business, after all, is business.

So the death of Bill Nye must have been some kind of aberration. A misunderstanding. Poring over footage from the moments leading up to the shooting, pundits and scholars puzzled over what inadvertent gesture or word Bill must have performed, to provoke that sudden, violent response.

"Remember how many times *human beings* misread each other, during the age of European exploration," one historian reminded. "And those were just different cultures within the same species! Something is going on here. Something we haven't figured out. And as the weaker ones, we had better figure it out, real soon."

Meanwhile, the visitors fanned out, most of them striding with amazing speed northward, out of the Florida peninsula, into America proper. Whether cross-country, by highway or through a dense urban center, the specific path seemed at first to make no difference. Only direction, each one seeking a single-minded goal.

Most people quickly got out of their way, though gawkers and the passionately curious shouted questions whenever a Martian loped by – tailed by frantic journalists and hurriedly-assembled teams of marshals, assigned to protect these alien visitors from our more unbalanced citizens. Almost fifty little swarms, like fast-moving and erratic movie stars chased by fans and paparazzi and bodyguards. The marshals had to work in relays in order to keep up.

All of that soon changed, however, when a motorist stopped abruptly near one of the creatures, flung open his passenger door and offered a ride – in exchange for a fistful of riches.

This caught the escorting marshals flat-footed, as the alien quickly agreed, tucking away its solar collector wings and folding its long legs inside.

The pickup truck sped off.

Nobody could think of any legal reason to stop it.

Frenzied phone calls brought in helicopters to keep the truck in sight. But soon, word somehow spread to the rest of the visitors. Wherever they were, other tall aliens abruptly headed for the nearest road and began sticking out their thumbs.

They must communicate, I thought at the time, pondering how well coordinated it all seemed.

Word spread quickly among humans, too. While a majority of citizens kept back in fear, there was no shortage of bold drivers, suddenly eager to pull over.

Hitchhiking Martians paid well for rides.

And for information – always seeking some person listed on one of those scrolls. Despite a rising sense of public unease, it wasn't hard for each alien to find someone – a shopkeeper or some passerby with a wireless link – willing to do a quick internet name-and-address search and then point the right way, often with a printed map.

Well, those diamonds were top quality.

Anyway, the government was loathe at first to interfere. This offered one way to find out why they had come and who they were looking for. No Martian asked for secrecy. So most of the information providers cashed-in twice by swiftly telling everything to the news media.

In a matter of hours we knew more than forty names.

What would *you* do, if you heard on TV that a Martian was looking for you?

After what we all witnessed at Cape Canaveral, acute interest focused on those who were asked-for. A diverse group, they shared one common trait – a passion for spaceflight. Only a few were scientists or engineers or NASA officials... some were school teachers, or accountants, or mechanics. But all believed in human expansion and adventure in the cosmos.

Not much to go on... though I began to wonder.

Any normal person, upon hearing that an alien was coming, would prudently stay away from home. Especially after what happened to Bill Nye. But as I said, those being sought weren't exactly normal. Most of them had dreamed of *first contact* from an early age, cutting their teeth on science fiction tales. Several, in fact, reacted to the news with excitement, hurrying *toward* their aliens, eager to meet them halfway.

By coincidence, the first two of these zealots reached their rendezvous within minutes of each other – thirty-one and a half hours after the ship from Mars arrived – several hundred miles apart.

"Are you Frank Martin?" A green visitor asked, near Gary, North Carolina.

"Yes I am," answered a well-known space engineer, grinning and holding out his hand.

Whereupon the creature shot him dead.

"I seek another individual," it then said, turning toward the appalled journalists while their cameras beamed a gruesome scene across the world. Nervous marshals and guardsmen drew their weapons while frantically consulting Washington. But the Martian just ignored them.

"I will pay for information leading me to a human named Danny Hillis."

Meanwhile, at almost the same moment in Gainesville, standing over the smoldering corpse of a fiction author named Joe Haldeman, another alien said:

"I will now pay for information leading to Penelope Boston."

There was no more ambiguity. No hope that Bill Nye's death was a fluke.

We now had a general idea why the Martians had come – with a narrowly focused sense of purpose. One by one, they aimed to hunt down and kill every person whose name appeared on a list.

But what list?

All of those mentioned so far were Americans, a fact that offered strange reassurance elsewhere. Across the globe, near-panic ebbed away, replaced with a rising sense of this-doesn't-directly-threaten-us interest...

accompanied perhaps by a kind of spectator *schadenfreude* at seeing the planet's Top Dog face its long-deserved come-uppance from dauntingly advanced extraterrestrials. Those who had been loudly demanding establishment of an International Contact Agency became less shrill. World leaders now urged patience – an attitude of watching, waiting.

That was fine for them. Within the borders of the United States, tension fizzed and nearly frothed-over. By now, forty-seven alien creatures had dispersed from coast to coast, with nine of them unaccounted-for, having vanished into some confusion of either traffic or countryside. We discovered the hard way that those photo-active wings of theirs had multiple uses. Wrapped around the body, they could suddenly go into a mode that mimicked the environs, turning a Martian almost invisible.

Army special forces augmented the marshals now, trying to keep a wide cordon around each alien, using bullhorns, warning people to stay back. It didn't always work, though. The creatures moved *fast*. Without notice, one of them might veer toward anyone in sight, offering a handful of treasure for information or a ride.

Most people ran away, but so what? Roughly one in a hundred consented. That was enough.

The third, fourth and fifth deaths occurred before two full days had passed. A dozen more of the targeted people barely left their homes in time. But always, some neighbor was willing to point helpfully in the direction they had fled. Others might shout "collaborator!" – but diamonds can help overcome hurt feelings. And no one could legally stop it. Or at least, nobody in authority could cite a law that fit a case like this.

People – even governments – are capable of acting quickly in an emergency. A special session of Congress was called, aimed at passing a quick national security bill to close the loopholes, outlawing cooperation with the Martians and confiscating whatever payments they made. Anyone who helped guide them to a victim could be prosecuted as an accessory. Instant polls showed huge public support, driven by disgust toward that self-serving minority among us who would cooperate in this alien death-hunt, betraying their neighbors for riches.

The President promised to sign the bill within twenty-four hours. She sent Secret Service agents to protect every person known to be a target.

That's when I phoned up Dan Jensen, in Senator Green's office.

"Dan, you've got to get me into the hearing tomorrow."

"I dunno," he answered. "It's crazy up here on the Hill. We're on war footing. The hearing is supposed to last just the morning, then we rush the bill to the floor. What's wrong? Not urgent enough?"

"Maybe too urgent. There's something they have to know, before passing that law. Something I think I figured out."

"You *think*? Buddy boy, you better —"

"I better get down there and talk to you in person tonight. Lay it out. Just do me - do us all - a favor. Set aside fifteen minutes for me to speak tomorrow morning. You can cancel if I don't convince you tonight."

It took some persuading. But I had that much pull.

I wound up getting ten minutes. I just prayed I'd be in time.

◇

"The names," I said, after being sworn-in, "are all included on a disk that was carried to the Martian surface aboard *Spirit* and *Opportunity*... the Mars Exploration Rover spacecraft, or MER... way back in January of 2003."

"On a disk?" one member of the committee asked. "For what purpose?"

"Public relations, Senator. Arranged by The Planetary Society, in collaboration with the LEGO Company. A mini-DVD, so small and light that it could be added without affecting mission performance or cost. It contained educational material, plus a *list* of space program supporters – people who signed on for the honor of having their names carried all the way to Mars."

"Some honor. But I don't get it. None of the footage from those rover-robots showed signs of intelligent life. Or any life at all."

"The Martians appear to be – well – extremely adaptable, Senator. As you might expect for beings that evolved in such a challenging envi- ronment. We witnessed them change shape before our eyes, just after arriving. And those cape-like *wings*, that they spread to absorb sunlight, can shift from perfect black to green to intricate patterns mimicking any background. There may have been Martians in plain sight, for all I know, or dwelling nearby underground. Certainly close enough to be offended by one of the MER machines, in some way we don't yet understand."

"And you think this disk filled with names... it covers everybody that the aliens have asked for?"

"So far. It's the only trait that every one of them has in common. It also explains how the Martians would have such a list in hand, the moment they arrived. They must have gotten it directly from the disk."

"Interesting. That's one mystery solved... and about a hundred still unexplained. Like *why* they seem determined to go around *killing* people on the list! Do you have any ideas about that, doctor?"

"Some possibilities come to mind. Perhaps they did not like the idea of machines landing to spy on their planet – though a dozen earlier probes never triggered such response. Perhaps they are angry over *where* the two probes landed. Or something bad happened when they did. Anyway, the truth should be easy enough to find out."

"Oh, how's that?"

"*Ask them*. They are traders, above all else. For the right price, I'm sure one of the Martians will explain it all, in detail."

The committee's chief counsel spoke up.

"We've tried to ask! They ignore our representatives."

"True enough. And yet they speak to private citizens."

"In order to bribe them! To hitch rides from traitors, or else buy directions that will help them hunt down some American! The same kind of nasty, treasonous help that we're going to outlaw."

"Right. Exactly. And I'm here to warn you... that could be a terrible mistake."

◇

Silence filled the conference room, until the chief counsel spoke again.

"You... *oppose* the bill currently before this committee?" He sounded perplexed, so unanimous had been the support up till now.

"I must oppose it, since the consequences of passing such a bill could be disastrous."

The senior senator from Oklahoma leaned forward, speaking softly.

"Could you please explain, doctor? So far, we've been careful not to shoot back at the creatures – though a public majority now wants massive retaliation next time another citizen is killed. This restraint is overwhelmingly difficult to maintain. "

"Indeed, Senator. I've been pleasantly surprised by the administration's wisdom in that regard. History warns that a weaker tribe *should* be cautious during first contact, especially not to let itself be provoked.

Pride can be fatally expensive. So can revenge. We may have to absorb pain... a lot of it, stoically... before we're ready to demand respect."

"Is *that* why you oppose the bill, doctor? But this proposed legislation has nothing to do with fighting back! All it will do is impose penalties on a few greedy humans, to deter them from helping the aliens. If we arrest the collaborators and seize all those little piles of gold and diamonds, so nobody profits... then who will step forward to help the aliens with information? It could take the creatures ages, wandering around, to find their victims. We'd have time to set up protection programs, offer new identities, and hide everybody on this list you told us about... how many people did you say are on it?"

"I didn't say, Senator."

A look of puzzled exasperation crossed the politician's face. "Well, could you please tell us, now? How many names were on those disks that *Spirit* and *Opportunity* carried to Mars?"

I coughed, feeling a sudden and powerful reluctance to speak. But then, the news media were probably looking it up already, on the web.

"How many? Um, senator, the disks held four million names."

◇

It took a while for the Sergeant at Arms to restore order. I fretted as the clock finished ticking out my allotted ten minutes. Would they stop me before I got around to my real point?

I needn't have worried. Nobody tried to usher me out of the room. All were attentive when Senator Green spoke for the first time.

"Four million? Why that's... more than one percent of our population."

Or ten percent of those who vote, I pondered during another long silence that finally broke when Senator Long distilled the general mood.

"Then this may *not* be a matter of just a few scientists and space aficionados. It could go on and on."

"So it seems," I answered. "Though let me correct one false impression that's going around. Only by a quirk of chance have the targets so far all been Americans. There are plenty of Europeans, Russians, Japanese and other nationalities represented on the list, just a little further down."

That brought a small murmur of satisfaction, amid the gloom. It can be comforting, when in pain, not to be alone.

182

"Still, *four million*. Could they really mean to hunt them *all* down, one by one?"

"I have no reason to think otherwise."

"Then appeasement is out of the question. The die is cast. We are at war."

I disagreed emphatically.

"No senator, we aren't *at war*.

"In fact, I doubt our Martian visitors know the true meaning of that word.

"But we could teach it to them, if you pass this bill."

I didn't succeed at getting the legislation killed. But they agreed to wait twenty-four hours.

It was enough.

Late that afternoon – on the third day after the landing at Cape Canaveral – another of the Martians caught up with the person it was seeking, in the suburbs of Lawrence, Kansas. Someone along the way, jumping at a chance for a little extra profit, had sold this creature a nifty little PDA with map feature and Global Positioning System, supplementing its already uncanny direction sense with good old human technical ingenuity.

Still, it wasn't exactly a surprise when the alien reached its destination. Forewarned, the news media were already there.

Though he had been alerted with plenty of time, the human quarry tried to be clever. He wasn't home when the alien showed up, but he did stay to watch from a neighbor's rooftop as a tall, green creature knocked at his front door, then broke the lock and bent over to step inside. There followed some brief crashing sounds – not exactly a rampage but an efficient search for hiding places. (All evidence so far showed that these creatures learned very fast.)

The Martian emerged, carrying a few scraps of paper... photos, book covers, some clippings from an album.

Standing on the front porch and turning the solar-collector wings on its shoulders to face the sun, it seemed to study the clippings carefully. Then, letting the papers fall, it stepped into the street and made a circle, scanning.

The man on the rooftop should have fled then, but he felt safe observing from the shadow of a neighbor's chimney. He would have been safe, from any Earthly hunter.

This alien had better eyes than any Earthly hunter. Whipping out a weapon, it swiftly and efficiently shot the poor fellow, burning a two centimeter-wide hole to the back of his head.

Then, almost without pause, it turned to find a helpful human – someone willing to sell information about the *next* person in a lengthy list.

Instead, within two blocks, the Martian ran straight into a vigilante mob.

This time, bullhorn warnings from marshals and secret service agents failed to keep back the angry crowd. Armed with everything from rifles to flaming torches, neighbors of the dead man approached the tall creature and began shooting.

"Damn if I'm gonna die for that thing," one marshal was heard saying as he joined the journalists, diving for cover. He had a first row seat for the spectacle that followed.

Quickly folding away its parasol-wings, the Martian seemed to become a blur, charging toward the irate rabble, plunging into their midst, tossing people right and left. Cries of wrath transformed to pain and dread as people fled in all directions, many of them limping.

In moments it was over, with the Martian striding off toward a nearby shopping mall in search of somebody more helpful. A couple of dozen people lay in its wake, clutching their sides, groaning or stanching the flow of blood. At first glance, it looked like a slaughter...

...till observers soon realized – nobody had died.

It took a couple of hours for experts to study footage from a dozen cameras, scrupulously analyzing each image at slow motion. Specialists traced the source of every bullet that passed near – or into – the Martian's body. In each case, no matter which human fired a weapon, that shooter came away from the melee with an injury, while those who did not fire were unharmed. The most accurate suffered worst, receiving excruciating puncture wounds, delivered by agile, merciless alien fingers.

Nobody died, though. And we started getting the message.

Though apparently unharmed, the Martian did not like to be attacked. For every assault, it had meted proportional retaliation. *Proportional* punishment.

"I think I know what's going on," I told Senator Green, who stood next to the President's Emergency Commissioner, watching reports from Lawrence.

"You've got to give me the next shot at making contact."

I had been making the same request for hours. This time, Green and the fellow from the White House looked at each other.

The President's guy shrugged.

"All right. Give it your best shot."

◇

They dropped me off a block from the Georgetown Alien. We knew where it was heading because someone had just sold out the head of NASA's Advanced Projects Division – a woman whose passion for space exploration was so great that she had remained a Planetary Society member, and now might pay for it with her life. She was number fourteen on the MER list.

I stepped out of the government van, wired and bugged to the gills. The Emergency Task Force could advise me through a button in one ear, listening to every word I said.

Not that they expected much to be achieved this time. No other envoy had succeeded, why should I?

It came around the street corner at a lope, trailed by truckloads of marshals and reporters. Most people scattered as soon as they caught sight of the creature with its iridescent-green winglets always turned sunward... though I glimpsed several individuals lingering bravely to jeer as it passed by. One or two seemed to have longing looks, as if tempted to run alongside for a while, as we had seen on TV – offering information in exchange for treasure. But this one seemed purposeful, as if it already knew what it needed, for now.

Anyway, word was crisscrossing the country, ever since Lawrence. The last three people to sell information had been caught and beaten by vigilantes, while police looked the other way. So the Anti-Collaboration Bill appeared unnecessary, after all. *Ad hoc* justice was doing the job.

That made what I was about to do even more dangerous.

As the alien drew near, running straight toward me, I couldn't help flashing back to that long ago morning at the Cape. Just this Tuesday? It felt like eons – or five minutes – since I stood in shock over Bill Nye's smoldering form.

How did I talk myself into this?

Prior envoys had tried all sorts of techniques. Blocking a Martian's path. Holding up placards. Or making formal declamations 'in the name of humanity.'

Instead of doing any of these things, I stepped slightly to one side. As the creature sped past, I spoke in a low voice.

"You have caused me personal injury. I demand compensation."

◇

It skidded to a halt like some cartoon character, raising a creditable screech against the pavement and swiveling with uncanny agility toward me.

They seem superior in nearly all ways, I thought, trying not to shake. What makes me imagine I can pull this off?

The Martian towered over me, standing close enough to touch, if I dared. Those shimmering solar collectors fluttered near, looming gorgeous, like enveloping webs. Or the wings spread by some magical bird of prey.

"What personal injury have I caused you? Explain."

My larynx threatened to shut down as I flashed on the creatures' propensity for quick violence. But I managed to croak.

"You must pay me for that information."

The viridian parasols flared and shimmered. Tilting its humanoid head, the alien appeared taken aback... or at least surprised.

"It is not customary to pay an accuser in order to learn a grievance. If you wish to make a claim, speak."

"That's the problem, then," I said carefully. "Our customs here must be different than yours."

Talk about an understatement. But the alien did not respond. Instead, it just stood there, looking down at me.

I recalled how one of the members of the Contact Committee had described them as 'super-intelligent but apparently devoid of curiosity.' Or at least curiosity about matters human. Clearly it was up to me to prod a reply, or else this attempt would end just like all the others, with the visitor turning contemptuously away, hurrying about its bloody business.

"Is the concept of cultural difference difficult for you to grasp? Your culture and people must be very old."

I was guessing, of course. A shot in the dark.

"You are attempting to extract information without payment," it replied. An accusation, and true enough. But I shook my head.

"I am engaging in a sophisticated human process called conversation. Information is exchanged between individuals in larger quantities, without formal negotiation over each datum. Instead, each party maintains a general sense that information flows are roughly equal, overall... or beneficially reciprocal."

The creature seemed to ponder for several long seconds. The photosynthetic wings drew back a little.

"This may explain why humans talk so much, in their television and radio broadcasts. Most of the content appears syntactically useless – void of practical value – except perhaps as indicator material, tracking the value exchange process itself."

"A valid presumption." Though rigid, they weren't stupid.

"Nevertheless, the procedure seems crude. Highly inefficient."

"Yes, inefficient. And yet, there are advantages. I note, for example, that you have just made a free statement in reply to one of my own. Both of us offered information without striking a deal or trading explicit economic payments. In other words, you have just engaged in a conversational exchange.

"To the best of my knowledge, it's the first time that a Martian has done so, since you people arrived."

In my left ear, I heard an excited buzz of commentary from experts on the Contact Team, as they tried to verify this. From their encouraging comments, it seemed they were happy with me, so far. I was on a good track.

"Notice is taken," the alien replied. "I find it discomforting to engage in a process in which reciprocal value remains so... inexplicit." Then, after another pause. "I voluntarily offer that commentary about my discomfort, speculating that you will reciprocate by answering a question, according to this vague custom of conversation."

"And I will reciprocate," I replied, "by attempting to answer your question... assuming that the question-and-answer are of similarly low value. Your discomfort is, after all, of little importance to me. I will not answer high-value questions without payment."

"Understood. I commence with my question. This method of information exchange – this technique called conversation – is it an example of what you call a cultural difference?"

I concentrated hard, shaping sentences in hope that the Martian would find all this interesting enough to stay and chat a while.

"It is. We have had a great many cultural differences within the human species, therefore the notion is very familiar to us. We expect even wider cultural gaps between species from different planets.

"You, on the other hand, despite your great agility and impressive mental powers, appear to find the very concept of cultural difference difficult. Even disturbing. Am I correct in concluding that you Martians have been *homogeneous* for a long time?"

Another excited buzz erupted in my ear, as our experts discussed this.

"Homogeneous. Similar. Same. Uniform. In comparison to human beings..." I could almost hear the synapses – or Martian equivalents – surge and grind. "This datum may be of great value to you, but I will risk that value against the vague possibility of recompense via conversation. Yes. By comparison to the young and ever-changing life forms of Earth, my species has been optimized for a long time."

"Optimized. Hm. For how long?"

Tension seemed to fill the tall body in front of me. This was clearly excruciatingly difficult, grappling with concepts long taken for-granted.

"You have asked two consecutive questions. Nevertheless, I shall answer.

"Optimization at near-perfection occurred two-hundred and thirty nine million of your years ago."

The noise in my ear was positively painful as members of the Contact team reacted. Surprise. Consternation. But above all joy that at last something was being learned.

So far, my handlers seemed happy with the way things were going.

I did not expect that to last.

"*Now answer a question of mine,*" the Martian said. "*Explain to me how this method called 'conversation' will help me to achieve my goal on this planet.*"

Damn if this guy wasn't single-minded.

"That question will be difficult to answer without knowing more about your goal. You appear to have come to Earth with a mission to kill people. I assume you have some grievance against those who were listed on the disks that were carried by the Mars Exploration Rovers."

Silence. I tried again.

"You make no accusation against these people when you kill them, so accusations are optional. You only accuse when you want compensation, by payment of some value. But the only thing that earthlings seem able to pay with is their lives. We don't have anything else that you want.

"So this is all about *revenge*, isn't it? Revenge that's direct. Personal."

The Martian took one step back. The parasol wings flared again.

"Instead of answering my question, you have posed a question of your own."

"B-but I'm just trying to narrow down how to answer. In conversation you first clarify –"

"Human style conversation appears to have no value. I will end this experiment in twenty seconds."

Desperation filled me. Clearly these creatures communicated with each other – buying and selling information by radio or some other channel our experts hadn't found. If I failed in this attempt, word would spread among Martians. Perhaps no other would stop to chat, ever.

A few blocks away, the next phase of this tragedy was already under preparation, as men with heavy weapons made ready to intervene with deadly force, the next time an American citizen was killed. Driven by rapidly shifting public opinion, momentum was building toward war.

I couldn't let it come to that. During the last urgent seconds that I had the creature's attention, even as it started to turn away, I quickly pulled out a paper envelope and blurted –

"You may be right about conversation. So let's make it a business deal, after all.

"I have here the locations of the first hundred people on that list. Up to the minute. You could sell the info to your fellow Martians, sorted geographically, so they can hunt more efficiently than before.

"Moreover, I can show you how to *keep* getting such information, evading all attempts at interference."

The screech in my left ear was so loud that I had to tear out the button-speaker. I guess I must have exceeded my official authority as a negotiator.

The rest of the monitoring gear followed, crushed under my foot as I watched the alien carefully.

It opened one of those seamless flesh-pockets, dipping into the limitless supply of nuggets and diamonds... but stopped when I waved a hand. The Martian seemed to comprehend my gesture of refusal at once. We had gone beyond such trifles.

"*State your price,*" it said.

◇

Time passes quickly when you're having fun.

I lay on a cot, tasting blood through the broken stumps of two teeth, when word came to my jail cell that the first of my payments had arrived.

Wages for selling out a fellow human, a fellow American. The first of a hundred. Possibly many more.

"We weren't able to move everybody in time," Senator Green said when I was finally dragged before the Emergency Committee. "Three more were killed in the last hour. Thanks to you."

He expected an answer, but I had learned from the Martians. Conversation is inefficient. Any comment I made would be superfluous.

"We fixed the mistake that let you access the protection database," said the President's representative. "The location of threatened individuals will be more secure."

I shrugged. "If you say so."

"We *will* protect our citizens."

That roused me a bit, in curiosity.

"How? By hiding four million people? By fighting?"

A general pounded the table. "If necessary, yes! They must be taught to respect us. Our laws and our lives."

"Very stirring," I answered. "How's that going?"

The general flushed without answering. No need. In my cell I'd watched TV footage from the slaughter in Seattle, when a National Guard armored company fought in the streets with heavy weapons, battling to protect a billionaire bookseller and space aficionado from a single lanky alien. This time, the Martian departed the *Battle of 12th Avenue* with a temporary limp... quite an accomplishment... though several tank crews died to achieve it. Along with the prominent book dealer.

Proportional punishment. Twenty brave men for one briefly inconvenient wound.

"I hope you at least took my advice about badges," I said, wincing as one of my broken teeth twinged.

The general glowered. But Senator Green nodded. "The soldiers wore no identifying markings. You still haven't explained why –"

"Why we should take advice from a collaborator and accomplice in cold blooded murder!" interjected the fellow from the White House. His attitude reflected a keen political sense of rising public will. The beating

190

I received upon being arrested was a mere taste of what would happen if I were released onto the street. Vigilantes would spare nothing larger than a hangnail.

"Why listen to me? Maybe because I'm the only one who seems to have a clue what's going on."

This time, the whole Committee lapsed into sullen quiet. You could scoop their hatred with a shovel.

"So." I broke the silence. Somebody had to. "Will anybody explain why I'm here? Why did you send for me?

"Wait," I continued, holding up a hand. "Let me guess the reason.

"They keep their word. They honor their debts.

"I've been paid."

Tight-lipped, grudgingly, Senator Green nodded to an assistant, who turned on a fancy live-access screen nearby. "A new web site appeared on the internet, twenty minutes ago. We can't trace the source. It contained only this video clip."

The screen flickered – a glitch at our end, I figure, since Earthling network technology would seem trivial to these ancient, advanced beings. When the static cleared, there stood a creature from another planet. One whose brain and form had already been "optimized" before our ancestors split off from dinosaurs.

It spoke rapidly and with characteristic efficiency – haloed by the iridescent-green fans, or wings, that fed it directly from the sun.

"The assistance proved helpful in accomplishing my immediate goal. I have also benefitted by selling updated location information to others of my kind.

"Despite this, some hunters report being inconvenienced by the clever evasiveness of those they seek. It appears increasingly likely that targets are being aided by other humans.

"I wish to know more about non-listed humans who interfere. I will pay for information about them. Their reasons for interfering. And for assistance adding their names to our List."

This was my first time watching the video. Everyone else in the room must have already seen it, many times. Even so, that last sentence drew a murmur of dismay.

"If you can help to identify those who interfere, contact me using the code words that you established," the Martian continued. *"Meanwhile, the assistance received so far has proved valuable. Hence, I will now pay the first installment of the agreed-upon price."*

I felt tension all around. Despite grueling interrogation, I had refused to explain what passed between me and the alien that morning, after I tore off the monitoring devices.

"You asked specific questions, requesting that I post answers on the crude planetary network. I deem that your help so far merits three answers. I will post more if success continues to result from your assistance."

In other words, further rewards would flow if the envelope that I handed over, early this morning, helped aliens to murder even more people in a long chain.

"Question Number One. Why have I come to Earth – a barbaric and unpleasant place – in search of human beings to kill?

"Answer. As you surmised, the motive is vengeance – a concept which human beings appear to understand, though in a typically gross and primitive manner, absent all subtlety, persistence, esthetics or depth.

"Someone of great importance to me died as a direct result of the arrival of a Mars Exploration Rover. Under the Calculus of Reprisal, I seek redress from those responsible. I shall exact payment from a sufficiently large number of humans to restore balance. At present that figure is eighty-nine thousand and seventy three – subject to change."

It was my turn to gasp, at the appalling number. Was that how small we seemed to them? Intelligent enough to be held accountable, yet not worthy of conversation. Bright enough to be punished, but only satisfying in large quantities.

One solace. Whatever calamity had come to Mars on that space probe, inadvertently wreaking harm – perhaps some terrestrial plague that took them by surprise – it did not slaughter *millions* as I had envisioned. Just forty, possibly fifty, or so of those ancient ones must have died. Maybe the same number as our invaders. Did each one come to avenge a single – loved one – by leaving a bloody swathe of dead humans?

The creature held up two fingers – an eerily humanlike gesture. *"Second question. What form of cooperative enterprise constructed the interplanetary vessel that brought me here?*

"Answer. Our craft was built by a collaborative association of the aggrieved. Sharing nearly identical motives, a number of us gathered – using ancient and long-dormant skills – in order to cross space, achieve vengeance and restore balance. Such collusion is distasteful. But imperative need overcame natural aversion.

"It has become apparent to me that Earthlings form collaborative associations with disgusting readiness, and hew to those associations rigidly. Like the association

of four million that sent the deadly Mars Exploration Rover. This cultural difference merits study. I will pay for further information about —"

"Stop!"

At my shout, the assistant tapped a key to freeze playback. Onscreen, the Martian remained motionless, warped slightly by video clutter.

"As I feared," I muttered. "We're in trouble."

Senator Green shook his head. "*Now* you say that? Or do you mean things are even worse than we thought? How do you conclude —"

"Never mind that!" the White House Guy growled. "We want to discuss the *third answer.*"

"Third answer?"

"The *next* one. Where the alien offers a few sentences about their *space drive.* That's the important one. Our physicists are all in a lather over what it says about *vacuum energy* and *neutralizing inertia.* A hundred theories are spouting all over the place, with no idea how to sort them out!"

I shrugged. "Well? What did you expect, detailed blueprints? A few sentences were all I had earned."

A murmur of disgust greeted the word. *Earned.* Yet they clearly felt torn, these men and women who were charged with finding a solution to humanity's worst crisis. I sympathized. But only to a point.

"If you want more hints — maybe even blueprints — I'm sure one Martian or another will sell them to you."

"Sell them... you mean like the way *you* bought these answers? Never!"

I felt too fatigued even to shrug again. "If you won't, then some-body else will, now that there's a more convenient way to do business with them. Frankly, I think we'll get a better deal if we do it carefully, in small stages, keeping the price high. Play them off each other..."

"You're talking about selling these invaders the lives of human beings!" shouted the general.

"In exchange for knowledge we desperately need. Yes. To race through a quarter billion years of catch-up. Call it a *reconnaissance* with moderate expected losses, General."

"Why, I never heard anything so monstrously —"

"Pragmatic?" With a sigh, I straightened, pulling my shoulders back. I had to try to get through to these people. If only in order to persuade them to send me a dentist.

"Senator, ladies, gentlemen, we need to ponder our own past. Espe-cially when European sailors and settlers arrived in Africa, Oceania, the

Americas. Few native peoples came through first or second contact very well. Many perished. And our differences then were nothing compared with the gaping chasm that separates us from extraterrestrials.

"Who managed best, among our ancestors facing those European strangers? Everyone suffered, but a few did better than average. The Japanese and Thais kept their independence and strove at great cost to catch up. The Cherokee and Iroquois carefully studied white newcomers, learning and borrowing whatever seemed to make sense.

"And yet, in our movies, books and modern myths, it is always the most obstinate tribes who are portrayed as noble, admirable, clinging to every aspect of their old ways, defying the clear need for flexibility, for adaptation. If we follow their example – proudly sticking by our own standards and customs, no matter what – we may *nobly* follow those tribes into extinction."

Amid the glowering faces, one woman – an anthropology professor I had met years ago at a conference – spoke in a voice deep with gloom.

"Many of us already reached that conclusion. The debate now is whether it will be *better* to go extinct, than do as you recommend. What good is surviving, if we pay with our souls?"

I nodded. "Our ancestors must have had similar conversations, in hogans and wigwams, in countless huts and palaces, from Lapland to Australia. It's an old story. Western civilization was luckier than most. But our luck has run out.

"I'm just glad it's not my decision. You leaders – and others like you – will make the call. I've simply laid out the choice, stark and bare."

"That you've done, sir. Ruthlessly."

"Judge me later," I snapped. "When you know all the facts. It's humanity that matters now. Not individuals, or nations.

"Anyway, do you honestly think you can protect the people on that list? Say you do finally succeed at killing one of these creatures. Won't that bring *more* Martians, seeking countless more human lives to atone? Ask Native Americans how well that math added up."

The glum spell that followed was punctuated by a sound I made sucking at one of my broken teeth. I couldn't help it, really, though it seemed disrespectful. In fact, part of me felt *glad* that these people were so unlike the pitiless clichéd authority figures of cinema. Instead, they seemed motivated by the highest values. Human values.

In my own way...

Senator Green spoke again.

194

"You don't seem curious about the answer to your third question."

"Should I be? A technical issue. Thrown in to interest scientists, the military. To show the Martians are so far ahead, they'll casually trade information we find precious. Like the Dutch, buying Manhattan Island for beads. It may take a great many such answers before we begin to know *how little* we know."

"Hm. And you've set it up so that now the aliens can trade information with treacherous humans via the internet."

"As if someone else wouldn't have done so, within hours. Even if you shut down the Net, that won't matter. They've learned not to offer baubles anymore. Nobody will sell out a neighbor for nuggets and gems that can be seized by police or vigilantes. But how about a new industrial process? Insight to disease? An advanced machine or weapon? I've shown that information can be swapped without personal contact, using some personal code words.

"Soon, others will catch on. How to get a few sentences of useful data from creatures who are eons ahead of us. You can't hide four million people from that kind of temptation. And now that the list is growing longer –"

"Longer," the general mused. "They add names of those who try to thwart them. Those who help the four million. Is that why you advised us to remove all badges –"

"It's worse, general. Much worse than that. Haven't you wondered why they came after *just* people on that Mars Exploration Rover list?"

Committee members looked at each other before turning back to glare at me. But I only felt the frozen presence on the big screen. Tall, enigmatic, impervious and almost perfect. *Optimized* so very long ago that its kind craved the warmth of no hearth, nor even atmosphere. So perfect that it made its own food, living in almost pure autonomy, scarcely needing any other.

How jealous I felt.

"What do you mean, worse?" the anthropologist finally asked.

"I mean that they seem not to comprehend how interdependent, cooperative and gregarious humans really are. We're individually so weak, so soft and frail, that we evolved these tendencies. We aggregate into large groups as a natural part of being what we are. Who we are."

"So?"

"So, the notion of *permanent* associations – including nations and states – may be the most alien thing about us, from their Martian point of view. They do know we're 'disgustingly' cooperative. When they examined the MER probe and found four million names, they naturally assumed that it was sent by a great big temporary consortium composed of those who *signed* the spacecraft —"

"You mean that's why —"

"— so that's who they've come to kill."

"So it's all a mistake! What if we explain these are innocent people. Space fans. Sci fi readers. They aren't responsible!"

"Then who *is* responsible, Professor? Who sent *Spirit?* Who sent *Opportunity,* and caused the death of fifty demigods?"

"Why, NASA did."

"With funds provided by — and representing —"

"Representing? Why, the people of the United States of Am...." Her voice trailed off.

This time, the silence stretched on and on. Finally, I turned away. Accompanied by two guards, I retraced my steps, back to the jail cell and my thoughts.

I won't stay here, of course. They can't hold me.

Things are moving fast and decisions will be made.

Perhaps they'll be pragmatic, as the Japanese were during the Meiji era, doing whatever it took to catch up with the West as quickly, systematically, and cold-bloodedly as possible. The logic is impeccable, after all. If those on the MER List are doomed anyway, perhaps we can get a best possible deal by doling them out to the aliens slowly, one by one, in exchange for information.

Buying lessons that we need to survive.

Or maybe our leaders will embrace the other course — one praised in legend and film. The noble path taken by so many of our ancestors when they faced similar choices — to go down fighting. Defending our customs and ways. Our fellow citizens. The innocent. Whatever the cost.

There are good arguments for choosing either course. Though judging from those people in the Committee Chamber, I'll bet on nobility winning over pragmatism.

How ironic that movies nearly always depict generals and statesmen as cold-blooded. Viciously practical. Perfect villains. But everyone in that room had been *raised* by the same films and legends. Underneath our modern-cynical gloss, most of us are romantics. Generous. Courageous. Capable of great sacrifice for other members of the tribe.

I admire it. Of course. I'm built the same way.

My sacrifice was to disagree. To make sure the other option was available. Maybe they'll realize it soon.

Anyway. I'm glad it's not my call.

◊

Ponder, what question would be worth a life to get answered? Would a Martian answer this one?

"If there are other intelligences than our two races, how might I make contact with the *next* closest race of imperfect beings that might actually become friendly to humans and help us?"

◊

Oh, the Martians aren't stupid. They operate under different assumptions, true. But soon – especially if we fight – they'll start to grasp how revoltingly gregarious humans really are. They'll figure out that 'laws' and 'nations' aren't just words that stand for temporary group-contracts, but powerful chains of obligation. Bonds that penetrate our tissue, bone and sinew.

Nor will it stop at the American border. Twenty nations contributed instruments to MER. And when you get down to sub-components...

Will *any* of us survive, once they realize that *all* of us are responsible?

As dark night settles through the narrow window of my cell, I squint at shadows, trying for analogies – the straws that a human mind clutches, when trying to fathom the strange. These Martians are like bears, I figure. Powerful, autonomous... needing little from each other or the environment... coming together only for special transactions, like mating. Ultimate libertarians. Damn.

From their perspective we're like ants, almost hive beings. An unpleasant image for one like me, raised to treasure individuality.

I envy *and* pity them. No perfect Martian will ever face the conflicts that roil me now. The regrets. Or the poignant satisfaction, knowing I'll be forgiven.

Somebody had to do what I did. Be the required Judas. Offer a second option, whether or not it's chosen. The bitter, pragmatic way.

It could only be someone with a number like mine – one hundred and twelve on the list.

◇

Awaiting my turn, I keep hoping one thing.

Get a good price for me.

No handful of beads. Make it something exciting, useful and interesting, like so many of us yearned to see from the space program. The reason we pooled so much human talent and enthusiasm, reaching for those lights that our imperfect eyes and caveman brains could barely make out, twinkling overhead.

If my death – and several million more – will bring us closer to the stars, well okay. I don't lament signing my name to a roll call of dreamers.

When our human descendants get 'optimized', will we turn our backs to the sky, as the Martians have? No way. We won't abandon curiosity. Or each other.

I hope.

Can't rest or sleep. I keep looking up, each time there's a noise beyond the dark window. Waiting for my own monster to come in its patient way, with the appearance – and godlike persistence – of some ageless, avenging angel. Come to spread its dark wings over me and collect my small value in vengeance, before moving on.

No battle this time. They won't try hard to save me – the soldiers, scientists and politicians charged with protecting humanity's future. Whichever course they choose – pragmatism or noble resistance – few will mourn my turn, I guess.

No matter.

Just get a good price for me.

Make it something cool.

Story Notes

This creepy "campfire story" was begun the very night that Mars passed closest to Earth in 50,000 years – during the October 2003 'planetary opposition.' It is too late to remove names or add them to MER. But this author invites you, if you dare, to join him in signing on to have your names enrolled aboard the next space probe. Take part by joining The Planetary Society at http://planetary.org

Next comes a little what-if tale about history and destiny. A contemplative piece that ponders whether (or not) a single individual can make a real difference.

A Professor at Harvard

◊

Dear Lilly,

This transcription may be a bit rough. I'm dashing it off quickly for reasons that should soon be obvious.

Exciting news! Still, let me ask that you please don't speak of this, or let it leak till I've had a chance to put my findings in a more academic format.

Since May of 2015, I've been engaged to catalogue the Thomas Kuiper Collection, which Harvard acquired in that notorious bidding war a couple of years ago, on eBay. The acclaimed astronomer-philosopher had been amassing trunkloads of documents from the late Sixteenth and early Seventeenth Centuries – individually and in batches – with no apparent pattern, rhyme or reason. Accounts of the Dutch Revolution. Letters from Johannes Kepler. Sailing manifests of ports in southern England. Ledgers and correspondence from the Italian Inquisition. Early documents of Massachusetts Bay Colony and narratives about the establishment of Harvard College.

The last category was what most interested the trustees, so I got to work separating them from the apparent clutter. That is, it *seemed* clutter, an unrelated jumble... till intriguing patterns began to emerge.

Let me trace the story as was revealed to me, in bits and pieces. It begins with the apprenticeship of a young English boy named Henry Stephens.

◊

Henry was born to a family of petit-gentry farmers in Kent, during the year 1595. According to parish records, his birth merited noting as *mirabilis* – he was premature and should have died of the typhus that claimed his mother. But somehow the infant survived.

He arrived during a time of turmoil. Parliament had passed a law that anyone who questioned the Queen's religious supremacy, or persistently absented himself from Anglican services, should be imprisoned or banished from the country, never to return on pain of death. Henry's father was a leader among the "puritan" dissenters in one of England's least tolerant counties. Hence, the family was soon hurrying off to exile, departing by ship for the Dutch city of Leiden.

Leiden, you'll recall, was already renowned for its brave resistance to the Spanish army of Philip II. As a reward, Prince William of Orange and the Dutch parliament gave the city a choice: freedom from taxes for a hundred years, or the right to establish a university. Leiden chose a university.

Here the Stephens family joined a growing expatriate community – English dissenters, French Huguenots, Jews and others thronging into the cities of Middelburg, Leiden, and Amsterdam. Under the Union of Utrecht, Holland was the first nation to explicitly respect individual political and religious liberty and to recognize the sovereignty of the people, rather than the monarch. (Both the American and French Revolutions specifically referred to this precedent).

Henry was apparently a bright young fellow. Not only did he adjust quickly – growing up multilingual in English, Dutch and Latin – but he showed an early flair for practical arts like smithing and surveying.

The latter profession grew especially prominent as the Dutch transformed their landscape, sculpting it with dikes and levees, claiming vast acreage from the sea. Overcoming resistance from his traditionalist father, Henry managed to get himself apprenticed to the greatest surveyor of the time, Willebrord Snel van Leeuwen – or Snellius. In that position, Henry would have been involved in a geodetic mapping of Holland – the first great project using triangulation to establish firm lines of location and orientation – applying methods still in use today.

While working for Snellius, Henry apparently audited some courses offered by Willebrord's father – Professor Rudolphus Snellius – at the University of Leiden. Rudolphus lectured on "Planetarum Theorica et Euclidis Elementa" and evidently was a follower of Copernicus. Meanwhile the son – also authorized to teach astronomy – specialized in the Almagest of Ptolemeus!

The Kuiper Collection contains a lovely little notebook, written in a fine hand – though in rather vulgar Latin – wherein Henry Stephens describes the ongoing intellectual dispute between those two famous Dutch scholars, Snellius elder and younger. Witnessing this intellectual tussle first-hand must have been a treat for Henry, who would have known how few opportunities there were for open discourse in the world beyond Leiden.

◇

But things were just getting interesting. For at the very same moment that a teenage apprentice was tracking amiable family quarrels over heliocentric versus geocentric astronomies, some nearby Dutchman was busy crafting the world's first telescope.

The actual inventor is unknown – secrecy was a bad habit practiced by many innovators of that time. Till now, the earliest mention was in September 1608, when a man 'from the low countries' offered a telescope for sale at the annual Frankfurt fair. It had a convex and a concave lens, offering a magnification of seven. So I felt a rising sense of interest when I read Henry's excited account of the news, dated six months earlier (!) offering some clues that scholars may find worth pursuing.

Later though. Not today. For you see, I left that trail just as soon as *another* grew apparent. One far more exciting.

Here's a hint: word of the new instrument, flying across Europe by personal letter, soon reached a certain person in northern Italy. Someone who, from description alone, was able to re-invent the telescope and put it to exceptionally good use.

Yes, I'm referring to the Sage of Pisa. Big *G* himself! And soon the whole continent was abuzz about his great discoveries – the moons of Jupiter, lunar mountains, the phases of Venus and so on. Naturally, all of this excited old Rudolphus, while poor grumpy Willebrord muttered that it seemed presumptuous to draw cosmological conclusions from such evidence. Both Snellius patris and filio agreed, however, that it would be a good idea to send a representative south, as quickly as possible, to learn first hand about any improvements in telescope design that could aid the practical art of surveying.

◇

So it was that in the year 1612, at age seventeen, young Henry Stephens of Kent headed off to Italy...

...and there the documented story stops for a few years. From peripheral evidence – bank records and such – it would appear that small amounts were sent to Pisa from Snel family accounts in the form of a 'stipend'. Nothing large or well-attributed, but a steady stream that lasted until about 1616, when "H. Stefuns" abruptly reappears in the employment ledger of Willebrord the surveyor.

What was Henry up to all that time? One might squint and imagine him counting pulse-beats in order to help time a pendulum's sway. Or using his keen surveyor's eye to track a ball's descent along an inclined plane. Did he help to sketch Saturn's rings? Might *his* hands have dropped two weights – heavy and light – over the rail of a leaning tower, while the master physicist stood watching below?

There is no way to tell. Not even from documents in the Kuiper Compilation.

There *is,* however, another item from this period that Kuiper missed, but that I found in a scan of Vatican archives. An early letter from the Italian scientist Evangelista Torricelli to someone he calls "Uncle Henri" – whom he apparently met as a child around 1614. Oblique references are enticing. Was this "Henri" the same man with whom Torricelli would have later adventures?

Alas, the letter has passed through so many collectors' hands over the years that its provenance is unclear. We must wait some time for Torricelli to enter our story in a provable or decisive way.

◇

Meanwhile, back to Henry Stephens. After his return to Leiden in 1616, there is little of significance for several years. His name appears regularly in account ledgers. Also on survey maps, now signing on his own behalf as people begin to rely ever-more on the geodetic arts he helped develop. Willibrord Snellius was by now hauling in f600 per annum and Journeyman Henry apparently earned his share.

Oh, a name very similar to Henry's can be found on the rolls of the Leiden Society, a philosophical club with highly distinguished membership. The spelling is slightly different, but people were lackadaisical about such things in those days. Anyway, it's a good guess that Henry kept up his interest in science, paying keen attention to new developments.

Then, abruptly, his world changed again.

Conditions had grown worse for dissenters back in England. Henry's father, having returned home to press for concessions from James I, was rewarded with imprisonment. Finally, the King offered a deal: amnesty in exchange for a new and extreme form of exile – participation in a fresh attempt to settle an English colony in the New World.

Of course everyone knows about the *Pilgrims*, their reasons for fleeing England and setting forth on the Mayflower, imagining that they were bound for Virginia, though by chicanery and mischance they wound up instead along the New England coast above Cape Cod. All of that is standard catechism in American History One-A, offering a mythic basis for our Thanksgiving Holiday. And much of it is just plain wrong.

For one thing, the Mayflower did not first set forth from Plymouth, England. It only stopped there briefly to take on a few more colonists and supplies, having actually begun its voyage in Holland. The expatriate community was the true source of people and material.

And right there, listed among the ship's complement, having obediently joined his father and family, you will find a stalwart young man of twenty-five – Henry Stephens.

Again, details are sketchy. After a rigorous crossing oft portrayed in book and film, the Pilgrims arrived at Plymouth Rock on December 21, 1620.

Professor Kuiper hunted among colonial records and found occasional glimpses of our hero. Apparently he survived that terrible first winter and did more than his share to help the young colony endure. Relations with the local natives were crucial and Professor Kuiper scribbled a number of notes which I hope to follow-up on later. One of them suggests that Henry went west for some time to live among the Mohegan and other tribes, exploring great distances, making drawings and collecting samples of flora and fauna.

If so, we may have finally discovered the name of the "American friend" who supplied William Harvey with his famous New World Collection, the core element upon which Edmond Halley later began sketching his Theory of Evolution!

Henry's first provable reappearance in the record comes in 1625, with his marriage to Prosper White-Moon Forest – a name that provokes interesting speculation. There is no way to verify that his wife was a Native American woman, though subsequent township entries show eight children, only one of whom appears to have died young – apparently a happy and productive family for the time. Certainly any bias or hostility toward Prosper must have been quelled by respect. Her name is noted prominently among those who succored the sick during the pestilence year of 1627.

Further evidence of local esteem came in 1629 when Henry was engaged by the new Massachusetts Bay Colony as official surveyor. This led to what was heretofore his principal claim for historical notice, as the architect who laid down the basic plan for Boston Town. A plan that included innovative arterial and peripheral lanes, looking far beyond the town's rude origins. As you may know, it became a model for future urban design that would be called the New England Style.

This rapid success might have led Henry directly to a position of great stature in the growing colony, had not events brought his tenure to an abrupt end in 1631. That was the year, you'll recall, when *Roger Williams* stirred up a hornet's nest in the Bay Colony, by advocating unlimited religious tolerance – even for Catholics, Jews and infidels.

Forced temporarily to flee Boston, Williams and his adherents established a flourishing new colony in Rhode Island – before returning to Boston in triumph in 1634. And yes, the first township of this new colony, this center of tolerance, was surveyed and laid out by you-know-who.

◇

It's here that things take a decidedly odd turn.

Odd? That doesn't half describe how I felt when I began to realize what happened next. Lilly, I have barely slept for the last week! Instead I popped pills and wore electrodes in order to concentrate as a skein of connections began taking shape.

For example, I had simply assumed that Professor Kuiper's hoard was so *eclectic* because of an obsessive interest in a certain period of time – nothing more. He seemed to have grabbed things randomly! So many documents, with so little connecting tissue between them.

Take the rare and valuable first edition that many consider the centerpiece of his collection – a rather beaten but still beautiful copy of "Dialogho Sopra I Due Massimi Sistemi Del Mondo" or "A Dialogue Concerning Two Systems Of The World."

(This document alone helped drive the aBay bidding war, which Harvard eventually topped because the Collection also contained many papers of local interest.)

A copy of the *Dialogue!* I felt awed just touching it with gloved hands. Did any other book do more to propel the birth of modern science? The debate between the Copernican and Ptolemaic astronomical systems reached its zenith within this publication, sparking a frenzy of reaction – not all of it favorable! Responding to this implicit challenge, the Papal Palace and the Inquisition were so severe that most of Italy's finest researchers emigrated during the decade that followed, many of them settling in Leiden and Amsterdam.

That included young Evangelista Torricelli, who by 1631 was already well-known as a rising star of physical science. Settling in Holland, Torricelli commenced rubbing elbows with friends of his "Uncle Henri" and performing experiments that would lead to invention of the barometer.

In correspondence that year, Torricelli shows deep worry about his old master, back in Pisa. Often he would use code words and initials. Obscurity was a form of protective covering in those days and he did not want to get the old man in even worse trouble. It would do no good for "G" to be seen as a martyr or *cause célèbre* in Protestant lands up north. That might only antagonize the Inquisition even further.

Still, Torricelli's sense of despondency grew evident as he wrote to friends all over Europe, passing on word of the crime being committed against his old master. Without naming names, Torricelli described the imprisonment of a great and brilliant man. Threats of torture, the coerced abjuration of his life's work... and then even worse torment as the gray-bearded *Professori* entered confinement under house arrest, forbidden ever to leave his home or stroll the lanes and hills, or even to correspond (except clandestinely) with other lively minds.

What does all of this have to do with that copy of *"Dialogho"* in the Kuiper Collection?

Like many books that are centuries old, this one has accumulated a morass of margin notes and annotations, scribbled by various owners over the years – some of them cogent glosses upon the elegant mathematical and physical arguments, and others written by perplexed or skeptical or hostile readers. But one large note especially caught my eye. Latin words on the flyleaf, penned in a flowing hand. Words that translate as:

> To the designer of Providence.
> Come soon, deliverance of our father.

All previous scholars who examined this particular copy of *"Dialogho"* have assumed that the inscription on the flyleaf was simply a benediction or dedication to the Almighty, though in rather unconventional form.

No one knew what to make of the signature, consisting of two large letters.

ET.

◇

Can you see where I'm heading with this?

Struck by a sudden suspicion, I arranged for Kuiper's edition of *"Dialogho"* to be examined by the Archaeology Department, where special interest soon focused on dried botanical materials embedded at the tight joining of numerous pages. All sorts of debris can settle into any book that endures four centuries. But lately, instead of just brushing it away, people have begun studying this material. Imagine my excitement when the report came in – pollen, seeds and stem residue from an array of plant types... nearly *all* of them native to New England!

It occurred to me that the phrase *"designer of Providence"* might not – in this case – have solely a religious import!

Could it be a coded salutation to an *architectural surveyor?* One who established the street plan of the capital of Rhode Island?

Might "father" in this case refer not to the Almighty, but instead to somebody far more temporal and immediate – the way two apprentices refer to their beloved master?

What I *can* verify from the open record is this. Soon after helping Roger Williams return to Boston in triumph, Henry Stephens hastily took his leave of America and his family, departing on a vessel bound for Holland.

◇

Why that particular moment? It should have been an exciting time for such a fellow. The foundations for a whole new civilization were being laid. Who can doubt that Henry took an important part in early discussions with Williams, Winthrop, Anne Hutchinson and others – deliberations over the best way to establish tolerance and lasting peace with native tribes. How to institute better systems of justice and education. Discussions that would soon bear surprising fruit.

And yet, just as the fruit was ripening, Stephens *left*, hurrying back to a Europe that he now considered decadent and corrupt. What provoked this sudden flight from his cherished New World?

It was July 1634. Antwerp shipping records show him disembarking there on the 5th.

On the 20th a vague notation in the Town Hall archive tells of a meeting between several guildmasters and a group of 'foreign doctors' – a term that could apply to any group of educated people from beyond the city walls. Only the timing seems provocative.

In early August, the Maritime Bank recorded a large withdrawal of 250 florins from the account of Willebrord Snellius, authorized in payment to 'H. Stefuns' by letter of credit from Leiden.

Travel expenses? Plus some extra for clandestine bribes? Yes, the clues are slim even for speculating. And yet we also know that at this time the young exiled scholar, Evangelista Torricelli, vacated his home. Bidding farewell to his local patrons, he then mysteriously vanished from sight forever.

So, temporarily, did Henry Stephens. For almost a year there is no sign of either man. No letters. No known mention of anyone seeing them...

...not until the spring of 1635, when Henry stepped once more upon the wharf in Boston Town, into the waiting arms of Prosper and their children. Sons and daughters who presumably clamored around their Papa, shouting the age-old refrain –

"What did you bring me? What did you bring me?"

What he brought them was the future.

◊

Oops, sorry about that, Lilly. You must be chafing for me to get to the point.

Or did you cheat?

Have you already done a quick mentat-scan of the archives, skipping past Henry's name on the *Gravenhage* ship manifest, looking to see who *else* disembarked along with him that bright April day?

No, it won't be that obvious. They were afraid, you see, and with good reason.

True, the Holy See quickly forgave the fugitive and declared him safe from retribution. But the secretive masters of the Inquisition were less eager to pardon a famous escapee. They had already proved relentless in pursuit of those who slip away. While pretending that he still languished in custody, they must have sent agents everywhere, searching...

So look instead for assumed names! Protective camouflage.

Try *Mr. Quicksilver*, which was the common word in English for mercury, a metal that is liquid at room temperature and a key ingredient in early barometers. Is the name familiar? It would be if you went to *this* university. And now it's plain – that had to be Torricelli! A flood of scholarly papers may come from this connection, alone. An old mystery solved.

But move on now to the real news. Have you scanned the passenger list carefully?

How about "Mr. Kinneret"?

Kinneret – one of the alternate names, in Hebrew, for the Sea of Galilee.

◇

Yes, dear. Kinneret.

I'm looking at his portrait right now, on the Wall of Founders. And despite obvious efforts at disguise – no beard, for example – it astonishes me that no one has commented till now on the resemblance between Harvard's earliest Professor of Natural Philosophy and the scholar who we are told died quietly under house arrest near Florence, way back in 1642.

It makes you wonder. Would a Catholic savant from "papist" Italy have been welcome in Puritan Boston – or on the faculty of John Harvard's new college – without the quiet revolution of reason that Roger Williams set in motion?

Would that revolution have been so profound or successful, without strong support from the Surveyor's Guild and the Seven United Tribes?

Lacking the influence of Kinneret, might the American tradition of excellence in mathematics and science have been delayed for decades? Maybe centuries?

◇

Sitting here in the Harvard University Library, staring out the window at rowers on the river, I can scarcely believe that less than four centuries have passed since the *Gravenhage* docked not far from here on that chilly spring morning of 1635. Three hundred and seventy nine years ago, to be exact.

Is that all? Think about it, just fifteen human generations, from those rustic beginnings to the dawn of a new millennium. How the world has changed.

Ill-disciplined, I left my transcriber set to record *Surface Thoughts*, and so these personal musings have all been logged for you to savor, if you choose high-fidelity download. But can even that convey the emotion I feel while marveling at the secret twists and turns of history?

If only some kind of time – or para-time – travel were possible, so history could become an observational... or even experimental... science! Instead we are left to use primitive methods, piecing together clues, sniffing and burrowing in dusty records, hoping the essential story has not been completely lost.

Yearning to shed a ray of light on whatever made us who we are.

◇

How much difference can one person make, I wonder? Even one gifted with talent and goodness and skill – and the indomitable will to persevere?

Maybe some group *other* than the Iroquois would have invented the steamboat and the Continental Train, even if James Watt hadn't emigrated and 'gone native'. But how ever could the Pan American Covenant have succeeded without Ben Franklin sitting there in Havana, to jest and soothe all the bickering delegates into signing?

How important was Abraham Lincoln's Johannesburg Address in rousing the world to finish off slavery and apartheid? Might the flagging struggle have failed without him? Or is progress really a team effort, the way Kip Thorne credits his AI colleagues – *meta-Einstein* and *meta-Feynman*

– claiming that he never could have created the Transfer Drive without their help?

Even this fine Widener Library where I sit – bequeathed to Harvard by one of the alumni who died when *Titanic* hit that asteroid in 1912 – seems to support the notion that things will happen pretty much the same, whether or not a specific individual or group happens to be on the scene.

No one can answer these questions. My own recent discoveries – following a path blazed by Kuiper and others – don't change things very much. Except perhaps to offer a sense of satisfaction – much like the gratification Henry Stephens must have felt the day he stepped down the wharf, embracing his family, shaking the hand of his friend Williams, and breathing the heady air of freedom in this new world...

... then turning to introduce his friends from across the sea. Friends who would do epochal things during the following twenty years, becoming legends while Henry himself faded into contented obscurity.

Can one person change the world?

Maybe not.

So instead let's ask; what would *Harvard* be like, if not for Professor Quicksilver-Torricelli?

Or if not for Professor Galileo Galilei.

Story Notes

This story – and the one after – falls into the category of a "contemplation." You take the What-If premise of science fiction and extrapolate some twist or change that affects the main character... but even more-so the world.

It is that possibility – the world will and must change – that distinguishes science fiction most from other genres, and *especially* from its cousin, fantasy. For example, despite all the action, drama and verve that you will find in an above-average fantasy tale, perhaps rooting for a good prince to overcome a dark lord, the deep premise of kings and lords will (almost) always be retained. Only in SF are you sometimes forced to consider how a small quirk of fate might transform everything. And sometimes it isn't the person who is most powerful or renowned who makes the greatest difference.

Our next tale, one of my collaborations with Gregory Benford, contemplates an even-more brash case of "let one character change everything."

I Could've Done Better

◇

by Gregory Benford & David Brin

1.

They didn't have to do this to me. Dump me in this place, with no chance of going home.

I told them I'd try harder. Really. Make up for my mistakes. Be a better person. They could choose someone else, easy.

But did they listen?

How I miss the things I'll never do again. Eat a hotdog at the ballpark. Take a flight out to the coast. Catch a Vegas show or watch a playoff game on TV. I suppose I could invent baseball or teach these people how to play poker. But they'd just let me win all the time, so where's the fun?

Here comes slender Mirimani now, carrying a basket of fresh fruit, followed by Deela—buxom Deela—with a pitcher of beer. I've grown used to the strong, bitter stuff they brew here, though I'd trade Tut's treasure right now for a cold, frothy Budweiser . . .

"It is time for my lord to have his morning massage," Deela says, leaning over me to fill a golden goblet. Her scent is mild musk and myrrh. Two more girls approach with linen towels and scented oils.

Mirimani smiles. She's leaner, more athletic.

"Or would the Father of the Nile prefer to bathe first?"

All right, I admit it. I used to get a kick out of talk like that, the first hundred or so times. Till I realized what an absolute pit it is to be Pharaoh.

"Not now," I respond. My Old Kingdom Egyptian has an Illinois accent, but no one complains. "What's on our schedule today?"

Mirimani can glide smoothly from seductive to pure business—one reason she's risen so high in my service.

"A new ambassador from Babylon wishes to present gifts."

"Right into my lapis, I suppose."

"My lord?"

"Never mind." Making puns in English, instead of my tortured Ancient Egyptian; I really am homesick today. "Okay, then what?"

"You grant clemency to the Libyan rebels."

"Clemency? Those guys gave me real trouble last summer, raiding caravans and burning my new schools. Remind me. Why was I planning to spare them?"

"In order to set an example, my lord. To illustrate your innovations called 'due process' and 'rehabilitation,' as I recall. Have you changed your mind?"

"Well . . . no, I guess not. It'd be more satisfying to set another kind of example, though. One involving hungry lions. Oh, never mind. Is there anything else?"

"Only an audience with the High Priestess of Isis, who craves a few moments from the Father of Waters."

At this I groan.

"Aw, man, do I really have to see *her?*"

Mirimani smiles gently. We've been through this before.

"No one commands the Pharaoh of all Egypt. But you have found the wisdom of Isis indispensable in the past."

Her phrasing tugs with bitter irony.

In the past, Mirimani?

Oh, if only you knew how far off you are.

2.

All right, picture this. Two babes come swaying into Mulligan's Bar, wearing identical black dresses with slit sides and plunging backs. One blond and the other with tightly curled hair that's a deep, almost black, henna red. They seem awkward on spike heels—wobbling a little—yet getting the hang of it fast. Athletic types. No. More than that.

Right away the old radar is up, beeping. They're knockouts. Tall, luminous, luscious . . . every male in the place takes notice. So does every female. You'd have to be dead not to.

Let me get something straight—I wasn't asking for trouble. Just stopping by the old haunt to relax with a brew—one!—after a racquetball match. I demolished poor Fred from Accounting pretty easy, 3–1, picking up fifty bucks on bets and feeling smug over grinding his nose in it. I'd been riding my underlings at work, too—working off the steam that kept building up in my life. The feeling that I should be doing more. More than middle management. More than this.

Sandy expected me home by six-thirty. I really meant to be prompt. Maybe put in some quality time with the kids.

The after-five crowd was trickling in. My fave time of day. Allowing for a twenty-minute commute, I had three quarters of an hour to just relax and be me. If I cut it close.

I had promised Sandy to do better, and really meant it this time. She had caught me chatting up an intern at the office picnic and raised hell. Then, two days later, I came home late and brewed up a bit. She didn't seem to understand that I was still a fun kinda guy. That's what originally drew us to each other, right? We sure had some wild times.

Only now she was auditioning for the role of Wounded Hausfrau and I hadn't changed. *Why should I?* part of me protested.

Another part answered—*Come on, sport, you know you've crossed the line a few times since you got hitched. She's worth some extra effort. So are the kids. Give it a rest.*

I'm sure every married guy has those conflicts, right? Well, a lot of us.

So there I was, just mulling it over, dealing with it, when the two lookers came in.

Lookers in both senses—they sat down and right away started looking at me.

Ah, those sheath dresses, hose and high heels—tight skirts, covering without concealing two great bodies. And the faces—just my type. High cheekbones, full lips, arching eyebrows, long hair. Redhead's dusky complexion set a nice contrast to the blonde's cool snow. Couldn't be better if I'd ordered them from a menu.

Okay, maybe I was a little irked with Sandy. Maybe I was tired. Give me credit—I went over there more out of curiosity than anything else. I mean, how often do two knockout babes send you pickup looks across a bar?

For just a moment, I recall, something about these two—the way they moved—made me think of... *soldiers*.

The thought was kind of weird. Unnerving.

It didn't stop me, though.

"Do I know you ladies?"

Not as amateur as it sounds. If they say no, turn it into a compliment, something about getting to start fresh with two such lovelies, blah blah. When I was in practice, I could come off even a routine opening with confidence, like answering a backhand serve.

Only the blonde surprises me.

"Oh, we know you. You're famous."

I gave her a quick look to see if this was irony, but she's beaming a big, white smile. Good teeth, great glossy lipstick, and not a hair out of place. Maybe they'd been in Mulligan's before and heard something.

I tossed it off with a disarming chuckle. "Whatever they're saying, officer, it ain't true."

"Oh, no, Alec," the redhead said, "you're renowned."

All right. A bit nervous now. They knew my name. I glanced around to see if any of the guys were giggling in a corner, having put these two up to it.

"Renowned, eh? How come I don't see myself on magazine covers?"

"Not now—in the future." And she motioned for me to sit down.

Now I know it's a gag. But nobody was cackling beyond the potted plants. Mulligan himself seemed unaware, busy with customers. I decided to play along, plopping in a chair.

"Oh, yeah?"

"We're serious," the blonde said. "We really are from your future."

"Sure, like in those movies." The guys knew I was a lifelong sci-fi fan. Whoever set this up, I'd have to come up with something good to top it.

"Indeed—" the redhead nodded, "—our research shows several cinematic dramas in your era approached the general concept, so you should easily grasp what we're talking about. Please do accept it. We are real, from two centuries ahead of this day."

I gave them a smile of disbelief, with a Cary Grant cock of the head. "Hm, well, they do make real beauties in the twenty-third century."

For the first time, something I said affected her. A modest blush, apparently sincere. I blinked, more surprised by that than anything she had said. This was no hired hooker or actress. She was nervous underneath and actually appreciated the compliment. My opinion meant something to her.

"So, are you ladies tourists? Come back in time to do a little slumming with the ancestors?"

The blonde was more businesslike. "We are not tourists, Alec. Our mission is serious. We are at war."

I blinked. A surprising turn. My latest theory had been that they were sorority pledges from a nearby college, pulling mind games on some locals as part of an initiation stunt. The future babes trip had just the right flavor for a tease fantasy. But this—

"At... war?"

"Yes. And we are losing."

"You . . ."

"We," she corrected. "All of us. Humanity."

"Uh huh, I think I saw that movie. You want me to go forward in time because I'm a typical primitive warrior type. Only a real man can defeat the alien invaders or rogue computers or mutant spiders, because your males are too civilized."

They gave me a don't-be-ridiculous look.

"Our warriors are strong, Alec," the redhead said, "both men and women. Indeed, many of our greatest heroes and most innovative thinkers are descended from you."

That made me blink a couple of times, momentarily at a loss for words. What a line! I should try it myself sometime. Somebody at the sorority had an imagination, all right.

Well, if they wanted to be outrageous, fine.

"Descended from . . . Oh, I get it now. You've come back in time to ask me for genetic samples?"

The blonde put her hand on my thigh, a pleasant warm pressure, and rather more alarming than I expected. Her smile broadened.

"Yes, but more than that, we need your help."

"No fighting aliens in the future? Shucks."

A small corner of me felt strangely disappointed. I kind of hankered after that.

"We would not risk your life. But you can save humanity, Alec. If you are willing to accept a most difficult, onerous, but ultimately rewarding task."

3.

The ambassador from Babylon brought mostly the same old crap. Jewelry that my kid might've spurned at a discount store, back home in Chicago. Some pathetic rugs. Spices to cover the smell when food starts to go stale.

We'll fix that problem by next year, if I keep making good progress setting up Pharaoh Laboratories, Inc. I think I can remember how to make a refrigerator and there's no lack of willing labor. Nor any corporate bean-counters or stockholders to hinder us. We'll keep trying till we get it right.

I'll have cold beer yet! You'll see.

The ambassador looked scared, trying desperately to impress me with his gifts. Well, can't blame him. Babylon and all the other ancient powers are pissing in their pants because Old Kingdom Egypt now has muzzle-loading cannon.

He seemed especially upset over the girls. He brought twenty of them. Real beauties. Didn't Pharaoh like 'em?

Shucks. The ever-efficient priestesses of Isis whisked them all away before I could even get a good look! Only those who actually *volunteer* – of their own free will – may come back to the palace, later. It's my own law, dammit.

To compensate, I enjoyed making the ambassador sweat some more. But not too much. To my surprise, I've found a little groveling goes a long way.

Anyway, the Libyan rebels were next. They should put on a good show.

4.

All right, so there we are in the bar, see? I'm getting into their little game—this time travel story thing. As I said, it just had to be a sorority prank. A sexy little mind tease. Even the "future war" scenario fit in.

Maybe they were "assigned to protect me" from some horrible android assassin. Why not play along? It wouldn't be sporting to spoil their fun, right?

Only part of me was getting worried. The part that knows people, often letting me manipulate them to my own advantage. The part that does well at poker. The part that knew these weren't ditzy sorority chicks out on a dare.

They were formidable women. Capable adults, serious and determined. Whatever they were up to, they meant to accomplish it.

Part of me already half believed them.

"Um . . . a task?"

"In another era."

"Another . . . right. You want me to come with you in a time machine."

"Not a machine. A time *beam*. Our greatest scientists managed to create just one, with an interference fringe here in your era and another at our final destination. So this has to work."

"Hm. Will it take long? My wife expects me home in less than an hour."

That's not like me. To mention Sandy, up front. First clue that I really am starting to take this crazy story as more than a joke.

"Your wife was destined to be disappointed tonight, whether or not we came to intervene. Do you see the brunette sitting behind me? Three tables back, trying to read a book."

"Yeah, so? I noticed her before."

"You were about to go to her and . . . what is your expression? Pick her up."

"No way."

"After your third beer . . . "

"I was just having one!"

" . . . one thing would lead to another. Amid the subsequent accusations, lies, and recriminations, a downward spiral would commence, with more such philandering episodes, more alienation, resulting in divorce and then two more failed marriages —"

"Hey!" This was getting weird. "I'm happy. All right, I need more control. And maybe I can be a bit self-centered. But I wouldn't spoil things like that! Not where it counts."

The redhead stayed serious. They were dividing roles.

"During the next month, by our records, everything will turn sour. You will go back to gambling, promiscuity—"

"No! I'm through with all that." Then I recall how I was feeling a minute ago. "Dammit, *you* started flirting with *me*. I was just having a beer, and . . . and I've been trying harder."

It sounded pretty lame, even to me, but I *had* been doing better. Really I had. Right up until that evening!

The blonde was merciless.

"Yes, but you will fail. If it helps, let me assure you that it isn't entirely your fault. Blame it on upbringing and a wretched environment—certainly not genes."

"What about my genes?" The weirder this got, the more I seemed compelled to stay and listen.

"Your traits are mostly outstanding and they manifest that way through all eight of your children. And their heirs, far downstream,"

"Eight!"

"I mentioned other marriages. That is how we know your genes are the critical factor, since you were not especially helpful to the mothers in any other way. Yet, all eight achieved wonders.

"Again, it's not really your fault, Alec. Twisted by your own past, you were merely a somewhat successful executive in this era, good at manipulating and defeating competitors, but also thwarted by those above you, who were put off by your drive and apparent amorality. At a root level, you have powerful leadership talents, inheritable traits that will prove crucial in our future. Your descendants will be mighty leaders, ambitious, innovative, demanding, and yet fair."

I couldn't even begin to imagine the point of this "joke" anymore. It was taking on a harshness that burned inside.

"What did you mean by twisted?"

"Our analysts believe your abilities—especially your sense of empathy for others—were stunted because of traumas you suffered while young."

Ouch. I felt a wrench in my stomach. How the hell could this bitch know about——

I very nearly got up at that moment. Got up and walked away from the lure of their beauty, the fascination of their teasing game. I almost stood up to go home, to where I knew I was loved in spite of my faults. At least up until that night. *Stand... up!* I commanded my muscles and bones. But they betrayed me.

"Those childhood traumas twisted your gifts, turning you into a user of others. Unpleasant traits you fought to overcome, beginning with your playground experience—you always felt badly about being a bully, didn't you? History gives you credit for that, Alec. And yet, you were never able to—"

"Hey, wait a second —"

The redhead injects with enthusiasm "—but what struck Special Projects HQ was how those very same traits ideally suit you for a special task! A role in saving all humanity."

I blink. Doubt, anger, and disbelief welled up in me. None of this made sense, even as an elaborate practical joke. It came rushing back: Tony Pasquetto beating the crap out of me in fifth grade, my seething anger, a bile from that simmered on and on. I took it out on others, roiling with both pleasure and guilt. One word from these two and presto— back it came. And worse, much worse from my own parents, too caught up in their war against each other to see what collateral damage they were doing to me inside.

I made myself take a deep breath. "I . . . had some rough times as a kid, sure, but that doesn't mean—"

The blonde's hand slid higher up my thigh, threatening to drive away all rational thought.

"Let us persuade you."

"Huh? Of what?"

"Of our purpose. Our resolve to make your decision obvious."

"Yes," the redhead added, leaning closer. "We are here to give you everything that you presently want. To fulfill your fantasies, such as they are."

"And you figure I want more than a good exec job and a wife and home?"

"We know you. Better than you know yourself, Alec," Red said with a slow, sly smile.

Struggling for some sense of control, I stretched, pretending nonchalance, knowing that I'm fooling no one.

"You ladies have got quite a line, I got to hand it to you."

"You do not believe us," the redhead said. "Of course, it is a fantastic tale."

"It's original, I'll give you that."

Blonde is all business. She leaned back, giving me a good long look at her perfectly proportioned body. "For now, let us see about collecting those samples you offered."

5.

The rebels groveled very well. Heads smacked on marble, moans of supplication echoed, they even trotted forward some women to offer—probably their poor frightened wives. I yawned.

My Western Frontier Advisor whispered, urging me to put them all on spikes. "As an example to others!" he finished.

"Have you watched an impalement?" I answered. I had made that mistake the first time I went along with this joker. They put the pointed shaft up the victim's bum and it takes the victim a full day to work down on it. I would still wake up in a sweat, years later, remembering their screams.

"Sire, for the good of the Kingdom—"

"Clemency is granted!" I said loudly. "One year at hard labor, helping to build the Great Library in Alec-Sandria, then back home on probation—and I better not hear of any more raided caravans! This rebellion stuff has got to stop. Get a life!"

Okay, not eloquent. But the expressions on their faces—and their wives'—made me feel like Abraham Lincoln. Sheesh, these ancient guys are easily pleased.

Not that I was always Mr. Nice Guy. Especially at the beginning, building a ragtag band of followers, then eventually taking over and ejecting the old Pharaoh. Had to show I was the kind of ruthless cutthroat that my growing army expected. Those first years were hungry, danger-packed, and tense, even with some modern tricks from the twenty-first century. And yet . . . it's funny how finally taking power didn't turn out to be as voluptuously satisfying as I thought it would be.

Who would have expected that I'm nowhere near the bully that I used to think I was?

The cries of gratitude from the rebels hardly faded away before the chief herald cried out. "Lo, the Priestess of Isis arrives!"

Damn! I had meant to slip away—

She came in at full swagger. And though she bowed low before me and uttered all the proper phrases, anyone could tell that she's my equal here.

Some may even suspect the truth.

The gold bracelets were striking, the ivory headdress and ebony belt gave her authority, and the figure . . . well nobody else in 1400 B.C. has anything like it.

But she was all business. How did I ever think she was so alluring, back in Mulligan's?

"Lord of All the Lands, I approach you with supplications."

Which meant work to do. With a sigh I sat back on my throne and answered in English.

"The usual?"

"I bring laws for you to proclaim. Matters that we discussed at our last monthly meeting. Regulations for fair trade in the Sinai. A better plan for Nile boats. Establishment of county and provincial fairs, for the open exchange of improvements. The apprenticeship and scholarship program for bright sons and daughters of the peasant class."

Yeah, yeah. Half of the ideas were mine. I'm not a complete puppet. Still, I winced when I saw a crimson scroll under her belt. The weekly quota of heirs for me to sire.

Dammit, I bet she was planning an increase! What am I, a machine?

"Look, what's the rush?" I mumbled. "We've already accomplished—"

"A great deal, proving that our estimates of your abilities were correct. You should trust—"

"Trust!" I laughed, without joy. "You tricked me! All of this, in order to—"

"In order to help guide society quickly toward a more advanced state, so that in three and a half millennia it will be capable of defeating a dire enemy from the stars."

None of the guards, deputies and ass-kissers around the throne room understood us, of course. They assumed we were talking in the Language of the Gods.

"Do remember the Enemy, O great Pharaoh."

I shivered. They had showed me a foe, all right—made me experience them in full. Not classic aliens or terrifying robo-devils, nothing you'd expect at all. They came from a world where smart mammals like us were herded. Not like cows, but more subtly. Symbiotic, they had mastered how to tap our deepest fears, using them against us. They ruled by immersing us in them. Imagine a chilly analytical engine, impersonally merciless as it uses you, only far worse to look at and impossible to look away from—because it's always there, slimy, inside.

The blonde and the redhead made me experience that. They showed me how humanity was losing.

But on this new timeline, we'll have an extra 3,000 years to get ready. Time enough, maybe, if we bypass the cruel stupidities and waste of the Assyrian and Roman and Ch'ing empires and all the dark ages between. If feudalism gets replaced by opportunity and science a whole lot earlier. Especially—they say—if that future has plenty of people with my traits. Traits that did me little good in my old life, but ones that would breed true, making great leaders in the future. Leaders not stunted the way I am—only good for simple tasks, like bullying primitives by the marshy borders of the Nile.

"One of your descendants invented the time beam," they had told me that night – it seemed like ages ago – as if I was supposed to be proud. "She knew this attempt would be our only chance."

"Well then, why not take *her* back in time? Or pick my son to be Pharaoh? He carries the same miracle genes, right? He's better and wiser than me, too, ain't that right? Anyway, if I leave, won't they vanish?"

"It is hard to explain the subtleties of temporal dynamics," the red-head had said. "All of your children made large contributions to our future. That timeline must continue to stand like a trellis for the new one to grow alongside. And it *will* continue to stand, even after you are removed."

I think of myself as flexible-minded, but this made my head hurt. You can't do time travel without a painful paradox, and the two savants in front of me were accommodating.

"But still . . . why me? Because that time beam had a … *fringe*… that appeared both in my era and here? I mean now?"

"That's part of it. Also, we must borrow the least important element. One whose suite of actions—personal choices and conscious involvement—can be spared, and yet someone capable of exercising fierce power in a primitive era, then growing into the job. All of those reasons pointed to you."

The least important element. Brutally frank, those gals were, once they knew they had me. Their futuristic personality analyzer told them I'd be fine leading a nation of millions, though in my real world I never made it beyond middle management. I could satisfy harems, but not one modern wife.

Go figure.

6.

It really came home to me later that day, in the privacy of my seraglio.

Did you ever work in an ice cream shop? First week you gorge. Second week you peck a little. Third week . . . well, I was getting that third week feeling again, real bad.

A voluptuous lady of the Levant, soft like pillows. A stately and dignified Nubian, like warm ebony. A leering, silky submissive of the West and a skilled contortionist from the Far East. All of them were volunteers, of course, never coerced. That moralist, Isis, made sure of their enthusiasm before any came to me. (What did she do with the others? I wondered.)

I had done the research every other man only dreams about, and learned a daunting truth: there is only a finite range of women, as there is of men. Probably Casanova learned the same lesson. Who would've figured the polygynous drive for variety turns out to be satiable, even in a rutting fool like me?

Eventually, it palls.

And then, dammit, you start dreaming every night of someone who actually loved you, who chose you, as an equal, despite knowing all your faults.

I tried to shake off the mood. It would be unseemly for Pharaoh not to watch the Parade of Lovelies, then show that he still has what it takes to govern. Sighing, I proceeded to do my best.

Later, the Priestess of Isis arrived for another consultation, this time accompanied by her redheaded companion, now the Priestess of Karnak, proudly bringing the latest crop of infants to show off. Each one a gift for the ages, or so that pair of eugenic time warriors crooned.

And yet, once again I wondered. They'd told me that a chain beginning in the year 2015 would not be long enough to create a new civilization with sufficient power by 2200. But three thousand years might suffice. We were growing a parallel timeline, a vine climbing alongside the world I had known. One that would be strong enough to battle a terrible foe. Too much High Concept for me, I'm afraid. But one nagging doubt kept bothering me—

I have only their word for it that I joined the right side in their war.

Looking at my latest offspring, one baby after another whom I would barely know, I found myself wishing with a pang that I hadn't missed so many of Bobby's Little League games. That I had gone to see Rachel win the science fair.

Who knew they'd turn out to be geniuses?

And who cared about that? I just missed them.

Oh, the blonde and redheaded time agents played me right. They offered power, which I enjoyed at first— till I got responsible. They knew it would happen. . . .

"Hey," I barked at both of them as they packed up their latest harvest of healthy, cooing princesses and princelings to depart. "I'm here running the Kingdom all day, begetting heirs all night, and meanwhile—what are you two doing in those temples of yours?"

The Priestess of Isis interrupted her inspection of a young heir. Her eyes became slits.

"We are organizing the women, Alec. Mind your own business."

I sighed as they left, ruminating yet again on my fate. And especially on one awful irony.

Somewhere deep down, way back in my former life, I always expected to be *punished*. For my faults. For my failings.

Now, despite pleasures that would have stunned Hefner, I couldn't escape feeling that way again. Exiled and condemned. Wishing... though I knew it was hopeless... for clemency.

A pardon.

For some way to go home.

"I could have done better," I muttered. "If only they left me alone. Really. I would have changed."

The pall lingered over me like a familiar cloud...

. . . till a nearby Grecian-primitive beauty gave me a slow, suggestive smile.

Ah, well. One endures.

Story Notes

The preceding story was created with my longtime collaborator Gregory Benford. Together, we wrote the deep-space novel Heart of the Comet. Of course, any collaboration results in a different "voice."

Science fiction features more collaborations than any other genre. I believe one reason is that – for all our notorious authorial egos – we really do care above all about story.

Story towers above all other considerations. If teamwork can make it succeed, then ego gives way to teamwork!

Next comes a light-hearted piece – another collaboration with Greg – in which we channel one of the greatest, early masters of our art, putting him in a "mash-up" with another maestro of newborn science fiction.

Paris Conquers All

◇

by Jules Verne
(As told to David Brin & Gregory Benford)

I commence this account with a prosaic stroll at eventide – a saunter down the avenues of *la Ville Lumière,* during which the ordinary swiftly gave way to the extraordinary. I was in Paris to consult with my publisher, as well as to visit old companions and partake of the exquisite cuisine, which my provincial home in Amiens cannot boast. Though I am now a gentleman of advanced age, nearing my 70th year, I am still quite able to favor the savories, and it remains a treat to survey the lovely demoiselles as they exhibit the latest fashions on the boulevards, enticing smitten young men and breaking their hearts at the same time.

I had come to town that day believing – as did most others – that there still remained weeks, or days at least, before the alien terror ravaging southern France finally reached the valley of the Seine. *Isle de France* would be defended at all costs, we were assured. So it came to pass that, tricked by this false complaisance, I was in the capital the very afternoon that the crisis struck.

Paris! It still shone as the most splendid exemplar of our progressive age – all the more so in that troubled hour, as tense anxiety seemed only to add to the city's loveliness – shimmering at night with both gas and electric lights, and humming by day with new electric trams, whose marvelous wires crisscrossed above the avenues like gossamer heralds of a new era.

I had begun here long ago as a young attorney, having followed into my father's profession. Yet that same head of our family had also accepted my urge to strike out on a literary road, in the theater and later down expansive voyages of prose.

"Drink your fill of Paris, my son!" the good man said, seeing me off from the Nantes railway station. "Devour these wondrous times. Your senses are keen. Share your insights. The world will change because of it."

Without such help and support, would I ever have found within myself the will, the daring, to explore the many pathways of the future, with all their wonders and perils? Ever since the Martian invasion began, I had found myself reflecting on an extraordinary life filled with such good fortune, especially now that *all* human luck seemed about to be revoked. With terror looming from the south and west, would it all soon come to nought? All that I had achieved? Everything humanity had accomplished, after so many centuries climbing upward from ignorance?

It was in such an uncharacteristically dour mood that I strolled in the company of M. Beauchamp, a gentleman scientist, that pale afternoon less than an hour before I had my first contact with the horrible Martian machines. Naturally, I had been following the eyewitness accounts which first told of plunging fireballs, striking the Earth with violence that sent gouts of soil and rock spitting upward, like miniature versions of the outburst at Krakatau. These impacts had soon proved to be far more than mere meteoritic phenomena, since there soon emerged, like insects from a subterranean lair, three-legged beings bearing incredible malevolence toward the life of this planet. Riding gigantic tripod mechanisms, these unwelcome guests rapidly set forth with one sole purpose in mind – destructive conquest!

The ensuing carnage, the raking fire, the sweeping flames – none of these horrors had yet reached the fair country above the river Loire... not yet. But reports all-too vividly told of villages trampled, farmlands seared black, and hordes of refugees cut down as they fled.

Invasion. The word called to mind vivid pain all too easily remembered. We of northern France knew the pain just twenty-eight years back, when Sedan fell and this sweet land trembled under an attacker's boot. Several Paris quarters still bear scars where Prussian firing squads tore moonlike craters out of plaster walls, mingling there the ochre life blood of communards, royalists and bourgeois alike.

Now Paris trembled before advancing powers so malign that, in contrast, those Prussians of 1870 were like beloved cousins, welcome to town for a picnic!

All of this I pondered while taking leave, with Beauchamp, of the Ecole Militaire, the national military academy, where a briefing had just been given to assembled dignitaries, such as ourselves. From the stone portico we gazed toward the Seine, past the encampment of the Seventeenth Corps of Volunteers, their tents arrayed across trampled grass and smashed flowerbeds of the ironically-named *Champs de Mars*. The meadow of the god of war.

Towering over this scene of intense (and ultimately futile) martial activity stood the tower of M. Eiffel, built for the recent exhibition – that marvelously fashioned testimonial to metal and ingenuity... and also target of so much vitriol.

"The public's regard for it may improve with time," I ventured, observing that Beauchamp's gaze lay fixed on the same magnificent spire.

My companion snorted with derision at the curving steel flanks. "An eyesore, of no enduring value," he countered, and for some time we distracted ourselves from more somber thoughts by arguing the relative merits of Eiffel's work, while turning east to walk toward the Sorbonne. Of late, experiments in the transmission of radio-tension waves had wrought unexpected pragmatic benefits, using the great tower as an *antenna*. I wagered Beauchamp there would be other advantages, in time.

Alas, even this topic proved no lasting diversion from thoughts of danger to the south. Fresh in our minds were reports from the wine districts. The latest outrage – that the home of Vouvray was now smashed, trampled and burning. This was my favorite of all the crisp, light vintages – better, even, than a fresh Sancerre. Somehow, that loss seemed to strike home more vividly than dry casualty counts, already climbing to the millions.

"There must be a method!" I proclaimed, as we approached the domed brilliance of *Les Invalides*. "There has to be a scientific approach to destroying the invaders."

"The military is surely doing its best," Beauchamp said.

"Buffoons!"

"But you heard of their losses. The regiments and divisions decimated –" Beauchamp stuttered. "The army dies for France! For humanity – of which France is surely the best example."

I turned to face him, aware of an acute paradox – that the greatest martial mind of all time lay entombed in the domed citadel nearby. Yet even he would have been helpless before a power that was not of this world.

"I do not condemn the army's courage," I assured.

"Then how can you speak—"

"No, no! I condemn their lack of imagination!"

"To defeat the incredible takes—"

"Vision!"

Timidly, for he knew my views, he advanced, "I saw in the Match that the British have consulted with the fantasist, Mr. Wells."

To this I could only cock an eyebrow. "He will give them no aid, only imaginings."

"But you just said —"

"*Vision* is not the same as dreaming."

At that moment the cutting smell of sulfuric acid wafted on a breeze from the reducing works near the river. (Even in the most beautiful of cities, rude work has its place.) Beauchamp mistook my expression of disgust for commentary upon the Englishman, Wells.

"He is quite successful. Many compare him to you."

"An unhappy analogy. His stories do not repose on a scientific basis. I make use of physics. He invents."

"In this crisis —"

"I go to the moon in a cannon ball. He goes in an airship, which he constructs of a metal that does away with the law of gravitation. Ca c'est tres joli! – but show me this metal. Let him produce it!"

Beauchamp blinked. "I quite agree – but, then, is not our present science woefully inadequate to the task at hand – defending ourselves against monstrous invaders?"

We resumed our walk. Leaving behind the crowds paying homage at Napoleon's Tomb, we made good progress along rue de Varenne, with the Petite Palais now visible across the river, just ahead.

"We lag technologically behind these foul beings, that I grant. But only by perhaps a century or two."

"Oh surely, more than that! To fly between the worlds —"

"Can be accomplished several ways, all within our comprehension, if not our grasp."

"What of the reports by astronomers of great explosions, seen earlier this year on the surface of the distant ruddy planet? They now think these were signs of the Martian invasion fleet being launched. Surely we could not expend such forces!"

I waved away his objection. "Those are nothing more than I have already foreseen in *From the Earth to the Moon*, which I would remind you

I published thirty-three years ago, at the conclusion of the American Civil War."

"You think the observers witnessed the belching of a great Martian cannon?"

"Of course! I had to make adjustments, engineering alterations, while designing my moon vessel. The shell could not be of steel, like one of Eiffel's bridges. So I conjectured that the means of making light projectiles of aluminum will come to pass. These are not basic limitations, you see" – I waved them away – "but mere details."

The wind had shifted, and with relief I now drew in a heady breath redolent with the smells of cookery rising from the city of cuisine. Garlic, roasting vegetables, the dark aromas of warming meats – such a contrast with the terror which advanced on the city and on our minds. Along rue St. Grenelle, I glanced into one of the innumerable tiny cafes. Worried faces stared moodily at their reflections in the broad zinc bars, stained by spilled absinthe. Wine coursed down anxious throats. Murmurs floated on the fitful air.

"So the Martians come by cannon, the workhorse of battle," Beauchamp murmured.

"There are other methods," I allowed.

"Your dirigibles?"

"Come, come, Beauchamp! You know very well that no air permeates the realm between the worlds."

"Then what methods do they employ to maneuver? They fall upon Asia, Africa, the Americans, the deserving British – all with such control, such intricate planning."

"Rockets! Though perhaps there are flaws in my original cannon ideas – I am aware that passengers would be squashed to jelly by the firing of such a great gun – nothing similar condemns the use of cylinders of slowly exploding chemicals."

"To steer between planets? Such control!"

"Once the concept is grasped, it is but a matter of ingenuity to bring it to pass. Within a century, Beauchamp, we shall see rockets of our own rise from this ponderous planet into the heavens. I promise you that!"

"Assuming we survive the fortnight," Beauchamp remarked gloomily. "Not to mention a century."

"To live, we must think. Our thoughts must encompass the entire range of possibility."

I waved my furled umbrella at the sky, sweeping it around and down *rue de Rennes,* toward the southern eminence of Montparnasse. By chance my gaze followed the pointing tip – and so I was among the first to spy one of the Martian machines, like a monstrous insect, cresting that ill-fated hill.

There is something in the human species that abhors oddity, the unnatural. We are double in arms, legs, eyes, ears, even nipples (if I may venture such an indelicate comparison; but remember, I am a man of science at all times). Two-ness is fundamental to us, except when Nature dictates singularity – we have but one mouth, and one organ of regeneration. Such biological matters are fundamental. Thus, the instantaneous feelings of horror at first sight of the *three-ness* of the invaders – which was apparent even in the external design of their machinery. I need not explain the revulsion to any denizen of our world. These were alien beings, in the worst sense of the word.

"They have broken through!" I cried. "The front must have collapsed."

Around us crowds now took note of the same dread vision, looming over the sooty Montparnasse railway station. Men began to run, women to wail. Yet, some courageous ones of both sexes ran the other way, to help bolster the city's slim, final bulwark, a line from which rose volleys of crackling rifle fire.

By unspoken assent, Beauchamp and I refrained from joining the general fury. Two old men, wealthier in dignity than physical stamina, we had more to offer with our experience and seasoned minds than with the frail strength of our arms.

"Note the rays," I said dispassionately, as for the first time we witnessed the fearful lashing of that horrid heat, smiting the helpless trains, igniting rail cars and exploding locomotives at a mere touch. I admit I was struggling to hold both reason and resolve, fastening upon details as a drowning man might cling to flotsam.

"Could they be like Hertzian waves?" Beauchamp asked in wavering tones.

We had been excited by the marvelous German discovery, and its early application to experiments in wireless signaling. Still, even I had to blink at Beauchamp's idea – for the first time envisioning the concentration of such waves into searing beams.

"Possibly," I allowed. "Legends say that Archimedes concentrated light to beat back Roman ships, at Syracuse... But the waves Hertz found were meters long, and of less energy than a fly's wingbeat. These –"

I jumped, despite my efforts at self-control, as another, much *larger* machine appeared to the west of the first, towering majestically, also spouting bright red torrents of destruction. It set fires on the far southern horizon, the beam playing over city blocks, much as a cat licks a mouse.

"We shall never defeat such power," Beauchamp said morosely.

"Certainly we do not have much time," I allowed. "But you put my mind into harness, my friend."

Around us people now openly bolted. Carriages rushed past without regard to panicked figures who dashed across the avenues. Horses clopped madly by, whipped by their masters. I stopped to unroll the paper from a Colombian cigar. Such times demand clear thinking. It was up to the higher minds and classes to display character and resolve.

"No, we must seize upon some technology closer to hand," I said. "Not the Hertzian waves, but perhaps something allied..."

Beauchamp glanced back at the destructive tripods with lines of worry creasing his brow. "If rifle and cannon prove useless against these marching machines –"

"Then we must apply another science, not mere mechanics."

"Biology? There are the followers of Pasteur, of course." Beauchamp was plainly struggling to stretch his mind. "If we could somehow get these Martians – has anyone yet seen one? – to drink contaminated milk..."

I had to chuckle. "Too literal, my friend. Would you serve it to them on a silver plate?"

Beauchamp drew himself up. "I was only attempting –"

"No matter. The point is now moot. Can you not see where the second machine stands, atop the very site of Pasteur's now ruined Institute?"

Although biology is a lesser cousin in the family of science, I nevertheless imagined with chagrin those fine collections of bottled specimens, now kicked and scattered under splayed tripod feet, tossing the remnants to the swirling winds. No help there, alas.

"Nor are the ideas of the Englishman, Darwin, of much use, for they take thousands of years to have force. No, I have in mind physics, but rather more recent work."

I had been speaking from the airy spot wherein my head makes words before thought has yet taken form, as often happens when a concept lumbers upward from the mind's depths, coming, coming...

Around us lay the most beautiful city in the world, already flickering with gas lamps lining the prominent avenues. Might that serve as inspiration? Poison gas? But no, the Martians had already proved invulnerable to even the foul clouds the Army had tried to deploy.

But then what? I have always believed that the solution to tomorrow's problems usually lay in plain sight, in materials and concepts already at hand – just as the essential ideas for submarines, airships, and even interplanetary craft, have been apparent for decades. The trick lies in formulating the right combinations.

As that thought coursed through my mind, a noise erupted so cacophonously as to over-ride even the commotion further south. A rattling roar (accompanied by the plaint of already-frightened horses) approached from the *opposite* direction! Even as I turned round toward the river, I recognized the clatter of an explosive-combustion engine, of the type invented not long ago by Herr Benz, now propelling a wagon bearing several men and a pile of glittering apparatus! At once I observed one unforeseen advantage of horseless transportation – to allow human beings to ride *toward* danger that no horse on Earth would ever approach.

The hissing contraption ground to a halt not far from Beauchamp and me. Then a shout burst forth in that most penetrating of human accents – one habituated to open spaces and vast expanses.

"Come on, you Gol-durned piece of junk! Fire on up, or I'll turn ya into scrap b'fore the Martians do!"

The speaker was dressed as a workman, with bandoliers of tools arrayed across his broad, sturdy frame. A shock of reddish hair escaped under the rim of a large, curve-brimmed hat, of the type affected by the troupe of Buffalo Bill, when that showman's carnival was the sensation of Europe, some years back.

"Come now Ernst," answered the man beside him, in a voice both more cultured and sardonic. "There's no purpose in berating a machine. Perhaps we are already near enough to acquire the data we seek."

An uneasy alliance of distant cousins, I realized. Although I have always admired users of the English language, for their boundless ingenuity, it can be hard to see the countrymen of Edgar Allen Poe as related to those of Walter Scott.

"What do you say, Fraunhoffer?" asked the Englishman of a third gentleman with the portly bearing of one who dearly loves his schnitzel, now peering through an array of lenses toward the battling tripods. "Can you get a good reading from here?"

"Bah!" The bald-pated German cursed. "From ze exploding buildings and fiery desolation, I get plenty of lines, those typical of combustion. But ze rays zemselves are absurd. Utterly absurd!"

I surmised that here were scientists at work, even as I had prescribed in my discourse to Beauchamp, doing the labor of sixty battalions. In such efforts by luminous minds lay our entire hope.

"Absurd how?" A fourth head emerged, that of a dark young man, wearing objects over his ears that resembled muffs for protection against cold weather – only these were made of wood, linked by black cord to a machine covered with dials. I at once recognized miniature speaker-phones, for presenting faint sounds directly to the ears. The young man's accent was Italian, and curiously calm. "What is absurd about the spectrum of-a the rays, Professor?"

"There *iss* no spectrum!" the German expounded. "My device shows just the one hue of red light we see with our naked eyes, when the rays lash destructive force. There are no absorption lines, just a single hue of brilliant red!"

The Italian pursed his lips in thought. "One *frequency*, perhaps...?"

"If you *insist* on comparing light to your vulgar Hertzian waves –"

So entranced was I by the discussion that I was almost knocked down by Beauchamp's frantic effort to gain my attention. I knew just one thing could bring him to behave so – the Martians must nearly be upon us! With this supposition in mind, I turned, expecting to see a disk-like foot of a leviathan preparing to crush us.

Instead, Beauchamp, white as a ghost, stammered and pointed with a palsied hand. "Verne, regardez!"

To my amazement, the invaders had abruptly changed course, swerving from the direct route to the Seine. Instead they turned left and were stomping swiftly toward the part of town that Beauchamp and I had only just left, crushing buildings to dust as they hurried ahead. At the time, we shared a single thought. The commanders of the battle tripods must have spied the military camp on the *Champs de Mars*. Or else they planned to wipe out the nearby military academy. It even crossed my mind that their objective might be the tomb of humanity's greatest general – to destroy that shrine, and with it our spirit to resist.

But no. Only much later did we realize the truth.

Here in Paris, our vanquishers suddenly had another kind of conquest in mind.

◇

Flames spread as evening fell. Although the Martian rampage seemed to have slackened somewhat, the city's attitude of *sang froid* was melting rapidly into frothy panic. The broad boulevards that Baron Haussmann gave the city, during the Second Empire, proved their worth as aisles of escape while buildings burned.

But not for all. By nightfall, Beauchamp and I found ourselves across the river at the new army headquarters, in the tree-lined Tuilleries, just west of the Louvre – as if the military had decided to make its last stand in front of the great museum, delaying the invaders in order to give the curators more time to rescue treasures.

A great crowd surrounded a cage wherein, some said, several captured Martians cowered. Beauchamp rushed off to see, but I had learned to heed my subconscious – (to use the terminology of the Austrian alienist, Freud) – and wandered about the camp instead. Letting the spectacle play in my mind.

While a colonel with a sooty face drew arrows on a map, I found my gaze wandering to the trampled gardens, backlit by fire, and wondered what the painter, Camille Pissarro, would make of such a hellish scene. Just a month ago I had visited his apartment at 204 rue de Rivoli, to see a series of impressions he had undertaken to portray the peaceful Tuilleries. Now, what a parody fate had decreed for these same gardens!

The colonel had explained that invader tripods came in two sizes, with the larger ones appearing to control the smaller. There were many of the latter kind, still rampaging the city suburbs, but all three of the great ones reported to be in Northern France had converged on the same site before nightfall, trampling back and forth across the *Champs de Mars*, presenting a series of strange behaviors that as yet had no lucid explanation. I did not need a military expert to tell me what I had seen with my own eyes... three titanic metal leviathans, twisting and capering as if in a languid dance, round and round the same object of their fierce attention.

I wandered away from the briefing, and peered for a while at the foreign scientists. The Italian and the German were arguing vehemently, invoking the name of the physicist Boltzmann, with his heretical theories of "atomic matter," trying to explain why the heat ray of the aliens should emerge as just a single, narrow color. But the discussion was over my head, so I moved on.

The American and the Englishman seemed more pragmatic, consulting with French munitions experts about a type of fulminating bomb that might be attached to a Martian machine's kneecap – if only some way could be found to carry it there... and to get the machine to stand still while it was attached. I doubted any explosive device devised overnight would suffice, since artillery had been next to useless, but I envied the adventure of the volunteer bomber, whoever it might be.

Adventure. I had spent decades writing about it, nearly always in the form of extraordinary voyages, with my heroes bound intrepidly across foaming seas, or under the waves, or over icecaps, or to the shimmering moon. Millions read my works to escape the tedium of daily life, and perhaps to catch a glimpse of the near future. Only now the future had arrived, containing enough excitement for anyone. We did not have to seek adventure far away. It had come to us. Right to our homes.

The crowd had ebbed somewhat, in the area surrounding the prisoners' enclosure, so I went over to join Beauchamp. He had been standing there for hours, staring at the captives, our only prizes in this horrid war, lying caged within stout iron bars, a dismal set of figures, limp yet atrociously fascinating.

"Have they any new ideas?" Beauchamp asked in a distracted voice, while keeping his eyes focused toward the four beings from Mars. "What new plans from the military geniuses?"

The last was spoken with thick sarcasm. His attitude had changed since noon, most clearly.

"They think the key is to be found in the Master Tripods, those that are right now stomping flat the region near Eiffel's Spire. Never have all three of the Master Machines been seen so close together. Experts suggest that the Martians may use *movement* to communicate. The dance they are now performing may represent a conference on strategy. Perhaps they are planning their next move, now that they have taken Paris."

Beauchamp grunted. It seemed to make as much sense as any other proposal to explain the aliens' sudden, strange behavior. While smaller tripods roamed about, dealing destruction almost randomly, the three great ones hopped and flopped like herons in a marsh, gesticulating wildly with their flailing legs, all this in marked contrast to the demure solidity of Eiffel's needle.

For a time we stared in silence at the prisoners, whose projectile had hurtled across unimaginable space only to shatter when it struck an unlucky hard place on the Earth, shattering open and leaving its occupants helpless, at our mercy. Locked inside iron, these captives did not look impressive, as if this world weighed heavy on their limbs. Or had another kind of languor invaded their beings? A depression of spirits, perhaps?

"I have pondered one thing, while standing here," Beauchamp mumbled. "An oddity about these creatures. We had been told that everything about them came in threes... note the trio of legs, and of arms, and of eyes –"

"As we have seen in newspaper sketches, for weeks," I replied.

"Indeed. But regard the one in the center. The one around which the others arrayed themselves, as if protectively... or perhaps in mutual competition?"

I saw the one he meant. Slightly larger than the rest, with a narrower aspect in the region of the conical head.

"Yes, it does seem different, somehow... but I don't see –"

I stopped, for just then I *did* see... and thoughts passed through my brain in a pell mell rush.

"Its legs and arms... there are *four!* Its symmetry is different! Can it be of another race? A servant species, perhaps? Or something superior? Or else..."

My next cry was of excited elation.

"Beauchamp! The Master Tripods... I believe I know what they are doing!

"Moreover, I believe this beckons us with opportunity."

◇

The bridges were sheer madness, while the river flowing underneath seemed chock-a-block with corpses. It took our party two hours to fight our way against the stream of panicky human refugees, before the makeshift expedition finally arrived close enough to make out how the dance progressed.

"They are closer, are they not?" I asked the lieutenant assigned to guide us. "Have they been spiraling inward at a steady rate?"

The young officer nodded. "Oui Monsieur. It now seems clear that all three are converging on Eiffel's Tower. Though for what reason, and whether it will continue...?"

239

I laughed, remembering the thought that had struck me earlier – a mental image of herons dancing in a swamp. The comparison renewed when I next looked upward in awe at the stomping, whirling gyrations of the mighty battle machines, shattering buildings and making the earth shake with each hammer blow of their mincing feet. Steam hissed from broken mains. Basements and ossuaries collapsed, but the dance went on. Three monstrous things, wheeling ever closer to their chosen goal... which waited quietly, demurely, like a giant metal ingénue.

"Oh, they will converge all right, lieutenant. The question is – shall we be ready when they do?"

My mind churned.

The essential task in envisioning the future is a capacity for wonder. I had said as much to journalists. These Martians lived in a future of technological effects we could but imagine. Only through such visualization could we glimpse their Achilles heel.

Now was the crucial moment when wonder, so long merely encased in idle talk, should spring forth to action.

Wonder... a fine word, but what did it mean? Summoning up an inner eye, which could scale up the present, pregnant with possibility, into...into...

What, then? Hertz, his waves, circuits, capacitors, wires –

Beauchamp glanced nervously around. "Even if you could get the attention of the military–"

"For such tasks the army is useless. I am thinking of something else." I said suddenly, filled with an assurance I could not explain. "The Martians will soon converge at the center of their obsession. And when they do, we shall be ready."

"Ready with what?"

"With what lies within our – " and here I thought of the pun, a glittering word soaring up from the shadowy subconscious "– within our *capacitance*."

◇

The events of that long night compressed for me. I had hit upon the kernel of the idea, but the implementation loomed like an insuperable barrier.

Fortunately, I had not taken into account the skills of other men, especially the great leadership ability of my friend, M. Beauchamp.

He had commanded a battalion against the Prussians, dominating his corner of the battlefield without runners. With more like him, Sedan would never have fallen. His voice rose above the streaming crowds, and plucked forth from that torrent those who still had a will to contest the pillage of their city. He pointed to my figure, whom many seemed to know. My heart swelled at the thought that Frenchmen–and French-women! – would muster to a hasty cause upon the mention of my name, encouraged solely by the thought that I might offer a way to fight back.

I tried to describe my ideas as briskly as possible... but alas, brevity has never been my chief virtue. So I suppressed a flash of pique when the brash American, following the impulsive nature of his race, leaped up and shouted –

"Of course! Verne, you clever old frog. You've got it!"

– and then, in vulgar but concise French, he proceeded to lay it all out in a matter of moments, conveying the practical essentials amid growing excitement from the crowd.

With an excited roar, our makeshift army set at once to work.

I am not a man of many particulars. But craftsmen and workers and simple men of manual dexterity stepped in while engineers, led by the Italian and the American, took charge of the practical details, charging about with the gusto of youth, unstoppable in their enthusiasm. In fevered haste, bands of patriots ripped the zinc sheets from bars and brasseries. They scavenged the homes of the rich in search of silver. No time to beat it into proper electrodes – they connected decanters and candlesticks into makeshift assortments. These they linked with copper wires, fetched from the cabling of the new electrical tramways.

The electropotentials of the silver with the copper, in the proper conducting medium, would be monstrously reminiscent of the original "voltaic" pile of Alessandro Volta. In such a battery, shape does not matter so much as surface area, and proper wiring. Working through the smoky night, teams took these rude pieces and made a miracle of rare design. The metals they immersed in a salty solution, emptying the wine vats of the district to make room, spilling the streets red, and giving any true Frenchman even greater cause to think only of vengeance!

These impromptu batteries, duplicated throughout the arrondise-ment, the quick engineers soon webbed together in a vast parallel circuit. Amid the preparations, M. Beauchamp and the English scientist inquired into my underlying logic.

"Consider the simple equations of planetary motion," I said. "Even though shot from the Martian surface with great speed, the time to reach Earth must be many months, perhaps a year."

"One can endure space for such a time?" Beauchamp frowned.

"Space, yes. It is mere vacuum. Tanks of their air – thin stuff, Professor Lowell assures us from his observations – could sustain them. But think! These Martians, they must have intelligence of our rank. They left their kind to venture forth and do battle. Several years without the comforts of home, until they have subdued our world and can send for more of their kind."

The Englishman seemed perplexed. "For more?"

"Specifically, for their families, their mates... dare I say their *wives?* Though it would seem that not *all* were left behind. At least one came along in the first wave, out of need for her expertise, perhaps, or possibly she was smuggled along, on the ill-fated missile that our forces captured."

Beauchamp bellowed. "Zut! The four-legged one. There are reports of no others. You are right, Verne. It must be rare to bring one of that kind so close to battle!"

The Englishman shook his head. "Even if this is so, I do not follow how it applies to this situation." He gestured toward where the three terrible machines were nearing the tower, their gyrations now tight, their dance more languorous. Carefully, reverentially, yet with a clear longing, they reached out to the great spire that Paris had almost voted to tear down, just a few years after the Grand Exhibition ended. Now all our hopes were founded in the city's wise decision to let M. Eiffel's masterpiece stand.

The Martians stroked its base, clasped the thick parts of the tower's curving thigh – and commenced slowly to climb.

Beauchamp smirked at the English scholar, perhaps with a light touch of malice. "I expect you would not understand, sir. It is not in your national character to fathom this, ah, ritual."

"Humph!" Unwisely, the Englishman used Beauchamp's teasing as cause to take offense. "I'll wager that *we* give these Martians a whipping before your lot does!"

"Ah yes," Beauchamp remarked. "Whipping is more along the lines of the English, I believe."

With a glance, I chided my dear friend. After all, our work was now done. The young, the skilled, and the brave had the task well in hand.

Like generals who have unleashed their regiments beyond recall, we had only to observe, awaiting either triumph or blame.

At dawn, an array of dozens and dozens of Volta batteries lay scattered across the south bank of the Seine. Some fell prey to rampages by smaller Martian machines, while others melted under hasty application of fuming acids. Cabling wound through streets where buildings burned and women wept. Despite obstacles of flame, rubble, and burning rays, all now terminated at Eiffel's tower.

The Martians' ardent climb grew manifestly amorous as the sun rose in piercing brilliance, warming our chilled bones. I was near the end of my endurance, sustained only by the excitement of observing Frenchmen and women fighting back with ingenuity and rare unity. But as the Martians scaled the tower – driven by urges we can guess by analogy alone – I began to doubt. My scheme was simple, but could it work?

I conferred with the dark Italian who supervised the connections.

"Potentials? Voltages?" He screwed up his face. "Who has had-a time to calculate? All I know, M'sewer, iz that we got-a plenty juice. You want-a fry a fish, use a hot flame."

I took his point. Even at comparatively low voltages, high currents can destroy any organism. A mere fraction of an Ampere can kill a man, if his skin is made a reasonable conductor by application of water, for example. Thus, we took it as a sign of a higher power at work, when the bright sun fell behind a glowering black cloud, and an early mist rolled in from the north. It made the tower slick beneath the orange lamps we had festooned about it.

And still the Martians climbed.

It was necessary to coordinate the discharge of so many batteries in one powerful jolt, a mustering of beta rays. Pyrotechnicians had taken up positions beside our command post, within sight of the giant, spectral figures which now had mounted a third of the way up the tower.

"Hey Verne!" The American shouted, with well-meant impudence. "You're on!"

I turned to see that a crowd had gathered. Their expressions of tense hope touched this old man's heart. Hope and faith in my idea. There would be no higher point in the life of a fabulist.

"Connect!" I cried. "Loose the hounds of electrodynamics!"

A skyrocket leaped forth, trailing sooty smoke – a makeshift signal, but sufficient.

Down by the river and underneath a hundred ruins, scores of gaps and switches closed. Capacitors arced. A crackling rose from around the city as stored energy rushed along the copper cabling. I imagined for an instant the onrushing mob of beta rays, converging on —

The invaders suddenly shuddered, and soon there emerged thin, high cries, screams that were the first sign of how much like us they were, for their wails rose in hopeless agony, shrieks of despair from mouths which breathed lighter air than we, but knew the same depths of woe.

They toppled one by one, tumbling in the morning mist, crashing to shatter on the trampled lawns and cobblestones of the ironically named *Champs de Mars*... marshaling ground of the god of war, and now grave-yard of his planetary champions.

The lesser machines, deprived of guidance, soon reeled away, some falling into the river, and many others destroyed by artillery, or even enraged mobs. So the threat ebbed from its horrid peak... at least for the time being.

As my reward for these services, I would ask that the site be renamed, for it was not the arts of battle that turned the metal monsters into burning slag. Nor even Zeus's lightning, which we had unleashed. In the final analysis, it was *Aphrodite* who had come to the aid of her favorite city.

What a fitting way for our uninvited guests to meet their end — to die passionately in Paris, from a fatal love.

Story Notes

Greg and I had a good time with this one — our contribution to a quirky anthology called *War of the Worlds: Global Dispatches*, edited by Kevin J. Anderson. That book's daring premise? Suppose the Martian invasion portrayed in H. G. Wells's *War of the Worlds* actually took place!

Moreover, what if this interplanetary conflict were reported from the viewpoints of other famous authors of the day — for example Rudyard Kipling, Joseph Conrad, or Mark Twain? We were among the modern scribblers recruited to make this concept come alive, trying to emulate the individual viewpoints and styles of Karl Marx, Sigmund Freud, and Jack London, when each of them found himself confronted by invaders from another world.

Greg and I had the good luck to draw from the most direct competitor and colleague of Wells, Jules Verne, co-inventor of modern science fiction and master of the can-do problem-solving tale, invoking the master's style and inherent positivity of spirit... along with some of his now-archaic ways of viewing the world.

Naturally, it was loads of fun.

About some of those archaic patterns of speech etc... may I offer an aside?

I am well-known for believing in progress and an ongoing expansion in our "horizons of otherness"... our willingness to include ever-more kinds of being within civilization's circle of protection and appreciation. Indeed, I have a book called "Otherness!" Those who push this process forward are definitely right, far more often than those who cling to ancient, frightened prejudices... and yet...

... yet there is a tendency to declare "I invented tolerance and diversity and social justice!" And to dismiss writers of an earlier age, because their patterns of assumption or speech do not pass modern litmust tests. That's silly. Judge past people by their efforts in the context of their time! Did they push the conversation forward? Were they several standard deviations better than their era? Did the feminists, civil-libertarians and environmentalists of those days call our authors of speculative literature allies?

Are we - who keep pushing otherness horizons outward - standing on their shoulders? By that standard, even Robert Heinlein – whose works read rather sexist today – comes out better than expected. A majority of past Hugo winners do rather well in fact, according to that measure.

Moving forward does not require proclaiming "WE invented fiction that's about tolerance!" No, you are only another link in our chain to the future, using great What-If stories to help humanity to self-uplift, out of darkness and into light.

And now let's polish off this section with a piece of meta-fiction based on "Paris Conquers all." We weren't quite finished with Verne, after all. He kinda took over our skulls, for a little while.

A Retrospective by Jules Verne

◇

(as told to Gregory Benford and David Brin)

In reflecting back on the terrible year described in these accounts, it may come to be seen as a fulcrum in time. The pivot, indeed, of modernity. That is if we, the thinking beings who stride under a common sun, learn to rise above ourselves.

About that single turn of an orbit, there tipped the fate of two worlds, two darkly different destinies. With the balm of three decades to heal the pain, one can perceive benefits – though bought at dear cost – in the tragic way that Mars first encountered Earth. Indeed it may have led to a better fate for humanity than might have been, had the tripods never come. For by uniting our genus against a shared foe, the Martians deflected those festering nationalist energies that had seemed aimed toward a Twentieth Century in which our finest tools would be used for beastly ends. Instead, the invaders forced us to join together, redirecting all ingenuity and will toward a common cause.

So we now have the world of marvels that you, dear reader, and I your humble editor, now inhabit. We blink in fulsome awe at palatial floating airships, at Cunard's ornate tourist-submersibles, at pneumatic tubes carrying mail rapidly from town to town – while our still-muddy roads thwart the steam-buses and cable lorries – so that even in the worst winter storms we all remain linked in a united world.

And of course there are the Great Cannons of Canaveral, Sumatra, Kourou and Kenya – those behemoths of iron who regularly bellow loud enough to be heard even in distant lands, filling the sky above with useful mirror-semaphores and other delights of the modern age.

A further benefit lies in literature – in a resurgent conviction that the world is illimitable and will obey reason, so that Man can improve upon it. This is remarkable in light of the waning decades of the 19th century, which saw futuristic thinking, in the hands of Mr. Wells and others, that leaned darker in texture and implication.

So it is in a reflective mood that I enter these very words onto the clicking kinetiscope array of my *tabula rasa* – the latest of modern wonders. It is two weeks before my hundredth birthday. Never would I have thought that I could reach the fantastical year of 1928!

My reflection is deepened further in contemplating the news received just hours ago by Hertzian wave from the first human interplanetary argonauts, scouts of the grand flotilla meant to return that "visit" we received from the red planet a generation – and an age – ago.

Mars proves, as we suspected, to be a sad, wounded place, ancient and dry. One can well imagine why a bitter, *paranoic* way of thinking would evolve there – if I might apply a term used by the new guild of professional mentalists. Relayed carbon-stripe images of Martian cities show the canals with which they desperately sought to stave off the ravages of time. The pictures also show structures of exquisite grace and beauty, unencumbered by Earthly gravity.

The same gravity that will make our warriors seem as titans when they land... unless the Martians finally drop their wretched, prideful silence.

They must agree to speak! They must help bridge the mental gulf between our races, yawning as wide as the vacuum straits between our worlds – or else we shall have no choice. Our actions will be fore-ordained and there will be an end to the makers of those fine towers.

Despite lingering wrathful unforgiveness on the part of some, it is mostly with reluctance that we ponder that genocidal option. For in learning to decipher their machines – and through dissection, their organic forms – there has grown among countless humans an unquenchable desire to fathom the inner splendor and grace of these hideous but strangely compelling beings. There are even fetishists, small in number but leaders in recent fashion, who seek to emulate the styles, speech and even the eerie ways of thought that some interpolate from salvaged Martian records.

To be sure, many disapprove of this effort at exaggerated empathy, but with my renown I assail such intolerance. Clearly, our celestial neighbors suffer from an inflexibility that cripples them far more than it ever harmed us – millions of deaths notwithstanding. If it is possible to cure them of this mortal flaw, it will only happen if youthful, flexible humankind manages to meet them more than halfway.

If I had my way, I would save as many of the poor creatures as I could from the two-legged wrath now descending toward the red world. If need be, I would have everyone – *go Martian* – just a little. In this, I recall what one of my own favorite characters, Captain Nemo, once said –

The true price of war is borne by mothers.

Or, in the words of my young friend and collaborator, Herbert George Wells –

Ignorance has caused more calamity than malignity.

An astronomical whole would be greater by far than the sum of our separate parts. We should not stride as conquerors, lonely in our righteous, vengeful vindication. We should not stand on the dry red plain of ashes that we have won. We should go to Mars to learn, even from the defeated.

Ponder the relations of the advanced nations of Europe and the Americas, and the vaster multitudes still enduring poverty and nescience around the rest of our troubled globe. We of the West have in a true, cultural sense, defeated the empires of ancient ignorance. They now cower in our shadow. But to gloat is to court death. For the liberated spirits of the East are rising now, and they will accept nothing less than equality, nor will the rousing minds of the great South. The Western world must reach out, here, to the rest, with the same ecumenical soulfulness and patience that I urge we'll take across interplanetary space.

In the oblique manner of lived history, we must now grasp that it is better to contemplate eventual reconciliation, world linked to world. And so brotherhood must come, in parallel, to Mars.

– Jules Verne
Amiens, France,
October 1928

WHO WE'LL MEET

◇

The following tale takes some guts...

Fortitude

◇

The aliens seemed especially concerned over matters of *genealogy*.

"It is the only way we can be sure with whom we are dealing," said the spokes-being for the Galactic Federation. Terran-Esperanto words emerged through a translator device affixed to the creature's speaking vent, between purple, compound eyes. "Citizen species of the Federation will have nothing to do with you humans. Not until you can be properly introduced."

"But *you're* speakin' to us, right now!" Jane Fingal protested. "You're not makin' bugger-all sense, mate."

Jane was our astronomer aboard the *Straits of Magellan*. She had first spotted the wake of the N'Gorm ship as it raced by, far swifter than any Earth vessel, and it had been Jane's idea to pulse our engines, giving off weak gravity waves to attract their attention. For several days she had labored to help solve the language problem, until a meeting could be arranged between our puny ETS survey probe and the mighty N'Gorm craft.

Still, I was surprised when Kwenzi Mobutu, the Zairean anthropologist, did not object to Jane's presence in the docking bubble, along with our official contact team. Kwenzi seldom missed a chance to play up tension between Earth's two greatest powers — Royal Africa and the Australian Imperium — even during this historic first encounter with a majestic alien civilization.

The alien slurped mucousy sounds into its mouthpiece, and out came more computer-generated words.

"You misunderstand. I am merely a convenience, a construct-entity, fashioned to be as much like you as possible, thereby to facilitate your evaluation. I have no name, and will return to the vats when this is done."

Fashioned to be like us? I must have stared. (Everyone else did.) The being in front of us was bipedal and had two arms. On top were objects and organs we had tentatively named ears and a mouth. Beyond that, he (She? It?) seemed about as alien as could be.

"Yipes!" Jane commented. "I'd hate to meet your *boss* in a dark alley, if you're the handsomest bloke they could come up with."

I saw Mobutu, the African aristocrat, smile. That's when I realized why he had not vetoed Jane's presence, but relished it.

He knows this meeting is being recorded for posterity. If she makes a fool of herself here, at the most solemn meeting of races, it could win points against Australians back home.

"As I have tried to explain," the alien reiterated. "You will not meet my "boss" or any other citizen entity. Not until we are satisfied that your lineage is worthy."

While our Israeli and Tahitian xenobiologists conferred over this surprising development, our Patagonian captain stared out through the docking bubble at the Federation ship whose great flanks arched away, gleaming, in all directions. Clearly, he yearned to bring these advanced technologies home to the famed shipyards of Tierra del Fuego.

"Perhaps I can be helpful in this matter," Kwenzi Mobutu offered confidently. "I have some small expertise. When it comes to tracking one's family tree, I doubt any other human aboard can match my own genealogy.

His smile was a gleaming white contrast against gorgeously-perfect black skin, the sort of rich complexion that trendy people from pole to pole had been using chemicals to emulate, when we left home.

"Even before the golden placards of Abijian were discovered, my family line could be traced back to the great medieval households of Ghana. But since the recovery of those sacred records, it has been absolutely verified that my lineage goes all the way to the black pharaohs of the XXth Dynasty – an unbroken chain of four thousand years."

Mobutu's satisfaction faded when the alien replied with a dismissive wave.

"That interval is far too brief. Nor are we interested in the time-thread of mere individuals. Larger groups concern us."

Jane Fingal chuckled, and Mobutu whirled on her angrily.

"Your attitude suits a mongrel nation whose ancestors were criminal transportees, and whose "emperor" is chosen at a *rugby match!*"

"Hey. Our king'd whip yours any day, even half-drunk and with 'is arse in a sling."

"Colleagues!" I hastened to interrupt. "These are serious matters. A little decorum, if you please?"

The two shared another moment's hot enmity, until Nechemia Meyers spoke up.

"Perhaps they refer to *cultural* continuity. If we can demonstrate that one of our social traditions has a long history, stretching back –"

"– five thousand years?" inserted Mohandas Nayyal, our linguist from Delhi Commune. "Of course the Hindi tradition, as carried by the Vedas, goes back easily that far."

"Actually," Meyers continued, a bit miffed. "I was thinking more along the lines of *six* thousand –"

He cut short as the alien let out a warbling sigh, waving both "hands."

"Once again, you misconstrue. The genealogy we seek *is* genetic, but a few thousand of your years is wholly inadequate."

Jane muttered – "Bugger! It's like dickering with a Pattie over the price of a bleeding iceberg... no offense, Skipper."

The captain returned a soft smile. Patagonians are an easy-going lot, til you get down to business.

"Well then," Mobutu resumed, nodding happily. "I think we can satisfy our alien friends, and win Federation membership, on a purely *biochemical* basis. For many years now, the Great Temple in Abijian has gathered DNA samples from every sub-race on Earth, correlating and sorting to trace out our genetic relationships. Naturally, African bloodlines were found to be the least mutated from the central line of inheritance –"

Jane groaned again, but this time Kwenzi ignored her.

"– stretching back to our fundamental common ancestor, that beautiful, dark ancestress of all human beings, the one variously called Eva, or M'tum, who dwelled on the eastern fringes of what is now the Zairean Kingdom, over *three million years ago!*"

So impressive was Mobutu's dramatic delivery that even the least sanguine of our crew felt stirred, fascinated and somewhat awed. But then the N'Gorm servant-entity vented another of its frustrated sighs.

"I perceive that I am failing in my mission to communicate with lesser beings. Please allow me to try once again.

"We in the Federation are constantly being plagued by young, upstart species, rising out of planetary nurseries and immediately yammering for attention, claiming rights of citizenship in our ancient culture. At times, it has been suggested that we should routinely sterilize such places – filthy little worlds – or at least eliminate noisy, adolescent infestations by targeting their early stages with radio-seeking drones. But the *Kutathi*, who serve as judges and law-givers in the Federation, have ruled this impermissible. There are few crimes worse than meddling in the natural progress of a nursery world. All we can do is snub the newcomers, and restrict them to their home systems until they have matured enough for decent company.

"That's *all?*" The Captain spoke for the first time, aghast at what this meant – an end to the Earth's bold ventures with interstellar travel. Crude our ships might be, by galactic standards, but humanity was proud of them. They were a unifying force, binding fractious nations in a common cause. It was awful to imagine that our expedition might be the last.

The translator apparently failed to convey the Captain's sarcasm. The alien envoy-entity nodded in solemn agreement.

"Yes, that is all. So you may rejoice, in your own pathetic way, that your world is safe for you to use up or destroy any way you see fit, since that is the typical way most puerile species finish their brief lifespans. If, by some chance, you escape this fate, you will eventually be allowed to send forth your best and brightest to serve in carefully chosen roles, earning eventual acceptance on the lowest rungs of proper society."

Jane Fingal growled. "Why you puffed-up pack of pseudo-pommie bast –"

I cut in with urgent speed. "Excuse me, but there is one thing I fail to understand. You spoke earlier of an "evaluation." Does this mean that our fate is *not* automatic?"

The alien emissary regarded me for a long time, as if pondering whether I deserved an answer, Finally, it must have decided I was not that much lower than my crewmates, anyway. It acknowledged my query with a nod.

"There *is* an exception – if you can prove a relationship with a citizen race. To determine that possibility was the purpose of my query about species-lineage."

"Ah, now it becomes clear," Mohandas Nayyal said. "You want to know if we are *genetically related* to one of your high-born castes. Does this imply that those legends may be true? That star beings have descended, from time to time, to engage in sexual congress with our ancestors? By co-mingling their seed with ours, they meant to generously endow and improve our..."

He trailed off as we all saw the N'Gorm quiver. Somehow, disgust was conveyed quite efficiently across its expressive "face."

"Please, do not be repulsive in your bizarre fantasies. The behavior you describe is beyond contemplation, even by the mentally ill. Not only is it physically and biologically absurd, but it assumes the high-born might *wish* to improve the stock of bestial nuisances. Why in the universe would they want to do such a thing?"

Ignoring the bald insult, Meyers, the exobiologist added —.

"It's unlikely for another reason. Human DNA has been probed and analyzed for three centuries. We have a pretty good idea where most of it came from. We're creatures of the Earth, no doubt about it."

When he saw members of the contact team glaring at him, Meyers shrugged. "Oh, it would all come out in time, anyway. Don't you think they'd analyze any claim we made?"

"Correct," buzzed the translator. "And we would bill you for the effort."

"Well, I'm still confused," claimed our Uzbecki memeticist. "You make it sound as if there is no way we could be related to one of your citizen-races, so why this grilling about our genealogy?"

"A formality, required by law. In times past, a few exceptional cases won status by showing that they possessed common genes with high-born ones."

"And how did these commonalities come about?" Mobutu asked, still miffed over the rejection of his earlier claims.

The N'Gorm whistled yet another sigh. "Not all individuals of every species behave circumspectly. Some, of noble birth, have been known to go down to planets, seeking thrills, or testing their mettle to endure filth and heavy gravity."

"In other words, they go slumming!" Jane Fingal laughed. "Now *those* are the only blokes I'd care to meet, in your whole damn Federation."

I caught Jane's eye, gesturing for restraint. She needn't make things worse than they already were. The whole of Earth would watch recordings of what passed here today.

Nechemia Meyers shook his head. "I can see where all this is leading. When galactics go *slumming*, as Jane colorfully put it, they risk unleashing alien genes into the ecosystem of a nursery world. This is forbidden interference in the natural development of such planets. It *also* makes possible a genetic link that could prove embarrassing later, when that world spawns a star-travelling race."

The translator buzzed gratification. "At last, I have succeeded in conveying the basic generalities. Now, before we take your ship in tow, and begin the quarantine of your wretched home system, I am required by law to offer you a chance. Do you wish formally to claim such a genetic link to one of our citizen races? Remember that we will investigate in detail, at your expense."

A pall seemed to settle over the assembled humans. This was not as horrible as some of the worst literary fantasies about alien contact, but it was pretty bad. Apparently, the galaxy was ruled by an aristocracy of age and precedence. One that jealously guarded its status behind a veneer of hypocritical law.

"How can we *know* whether or not to make such a claim!" Kwenzi Mobutu protested. "Unless we meet your high castes for ourselves."

"That will not happen. Not unless your claim is upheld."

"But —"

"It hardly matters," inserted Nechemia, glumly.

We turned and the Captain asked — "What do you mean?"

"I mean that we cannot make such a claim. The evidence refutes it. All we need is to look at the history of life on Earth.

"Consider, friends. Why did we think for so long that we were alone in the cosmos? It wasn't just that our radio searches for intelligent life turned up nothing, decade after decade. Aliens *could* have efficient technologies that make them abandon radio, the way we gave up signal-drums. This is exactly what we found to be the case.

"No, a much stronger argument for our uniqueness lay in the sedimentary rocks of our own world.

"If intelligent life was plentiful, someone would invent starships and travel. Simple calculations showed that just one such outbreak, if it flourished, could fill the galaxy with its descendants in less than fifty million years... and that assumed ship technology far cruder than this N'Gorm dreadnought hovering nearby."

He gestured toward the sleek, gleaming hull that had accelerated so nimbly in response to Jane Fingal's hail.

"Imagine such a life-swarm, sweeping across the galaxy, settling every habitable world in sight. It's what we *humans* thought we'd do, once we escaped Earth's bonds, according to most science fiction tales. A prairie fire of colonization that radically changes every world it touches, forever mixing and re-shuffling each planet's genetic heritage."

The emissary conceded. "It is illegal, but it has happened, from time to time."

Meyers nodded. "Maybe it occurred elsewhere, but not on Earth."

"How can you be sure?" I asked.

"Because we can read Earth's biography in her rocks. For more than two billion years, our world was "prime real estate," as one great 20th century writer once put it. Our planet had oceans and a decent atmosphere, but no living residents higher than crude prokaryotes – bacteria and algae – simmering in the sea. In all that time, until the Eukaryotic Explosion half a billion years ago, any alien interference would have profoundly changed the course of life on our world."

Sullen silence reigned, until Jane Fingal edged forward.

"This 'explosion' you spoke of. What was that?"

"The *Eukaryotic Explosion*," Meyers explained, "occurred about 560 million years ago, when there suddenly evolved nucleated cells, crammed with sophisticated organelles. Soon after, there arose multi-celled organisms, invertebrates, vertebrates, fishes, dinosaurs, and primates. But the important datum is the two billion years before that, when even the most careful of colonizations, or even brief visits, would have utterly changed Earth's ecology, by infecting it with advanced alien organisms we would later see in sediments. Even visitors who flushed their *toilets* carelessly..."

Meyers trailed off as our astronomer made choking sounds, covering her mouth. Finally, Jane burst out with deep guffaws, laughing so hard that she nearly doubled over. We waited until finally Jane wiped her eyes and explained.

"Sorry, mates. It's just that... well, somethin' hit me when Nechemia mentioned holy altars."

I checked my memory files and recalled the euphemism, popular in Australian English. Every Aussie home is said to contain at least one porcelain "altar," where adults who have over-indulged with food or drink often kneel and pray for relief, invoking the beer deities, "Ralph" or "Ruth." Most of the time, these altars have other, more mundane uses.

Kwenzi Mobutu seemed torn between outrage over Jane's behavior and delight that it was all being recorded.

"And what insight did this offer you?" He asked with a tightly controlled voice.

"Oh, with your interest in genealogy you'll love this, Kwenzi," Jane assured, in a friendly tone.

She turned to Nechemia.

"You say there couldn't have been any alien interference before the Eukaryotic Explosion, and after that, everything on Earth seems to be part of the same tree of life, right? Neither of those long periods seem to show any trace of outside interference."

The Israeli nodded, and Jane smiled.

"But what about the explosion, itself? Isn't that *just* the sort of sudden event you say would be visible in rocks, if alien garbage ever got dumped on Earth?"

Meyers frowned, knotting his brow.

"Well... ye-e-e-es. Off hand, I cannot think of any perfect refutation, providing you start out assuming a general similarity in amino and nucleic acid coding... and compatible protein structures. That's not too far-fetched.

"From that point on, prokaryotic and early eukaryotic genes mixed, but the eukaryote seed stock *might* have come, quite suddenly –"

A short squeal escaped the alien emissary.

"This is true? Your life history manifested such a sudden transformation on so basic a level? From un-nucleated to fully competent multicellular organisms? How rapid was this change?"

Meyers shook his head. "No one has been able to parse the boundary thinly enough to tell. But clearly it was on the order of a million years, or perhaps much less. Some hypothesize a chain of fluke mutations, leveraging on each other rapidly. But that explanation *did* always seem a bit too pat. There are just too many sudden, revolutionary traits to explain..."

He looked up at Jane, with a new light in his eyes.

"You aren't joking about this, are you? I mean, we could be onto something! I wonder why this never occurred to us before?"

The Captain uttered a short laugh.

"Trust an Australian to think of it. They don't give a damn *what* you think about their ancestors."

A flurry of motion drew our eyes to the tunnel leading to the N'Gorm ship, just in time to catch sight of the envoy-entity, fleeing our presence in a state of clear panic. A seal hissed shut and vibrations warned that the huge vessel was about to detach. We made our own prudent exit, hurrying back to our ship.

Last to re-board was Kwenzi Mobutu, wearing a bleak look on his face, paler than I had ever seen him. The African aristocrat winced as Jane Fingal offered a heartfelt, Australian prayer of benediction, aimed at the retreating N'Gorm frigate.

"May Ruth follow you everywhere, mate, and keep you busy at her altar."

Jane laughed again, and finished with a slurpy, *flushing* sound.

Many years have passed since that epiphany on the spacelanes. Of all of the humans present when we held the fateful meeting, only I, the one made of durable silicon and brass, still live to tell an eyewitness-tale.

By the laws of Earth, I am equal to any biological human being, despite galactic rules that would let me be enslaved. No noble genes lurk in *my* cells. No remnants of ruffians who went slumming long ago, merging their heritage with scummy mats at the fringes of a tepid sea. I carry no DNA from those alien rapscallions, those high-born ones who carelessly gave Earth an outlawed gift, a helpful push. But my kind was *designed* by the heirs of that little indiscretion, so I can share the poignant satisfaction brought by recent events.

For decade after decade, ever since that fateful meeting between the stars, we have chased Federation ships, who always fled like scoundrels evading a subpoena. Sometimes our explorers would arrive at one of their habitat clusters, only to find vast-empty cities, abandoned in frantic haste to avoid meeting us, or to prevent our emissaries from uttering one terrible word –

Cousin!

It did them no good in the long run. Eventually, we made contact with the august, honest *Kutathi*, the judges, who admitted our petition before them.

The galactic equivalent of a cosmo-biological *paternity suit*.

And now, the ruling has come down at last, leaving Earth's accountants to scratch their heads in awe over the damages we have been awarded, and the official status we have won.

As for our unofficial *social position,* that is another matter. Our having the right to vote in high councils will not keep most of the haughty aliens from snubbing Earthlings for a long time to come. (Would *we* behave any better, if a strain of our intestinal flora suddenly began demanding a place at the banquet table? I hope so, but you can never tell until you face the situation for yourself.)

None of that matters as much as the freedom – to come and go as we please. To buy and sell technologies. To learn... and eventually to teach.

The Kutathi judges kindly told our emissaries that humans seem to have a knack, a talent, for *the law.* Perhaps it will be our calling, the Kutathi said. It makes an odd kind of sense, given the jokes people have long told about the genetic nature of lawyers.

Well, so be it.

Among humans of all races and nations, there is agreement. There is common cause. Something has to change. The snooty ways of high-born clans must give way, and we are just the ones to help make it happen. We'll find other loopholes in this rigid, inane class system, other ways to help spring more young races out of quarantine, until at last the stodgy old order crumbles.

Anyway, who cares what aristocrats think of us, their illegitimate cousins, the long-fermented fruit of their bowels?

Jane Fingal wrote our anthem, long ago. It is a stirring song, hauntingly kindred to *Waltzing Matilda,* full of verve, gumption, and the spirit of rebellion. Like the *1812 Overture,* it can't properly be played without an added instrument. Only in this case, the guest soloist plays no cannon, but a porcelain *altar,* one that swishes, churns and gurgles with the soulful strains of destiny.

Story Notes

Do I return, now and again, to themes of rebellion?

It occurs to me only now, while editing stories for this volume, that resistance against unfair authority may be one of my literary obsessions. Well, that's no shocker. A lot of authors share the same reflex. For one thing, Suspicion of Authority (SoA) is a core tradition in western storytelling. For another – well – nothing helps propel a pulse-pounding plot better than villainy by an oppressive-elite!

Still, I hope to think my rebellions at least have some originality... like the proudly-porcelain angle in "Fortitude."

Of course that story also fits into another of my ongoing themes, that of First Contact. Looking back, I see that the "alien" has always obsessed me. In my choice of astrophysics as a core professional career, plus 35 years engagement in SETI. (Publishing the main review article in the field, tabulating 100+ explanations for the Fermi Paradox.) And, of course, in science fiction explorations of this possible encounter scenario... then that one... and then...

The stories in this section – Who We'll Meet – are mostly "think-pieces" – in which some matter of logic or science plays a role, fully as important as any of the characters or, indeed, plot. Einstein called this process "gedankenexperiment" or thought-experimentation. It may not be the highest form of literature... but there has always been a place, in science fiction, for taking pure joy just by exploring ideas.

Next, we have another simple tale in which Contact comes with a cosmological twist.

An Ever-Reddening Glow

◇

1.

We were tooling along at four nines to c, relative to the Hercules Cluster, when our Captain came on the intercom to tell us we were being tailed.

The announcement interrupted my afternoon lecture on Basic Implosive Geometrodynamics, as I explained principles behind the *Fulton's* star drive to youths who had been children when we boarded, eight subjective years ago.

"In ancient science fiction," I had just said, "you can read of many fanciful ways to cheat the limit of the speed of light. Some of these seemed theoretically possible, especially when we learned how to make microscopic singularities by borrowing and twisting spacetime. Unfortunately, wormholes have a nasty habit of crushing anything that enters them, down to the size of a Planck unit, and it would take a galaxy-sized mass to "warp" space over interstellar distances. So we must propel ourselves along through normal space the old-fashioned way, by Newton's law of action and reaction... albeit in a manner our ancestors would never have dreamed."

I was about to go on, and describe the physics of metric-surfing, when the Captain's voice echoed through the ship.

"It appears we are being followed," he announced. "Moreover, the vessel behind us is sending a signal, urging us to cut engines and let them come alongside."

It was a microscopic ship that had been sent flashing to intercept us, massing less than a microgram, pushed by a beam of intense light from a nearby star. The same light (thoroughly red-shifted) was what we had seen reflected in our rear-viewing mirrors, causing us to stop our BIG motors and coast, awaiting rendezvous.

Picture that strange meeting, amid the vast, yawning emptiness between two spiral arms, with all visible stars crammed by the Doppler effect into a narrow, brilliant hoop, blue along its forward rim and deep red in back. The *Fulton* was like a whale next to a floating wisp of plankton as we matched velocities. Our colony ship, filled with humans and other Earthlings, drifted alongside a gauzy, furled umbrella of ultra-sheer fabric. An umbrella that *spoke*.

"Thank you for acceding to our request," it said, after our computers established a linguistic link. "I represent the intergalactic Corps of Obligate Pragmatism."

We had never heard of the institution, but the Captain replied with aplomb.

"You don't say? And what can we do for you?"

"You can accommodate us by engaging in a discussion concerning your star drive."

"Yes? And what about our star drive?"

"It operates by the series-implosion of micro-singularities, which you create by borrowing spacetime-metric, using principles of quantum uncertainty. Before this borrowed debit comes due, you allow the singularities to re-collapse behind you. This creates a spacetime ripple, a wake that propels you ahead without any need on your part to expend matter or energy."

I could not have summarized it better to my students.

"Yes?" The Captain asked succinctly. "So?"

"This drive enables you to travel swiftly, in relativistic terms, from star system to star system."

"It has proved rather useful. We use it quite extensively."

"Indeed, that is the problem," answered the wispy star probe. "I have chased you across vast distances in order to ask you to stop."

No wonder it had used such a strange method to catch up with us! The C.O.P. agent claimed that our BIG drive was immoral, unethical, and dangerous!

"There are alternatives," it stressed. "You can travel as I do, pushed by intense beams cast from your point of origin. Naturally, in that case you would have to discard your corporeal bodies and go about as software entities. I contain about a million such passengers, and will happily make room for your ship's company, if you wish to take up the offer of a free ride."

"No thank you," the Captain demurred. "We like corporeality, and do not find your means of conveyance desirable or convenient."

"But it is ecologically and cosmologically sound! Your method, to the contrary, is polluting and harmful."

This caught our attention. Only folk who have sensitivity to environmental concerns are allowed to colonize, lest we ruin the new planets we take under our care. This is not simply a matter of morality, but of self-interest, since our grandchildren will inherit the worlds we leave behind.

Still, the star probe's statement confused us. This time, I replied for the crew.

"Polluting? All we do is implode temporary micro black holes behind us and surf ahead on the resulting recoil of borrowed spacetime. What can be *polluting* about adding a little more space to empty space?"

"Consider," the COP probe urged. "Each time you do this, you add to the net distance separating your origin from your destination!"

"By a very small fraction," I conceded. "But meanwhile, we experience a powerful pseudo-acceleration, driving us forward nearly to the speed of light."

"That is very convenient for you, but what about the rest of us?"

"The ... rest... The rest of *whom?*"

"The rest of the universe!" the probe insisted, starting to sound petulant. "While you speed ahead, you increase the distance from point A to point B, making it marginally harder for the next voyager to make the same crossing."

I laughed. "*Marginally* is right! It would take millions of ships... *millions* of millions... to begin to appreciably affect interstellar distances, which are already increasing anyway, due to the cosmological expansion –"

The star-probe cut in.

"And where do you think that expansion comes from?"

⟡

I admit that I stared at that moment, speechless, until at last I found my voice with a hoarse croak.

"What..." I swallowed. "What do you mean by that?"

◊

The COPS have a mission. They speed around the galaxies – not just this one, but most of those we see in the sky – urging others to practice restraint. Beseeching the short-sighted to think about tomorrow. To refrain from spoiling things for future generations.

They have been at it for a very, very long time.

"You're not having much success, are you?" I asked, after partly recovering from the shock.

"No, we are not," the probe answered, morosely. "Every passing eon, the universe keeps getting larger. Stars get farther apart, making all the old means of travel less and less satisfying, and increasing the attraction of wasteful metric-surfing. It is so easy to do. Those who refrain are mostly older, wiser species. The young seldom listen."

I looked around the communications dome of our fine vessel, thronging with the curious, with our children, spouses and loved ones – the many species of humanity and its friends who make up the vibrant culture of organic beings surging forth across this corner of the galaxy. The COP was saying that we weren't alone in this vibrant enthusiasm to move, to explore, to travel swiftly and see what there was to see. To trade and share and colonize. To *go!*

In fact, it seemed we were quite typical.

"No," I replied, a little sympathetically this time. "I don't suppose they do."

2.

The morality-probes keep trying to flag us down, using entreaties, arguments and threats to persuade us to stop. But the entreaties don't move us. The arguments don't persuade. And the threats are as empty as the gaps between galaxies.

After many more voyages, I have learned that these frail, gnat-like COPS are ubiquitous, persistent, and futile. Most ships simply ignore the flickering light in the mirror, dismissing it as just another phenomenon of relativistic space, like the Star-Bow, or the ripples of expanding metric that throb each time we surge ahead on the exuberant wake of collapsing singularities.

I admit that I do see things a little differently, now. The universal expansion, that we had thought due to a "big bang" – accelerated by "dark energy" – is in fact, at least 50% exacerbated by vessels like ours, riding along on waves of pollution, filling space with more space, making things harder for generations to come.

It is hard for the mind to grasp – so *many* starships. So many that the universe is changing, every day, year, and eon that we continue to go charging around, caring only about ourselves and our immediate gratification.

Once upon a time, when everything was much closer, it might have been possible to make do with other forms of transportation. In those days, beings *could* have refrained. If they had, we might not need the BIG drive today. If those earlier wastrels had shown some restraint.

On the other hand, I guess they'll say the same thing about *us* in times to come, when stars and galaxies are barely visible to each other, separated by the vast gulfs that *we* of this era short-sightedly create.

Alas, it is hard to practice self-control when you are young, and so full of a will to see and do things as fast as possible. Besides, everyone *else* is doing it. What difference will our measly contribution make to slowing the mighty expansion of the universe? It's not as if we'd help matters much, if we alone stopped.

Anyway, the engines hum so sweetly. It feels good to cruise along at the redline, spearing the star-bow, pushing the speed limit all the way against the wall.

These days, we hardly glance in that mirror anymore... or pause to note the ever-reddening glow.

Story Notes

This story falls into the general category of "hard" science fiction, where the central issue is a technical or scientific question or possibility. SF can sometimes be used to illustrate such issues with delightful vividness and efficiency, doing more than just reiterating "eternal verities"!

In "An Ever-Reddening Glow," the one strong, stylistic component is irony.

Indeed, look around yourself.

Clearly, irony is one of the heaviest elements in the universe.

The following tale first appeared in the book *Isaac's Universe Volume One: The Diplomacy Guild*, an anthology of stories set in the Erthumoi universe of Isaac Asimov, a special edition published in his honor. My tale – another think-piece – was intended to work out the implications of an idea. Still...

The Diplomacy Guild

◇

"I have heard it suggested that you humans undergo this queer obsession because you live so hot and fast. You sense time's current at your backs, and so feel you must *copy* yourselves, in order to be two places at once."

Phss'aah's words flowed so musically from the translator grille that it was easy to lose the Cephallon philosopher's meaning in the harmonies. Anyway, I had been distracted for a moment by the whining of my other guest, a miserable Crotonite huddled in the corner – a pathetic figure, whimpering and uselessly flexing broken stubs that had once been powerful wings.

One more burdensome responsibility. I cursed fate and my boss's meddling for saddling me with the creature – cruelly scorned by its own kind, and yet Ambassador Plenipotentiary from a powerful interstellar race.

Phss'aah's words shook me from perusing my newest guest. I turned back to the huge tank taking up half the ship's Visitor Suite, where a vaguely porpoise-like form flailed oxygen-rich water into a froth.

"I'm sorry..." and I made the wet sound approximating Phss'aah's name as near as a descendant of Earth humans could form it. "I didn't quite catch that last remark."

Bubbles rose from the Cephallon's twin exhalation slits, and now I read what might be mild exasperation in the flex of his long snout. Instead of repeating himself, Phss'aah waved a four fingered flipper-arm toward the aqua-bot that shared his tank. The bulbous machine planted a sucker on the glassy wall and spoke in its owner's stead.

"I believe Master Phss'aah is proposing a hypothesis as to why humans – you Erthuma – were the only one of the Six Starfaring Races to invent true autonomous robots. He suggests it is because you have such short natural lifespans. Being ambitious, your race sought ways to extend itself artificially. In order to be many places at once, they put much of themselves into their machines."

I shook my head. "But our lives aren't any shorter than Locrians, or Nexians..."

"Correction," the robot interrupted. "You are counting up an individual's sum span of years, including all of his or her consecutive natural lifetimes. You've had four renewals, Ambassador Dorning, totaling three hundred and four standard Earth years.

"But my master apparently thinks your Erthumoi worldview is still colored by the way existence was for you during the ages leading to High Civilization. In any event, your race invented artificially intelligent constructs like me well before learning how to Renew."

The machine – and Phss'aah – did have a point. Not for the first time I tried to imagine what it must have been like for my ancestors, facing certain death after only a single span of less than nine standard decades. Why, at my first Renewal, I was still barely formed... an infant! I'd only completed one profession by then.

How strange that most humans, back in olden times, became parents as early as thirty years of age. In most modern nations of the modern Galactic Erthuma, you weren't even supposed to *think* about breeding until the middle of your second life.

All this time Phss'aah watched me through the glass with one eye, milky blue and inscrutable. I almost regretted the human-invented technology that enabled the Cephallon to use his robot mouthpiece as yet another veil to shelter behind. Though, of course, getting Phss'aah to rely on this fancy assistant-drone was actually quite a coup. The idea was to sell large numbers of such machines to the water race, and then each of the other Big Five, so they'd get used to what some called the "bizarre Erthumoi notion" of intelligent devices... robots. Frankly, we newcomer humans could use the trade credits.

"Hmm." I answered cautiously. "But the Crotonites –" I nodded toward my unwanted guest in the corner. "– have even shorter lifespans than natural, old style humans, and they don't renew! Why then, didn't *they* invent robots? It's not for lack of skill with machines. They're more nimble than anyone, with unsurpassed craftsmanship. And Space knows they have easily as much ambition as anyone."

The Cephallon surfaced to breathe, and returned trailing bubbles. When he spoke, the wall unit conveyed an Erthumoi translation, this time bypassing the robot.

"You reply logically and well for one of your kind. Certainly you and the Crotonites share the quick metabolisms characteristic of breathers of supercharged oxygen atmospheres. They, however, are oviparous flyers, while you are descended from arboreal mammals. Mammals are gregarious..."

"*Some* mammals."

"Indeed." And some of Phss'aah's irritation briefly showed. Cephallons do not like being interrupted while pontificating. That was exactly why I did it.

Diplomacy is such a delicate business.

"Perhaps another reason you invented intelligent machines was because –"

This time the interruption wasn't my fault. The door behind me hissed open and my own secretary 'bot hovered into the Guest Suite.

"Yes, Betty, what is it?" I asked.

"Messages received," she said tersely. "High priority, from Erthuma Diplomatic Guild, Long-Last Station."

Oblong, suspended in a cradle of invisible force, the machine looked nothing like her namesake, my most recent demi-wife on Long-Last. But, as it was imprinted with her voice and twenty of her personality engrams, this was a device one had to think of as possessing gender, and even a minimal right to courtesy. "Thank you," I told the auto-sec. "I'll be right up."

Assuming dismissal, Betty turned and departed. From the corner of the suite, the Crotonite lifted his head and watched the machine briefly. Something in those cat-like eyes seemed to track it as a hunter might follow prey. But this Crot wasn't going to be chasing flitting airborne victims above the forests of any thick-aired world. Never again. Where once he had carried great, tent-like wings, powerfully muscled and heavier than his torso, now the short, deep-chested being wore mere nubs – scarred from recent amputation.

The Crotonite noticed my look, and snarled fiercely. "Plant-eating grub! Turn away your half-blind, squinty orbs. You have no status to cast them on my shame!"

That was in Crotonoi, of course. Few Erthumoi would have understood so rapid and slurred an alien diatribe. But my talents and training had won me this post. Cursed talents. Double cursed training!

By my own species' standards of politeness I'd have accepted the rebuke and turned away, respecting his privacy. Instead, I snapped right back in my own language.

"*You* dare throw insults at me? You who are broken and wingless and shall never again fly? *You* who shame your race by neglecting the purpose for which you were cast down? Here, try doing this!"

I flexed my strong legs and bounded high in the half gravity of the Guest Suite. The cripple, of course, could not manage it with his puny legs. I landed facing him.

"You're a diplomat, Jirata. You won your fallen state by being *better* than your peers, the first so chosen for a bold new experiment. Your job is now to try something new to your folk... to *empathize* with ground-walking life forms like me, and even swimming forms like Phss'aah. To make that effort, you were assigned to me, a burden I did not ask for, nor welcome. Nor do I predict success.

"Still, you can *try*. It's the purpose of your existence. The reason your people didn't leave you beneath some tree to starve, and instead still speak your name to the winds, as if you were alive.

"*Try*, Jirata. Just try, and the least you'll win is that I, personally, will stop being cruel to you."

The Crotonite looked away, but I could tell he was struggling with a deep perplexity.

"Why should you stop being cruel?" he asked. "You have every advantage."

I sighed. This was going to take time.

"Because I'd rather like you than hate you, Jirata. And if you don't understand that, consider this. Your job is to investigate a new mode of diplomacy for your people. *Empathy* is what you must discover to succeed. So while I'm away, why not converse with Phss'aah? I'm sure he'll be patient with you. He doesn't know how to be anything else."

That was untrue of course. Phss'aah gave me a look of exasperation at this unwelcome assignment. For his part, Jirata glanced at the Cephallon, floating in all that water, and let out a keening of sheer disgust.

I left the room.

◇

"Actually, there are two messages of Red Priority," Captain Smeet told me. She handed over a pair of decoded flimsies. I thanked her, went to the privacy corner of the ship's bridge, and laid the first of the shimmering, gauzy message films over my head. Immediately, the gossamer fabric wrapped my face, covering eyes and ears, leaving only my nostrils free. It began vibrating and, after a momentary blurriness, sight and sound enveloped me.

My boss – the slave driver whose faith in my abilities was anything but reassuring – looked across his desk. He seemed to feel there was no end to the number of tasks I could take on at once.

"Patty," he said. "Sorry about dumping the Crotonite on you. He's part of an experimental program initiated by the Seven Sovereigns' League. You'll recall that particular Crotoni confederacy suffered rather badly for bungling the negotiations at Maioplar, fifty years ago. In desperation, they're trying something radical to revise their way of dealing with other races. I guess they're testing it on us Erthuma because we're the least influential of the Six. If it flops, our opinion won't matter much.

"In answer to your last query – I have no idea if the Seven Sovereigns cleared this with the other Crotonite nation-states, or if they're doing it on their own. Crot intra-race politics is such a tangle, who can tell? That's why the Diplomacy Guild decided to farm out Jirata and the others like him to our roving emissaries. Try to figure out what's going on, far away from media and the like. I'm sure you understand."

"Right, Maxwell." I gave a very un-ladylike snort. Back on Long-Last, Betty used to chastise me for that. But I never heard any of our husbands complain.

"Excellent, Patty," he went on, as if he was sure my reaction would be complete enthusiasm. "Who knows, maybe the League's idea of using crippled bats as envoys may work, so let's put it on high priority, okay?"

"As high as preventing a break in the Essential Protocols?" I muttered. But I knew the answer.

"Of course, nothing is to stand in the way of getting King Zardee to toe the line on replicants. If he gives you any trouble, just tell that freon-blooded son of a b–"

I'd heard enough and ripped the flimsy off. It instantly began dissolving into inert gas.

"Orders, madam?" Captain Smeet looked at me coolly, expectantly.

"Proceed to Planet Nine of this system, and please beam to King Zardee that I'll wait no longer for him to prepare for my arrival. If he plans to shoot us out of the sky, let him do so and live with the consequences."

Smeet nodded. I could have asked her to take me wet-diving in the nearby sun of Prongee System and she'd have found a way to do it, keeping her opinion of crazy diplomats to herself. That was more than *I* sometimes was able to do, after listening to Maxwell for a while.

Why success followed that awful old man around so, I could never understand.

◇

An angry visage greeted me, glaring out of the communications tank. I had been sent on this mission because, among all the different styles of government used by various Erthumoi nation-worlds, royal-inheritance domains were among the quirkiest, and I had the most experience in our sector dealing with arrogant creatures known as kings.

Some were smooth. But this one actually reminded me of Jirata as he growled. "We are not accustomed to being made to wait," he said as I stepped into the Communications Lounge. Ignoring the remark, I curtsied in the manner customary for women in his commonwealth.

"Your majesty would not have liked to see me dressed as I was when you called. It took a few moments to make myself presentable."

Zardee grunted. I felt his eyes survey me like a piece of real estate, and recognized covetousness in them. I always find it amazing how many Erthumoi societies left their males with these unaltered, visually stimulated lust patterns. And Zardee was nearly eight hundred standard years old!

Never mind. I'd use whatever chinks in his armor I could find.

"I accept your apology," he said in a softer tone. "And I must offer my regrets in turn for keeping such a comely and accomplished lady waiting at the boundary. I now invite you to join me on my yacht for some refreshment and entertainment I'm sure you'll find distracting."

"You are most gracious, Your Majesty. However, first I really must inspect your mining establishment on the ninth planet of this system."

His visage transformed once more to anger, and again I felt astonishment this system's folk put up with such a monarch. The attractions of kingship are well documented, but sentimental indulgence can become an illness if it isn't looked to.

"There's nothing on my mining world of interest to the Diplomacy Guild!" he snapped. "You have no authority to force yourself upon me!"

This from a fellow so atavistic, I had no doubt he would chain me to a bed in his seraglio, were it in his power. I kept my amusement to myself. "I'm sure, Your Majesty, that you wouldn't want it to get out among your Erthumoi and Nexian neighbors that you have something to hide..."

"*All* kingdoms and sovereign worlds have secrets, foolish woman. I have a right to keep vital security information from the prying eyes of outsiders."

I nodded. "But not when those secrets violate the Essential Protocols of the Erthuma. Or is it your intention to join the Outlaw Worlds, foregoing the services of my Guild?"

For a moment it looked as if he might declare just such intentions. But he stopped. Commercial repercussions would be catastrophic. That step might push his people too far.

"The Essential Protocols don't cover much," he said, slowly. "My subjects have access to Erthumoi ombudsmen. I vet my treaties past Guild lawyers, and my ship captains report to the Guild on activities observed among the Other Five races. That is all that's required of me."

"You are forgetting Article Six of the Protocols," I said.

Blinking, Zardee spoke slowly. "Exactly what do you accuse me of, Ambassador?"

I shrugged. "Such a strong word. There are rumors, Majesty... that *someone* is violating the rule against creating fully autonomous replicants."

His face reddened three shades. I did not need a Nexian's insight or Cephallon's empathy to tell I'd struck home. At the same time though, it was not *guilt* I read in the monarch's eyes, but rather something akin to *shame*. I found the reaction most interesting.

"I'll rendezvous with your ship above the ninth planet," he said tersely, and cut the channel. No doubt Captain Smeet and the king's captain were already exchanging coordinates by the time I departed the lounge and headed for the Guest Suite, to see how things were progressing there.

I shouldn't have expected miracles from Phss'aah. After all, Jirata the Crotonite was my responsibility, not his. But, at least, I might have hoped for *tact* from a Cephallon diplomat. Instead, I returned to find Phss'aah carrying on a long monologue directed at the crippled Croton, who huddled in his corner glaring back at the creature in the tank. And if looks could maim there wouldn't have been much of anything left but bloody water.

"... so unlike the other Starfaring Races, we Cephallons find this human innovation of articulate, intelligent machines useful and fascinating, even if it is also puzzling and bizarre. Take your own case, Jirata. Would not a loyal mechanical surrogate be of use to one such as you, especially in your present condition? Helping you fend for..."

Phss'aah noticed my return and interrupted his monologue. "Ah, Patty. You have returned. I was just explaining to our comrade here how useful it is to have machines able to anticipate your requirements, and of repairing and maintaining themselves. Even the Crotonites' marvelous, intricate devices, hand-made and unique, lack that capability."

"We do not need it!" Jirata spat. "A machine should be elegant, light, compact, efficient. It should be a thing of beauty and craftsmanship! Pah! What pride can a human have in such a monster as a robot? Why, I hear they even allow the things to design and build *more* robots, which build still others! What can come about when an engineer lets his creations pass beyond personal control?"

I felt an eerie chill. Glad as I was that Jirata seemed, in his own style, to be emerging from his funk, I didn't like the direction this conversation was headed.

"What about that, Patty?" Phss'aah asked, turning to face me. "I have consulted much Erthumoi literature having to do with man-created machine intelligence, and there runs through much of it a thread of warning. Philosophers speak of the very fear Jirata expressed... calling it the "Frankenstein Syndrome." I do not know the origins of that term, but it has an apt sound for dread of destruction at the hands of one's own creations."

I nodded. "Fortunately, we Erthuma have a tradition of *liking* to frighten ourselves with scary stories, then finding ways to avoid the very scenario described. It's called Warning Fiction, and historians now credit that art form with our species' survival across the bomb-to-starship crisis time."

"Most interesting. But tell me please, how did you come to choose a way to keep control over your creations? The Locrians certainly have trouble, whenever a clutch of male eggs is neglectfully laid outside the careful management of professional brooders, and the Samians have their own problems with gene-bred animals. How do you manage your robots then?"

How indeed? I wondered at the way this discussion had, apparently naturally, just happened upon a topic so deadly and coincidentally apropos to my other concerns.

"Well, one approach is to have the machines programmed with deeply coded fundamental operating rules, or robotic laws, which they cannot disobey without causing paralysis. This method serves well as a first line of defense, especially for simple machines.

Unfortunately, those *laws of robotics* proved tragically inadequate when the machines' growing intelligence enabled them to *interpret* those laws in new, rather distressing ways. Lawyer programs can be terribly tricky, we found. Today, unleashing a new one without proper checks is punishable by death."

"I understand. We Cephallons reserve that punishment for the lawyers themselves. I'll remember to advise my Council about this, if we decide to buy more of your high-end robots. Do continue."

"Well, one experimental approach, with the very brightest machines, has been to actually raise them as if they were Erthumoi children. In one of our confederations there are several thousand robots that have been granted provisional status as junior citizens –"

"Obscenity!" Jirata interrupted with a shout.

I merely shrugged. "It's an experiment. The idea is that we'll have little to fear from super-smart robots if they think of themselves as fellow Erthuma, who just happen to be built differently. Thus the hope is that they'll be as loyal as our grand-children, and like our grand-children, pose no threat even if they grow smarter than us."

"Fascinating!" the Cephallon cried. "But then, what happens when..."

Point after point, he spun out the logical chain. I was drawn into Phss'aah's intellectual enthusiasm. This was one of the reasons I entered the Diplomacy Guild, after all... in order to see old things in entirely new light, through alien eyes, as if for the first time.

In his corner, I sensed even Jirata paying attention, almost in spite of himself. I had never before seen a Crotonite willing to sit and listen for so long. Perhaps this cruel and desperate experiment of theirs might actually bear fruit?

Then Jirata exploded with another set of disdainful curses, deriding one of Phss'aah's extrapolations. And I knew that, even if the experiment worked, it was going to be a long struggle.

Meanwhile, I felt the minutes flicker by, counting down to my encounter with Zardee.

◇

Even with hyperdrive it's next to impossible to run anything like an "Empire," in the ancient sense of the word. Not across starlanes as vast as the Galaxy. Left to their own devices, the scattered colony worlds – daughters of faraway Earth – would probably have diverged long ago... each choosing a separate path, conservative or outlandish, into a unique destiny. Without opposition, we humans do tend to fraction our loyalties.

But there *was* opposition of sorts, when we emerged into space. The Other Five were already there. Strange, barely knowable creatures with technologies at first quite a bit ahead of ours. In playing a furious game of catch-up, the Erthumoi worlds nearly all agreed to a pact... a loose confederation bound together by a civil service. Foremost of these is the Diplomacy Guild.

And foremost among the rules agreed to by all signatories to the Essential Protocol is this – not to undertake any unilateral actions which might unite other starfaring cultures against the Erthuma. In my lifetime, four crises have loomed which caused strife over this provision – in which some community of Earth-descent was found to be engaged in dangerous or inciteful activities. Once, a small trade alliance of Erthumoi worlds almost provoked a Locrian Queendom to the point of violence. Each time, the episode was soothed over by the Guild, but on two of those occasions it took severe threats... arraying all of the offending community's Erthumoi neighbors in a united show of intimidation... before the reckless ones backed down.

Now I feared it was about to happen again. And this time, the conditions for a quick and simple solution weren't encouraging. Zardee's system lay nearby a cluster of stars very rich in material resources, heavy elements given off by a spate of supernovas a few million years ago. Asteroids abundant in every desirable mineral were plentiful there.

Now normally, this wouldn't matter much. The galaxy is not resource poor. We are not living in Earth's desperate Twenty-first Century, after all.

But what if one of the Six embarked on a population binge? Still fresh among we Erthuma is memory of such a calamity. Earth's frail ecosystem is still recovering from the stress laid on her before we grew up and moved away to give our ancient mother a rest.

Of course the galaxy is vast beyond all planetary measure. Still, it doesn't take much computer time to extrapolate what could happen if any of the Six Starfarers decided to have fun making babies fast. Take our own species as an example. At human breeding rates typical of pre-spacefaring Earth, and given the efficiency of hyperdrive to speed colonization, we could fill every Earthlike world in the galaxy within a million years. Among the catastrophic consequences of such a hasty, uncontrolled expansion would be destruction of various lifeforms already in existence on those worlds.

Whereupon, of course, our descendants would run out of Earth-like planets. What then? Might they not chafe at the limitations on ter-raforming... the agreement among the Six only to convert dead worlds, never worlds already bearing life?

Consider the fundamental reason why there has never been a major war among the Six. It's their *incompatibility* – the fact that each others' worlds are respectively unpleasant or deadly to the other five – that maintains the peace. But what if overpopulation started us imagining we could get away with turning a high CO_2 world into an Oxy-rich planet, say. How would the Locrians react to that?

The same logic applied to the Other Five, each capable of its own population burst. Only their irascible temperaments and short life-spans keep the Crotonites from over-breeding, for instance. And the Locrians, first of the Six upon the spacelanes, admitted once in rare candor that the urge to spew forth a myriad of eggs is still powerful within them, constrained only by social and religious pressures.

The problem is this – what seems at first to be a stable situation is anything but stable. If the Locrians seem ancient from our Erthumoi perspective, by the clock of the stars they are nearly as recent as we. Three hundred thousand years is a mere eyeblink. The coincidence of all Six appearing virtually at the same time is one that has Erthumoi and Cephallon and Naxian scholars completely puzzled.

Yes, we're all at peace now. But computer simulations show utter calamity if any race looks about to take off on a population binge. And despite the Erthumoi monopoly on self-aware machines, all of the Six do have computers.

As my ship docked with the resplendent yacht of the King of Prongee, I looked off in the direction of the Gorch Cluster, with its rainbow of bright, metal rich stars, and its promise of riches beyond what anyone alive might need.

Beyond present needs, yes. But perhaps not beyond what any one man might *want*.

Captain Smeet signaled the locks would open in a few minutes. I took advantage of that interval to use a viewer and check in on my guests.

Within his tank, Phss'aah was getting another rub-down from his personal robot valet. Meanwhile, the Cephallon continued an apparent monologue.

"... how mystics of several races explain the sudden and simultaneous appearance of starfarers in the galaxy. After all, is it not puzzling that awkward creatures such as we water dwellers, or the Samians, took to the stars, when so many skilled, mechanically minded races, such as the Lenglils and Forttts, never even thought of it, and rejected spaceflight when it was offered them?"

From his corner of the room, Jirata flapped his wing nubs as if dismissing an unpleasant thought. "It is obscene that any but those who personally fly should ever have achieved the heights."

I felt pleased. By Crotonite standards, Jirata was being positively outgoing and friendly. Like a good Cephallon diplomat, Phss'aah seemed not to notice the insults.

Captain Smeet signaled and I shut off the viewer reluctantly. There were times when, irritating as he was, Phss'aah could be fascinating to listen to. Now though, I had business to discuss, and no lesser matter, possibly, than the long-term survival of the Erthuma.

"My industrial robots are mining devices, pure and simple. They threaten no one!"

I watched the activity on the surface of the ninth planet. Although it was an airless body, crater-strewn and wracked by ancient lava seams, it seemed at first that I was looking down on the veldt of some prairie world, covered from horizon to horizon with roaming herds of ungulates. Though these ruminants were not living creatures, they moved as if they were. I even saw "mothers" pause in their grazing to "nurse" their "offspring".

Of course what they were grazing on was the dusty, metal-rich surface soil of the planet. Across their broad backs, solar collectors powered the conversion of those raw materials into refined parts. Within each of these browsing cows there grew a tiny duplicate of itself, which the artificial beasts then gave birth to, and then fed still more refined materials straight through to adulthood.

There was nothing particularly unusual about this scene so far. Back before we Erthuma achieved starflight it was machines such as these that changed our destiny, from paupers on a half-ruined world, short of resources, to beings wealthy enough to demand a place among the Six.

An ancient mathematician named John Von Neumann had predicted the eventuality of robots able to make copies of themselves. When such creatures were let loose on the Earth's moon, within a few years they had multiplied into the millions. Then, half of them had been reprogrammed to make consumer goods instead — and suddenly our wealth was, compared to what it had been, as Twentieth Century man's had been to the Neanderthal.

But in every new thing there are always dangers. We found this out when some of the machines *refused* their new programming, and even began evading the harvesters.

"I see no hound mechanisms," I told King Zardee. "You have no mutant-detecting dog-bots patrolling the herds? Searching for mutants?"

He shrugged. "A useless, needless expense. We're in a part of the galaxy low in cosmic rays, and our design is well shielded. I've shown you the statistics. Our new replicants demonstrate breakthroughs in both efficiency and stability."

I shook my head, unimpressed. Figures were one thing. Galactic survival was another matter entirely.

"Please show me how the mechanisms are fitted with their enabling and remote shut-down keys, your Majesty. I don't see any robo-cowboys at work. How and when are the calves converted into adults? Are they called in to a central point?"

"It happens right out on the range," Zardee said proudly. "I see no reason to force every calf to go to a factory in order to get its keys. We program each cow to manufacture its calf's keys on the spot."

Madness! I balled my hands into fists in order to keep my diplomat's reserve. The idiot!

With deliberate calmness I faced him. "Your Majesty, that makes the keys completely meaningless. Their original and entire *purpose* is to make sure that no Von Neumann replicant device ever reaches maturity without coming to an Erthumoi-run facility for inspection. It's our ultimate guarantee the machines remain under our control, and that their numbers do not explode."

Zardee laughed. "I've heard it before, this fear of fairy tales. My dear beautiful young woman, surely you don't take seriously those Frankenstein stories in the pulp flimsies, about replicants running away and devouring planets? Entire solar systems?" He guffawed.

I shrugged. "It does not matter how likely or unlikely such scenarios are. What matters is how the prospect *appears* to the Other Five. For twelve centuries we've downplayed this potential outcome of automation, because our best alienists think the Others would find it appalling. It's the reason replicant restrictions are written into the Protocols, your Majesty."

I gestured at the massed herds down below. "What you've done here is utterly irresponsible..."

I stopped, because Zardee was smiling.

"You fear a chimera, dear diplomat. For I've already proven you have nothing to worry about in regard to alien opinion."

"What do you mean?"

"I mean that I've *already* shown these devices to representatives of many Locrian, Samian, and Nexian communities, several of whom have already taken delivery of breeding stock."

My mouth opened and closed. "But... but what if they equip the machines with space-transport ability? You..."

Zardee blinked. "What are you talking about? Of *course* the models I provided are space adapted. Their purpose is to be asteroid mining devices, after all. It's a breakthrough! Not only do they reproduce rapidly and efficiently, but they also transport themselves wherever the customer sets his beacon..."

I did not stay to listen to the rest. Filled with anger and despair, I turned away and left him to stammer into silence behind me. I had calls to make, without any delay.

◇

Maxwell took the news well, all considered.

"I've already traced three of the contracts," he told me by hyperwave. "We've managed to get the Naxians to agree to a delay, long enough for us to lean on Zardee and alter the replicants' key system. The Naxians didn't understand why we were so concerned, though they could tell we were worried. Clearly they haven't thought out the implications yet, and we're naturally reluctant to clue them in.

"The other contracts are going to be much harder. Two went to small Locrian Queendoms. One to a Samian solidity, and one to a Cephallon super-pod. I'm putting prime operatives onto each, but I'm afraid it's likely the replicants will go through at least five generations before we accomplish anything. By then it will probably be too late."

"You mean by then some will have mutated and escaped customer control?" I asked.

He shook his head. "According to Zardee's data, it should take longer than that to happen. No, by then I'm afraid our projections show each of the customers will be getting a handsome profit from his investment. The replicants will become essential to them, and impossible for us to regain control over."

"So what do you want me to do?"

Maxwell sighed. "You stay by Zardee. I'll have a sealed alliance of his Erthumoi neighbors for you by tomorrow, to get him deposed if he won't cooperate. Problem is, the cat's already out of the bag."

I, too, had studied Ancient Earth Expressions during one of my lives. "Well, I'll close the barn door, anyway."

Maxwell did not bother with a salutation. He signed off more weary-looking than I'd ever seen him. And our labors were only just beginning.

The Cephallon and the Crotonite weren't exactly making love when I returned to the Guest Suite. (What an image!) Still, they hadn't murdered each other, either.

Jirata had become animated enough to attend to the internal environments controller in his corner of the chamber. He had dismantled the wall panel and was experimenting – creating a partition, then a bed-pallet, then an excretarium. Immersed in mechanical arts, his bat-like face almost took on a look of serenity as he customized the machinery, converting the insensitively mass-produced into something individualized, with character and uniqueness.

It was a rare epiphany, watching him so and coming to realize that even so venal and disgusting a race as his could cause me wonder.

Oh, no doubt I was over-simplifying. Perhaps it was the replicant crisis that had me primed to feel this way. Ironically, though they were the premier mechanics among the Six, the Crotonites' technical and scientific level was not particularly high. And they would be among the *last* ever to understand what a Von Neumann machine was about. From their point of view, autonomy and self-replication were for Crotonites – and in anyone or anything else they were obscenities.

I wondered if this experiment, which had caused a noble and high-caste creature of his community to be cast down so in a desperate attempt to learn new ways, would ever meet any degree of success. What would be the analogy for a person like me... to be surgically grafted crude gills instead of lungs, and dwell forever underwater, less mobile than a Cephallon? Would I, *could* I ever volunteer for so drastic an exile, even if my homeworld depended on it?

Yes, I conceded, watching Jirata work. There was nobility here, of a sort. And at least the Crotonites had not unleashed upon the galaxy a thing that could threaten all Six Spacefarers... and the million other intelligent life forms without starships.

Phss'aah awakened from a snooze at the pool's surface and descended to face me. But it was his robot that spoke.

"Patty, my master hopes your business in this system has been successfully concluded."

"Alas, no. Crises develop lives of their own. Soon, however, I expect permission to confide this matter in him. When that happens, I hope to benefit from his insight."

Phss'aah acknowledged the compliment with a bare nod. Then he spoke for himself. "You must not despair, my young Erthumoi colleague. Look, after all, to your *other* accomplishments. I have decided, for instance, to go ahead and purchase a sample order of thirty thousand of these delightful machines for my own community. And if they work out there, perhaps others in the Cephallon Supreme Pod will buy. Is this not a coup to make you happy?"

For a moment I could not answer. What could I say to Phss'aah? That soon robots such as these might be so cheap that they could be had for a song? That soon a flood of wealth would sweep the galaxy, so great that no creature of any starfaring race would ever want for material goods?

Or should I tell him that the seeds strewn to grow this cornucopia were doomed to mutate, to change, to seek paths of their own... paths down which no foreseeing could follow?

"That's nice," I finally said. "I'm glad you like our machines. You can have as many as you need."

And I tried to smile. "You can have as many as you want."

Story Notes

Think pieces — stories that revolve around an idea, more than plot or character — have their place. But that does not mean one has to do without irony, poignancy, or any of the other virtues.

"The Diplomacy Guild" had to bridge a story arc, connecting works by other authors, so that the whole might make satisfying sense. Still, the concept made me ponder, night after night.

Our next tale, "The Other Side of the Hill," is one of my oldest, having appeared in Analog Magazine shortly after I published my first novel, Sundiver. It harkens to the underlying reason why some so eagerly sift the sky, hoping to find wisdom of another sort, out there.

This story may not be high art, but nothing has happened to make the central point obsolete. We still face the fundamental truth —

— that a people who deserve the stars will be those who first learned to be wise at home.

The Other Side of the Hill

◊

"**D**eserts grow.

"The sky glowers with deadly rays and the seas grow poisonous.

"Today I have come to tell you of our decision.

"You will get your way. Our people have no choice but to depart with the rest of you. To flee this unhappy, cursed world."

Head bowed, calloused hands clasped before him, Mu Wathengria spoke from the High Council's circle of deliberation, his voice heavy with age and defeat.

"North Glacier Clan submits to majority will," he concluded. "We will join the exodus."

The other members of the Council shared looks of astonishment, having grown accustomed to decades of righteous northern stubbornness. At last, Keliangeli, the Grand Mu of Farfields Clan, thumped the stone floor with her staff, and exclaimed.

"We are united, then! All can join now, without bitterness or anguish over leaving kinfolk behind."

Wathengria answered with an acquiescent drooping of his ear-fringes.

"No clan or colony will stay on Bharis, Mu Keliangeli," he agreed. "My people will now help build the ships. We will participate in the abandonment of our mother world. But only because it is too late to turn back."

The stooped, gray-fringed Mu appeared not to hear him, so excited was she. "With the resources of North Glacier no longer wasted, we can push the schedule forward two years, and leave before another famine comes!"

Mu Wathengria nodded gravely. It would be rude, having submitted, to voice doubts now. Anyway, he was tired. Keliangeli called it "waste" to set aside some of the last arable land on Bharis, sparing it the kind of intense overuse that had ruined a once-beautiful planet. Starvation and pestilence now twisted judgment and reason. Keliangeli and her followers were desperate enough to try anything, even use up what was left of this world in order to flee toward a distant star.

North Glacier, with its fresh water and abundant ores, had long held out. But the siren song of a robot probe, circling a faraway globe, now beckoned with lush green images of a better place, only a few light years away. Shipbuilding became a planet-wide mania, heedless of new damage.

"My ecologists tell me that once the ships are built, and the exodus prepared, little more than seven hundredths of the land on Bharis will remain suitable to support life in any decency. You, all of you, have thrown our lives like dice into the wind. They tumble even now, up in the sky."

He pointed to the Fleet, which glittered in orbit overhead, like gems in early evening, crossing the heavens much swifter than the stars. "North Glacier must join the cast."

"We are overjoyed to have you with us, Mu Wathengria." the Bas of Sheltered Oasis cried out, oblivious to Wathengria's irony. "Oh, yes!" Mu Keliangeli added. "On our new home, you will help teach us how to keep and preserve it against the sorts of mischief our ancestors unleashed on Bharis. You will be our conscience."

Wathengria suppressed a hot response. True, their ancient forebears had done the worst harm, with their wars, noxious pollution and mismanagement. But today's folk were multiplying the damage, even as they sought to flee.

"My specialists will accompany you to the new world. Perhaps you will learn from them, although I doubt it. As for myself, I plan to stay and take the Lesser Death. I will sleep, in frozen stasis within the hall of my ancestors. One of our race should remain to explain this wasteland, should the ancient gods of myth ever return, to look in dismay upon poor, ruined Bharis."

The Mu coursed his eyes around the circle. On a few faces, he noted signs of shame. But within moments of turning and departing the hall, he heard their voices rise again behind him, the moment forgotten amid new, excited plans.

I notice no one even protested my personal decision to stay, he thought. *Probably, they're all relieved to hear the last of my carping. My caustic criticism.*

From his transport, Mu Wathengria looked down on the valley of Lansenil. The Council Chambers stood next to one of the few remaining sites of untarnished beauty on Bharis. If they had chosen a more desolate and representative place, Mu Wathengria might have been more optimistic for his race.

Forested slopes gave way to the paler shades of crops and pocket gardens, and then the harbor spires of Sea Haven, one of three remaining cities. Haven was not yet a desert of wind-blown dust. Still, Mu Wathengria tried not to look closely as his machine passed over cracked marble monuments, stained by ancient pollution and more recent, inexorable decay. Squinting past the fuming shipworks, he peered instead with his mind's inner eye toward the better days of his youth.

Longingly, he filled his mind with remembered beauty to take with him to an icy tomb.

One compensation. The animals and plants that remain will have peace at last. We "thinking creatures" will no longer be a menace.

Too late, alas. Much, much too late.

◇

Sounds of celebration continued even after the airlock sealed, cutting off the noise of continuing revelry aboard the mother ship. The crew on Ras Gafengria's exploration craft were on duty and free of intoxicants, but that did not make them sober. They went grinning to their tasks, babbling excitedly, drunk on hope.

It was tempting to give in to the contagious happiness. Joy at the prospect of landing on such a beautiful world after half an aeon of cold sleep! Most of the refugees from Bharis had dreamed, during the long voyage to this new home. And now their hopes had come true.

Orbital surveys had already confirmed what the robot probes earlier promised. More than twice as much of this planet's surface area supported life as tired old Bharis! Green regions ran like thick veins across every continent. As for the oceans — no one living had ever seen so much good water. The cartographer kept muttering happily, over and over — seas covered nearly a third of the globe!

Ras Gafengria wanted to share the others' covetous triumph. She could appreciate the wonder of this place. After all, here was an entire ecosystem to study... and perhaps take better care of, if she and others like her had their way.

But the message, she thought. *It's hard to take pleasure in any of this, after seeing my father's message.*

The pilots banked the landing boat into an aerodynamic braking dive, to save fuel. Soon they were passing high over an ocean. Instruments detected planktonic life, something they could not have done an equal distance above old Bharis. Amazing.

Yet, Gafengria's thoughts kept pulling back to the image she had seen only an hour ago, in the viewing tank of the mother ship... an image of Mu Wathengria. The old man's face seemed almost unchanged from when she had seen it last, impassively watching his people march into the ships.

On the day they blasted off, leaving him behind. Alone.

Who could have imagined that he would send a message later... at the speed of light... and it would be waiting when they arrived at their new home?

The Council had not wanted to distract from the joy of a million newly-awakened exiles. So the leaders only invited a few to come see the strange message that had caught up with their fleet while passengers and crew slept. Patient computers had stored the transmission until arrival, when the officers and councilors wakened to view it.

The first thing Gafengria had noticed was the date – five hundred and forty turns after Departure! So, the old man's stasis unit had held, even without anyone around to perform routine maintenance.

She had expected words, but what happened next was far more startling. Her father's wrinkled sardonic visage shrank as he stepped back from the camera, and... into the holo tank next to him appeared the image of an alien creature!

The figure was tall, bipedal and slender, with dark cranial filaments that lay motionless atop its scalp. The narrow, fleshy face was inset with two small but penetrating eyes, above and on both sides of a fleshy, protruding nose.

Wathengria remained silent for a long interval, as if knowing the effect this scene would have on those to later view it. Only when the shock had abated slightly did his speech begin.

"My dear, departed people," the Mu had said. *"I hope your new world is everything you prayed for. If, indeed, you've learned a lesson, perhaps you will take better care of it than you did our poor beloved Bharis. You'll notice, though, I haven't held my breath!"*

The message went on. *"By the time you see this, another several hundred years will have passed. Nevertheless, I'm giving in to a little hastiness, rushing to transmit. Because I want to introduce you to Bharis's new tenants.*

"They are called Hu-Mhenn. And they seem to adore our tired old world! They've settled into Sea Haven now, and they want you to know..."

The chief pilot interrupted Gafengria's recollection. "We're approaching the coast now, noble Ras," he said. A collective sigh filled the cabin as the shoreline neared. Scattered vegetation grew upon the dun slopes, left and right as far as the eye could see, even from this great height. None of the people had ever encountered such a sight.

"Over there!" One of the pilots pointed to the eastern horizon. "One of the anomaly clusters! Shall we fly closer?"

Gafengria assented and they adjusted course toward an elevated clump of brown and tan shapes, shinier than the surrounding dunes. From space, the regular, geometric features had caused some to speculate they might be cities. Were there inhabitants with prior claims to this planet?

That prospect disturbed the Council... though such a rich world surely had room enough for two races.

The youngest pilot gasped. "They *are* habitations!"

The chief pilot magnified the screen. "Perhaps, once. But they look long abandoned."

The ship cautiously slowed, skirting some distance from the rounded stone shapes. The extant of the constructions soon left no doubt this had been a great city, indeed. Giant, spidery bridges and archways still connected many of the concave structures, whose blank, oval windows stared empty, like the eye sockets in a skull. The alienness of the architecture was almost as eerie as was the desolate loneliness of total abandonment.

The younger pilot pointed again, this time to a broad, flattened area not far away. "Firing pits," he pronounced. "A launching field."

"Don't jump to conclusions. We can't be sure..." The senior pilot abruptly stopped and stared. The cartographer gasped.

As they topped a gentle rise, an immense cube of shining metal came into view, glittering under the slanting sunshine. Gafengria covered her eyes, wishing the giant thing would go away. She had a premonition about it, which caused her fringes to shrink down to their roots. It did not feel good.

"The Council calls," their comm operator said. "The elders command us to approach the artifact. Shipboard image enhancement indicates *writing* along the sides!"

In hushed awe, the pilots brought the boat nearer. Ras Gafengria sank back in her seat, while the comm operator tuned to the frequency of the linguists, onboard the mother ship. Those experts babbled urgently about ciphers and contexts and translation possibilities. About analogies and similarities....

"*It's all terribly ironic*," Gathengria recalled her father pronouncing across the light years. "*These Hu-Mhenn are also refugees! They, too, fled a world that could barely support them. They didn't use robot probes to search for a new planet. Their method appears to have been more direct, though I can't say I really understand it well enough to explain it.*

"*Anyway, here they are. They awakened me, and I told them where you'd all gone. They're very much like us, you know.* " His smile had been bitter. "*They may look strange, but it's uncanny how much like us they truly are.*"

◇

Holograms from the cubic artifact filled the tank in front of Ras Gafengria. It was a full body portrait of an alien being, a roundish shape coated with tentacles. To her surprise and relief, those who had left this monolith weren't at all similar in appearance to the "Hu-Mhenn" shown in her father's message.

Thank the gods, Ras sighed. *That* irony would have been too much to bear – that one species should deplete its home world in order to fly to a refuge that had been depleted by another race in *its* own desperate effort to flee to the first... A terrible trade.

As a matter of fact, that tragedy was logically impossible. For one thing, the Hu-Mhenn had come from a direction opposite to the one the people had fled towards. And anyway, her father had said the Hu-Mhenn were *pleased* with Bharis. In fact, the poor creatures had seemed pathetically ecstatic, calling their new home a "paradise."

How devastated their own planet must have been, then, for them to think so highly of tired old Bharis!

Ras noticed that the others on the boat had stopped talking. "What
–?" she began.

The cartographer turned and whispered. "The translation, noble
Ras! They've translated the inscription!"

"Show me the translation," she commanded, though she feared
what it would say.

Blinking, she saw that the round alien figure in the holo tank was
moving, waving its tentacles! A tinny voice accompanied the movements,
soft and lilting. Below the figure flowed text from the mother ship's
translation of words that these creatures must have written a million
years ago.

> **... So we were forced to decide... to remain and face
> continued famine, or to take a desperate gamble,
> squandering our last resources to fling our race
> of heroes across the stars... The** (undefined term)
> **choice was obvious to all but a few** (undefined
> term)**... By the time the necessary** (undefined term)
> **transmitters were completed, our world was hum-
> bled... ruined... less than a quarter of her land ara-
> ble... dead in so many...**

"Less than a *quarter?*" The voice of the assistant ecologist voice
cracked. "They call that ruined? The message can't be correctly
translated!"

But Ras Gafengria sighed, seeing it all in utter clarity. The terrible
truth. They had been spared the irony that was superficially most cruel,
only so they might have nightmares over a far more subtle joke the Universe had played on them.

Or the joke that we all played on the Universe.

She closed her eyes and wished the former denizens of this world
good luck in their quest.

*May they find their bountiful new home. Though to satisfy them, it need be so
rich as to stagger my imagination. They don't deserve success, of course, but neither
did we... nor the Hu-Mhenn, presumably.*

In her mind she envisioned a chain of intelligent but short-sighted
races, each getting more mercy than it merited, joyful to inherit the leav-
ings of the one ahead of it in line. Each of them so poor and hungry,
they would see the next, leftover wasteland as a heaven!

She thought of Wathengria's wry words, and wished he had not taught her so well the burdensome gift of honesty.

"*The Hu-Mhenn had a terrible time,*" the Mu had said. "*But they kept faith, and knew they would find a world as nice as Bharis, someday. Amongst them, there is a saying almost as old as their race. When times were hard, they repeated it to one another for encouragement. For the courage to move on. Loosely translated, it goes something like this —*

"'*Over the mountain, the plant life will be a more pleasant shade of green.*'

"So, now I must end this message, and begin trying to teach the new tenants of Bharis how to take care of her. Perhaps this time I will have better luck.

"May fate bless you, my wayward children.

"As little as you deserve it, may you also find the grass greener, and the waters sweeter... on the other side of the hill."

WHERE WE WILL GO

◇

After a section devoted to "think pieces" about contact with aliens, how about some adventure?

The following long novella is from my Uplift Universe of Startide Rising, Sundiver *and* The Uplift War. *This stand-alone story is set on the world – Jijo – where most of the action takes place in* Brightness Reef *and* Infinity's Shore.

When the Earth starship – Streaker – escapes from Jijo, in Heaven's Reach, some members of its dolphin crew are left behind, sharing exile with six previous races, all of them hiding on that isolated world.

For those of you who have been asking for more about Jijo and its role in Galactic destiny, here's a down payment... along with startling information about the meddlesome alien Buyur....

Temptation

◇

A Novella in the Uplift Universe

Makanee

Jijo's ocean stroked her flank like a mother's nuzzling touch or a lover's caress. Though it seemed a bit disloyal, Makanee felt this alien ocean had a silkier texture and finer taste than the waters of Earth, the home-world she had not seen in years.

With gentle beats of their powerful flukes, she and her companion kept easy pace beside a tremendous throng of fishlike creatures – red-finned, with violet gills and long, translucent tails that glittered in the slanted sunlight like plasma sparks behind a starship. The school seemed to stretch forever, grazing on drifting clouds of plankton, moving in unison through coastal shallows like the undulating body of a vast complacent serpent.

The creatures were beautiful... and delicious. Makanee performed an agile twist of her sleek gray body, lunging to snatch one from the teeming mass, provoking only a slight ripple from its nearest neighbors. Her casual style of predation must be new to Jijo, for the beasts seemed quite oblivious toward the dolphins. The rubbery flesh tasted like exotic mackerel.

"I can't help feeling guilty," she commented in Underwater Anglic, a language of clicks and squeals that was well-suited to a liquid realm where sound ruled over light.

Her companion rolled alongside the school, belly up, with ventral fins waving languidly as he grabbed one of the local fish for himself.

"Why guilty?" Brookida asked, while the victim writhed between his narrow jaws. Its soft struggle did not interfere with his train of word-glyphs, since a dolphin's mouth plays no role in generating sound. Instead a rapid series of ratcheting sonar impulses emanated from his brow.

"Are you ashamed because you live? Because it feels good to be outside again, with a warm sea rubbing your skin and the crash of waves singing in your dreams? Do you miss the stale water and moldy air aboard ship? Or the dead echoes of your cramped stateroom?"

"Don't be absurd," she snapped back. After three years confined aboard the Terran survey vessel, *Streaker*, Makanee had felt as cramped as an overdue fetus, straining at the womb. Release from that purgatory was like being born anew.

"It's just that we're enjoying a tropical paradise while our crewmates —"

"— must continue tearing across the cosmos in foul discomfort, chased by vile enemies, facing death at every turn. Yes, I know."

Brookida let out an expressive sigh. The elderly geophysicist switched languages, to one more suited for poignant irony.

* Winter's tempest spends
　　* All its force against the reef,
　　　　* Sparing the lagoon. *

The Trinary haiku was expressive and wry. At the same time though, Makanee could not help making a physician's diagnosis. She found her old friend's sonic patterns rife with undertones of Primal — the natural cetacean demi-language used by wild *Tursiops truncatus* dolphins back on Earth — a dialect that members of the modern amicus breed were supposed to avoid, lest their minds succumb to tempting ancient ways. Mental styles that lured with rhythms of animal-like purity.

She found it worrisome to hear Primal from Brookida, one of her few companions with an intact psyche. Most of the other dolphins on Jijo suffered to some degree from stress-atavism. Having lost the cognitive focus needed by engineers and starfarers, they could no longer help *Streaker* in its desperate flight across five galaxies. Planting this small colony on Jijo had seemed a logical solution, leaving the regressed ones for Makanee to care for in this gentle place, while their shipmates sped on to new crises elsewhere.

She could hear them now, browsing along the same fishy swarm just a hundred meters off. Thirty neo-dolphins who had once graduated from prestigious universities. Specialists chosen for an elite expedition – now reduced to splashing and squalling, with little on their minds but food, sex, and music. Their primitive calls no longer embarrassed Makanee.

After everything her colleagues had gone through since departing Terra – on a routine one-year survey voyage that instead stretched into a hellish three – it was surprising they had any sanity left at all.

Such suffering would wear down a human, or even a Tymbrimi. But our race is just a few centuries old. Neo-dolphins have barely started the long Road of Uplift. Our grip on sapience is still slippery.

And now another trail beckons us.

After debarking with her patients, Makanee had learned about the local religion of the Six Races who already secretly settled this isolated world, a creed centered on the Path of Redemption – a belief that salvation could be found in blissful ignorance and non-sapience.

It was harder than it sounded. Among the "sooner" races who had come to this world illegally, seeking refuge in simplicity, only one had succeeded so far, and Makanee doubted that the human settlers would ever reclaim true animal innocence, no matter how hard they tried. Unlike species who were uplifted, humans had earned their intelligence the hard way on Old Earth, seizing each new talent or insight at frightful cost over the course of a thousand harsh millennia. They might become ignorant and primitive – but never simple. Never innocent.

We neo-dolphins will find it easy, however. We've only been tool-users for such a short time – a boon from our human patrons that we never sought. It's simple to give up something you received without struggle. Especially when the alternative – the Whale Dream – calls seductively, each time you sleep.

An alluring sanctuary. The sweet trap of timelessness.

From clackety sonar emanations, she sensed her assistants – a pair of fully conscious volunteers – keeping herd on the reverted ones, making sure the group stayed together. Things seemed pleasant here, but no one knew for sure what dangers lurked in Jijo's wide sea.

We already have three wanderers out there somewhere. Poor little Peepoe and her two wretched kidnappers. I promised Kaa we'd send out search parties to rescue her. But how? Zhaki and Mopol have a huge head start, and half a planet to hide in.

Tkett's out there looking for her right now, and we'll start expanding the search as soon as the patients are settled and safe. But they could be on the other side of Jijo by now. Our only real hope is for Peepoe to escape that pair of dolts somehow, and get close enough to call for help.

It was time for Makanee and Brookida to head back and take their own turn shepherding the happy-innocent patients. Yet, she felt reluctant. Nervous.

Something in the water rolled through her mouth with a faint metallic tang, tasting like expectancy.

Makanee swung her sound-sensitive jaw around, seeking clues. At last she found a distant tremor. A faintly familiar resonance, coming from the west.

Brookida hadn't noticed yet.

"Well," he commented. "It won't be long until we are truly part of this world, I suppose. A few generations from now, none of our descendants will be using Anglic, or any Galactic language. We'll be guileless innocents once more, ripe for re-adoption and a second chance at uplift. I wonder what our new patrons will be like."

Makanee's friend was goading her gently with the bitter-sweet destiny anticipated for this colony, on a world that seemed made for cetaceans. A world whose comfort was the surest way to clinch a rapid devolution of their disciplined minds. Without constant challenges, the Whale Dream would surely reclaim them. Brookida seemed to accept the notion with an ease that disturbed Makanee.

"We still have patrons," she pointed out. "There are humans living right here on Jijo."

"Humans, yes. But uneducated, lacking the scientific skills to continue guiding us. So our only remaining option must be –"

He stopped, having at last picked up that rising sound from the west. Makanee recognized the unique hum of a speed sled.

"It is Tkett," she said. "Returning from his scouting trip. Let's go hear what he found out."

Thrashing her flukes, Makanee jetted to the surface, spuming the moist, stale air from her lungs and drawing in a deep breath of sweet oxygen. Then she spun about and kicked off toward the engine noise, with Brookida following close behind.

In their wake, the school of grazing fishoids barely rippled in its endless, sinuous dance, darting in and out of luminous shoals, feeding on whatever the good sea pressed toward them.

The archaeologist had his own form of mental illness – wishful thinking.

Tkett had been ordered to stay behind and help Makanee with the reverted ones, partly because his skills weren't needed in *Streaker's* continuing desperate flight across the known universe. In compensation for that bitter exile, he had grown obsessed with studying the Great Midden, that deep underwater trash heap where Jijo's ancient occupants had dumped nearly every sapient-made object when this planet was abandoned by starfaring culture, half a million years ago.

"I'll have a wonderful report to submit when we get back to Earth," he rationalized, in apparent confidence that all their troubles would pass, and eventually he would make it home to publish his results.

It was a special kind of derangement, without featuring any sign of stress-atavism or reversion. Tkett still spoke Anglic perfectly. His work was flawless and his demeanor cheerful. He was pleasant, functional, and mad as a hatter.

Makanee met the sled a kilometer west of the pod, where Tkett pulled up short in order not to disturb the patients.

"Did you find any traces of Peepoe?" she asked when he cut the engine.

Tkett was a wonderfully handsome specimen of *Tursiops amicus*, with speckled mottling along his sleek gray flanks. The permanent dolphin-smile presented twin rows of perfectly white, conical teeth. While still nestled on the sled's control platform, Tkett shook his head left and right.

"Alas, no. I went about two hundred klicks, following those faint traces we picked up on deep-range sonar. But it grew clear that the source wasn't Zhaki's sled."

Makanee grunted disappointment. "Then what was it?" Unlike the clamorous sea of Earth, this fallow planet wasn't supposed to have motor noises permeating its thermal-acoustic layers.

"At first I started imagining all sorts of unlikely things, like sea monsters, or Jophur submarines," Tkett answered. "Then the truth hit me."

Brookida nodded nervously, venting bubbles from his blowhole. "Yesssss?"

"It must be a starship. An ancient, piece-of-trash wreck, barely puttering along –"

"Of course!" Makanee thrashed her tail. "Some of the decoys didn't make it into space."

Tkett murmured ruefully over how obvious it now seemed. When *Streaker* made its getaway attempt, abandoning Makanee and her charges on this world, the earthship fled, concealed in a swarm of ancient relics that dolphin engineers had resurrected from trash heaps on the ocean floor. Though Jijo's surface now was a fallow realm of savage tribes, the deep underwater canyons still held thousands of battered, abandoned spacecraft and other debris from when this section of Galaxy Four had been a center of civilization and commerce. Several dozen of those derelicts had been re-activated in order to confuse *Streaker's* foe – a fearsome Jophur battleship – but some of the hulks must have failed to haul their bulk out of the sea when the time came. Those failures were doomed to drift aimlessly underwater until their engines gave out and they tumbled once more to the murky depths.

As for the rest, there had been no word whether *Streaker's* ploy succeeded beyond luring the awful dreadnought away toward deep space. At least Jijo seemed a friendlier place without it. For now.

"We should have expected this," the archaeologist continued. "When I got away from the shoreline surf noise, I thought I could detect at least three of the hulks, bumping around out there almost randomly. It seems kind of sad, when you think about it. Ancient ships, not worth salvaging when the Buyur abandoned Jijo, waiting in an icy, watery tomb for just one last chance to climb back out to space. Only these couldn't make it. They're stranded here."

"Like us," Makanee murmured.

Tkett seemed not to hear.

"In fact, I'd like to go back out there and try to catch up with one of the derelicts."

"Whatever for?"

Tkett's smile was still charming and infectious... which made it seem even crazier, under these circumstances.

"I'd like to use it as a scientific instrument," the big neo-dolphin said.

Makanee felt utterly confirmed in her diagnosis.

Peepoe

Captivity wasn't as bad as she had feared.

It was worse.

Among natural, pre-sapient dolphins on Earth, small groups of young males would sometimes conspire to isolate a fertile female from the rest of the pod, herding her away for private copulation – especially if she was about to enter heat. By working together, they might monopolize her matings and guarantee their own reproductive success, even if she clearly preferred a local alpha-ranked male instead. That ancient behavior pattern persisted in the wild because, while native *tursiops* had both traditions and a kind of feral honor, they could not quite grasp or carry out the concept of law – a code that all must live by – for the entire community has a memory transcending any individual.

But modern, uplifted *amicus* dolphins did have law! And when young hoodlums occasionally let instinct prevail and tried that sort of thing back home, the word for it was rape. Punishment was harsh. As with human sexual predators, just one of the likely outcomes was permanent sterilization.

Such penalties worked. After three centuries, some of the less desirable primal behaviors were becoming rare. Yet, uplifted neo-dolphins were still a young race. Great stress could yank old ways back to the fore, from time to time.

And we Streakers have sure been under stress.

Unlike some devolved crewmates, whose grip on modernity and rational thought had snapped under relentless pressure, Zhaki and Mopol suffered only partial atavism. They could still talk and run complex equipment, but they were no longer the polite, almost shy junior ratings she had met when *Streaker* first set out from Earth under Captain Creideiki, before the whole cosmos seemed to implode all around the dolphin crew.

In abstract, she understood the terrible strain that had put them in this state. Perhaps, if she were offered a chance to kill Zhaki and Mopol, Peepoe might call that punishment a bit too severe.

On the other fin, sterilization was much too good for them.

Despite sharing the same culture - and a common ancestry as Earth mammals - dolphins and humans looked at many things differently. Peepoe felt more annoyed at being kidnapped than violated. More pissed-off than traumatized. She wasn't able to stymie their lust completely, but with various tricks – playing on their mutual jealousy and feigning illness as often as she could – Peepoe staved off unwelcome attentions for long stretches.

But if I find out they murdered Kaa, I'll have their entrails for lunch.

Days passed and her impatience grew. Peepoe's real time limit was fast approaching. *My contraception implant will expire. Zhaki and his pal have fantasies about populating Jijo with their descendants, but I like this planet far too much to curse it that way.*

She vowed to make a break for it. But how?

Sometimes she would swim to a channel between the two remote islands where her kidnappers had brought her, and drift languidly, listening. Once, Peepoe thought she made out something faintly familiar – a clicking murmur, like a distant crowd of dolphins. But it passed, and she dismissed it as wishful thinking. Zhaki and Mopol had driven the sled at top speed for days on end with her strapped to the back, before they halted by this strange archipelago and removed her sonar-proof blindfold. She had no idea how to find her way back to the old coastline where Makanee's group had settled.

When I do escape these two idiots, I may be consigning myself to a solitary existence for the rest of my days.

Oh well, you wanted the life of an explorer. There could be worse fates than swimming all the way around this beautiful world, eating exotic fish when you're hungry, riding strange tides and listening to rhythms no dolphin ever heard before.

The fantasy had a poignant beauty – though ultimately, it made her lonely and sad.

◇

The ocean echoed with anger, engines, and strange noise.

Of course it was all a matter of perspective. On noisy Earth, this would have seemed eerily quiet. Terran seas buzzed with a cacophony of traffic, much of it caused by her own kind as neo-dolphins gradually took over managing seventy percent of the home planet's surface. In mining the depths, or tending fisheries, or caring for those sacredly complex simpletons called whales, more and more responsibilities fell to uplifted 'fins using boats, subs and other equipment. Despite continuing efforts to reduce the racket, home was still a raucous place.

In comparison, Jijo appeared as silent as a nursery. Natural sound-carrying thermal layers reported waves crashing on distant shorelines and intermittent groaning as minor quakes rattled the ocean floor. A myriad buzzes, clicks and whistles came from Jijo's own subsurface fauna – fishy creatures that evolved here, or were introduced by colonizing leaseholders like the Buyur, long ago. Some distant rumbles even hinted at large entities, moving slowly, languidly across the deep... perhaps pondering long, slow thoughts.

As days stretched to weeks, Peepoe learned to distinguish Jijo's organic rhythms... punctuated by a grating din whenever one of the boys took the sled for a joy ride, stampeding schools of fish, or careening along with the load indicator showing red. At this rate the machine wouldn't stand up much longer, though Peepoe kept hoping one of them would break his fool neck first.

With or without the sled, Zhaki and Mopol could track her down if she just swam away. Even when they left piles of dead fish to ferment atop some floating reeds, and got drunk on the foul carcasses, the two never let their guard down long enough to let her steal the sled. It seemed that one or the other was always sprawled across the saddle. Since dolphins sleep only one brain hemisphere at a time, it was impossible to take them completely by surprise.

◊

Then, after two months of captivity, she detected signs of something drawing near.

Peepoe had been diving in deeper water for a tasty kind of local soft-shell crab when she first heard it. Her two captors were having fun a kilometer away, driving their speedster in tightening circles around a panicked school of bright silvery fishoids. But when she dived through a thermal boundary layer, separating warm water above from cool, saltier liquid below – the sled's racket abruptly diminished.

Blessed silence was one added benefit of this culinary exploit. Peepoe had been doing a lot of diving lately.

This time, however, the transition did more than spare her the sled's noise for a brief time. It also brought forth a new sound. A distant rumble, channeled by the chilly stratum. With growing excitement, Peepoe recognized the murmur of an engine! Yet the rhythms struck her as unlike any she had heard on Earth or elsewhere.

Puzzled, she kicked swiftly to the surface, filled her lungs with fresh air, and dived back down to listen again.

This deep current offers an excellent sonic groove, she realized, *focusing sound rather than diffusing it. Keeping the vibrations well-confined. Even the sled's sensors may not pick it up for quite a while.*

Unfortunately, that also meant she couldn't tell how far away the source was.

If I had a breather unit... if it weren't necessary to keep surfacing for air... I could swim a great distance masked by this thermal barrier. Otherwise it seems hopeless. They can use the sled's monitors on long-range scan to detect me when I broach and exhale.

Peepoe listened for a while longer, and decided.

I think it's getting closer... but slowly. The source must still be far away. If I make a dash now, I won't get far before they catch me.

And yet, she daren't risk Mopol and Zhaki picking up the new sound. If she must wait, it meant keeping them distracted 'til the time was right.

There was just one way to accomplish that.

Peepoe grimaced. Rising toward the surface, she expressed disgust with a vulgar Trinary demi-haiku.

> * May sun roast your backs,
> > * And hard sand scrape your bottoms,
> > * Til you itch madly... *
> * ... as if with a good case of the clap! *

Makanee

She sent a command over her neural link, ordering the tools of her harness to fold away into streamlined recesses, signaling that the inspection visit was over.

The chief of the kiqui, a little male with purple gill-fringes surrounding a squat head, let himself drift a meter or so under the water's surface, spreading all four webbed hands in a gesture of benediction and thanks. Then he thrashed around to lead his folk away, back toward the nearby island where they made their home. Makanee felt satisfaction as she watched the small formation of kicking amphibians, clutching their stone-tipped spears.

Who would have thought that we dolphins, youngest registered sapient race in the Civilization of Five Galaxies, would become patrons ourselves, just a few centuries after humans started uplifting us.

The Kiqui were doing pretty well on Jijo, all considered. Soon after being released onto a coral atoll, not far offshore, they started having babies.

Under normal conditions, some elder race would find an excuse to take the Kiqui away from dolphins, fostering such a promising pre-sapient species into one of the rich, ancient family lines that ruled oxygen-breathing civilization in the Five Galaxies. But here on Jijo things were different. They were cut off from starfaring culture, a vast bewildering society of complex rituals and obligations that made the ancient Chinese Imperial court seem like a toddler's sandbox, by comparison. There were advantages and disadvantages to being a castaway from all that.

On the one hand, Makanee would no longer have to endure the constant tension of running away from huge oppressive battlefleets or aliens whose grudges went beyond Earthling comprehension.

On the other hand, there would be no more performances of symphony, or opera, or bubble-dance for her to attend.

Never again must she endure disparaging sneers from exalted patron-level beings, who considered dolphins little more than bright beasts.

Nor would she spend another lazy Sunday in her snug apartment in cosmopolitan Melbourne-Under, with multicolored fish cruising the coral garden just outside her window while she munched salmon patties and watched an all-dolphin cast perform Twelfth Night on the tellie.

Makanee was marooned, and would likely remain so for the rest of her life, caring for two small groups of sea-based colonists, hoping they could remain hidden from trouble until a new era came. An age when both might resume the path of uplift.

Assuming some metal nutrient supplements could be arranged, the Kiqui had apparently transplanted well. Of course, they must be taught tribal taboos against over-hunting any one species of local fauna, so their presence would not become a curse on this world. But the clever little amphibians already showed some understanding, expressing the concept in their own, emphatic demi-speech.

> ## Rare is precious! ##
> ## Not eat-or-hurt rare/precious things/fishes/beasts! ##
> ## Only eat/hunt many-of-a-kind! ##

She felt a personal stake in this. Two years ago, when *Streaker* was about to depart poisonous Kithrup, masked inside the hulk of a crashed Thennanin warship, Makanee had taken it upon herself to beckon a passing tribe of Kiqui with some of their own recorded calls, attracting the curious group into *Streaker's* main airlock just before the surrounding water boiled with exhaust from revving engines. What then seemed an act of simple pity turned into a kind of love affair, as the friendly little amphibians became favorites of the crew. Perhaps now their race might flourish in a kinder place than unhappy Kithrup. It felt good to know *Streaker* had accomplished at least one good thing out of its poignant, tragic mission.

As for dolphins, how could anyone doubt their welcome in Jijo's warm sea? Once you learned which fishoids were edible and which to avoid, life became a matter of snatching whatever you wanted to eat, then splashing and lolling about. True, she missed her holoson unit, with its booming renditions of whale chants and baroque chorales. But here she could take pleasure by listening to an ocean whose sonic purity was almost as fine as its vibrant texture.

Almost...

Reacting to a faint sensation, Makanee swung her sound-sensitive jaw around, casting right and left.

There! She heard it again. A distant rumbling that might have escaped notice amid the underwater cacophony on Earth. But here it seemed to stand out from the normal swish of current and tide.

Her patients – the several dozen dolphins whose stress atavism had reduced them to infantile innocence – called such infrequent noises *boojums*. Or else they used a worried upward trill in Primal Delphin – one that stood for strange monsters of the deep. Occasionally the far off grumbles did seem to hint at some huge, living entity, rumbling with basso-profundo pride, complacently assured that it owned the entire vast sea. Or else it might be just frustrated engine noise from some remnant derelict machine, wandering aimlessly in the ocean's immensity.

Leaving the kiqui atoll behind, Makanee swam back toward the underwater dome where she and Brookida, plus a few still-sapient nurses, maintained a small base to keep watch over their charges. It would be good to get out of the weather for a while. Last night she had roughed it, keeping an eye on her patients during a rain squall. An unpleasant, wearying experience.

We modern neo-fins are spoiled. It will take us years to get used to living in the elements, accepting whatever nature sends our way, without complaining or making ambitious plans to change the way things are.

That human side of us must be allowed to fade away.

Peepoe

She made her break around mid-morning the next day.

Zhaki was sleeping off a hangover near a big mat of driftweed, and Mopol was using the sled to harass some unlucky penguin-like sea birds, who were trying to feed their young by fishing near the island's lee shore. It seemed a good chance to slip away, but Peepoe's biggest reason for choosing this moment was simple. Diving deep below the thermal layer, she found that the distant rumble had peaked, and appeared to have turned away, diminishing with each passing hour.

It was now or never.

Peepoe had hoped to steal something from the sled first. A utensil harness perhaps, or a breather tube, and not just for practical reasons. In normal life, few neo-dolphins spent a single day without using cyborg tools, controlled by cable links to the brain's temporal lobes. But for months now her two would-be "husbands" hadn't let her connect to anything at all! The neural tap behind her left eye ached from disuse.

Unfortunately, Mopol nearly always slept on the sled's saddle, barely ever leaving except to eat and defecate.

He'll be desolated when the speeder finally breaks down, she thought, taking some solace from that.

So the decision was made, and Ifni's dice were cast. She set out with all the gifts and equipment nature provided – completely naked – into an uncharted sea.

For Peepoe, escaping captivity began unlike any human novel or fantasholo. In such stories, the heroine's hardest task was normally the first part, sneaking away. But here Peepoe faced no walls, locked rooms, dogs or barbed wire. Her "guards" let her come and go as she pleased. In this case, the problem wasn't getting started, but winning a big enough head start before Zhaki and Mopol realized she was gone.

Swimming under the thermocline helped mask her movements at first. It left her vulnerable to detection only when she went up for air. But she could not keep it up for long. The *Tursiops* genus of dolphins weren't deep divers by nature, and her speed at depth was only a third what it would be skimming near the surface.

So, while the island was still above the horizon behind her, Peepoe stopped slinking along silently below and instead began her dash for freedom in earnest – racing toward the sun with an endless series of powerful back archings and fluke-strokes, going deep only occasionally to check her bearings against the far-off droning sound.

It felt exhilarating to slice through the wavetops, flexing her body for all it was worth. Peepoe remembered the last time she had raced along this way – with Kaa by her side – when Jijo's waters had seemed warm, sweet, and filled with possibilities.

Although she kept low-frequency sonar clickings to a minimum, she did allow herself some short-range bursts, checking ahead for obstacles and toying with the surrounding water, bouncing reflections off patches of sun-driven convection, letting echoes wrap themselves around her like rippling memories. Peepoe's sonic transmissions remained soft and close – no louder than the vibrations given off by her kicking tail – but the patterns grew more complex as her mind settled into the rhythms of movement. Before long, returning wavelets of her own sound meshed with those of current and tide, overlapping to make phantom sonar images.

Most of these were vague shapes, like the sort that one felt swarming at the edges of a dream. But in time several fell together, merging into something larger. The composite echo seemed to bend and thrust when she did – as if a spectral companion now swam nearby, where her squinting eye saw only sunbeams in an empty sea.

Kaa, she thought, recognizing a certain unique zest whenever the wraith's bottlenose flicked through the waves.

Among dolphins, you did not have to die in order to come back as a ghost... though it helped.

Sometimes the only thing required was vividness of spirit – and Kaa surely was, or had been, vivid.

Or perhaps the nearby sound-effigy fruited solely from Peepoe's eager imagination.

In fact, dolphin logic perceived no contradiction between those two explanations. Kaa's essence might be there – and not be – at the same time. Whether real or mirage, she was glad to have her lover back where he belonged – by her side.

I've missed you, she thought.

Anglic wasn't a good language for phantoms. No human grammar was. Perhaps that explained why the poor bipeds so seldom communed with their beloved lost.

Peepoe's visitor answered in a more ambiguous, innately delphin style.

> * 'Til the seaweed's flower
>   * Shoots forth petals made of moonbeams
>   * I will swim with you *

Peepoe was content with that. For some unmeasured time, it seemed as if a real companion, her mate, swam alongside, encouraging her efforts, sharing the grueling pace. The water divided before her, caressing her flanks like a real lover.

Then, abruptly, a new sound intruded. A distant, grating whine that threatened to shatter all illusions.

Reluctantly, she made herself clamp down, silencing the resonant chambers surrounding her blowhole. As her own sonar vibrations ceased, so did the complex echoes, and her phantom comrade vanished. The waters ahead seemed to go black as Peepoe concentrated, listening intently.

There it was.

Coming from behind her. Another engine vibration, this one all-too familiar, approaching swiftly as it skimmed across the surface of the sea.

They know, she realized. *Zhaki and Mopol know I'm gone, and they're coming after me.*

Peepoe wasted no more time. She bore down with her flukes, racing through the waves faster than ever. Stealth no longer mattered. Now it was a contest of speed, endurance, and luck.

Tkett

It took him most of a day and the next night to get near the source of the mysterious disturbance, pushing his power sled as fast as he dared. Makanee had ordered Tkett not to over-strain the engine, since there would be no replacements when it wore out.

"Just be careful out there," the elderly dolphin physician had urged, giving permission for this expedition. *"Find out what it is... whether it's one of the*

derelict spacecraft that Suessi and the engineers brought back to life as decoys. If so, don't mess with it! Just come back and report. We'll discuss where to go from there."

Tkett did not have disobedience in mind. At least not explicitly. But if it really was a starship making the low, uneven grumbling noise, a host of possibilities presented themselves. What if it proved possible to board the machine and take over the makeshift controls that *Streaker's* crew had put in place?

Even if it can't fly, it's cruising around the ocean. I could use it as a submersible and visit the Great Midden.

That vast undersea trench – where the Buyur had dumped most of the dross of their mighty civilization, when it came time for them to abandon Jijo and return its surface to fallow status. After packing up to leave, the last authorized residents of this planet used titanic machines to scrape away their cities, then sent all their buildings and other works tumbling into an abyss where the slow grinding of tectonic plates would draw the rubble inward, melting and reshaping new ores to be used by others, in some future era, when Jijo was opened for legal settlement once again.

To an archaeologist, the Midden seemed the opportunity of a lifetime.

I'd learn so much about the Buyur! We might examine whole classes of tools that no Earthling has ever seen. The Buyur were rich and powerful. They could afford the very best in the Civilization of Five Galaxies, while we Terran newcomers can only buy dregs. Even stuff the Buyur threw away – their toys and broken trinkets – could provide valuable data for the Terragens Council.

Tkett wasn't a complete fool. He knew what Makanee and Brookida thought of him.

They consider me crazy to be optimistic about going home. To believe any of us will see Earth again, or let the industrial tang of its waters roll through our open jaws, or once more surf the rip tides of Ranga Roa.

Or give a university lecture. Or dive through the richness of a worldwide data network, sharing ideas with a fecund civilization at light-speed. Or hold challenging conversations with others who share your intellectual passions.

He had signed aboard *Streaker* to accompany Captain Creideiki and a neo-dolphin intellectual elite in the greatest mental and physical adventure any group of cetaceans ever faced – the ultimate test of their new sapient race. Only now Creideiki was gone, presumed dead, and Tkett had been ejected by *Streaker's* new commander, exiled from the ship at its worst moment of crisis. Makanee might feel complacent over being put ashore as "non-essential" personnel, but it churned Tkett's guts to be spilled into a warm, disgustingly placid sea while his crewmates were still out there, facing untold dangers among the bleeding stars.

A voice broke in from the outside, before his thoughts could spiral any further toward self-pity.

> # give me give me GIVE ME
> # snout-smacking pleasure
> # of a good fight! #

That shrill chatter came from the sled's rear compartment, causing Tkett's flukes to thrash in brief startlement. It was easy to forget about his quiet passenger for long stretches of time. Chississ spoke seldom, and then only in the throwback proto-language, Primal Delphin.

Tkett quashed his initial irritation. After all, Chissis was unwell. Like several dozen other members of the crew, her modern mind had crumpled under the pressure of *Streaker's* long ordeal, taking refuge in older ways of thought. One had to make allowances, even though Tkett could not imagine how it was possible for anyone to abandon the pleasures of rationality, no matter how insistently one heard the call of the Whale Dream.

After a moment, Tkett realized that her comment had been more than just useless chatter. Chissis must have sensed some meaning from his sonar clicks. Apparently she understood and shared his resentment over Gillian Baskin's decision to leave them behind on Jijo.

"You'd rather be back in space right now, wouldn't you?" He asked. "Even though you can't read an instrument panel anymore? Even with Jophur battleships and other nasties snorting down *Streaker's* neck, closing in for the kill?"

His words were in Underwater Anglic. Most of the reverted could barely comprehend it anymore. But Chissis squawled from the platform behind Tkett, throwing a sound burst that sang like the sled's engine, thrusting ever-forward, obstinately defiant.

> # smack the jophur! smack the sharks!
> # SMACK THEM! #

Accompanying her eager-repetitive message squeal, there came a sonar image crafted by the fatty layers of her brow, casting a brief veil of illusion around Tkett. He briefly visualized Chissis, joyfully ensconced in the bubble nose of a lamprey class torpedo, personally piloting it on course toward a huge alien cruiser, penetrating all of the cyber-disruptive fields that Galactic spacecraft used to stave off digital guidance systems, zeroing in on her target with all the instinct and native agility that dolphins inherited from their ancestors.

Loss of speech apparently had not robbed some "reverted" ones of either spunk or ingenuity. Tkett sputtered laughter. Gillian Baskin had made a real mistake leaving this one behind! Apparently you did not need an engineer's mind in order to have the heart of a warrior.

"No wonder Makanee let you come along on this trip," he answered. "You're a bad influence on the others, aren't you?"

It was her turn to emit a laugh — sounding almost exactly like his own. A ratcheting raspberry-call that the masters of uplift had left alone. A deeply cetacean shout that defied the sober universe for taking so many things too seriously.

> # Faster faster FASTER!
> # Engines call us...
> # offering a ride... #

Tkett's tail thrashed involuntarily as her cry yanked something deep within. Without hesitating, he cranked up the sled's motor, sending it splashing through the foamy white-tops, streaking toward a mysterious object whose song filled the sea.

Peepoe

She could sense Zhaki and Mopol closing in from behind. They might be idiots, but they knew what they wanted and how to pilot their sled at maximum possible speed without frying the bearings. Once alerted to her escape attempt, they cast ahead using the machine's deep range sonar. She felt each loud ping like a small bite along her backside. By now they knew exactly where she was. The noise was meant to intimidate her.

It worked. *I don't know how much longer I can keep on,* Peepoe thought, while her body burned with fatigue. Each back-arching plunge through the waves seemed to take more out of her. No longer a joyful sensation, the ocean's silky embrace became a clinging drag, taxing and stealing her hard-won momentum, making Peepoe earn each dram of speed over and over again.

In comparison, the hard vacuum of space seemed to offer a better bargain. What you bought, you got to keep. Even the dead stayed on trajectory, tumbling ever onward. Space travel tended to promote belief in "progress," a notion that old-style dolphins used to find ridiculous, and still had some trouble getting used to.

I should be fairly close to the sound I was chasing... whatever's making it. I'd be able to tell, if only those vermin behind me would turn off the damned sonar and let me listen in peace!

Of course the pinging racket was meant to disorient her. Peepoe only caught occasional sonic-glimpses of her goal, and then only by diving below the salt-boundary layer, something she did as seldom as possible, since it always slowed her down.

The noise of the sled's engine sounded close. Too damned close. At any moment Zhaki and Mopol might swerve past to cut her off, then start spiraling inward, herding her like some helpless sea animal while they chortled, enjoying their macho sense of power.

I'll have to submit... bear their punishment... put up with bites and whackings 'til they're convinced I've become a good cow.

None of that galled Peepoe as much as the final implication of her recapture.

I guess this means I'll have to kill the two of them.

It was the one thing she'd been hoping to avoid. Murder among dolphins had been rare in olden times, and the genetic engineers worked to enhance this innate distaste. Anyway, a clean getaway would have sufficed.

She didn't know how she'd do it. Not yet.

But I'm still a Terragens officer, while they relish considering themselves wild beasts. How hard can it be?

Part of her knew that she was drifting, fantasizing. This might even be the way her subconscious was trying to rationalize surrendering the chase. She might as well give up now, before exhaustion claimed all her strength.

No! I've got to keep going.

Peepoe let out a groan as she redoubled her efforts, bearing down with intense drives of her powerful tail flukes. Each moment that she held them off meant just a little more freedom. A little more dignity.

It couldn't last, of course. Though it felt exultant and defiant to give one more hard push, the burst of speed eventually faded as her body used up its last reserves. Quivering, she fell at last into a languid glide, gasping for air to fill her shuddering lungs.

Too bad. I can hear it... the underwater thing I was seeking... not too far away now.

But Zhaki and Mopol are closer still....

What took Peepoe some moments to recall was that the salt-thermal barrier deadened sound from whatever entity was cruising the depths below. For her to hear it now, however faintly, meant that it had to be —

A tremor rocked Peepoe. She felt the waters bulge around her, as if pushed aside by some massive creature, far under the ocean's surface. Realization dawned, even as she heard Zhaki's voice, shouting gleefully only a short distance away.

It's right below me. The thing! It's passing by, down there in the blackness.

She had only moments to make a decision. Judging from cues in the water, it was both very large and very far beneath her. Yet Peepoe felt nowhere near ready to attempt a deep dive while each breath still sighed with ragged pain.

She heard and felt the sled zoom past, spotting her two tormentors sprawled on the machine's back, grinning as they swept by, dangerously close. Instinct made her want to turn away and flee, or else go below for as long as her lungs could hold out. But neither move would help, so she stayed put.

They'll savor their victory for a little while, she thought, hoping they were confident enough not to use the sled's stunner on her. Anyway, at this short range, what could she do?

It was hard to believe they hadn't picked up any signs of the behemoth by now. Stupid, single-minded males, they had concentrated all of their attention on the hunt for her.

Zhaki and Mopol circled around her twice, spiraling slowly closer, leering and chattering.

Peepoe felt exhausted, still sucking air for her laboring lungs. But she could afford to wait no longer. As they approached for the final time, she took one last, body-stretching gasp through her blowhole, arched her back, and flipped over to dive nose-first into the deep.

At the final instant, her tail flukes waved at the boys. A gesture that she hoped they would remember with galling regret.

Blackness consumed the light and she plunged, kicking hard to gain depth while her meager air supply lasted. Soon, darkness welcomed Peepoe. But on passing the boundary layer, she did not need illumination any more. Sound guided her, the throaty rumble of something huge, moving gracefully and complacently through a world where sunshine never fell.

Tkett

He had several reasons to desire a starship, even one that was unable to fly. It could offer a way to visit the Great Midden, for instance, and explore its wonders. A partly operational craft might also prove useful to the Six Races of Jijo, whose bloody war against Jophur aggressors was said to be going badly ashore.

Tkett also imagined using such a machine to find and rescue Peepoe.

No one held out much hope of finding the beautiful dolphin medic, one of Makanee's assistants, kidnapped shortly before *Streaker* departed. The two dolphin felons – Mopol and Zhaki – had an immensity to conceal her in. But that gloomy calculation assumed searchers must travel by sled!

A *ship* on the other hand – even a wreck that had lain on an ocean floor garbage dump for half a million years – could cover a lot more territory and listen with big underwater sonaphones, combing for telltale sounds from Peepoe and her abductors. It might even be possible to sift the waters for Earthling DNA traces. Tkett had heard of such techniques available for a high price on Galactic markets. Who knew what wonders the fabled Buyur took for granted on their elegant starcraft?

Unfortunately, the trail kept going hot and cold. Sometimes he picked up murmurs that seemed incredibly close, channeled by watery layers that focused sound. Other times they vanished altogether.

Frustrated, Tkett was willing to try anything. So when Chissis started getting agitated, squealing in Primal that a great beast prowled to the southwest, he willingly turned the sled in the direction she indicated.

And soon he was rewarded. Indicators began flashing on the control panel and down his neural-link cable, connecting the sled to an implanted socket behind his left eye. In addition to a surge of noise, mass displacement anomalies suggested something of immense size was moving ponderously just ahead, and perhaps a hundred meters down.

"I guess we better go find out what it is," he told his passenger, who clicked her agreement.

go chase go chase go chase ORCAS!

She let out squalls of laughter at her own cleverness. But minutes later, as they plunged deeper into the sea – both listening and peering down the shaft of the sled's probing headlights – Chissis ceased chuckling and became silent as a tomb.

Great Dreamers! Tkett stared in awe and surprise at the object before them. It was unlike any starship he had ever seen before. Sleek metallic sides seemed to go on and on forever as the titanic machine trudged onward across the sea floor, churning up mud with thousands of shimmering, crystalline legs!

As if sensing their arrival, a mammoth hatch began irising open – in benign welcome, he hoped.

No resurrected starship. Tkett began to suspect he had come upon something entirely different.

Peepoe

Her ribcage heaved.

Peepoe's lungs filled with a throbbing ache as she forced herself to dive ever deeper, much lower than would have been wise, even if she weren't fatigued to the very edge of consciousness.

The sea at this depth was black. Her eyes made out nothing. But that was not the important sense, underwater. Sonar clicks, emitted from her brow, grew more rapid as she scanned ahead, using her sensitive jaw as an antenna to sift reflections.

It's big.... she thought when the first signs returned.

Echo outlines began coalescing and she shivered.

It doesn't sound like metal. The shape... seems less artificial than something –

A thrill of terror coursed her spine as she realized that the thing ahead had outlines resembling a gigantic living creature! A huge mass of fins and trailing tentacles, resembling some monster from the stories dolphin children would tell each other at night, secure in their rookeries near one of Earth's great port cities. What lay ahead of Peepoe, swimming along well above the canyon floor, seemed bigger and more intimidating than the giant squid who fought Physeter sperm whales, mightiest of all the cetaceans.

And yet, Peepoe kept arching her back, pushing hard with her flukes, straining ever downward. Curiosity compelled her. Anyway, she was closer to the creature than the sea surface, where Zhaki and Mopol waited.

I might as well find out what it is.

Curiosity was just about all she had left to live for.

When several tentacles began reaching for her, the only remaining question in her mind was about death.

I wonder who I'll meet on the other side.

Makanee

The dolphins in the pod – her patients – all woke about the same time from their afternoon siesta, screaming.

Makanee and her nurses joined Brookida, who had been on watch, swimming rapid circles around the frightened reverts, preventing any of them from charging in panic across the wide sea. Slowly, they all calmed down from a shared nightmare.

It was a common enough experience back on Earth, when unconscious sonar clicks from two or more sleeping dolphins would sometimes overlap and interfere, creating false echoes. The ghost of something terrifying. It did not help that most cetaceans sleep with just one brain hemisphere at a time. In a way, that seemed only to make the dissonance more eerie, and the fallacious sound-images more credibly scary.

Most of the patients were inarticulate, emitting only a jabber of terrified Primal squeals. But there were borderline cases who might even recover their full faculties someday. One of these moaned nervously about Tkett and a city of spells.

Another one chittered nervously, repeating over and over, the name of Peepoe.

Tkett

Well, at least the machine has air inside, he thought. *We can survive here and learn more.*

In fact, the huge underwater edifice – bigger than all but the largest starships – seemed rather accommodating, pulling back metal walls as the little sled entered a spacious airlock. The floor sank in order to provide a pool for Tkett and Chissis to debark from their tight cockpits and swim around. It felt good to get out of the cramped confines, even though Tkett knew that coming inside might be a mistake.

Makanee's orders had been to do an inspection from the outside, then hurry home. But that was when they expected to find one of the rusty little spacecraft that *Streaker's* engineers had resurrected from some sea floor dross pile. As soon as Tkett saw this huge cylindrical thing, churning along the sea bottom on a myriad caterpillar legs that gleamed like crystal stalks, he knew that nothing on Jijo could stand in the way of his going aboard.

Another wall folded aside, revealing a smooth channel that stretched ahead – water below and air above – beckoning the two dolphins down a hallway that shimmered as it continued transforming before their eyes. Each panel changed color with the glimmering luminescence of octopus skin, seeming to convey meaning in each transient, flickering shade. Chissis thrashed her tail nervously as objects kept slipping through seams in the walls. Sometimes these featured a camera lens at the end of an articulated arm, peering at them as they swam past.

Not even the Buyur could afford to throw away something as wonderful as this, Tkett thought, relishing a fantasy of taking this technology home to Earth. At the same time, the mechanical implements of his tool harness quivered, responding to nervous twitches that his brain sent down the neural tap. He had no weapons that would avail in the slightest, if the owners of this place proved to be hostile.

The corridor spilled at last into a wide chamber with walls and ceiling that were so corrugated that he could not estimate its true volume. Countless bulges and spires protruded inward, half of them submerged, and the rest hanging in midair. All were bridged by cables and webbing that glistened like spider webs lined with dew. Many of the branches carried shining spheres or cubes or dodecahedrons that dangled like geometric fruit, ranging from half a meter across to twice the length of a bottlenose dolphin.

Chissis let out a squall, colored with fear and awe.

coral that bites! coral bites bites!
See the critters, stabbed by coral!

When he saw what she meant, Tkett gasped. The hanging "fruits" were mostly transparent. They contained things that moved... creatures who writhed or hopped or ran in place, churning their arms and legs within the confines of their narrow compartments.

Adaptive optics in his right eye whirred, magnifying and zooming toward one of the crystal-walled containers. Meanwhile, his brow cast forth a stream of nervous sonar clicks – useless in the air – as if trying to penetrate this mystery with yet another sense.

I don't believe it!

He recognized the shaggy creature within a transparent cage.

Ifni! It's a hoon. A miniature hoon!

Scanning quickly, he found individuals of other species... four-legged urs with their long necks whipping nervously, like muscular snakes... minuscule traeki that resembled their Jophur cousins, looking like tapered stacks of doughnuts, piled high... and tiny versions of wheeled g'Keks, spinning their hubs madly, as if they were actually going somewhere. In fact, every member of the Commons of Six Races of Jijo – fugitive clans that had settled this world illegally during the last two thousand years – could be seen here, represented in Lilliputian form.

Tkett's spine shuddered when he made out several cells containing slim bipedal forms. Bantam-weight *human beings*, whose race had struggled against lonely ignorance on old Terra for so many centuries, nearly destroying the world until they finally matured enough to lead the way toward true sapiency for the rest of Earthclan.

Before Tkett's astonished eye, these members of the patron race were now reduced to leaping and cavorting with the confines of dangling crystal spheres.

Peepoe

Death would not be so mundane... nor hurt in such familiar ways. When she began regaining consciousness, there was never any doubt which world this was. The old cosmos of life and pain.

Peepoe remembered the sea monster, an undulating behemoth of fins, tendrils and phosphorescent scales, more than a kilometer long and nearly as wide, flapping wings like a manta ray as it glided well above the sea floor. When it reached up for her, she never thought of fleeing toward the surface, where mere enslavement waited. Peepoe was too exhausted by that point, and too transfixed by the images – both sonic and luminous – of a true leviathan.

The tentacle was gentler than expected, in grabbing her unresisting body and drawing it toward a widening beaklike maw. As she was pulled between a pair of jagged-edged jaws, Peepoe had let blackness finally claim her, moments before the end. The last thought to pass through her head was a Trinary haiku.

> *Arrogance is answered*
> > *When each of us is reclaimed.*
> > > *Rejoin the food chain! **

Only there turned out to be more to her life, after all. Expecting to become pulped food for huge intestines, she wakened instead, surprised to find herself in another world.

A blurry world, at first. She lay in a small pool. That much was evident. But it took moments to restore focus. Meanwhile, out of the pattern of her bemused sonar clickings, a reflection seemed to mold itself, unbidden, surrounding Peepoe with Trinary philosophy.

> *In the turning of life's cycloid,*
> > *Pulled by sun and moon insistence,*
> *Once a springtime storm may toss you,*
> > *Over reefs that have no channel,*
> *Into some lagoon untraveled,*
> > *Where strange fishes, spiny-poisoned,*
> > *Taunt you, forlorn, isolated... **

It wasn't an auspicious thought-poem, and Peepoe cut it off sharply, lest such stark sonic imagery trigger panic. The Trinary fog clung hard, though. It dissipated only with fierce effort, leaving a sense of dire warning in its wake.

Rising to the surface, Peepoe lifted her head and inspected the pool, lined by a riot of vegetation. Dense jungle stretched on all sides, brushing the rough-textured ceiling and cutting off her view beyond a few meters. Flickering movements and skittering sounds revealed the presence of small inhabitants, from flying insectoids to clambering things that peered at her shyly from behind sheltering leaves and shadows.

A habitat, she realized. Things lived here, competed, preyed on each other, died, and were recycled in a familiar ongoing synergy. The largest starships often contained ecological life-support systems, replenishing both food and oxygen supplies in the natural way.

But this is no starship. It can't be. The huge shape I saw could never fly. It was a sea beast, meant for the underwater world. It must have been alive!

Well, was there any reason why a gigantic animal could not keep an ecology going inside itself, like the bacterial cultures that helped Peepoe digest her own food?

So now what? Am I supposed to take part in all of this somehow? Or have I just begun a strange process of being digested?

She set off with a decisive push of her flukes. A dolphin without tools wasn't very agile in an environment like this. Her monkey-boy cousins – humans and chimps – would do better. But Peepoe was determined to explore while her strength lasted.

A channel led out of the little pool. Maybe something more interesting lay around the next bend.

Tkett

One of the spiky branches started moving, bending and articulating as it bowed lower toward the watery surface where he and Chissis waited. At its tip, one of the crystal "fruits" contained a quadrupedal being – an *urs* whose long neck twisted as she peered about with glittering black eyes.

Tkett knew just a few things about this species. For example, they hated water in its open liquid form. Also the females were normally as massive as a full-grown human, yet this one appeared to be as small as a diminutive urrish male, less than twenty centimeters from nose to tail. Back in the Civilization of Five Galaxies, urs were known as great engineers. Humans didn't care for their smell (the feeling was mutual), but interactions between the two starfaring clans had been cordial. Urs weren't among the persecutors of Earthclan.

Tkett had no idea why an offshoot group of urs came to this world, centuries ago, establishing a secret and illegal colony on a planet that had been declared off-limits by the Migration Institute. As one of the Six Races, they now galloped across Jijo's prairies, tending herds and working metals at forges that used heat from fresh volcanic lava pools. To find one here, under the sea, left him boggled and perplexed.

The creature seemed unaware of the dolphins who watched from nearby. Tkett guessed that the glassy confines of the enclosure were transparent only in one direction. Flickering scenes could be made out, playing across the opposite internal walls. He glimpsed hilly countryside covered with swaying grass. The little urs galloped along, as if unencumbered and unenclosed.

The sphere dropped closer, and Tkett saw that it was choked with innumerable microscopic threads that crisscrossed the little chamber. Many of these terminated at the body of the urs, especially the bottoms of her flashing hooves.

Resistance simulators! Tkett recognized the principle, though he had never seen such a magnificent implementation. Back on Earth, humans and chimps would sometimes put on full body suits and VR helmets before entering chambers where a million needles made up the floor, each one computer controlled. As the user walked along a fictitious landscape, depicted visually in goggles he wore, the needles would rise and fall, simulating the same rough terrain underfoot. Each of these small crystal containers apparently operated in the same way, but with vastly greater texture and sophistication. So many tendrils pushing, stroking or stimulating each patch of skin, could feign wind blowing through urrish fur, or simulate the rough sensation of holding a tool... perhaps even the delightful rub and tickle of mating.

Other stalks descended toward Tkett and Chissis, holding many more virtual reality fruits, each one containing a single individual. All of Jijo's sapient races were present, though much reduced in stature. Chissis seemed especially agitated to see small humans that ran about, or rested, or bent in apparent concentration over indiscernible tasks. None seemed aware of being observed.

It all felt horribly creepy, yet the subjects did not give an impression of lethargy or unhappiness. They seemed vigorous, active, interested in whatever engaged them. Perhaps they did not even know the truth about their peculiar existence.

Chissis snorted her uneasiness, and Tkett agreed. Something felt weird about the way these micro-environments were being paraded before the two of them, as if the mind – or minds – controlling the whole vast apparatus had some point it was trying to make, or some desire to communicate.

Is the aim to impress us?

He wondered about that, then abruptly realized what it must be about.

... all of Jijo's sapient races were present...

In fact, that was no longer true. Another species of thinking beings now dwelled on this world, the newest one officially sanctioned by the Civilization of Five Galaxies.

Neo-dolphins.

Oh, certainly the reverts like poor Chissis were only partly sapient anymore. And Tkett had no illusions about what Dr. Makanee thought of his own mental state. Nevertheless, as stalk after stalk bent to present its fruit before the two dolphins, showing off the miniature beings within – all of them busy and apparently happy with their existence – he began to feel as if he was being wooed.

"Ifni's boss..." he murmured aloud, amazed at what the great machine appeared to be offering. "It wants us to become part of all this!"

Peepoe

A village of small grass huts surrounded the next pool she entered.

Small didn't half describe it. The creatures who emerged to swarm around the shore stared at her with wide eyes, set in skulls less than a third of normal size.

They were humans and hoons, mostly... along with a few traeki and a couple of glavers... all races whose full sized cousins lived just a few hundred kilometers away, on a stretch of Jijo's western continent called The Slope.

As astonishing as she found these Lilliputians, they stared in even greater awe at her. *I'm like a whale to them*, she realized, noting with some worry that many of them brandished spears or other weapons.

She heard a chatter of worried conversation as they pointed at her long gray bulk. That meant their brains were large enough for speech. Peepoe noted that the creatures' heads were out of proportion to their bodies, making the humans appear rather child-like... until you saw the men's hairy, scarred torsos, or the women's breasts, pendulous with milk for hungry babies. Their rapid jabber grew more agitated by the moment.

I'd better reassure them, or risk getting harpooned.

Peepoe spoke, starting with Anglic, the wolfling tongue most used on Earth. She articulated the words carefully with her gene-modified blowhole.

"Hello f-f-folks! How are you doing today?"

That got a response, but not the one she hoped for. The crowd onshore backed away hurriedly, emitting upset cries. This time she thought she made out a few words in a time-shifted dialect of Galactic Seven, so she tried again in that language.

"Greetings! I bring you news of peaceful arrival and friendly intentions!"

This time the crowd went nearly crazy, leaping and cavorting in excitement, though whether it was pleasure or indignation seemed hard to tell at first.

Suddenly, the mob parted and went silent as a figure approached from the line of huts. It was a hoon, taller than average among these midgets. He wore an elaborate headdress and cape, while the dyed throat sac under his chin flapped and vibrated to a sonorous beat. Two human assistants followed, one of them beating a drum. The rest of the villagers then did an amazing thing. They all dropped to their knees and covered their ears. Soon Peepoe heard a rising murmur.

They're humming. I do believe they're trying not to hear what the big guy is saying!

At the edge of the pool, the hoon lifted his arms and began chanting in a strange version of Galactic Six.

"Spirits of the sky, I summon thee by name... Kataranga!

"Spirits of the water, I beseech thy aid... Dupussien!

"By my knowledge of your secret names, I command thee to gather and surround this monster. Protect the people of the True Way!"

This went on for a while. At first Peepoe felt bemused, as if she were watching a documentary about some ancient human tribe, or the Prob'shers of planet Horst. Then she began noticing something strange. Out of the jungle, approaching on buzzing wings, there appeared a variety of insect-like creatures. At first just a few, then more. Flying zig-zag patterns toward the chanting shaman, they started gathering in a spiral-shaped swarm.

Meanwhile, ripples in the pool tickled Peepoe's flanks, revealing another convergence of ingathering beasts – this time swimmers – heading for the point of shore nearest the summoning hoon.

I don't believe this, she thought. It was one thing for a primitive priest to invoke the forces of nature. It was quite another to sense those forces responding quickly, unambiguously, and with ominous threatening behavior.

Members of both swarms, the fliers and the swimmers, began making darting forays toward Peepoe. She felt several sharp stings on her dorsal fin, and some more from below, on her ventral side.

They're attacking me!

Realization snapped her out of a bemused state.

Time to get out of here, she thought as more of the tiny native creatures could be seen arriving from all directions.

Peepoe whirled about, shoving toward shore a wavelet that interrupted the yammering shaman, sending him scurrying backward with a yelp. Then, in a surge of eager strength, she sped away from there.

Tkett

Just when he thought he had seen enough, one of the crystal fruits descended close to the pool where he and Chissis waited, stopping only when it brushed the water, almost even with their eyes. The walls vibrated for a moment... then spilt open!

The occupant, a tiny g'Kek with spindly wheels on both sides of a tapered torso, rolled toward the gap, regarding the pair of dolphins with four eye stalks that waved as they peered at Tkett. Then the creature spoke in a voice that sounded high-pitched but firm, using thickly-accented Galactic Seven.

"We were aware that new settlers had come to this world. But imagine our surprise to discover that this time they are swimmers, who found us before we spotted them! No summoning call had to be sent through the Great Egg. No special collector robots dispatched to pick up volunteers from shore. How clever of you to arrive just in time, only days and weeks before the expected moment when this universe splits asunder!"

Chissis panted nervously, filling the sterile chamber with rapid clicks while Tkett bit the water hard with his narrow jaw.

"I... have no idea what y-y-you're talking about," he stammered in reply.

The miniature g'Kek twisted several eye stalks around each other. Tkett had an impression that it was consulting or communing with some entity elsewhere. Then it rolled forward, unwinding the stalks to wave at Tkett again.

"If an explanation is what you seek, then that is what you shall have."

Peepoe

The interior of the great leviathan seemed to consist of one leaf-shrouded pool after another, in a complex maze of little waterways. Soon quite lost, Peepoe doubted she would ever be able to find her way back to the thing's mouth.

Most of the surrounding areas consisted of dense jungle, though there were also rocky escarpments and patches of what looked like rolling grassland. Peepoe had also passed quite a few villages of little folk. In one place an endless series of ramps and flowing bridges had been erected through the foliage, comprising what looked like a fantastic scale-model roller coaster, interweaved amid the dwarf trees. Little g'Keks could be seen zooming along this apparatus of wooden planks and vegetable fibers, swerving and teetering on flashing wheels.

Peepoe tried to glide innocuously past the shoreline villages, but seldom managed it without attracting some attention. Once, a war party set forth in chase after her, riding upon the backs of turtle-like creatures, shooting tiny arrows and hurling curses in quaint-sounding jargon she could barely understand. Another time, a garishly attired urrish warrior swooped toward her from above, straddling a flying lizard whose wings flapped gorgeously and whose mouth belched small but frightening bolts of flame! Peepoe retreated, overhearing the little urs continue to shout behind her, challenging the "sea monster" to single combat.

It seemed she had entered a world full of beings who were as suspicious as they were diminished in size. Several more times, shamans and priests of varied races stood at the shore, gesturing and shouting rhythmically, commanding hordes of beelike insects to sting and pursue her until she fled beyond sight. Peepoe's spirits steadily sank... until at last she arrived at a broad basin where many small boats could be seen, cruising under brightly painted sails.

To her surprise, this time the people aboard shouted with amazed pleasure upon spotting her, not fear or wrath! With tentative but rising hope, she followed their beckonings to shore where, under the battlements of a magnificently ornate little castle, a delegation descended to meet her beside a wooden pier.

Their apparent leader, a human wearing gray robes and a peaked hat, grinned as he gestured welcome, enunciating in an odd but lilting version of Anglic.

"Many have forgotten the tales told by the First. But we know you, oh noble dolphin! You are remembered from legends passed down since the beginning! How wonderful to have you come among us now, as the Time of Change approaches. In the name of the Spirit Guides, we offer you our hospitality and many words of power!"

Peepoe mused on everything she had seen and heard.

Words, eh? Words can be a good start.

She had to blow air several times before her nervous energy dispelled enough to speak.

"All right then. Can you start by telling me what in Ifni's name is going on here?"

Givers of Wonder

A Time of Changes comes. Worlds are about to divide.

Galaxies that formerly were linked by shortcuts of space and time will soon sunder apart. The old civilization — including all the planets you came from — will no longer be accessible. Their ways won't dominate this part of the cosmos, anymore.

Isolated, this island realm of one hundred billion stars (formerly known as Galaxy Four) will soon develop its own destiny, fostering a bright new age. It has been foreseen that Jijo will provide the starting seed for a glorious culture, unlike any other. The six... and now seven!... sapient species who came sneaking secretly to this world as refugees — skulking in order to hide like criminals on a forbidden shore — will prosper beyond all their wildest imaginings. They will be co-founders of something great and wonderful. Forerunners of all the starfaring races who may follow in this fecund stellar whirlpool.

But what kind of society should it be? One that is a mere copy of the noisy, bickering, violent conglomeration that exists back in "civilized" space? One based on crude so-called sciences? Physics, cybernetics, and biology? We have learned that such obsessions lead to soullessness. A humorless culture, operated by reductionists who measure the cost/benefit ratios of everything and know the value of nothing!

There must be something better.

Indeed, consider how the newest sapient races — fresh from uplift — look upon their world with a childlike sense of wonder! What if that feeling could be made to last?

To those who have just discovered it, the power of speech itself is glorious. A skill with words seems to hold all the potency anyone should ever need! Still heedful of their former animal ways, these infant species often use their new faculty of self-expression to perceive patterns that are invisible to older, "wiser" minds. Humans were especially good at this, during the long ages of their lonely abandonment, on isolated Earth. They had many names for their systems of wondrous cause-and-effect, traditions that arose in a myriad land-bound tribes. But nearly all of these systems shared certain traits in common:

a sense that the world is made of spirits, living in each stone or brook or tree.

an eager willingness to perceive all events, even great storms and the movements of planets, as having a personal relationship with the observer.

a conviction that nature can be swayed by those favored with special powers of sight, voice, or mind, raising those elite ones above other mere mortals.

a profound belief in the power of words to persuade and control the world.

"Magic" was one word that humans used for this way of looking at the universe. We believe it is a better way, offering drama, adventure, vividness, and romance. Yet magic can take many forms. And there is still some dispute over the details....

Alternating Views of Temptation

Tkett found the explanation bizarre and perplexing at first. How did it relate to this strange submersible machine whose gut was filled with crystal fruit, each containing an intelligent being who leaped about and seemed to focus fierce passion on things only he or she could see?

Still, as an archaeologist he had some background studying the tribal human past, so eventually a connection clicked in his mind.

"You... you are using technology to give each individual a private world! B-but there's more to it than that, isn't there? Are you saying that every hoon, or human, or traeki inside these crystal c-containers gets to cast magic spells? They don't just manipulate false objects by hand, and see tailored illusions... they also shout incantations and have the satisfaction of watching them come true?"

Tkett blinked several times, trying to grasp it all.

"Take that woman over there." He aimed his rostrum at a nearby cube wherein a female human grinned and pointed amid a veritable cloud of resistance threads.

"If she has an enemy, can she mold a clay figure and stick pins in it to cast a spell of pain?"

The little g'Kek spun its wheels before answering emphatically.

"True enough, oh perceptive dolphin! Of course she has to be creative. Talent and a strong will are helpful. And she must adhere to the accepted lore of her simulated tribe."

"Arbitrary rules, you mean."

The eye stalks shrugged gracefully. "Arbitrary, but elegant and consistent. And there is another requirement. Above all, our user of magic must intensely believe."

◇

Peepoe blinked at the diminutive wizard standing on the nearby dock, in the shadow of a fairytale castle.

"You mean people in this place can command the birds and insects and other beasts using words alone?"

She had witnessed it happen dozens of times, but to hear it explained openly like this felt strange.

The gray-cloaked human nodded, speaking rapidly, eagerly. "Special words! The power of secret names. Terms that each user must keep closely guarded."

"But —"

"Above all, most creatures will only obey those with inborn talent. Individuals who possess great force of will. Otherwise, if they heeded everybody, where would be the awe and envy that lie at the very heart of sorcery? If everyone can do a thing, it soon loses all worth. A miracle palls when it becomes routine.

"It is said that technology used to be like that, back in the Old Civilization. Take what happened soon after Earth-humans discovered how to fly. Soon all people could soar through the sky, and they took the marvel for granted. How tragic! That sort of thing does not happen here. We preserve wonder like a precious resource."

Peepoe sputtered.

"But all this –" She flicked her jaws, spraying water toward the jungle and the steep, fleshy cliffs beyond. "All of this smacks of technology! That absurd fire-breathing dragon, for instance. Clearly bio-engineered! Somebody set up this whole thing as... as an..."

"As an experiment?" The gray-clad mage conceded with a nod. His beard shook as he continued with eager fire in his piping voice.

"That has never been secret! Ever since our ancestors were selected from among Jijo's land-bound Six Races, to come dwell below the sea in smaller but mightier bodies, we knew that one purpose would be to help the Buyur fine-tune their master plan."

◇

Tkett reared back in shock, churning water with his flukes. He stared at the many-eyed creature who had been explaining this weird chamber-of-miniatures.

"The B-Buyur! They left Jijo half a million years ago. How could they even know about human culture, let alone set up this elaborate –"

"Of course the answer to that question is simple," replied the little g'Kek, peering with several eye stalks from its cracked crystal shell. "Our Buyur lords never left! They have quietly observed and guided this process ever since the first ship of refugees slinked down to Jijo, preparing for the predicted day when natural forces would sever all links between Galaxy Four and the others."

"But –"

"The great evacuation of starfaring clans from Galaxy Four – half an eon ago – made sure that no other techno-sapiens remain in this soon-to-be-isolated starry realm. So it will belong to *our* descendants who inherit! In a culture far different than the dreary one our ancestors belonged to."

Tkett had heard of the Buyur, of course – among the most powerful members of the Civilization of Five Galaxies, and one of the few elder races known for a sense of humor... albeit a strange one. It was said that they believed in long jokes, that took ages to plan and execute.

Was that because the Buyur found Galactic culture stodgy and stifling? (Most Earthlings would agree.) Apparently they foresaw all of the changes and convulsions that were today wracking the linked starlanes, and began preparing millennia ago for an unparalleled opportunity to put their own stamp on an entirely new branch of destiny.

⬦

Peepoe nodded, understanding part of it at last.

"This leviathan... this huge organic beast... isn't the only experimental container cruising below the waves. There are others! Many?"

"Many," confirmed the little gray-bearded human wizard. "The floating chambers take a variety of forms, each accommodating its own colony of sapient beings. Each habitat engages its passengers in a life that is rich with magic, though in uniquely different ways.

"Here, for instance, we sapient beings experience physically active lives, in a totally real environment. It is the wild creatures around us who were altered! Surely you have heard that the Buyur were master gene-crafters? In this experimental realm, each insect, fish and flower knows its own unique and secret name. By learning and properly uttering such names, a mage like me can wield great power."

⬦

Tkett listened as the cheerful g'Kek explained the complex experiment taking place in the chamber of crystalline fruits.

"In *our* habitat, each of us gets to live in his or her own world – one that is rich, varied, and physically demanding, even if it is mostly a computer-driven simulation. Within such an ersatz reality every one of us can be the lead magician in a society or tribe of lesser peers. Or the crystal fruits can be linked, allowing shared encounters between equals. Either way, it is a vivid life, filled with more excitement than the old way of so-called engineering.

"A life in which the mere act of believing can have power, and wishing sometimes makes things come true!"

⬦

Peepoe watched the gray magician stroke his beard while describing the range of Buyur experiments.

"There are many other styles, modes, and implementations being tried out, in scores of other habitats. Some emphasize gritty 'reality,' while others go so far as to eliminate physical form entirely, encoding their subjects as digital personae in wholly computerized worlds."

Downloading personalities. Peepoe recognized the concept. It was tried back home and never caught on, even though boosters said it ought to, logically.

"There is an ultimate purpose to all of these experiments," the human standing on the nearby pier explained, like a proselyte eager for a special convert. "We aim to find exactly the right way to implement a new society that will thrive across the starlanes of Galaxy Four, once separation is complete and all the old hyperspatial transit paths are gone. When this island whirlpool of a hundred billion stars is safe at last from interference by the Old Civilization, it will be time to start our own. One that is based on a glorious new principle.

"By analyzing the results of each experimental habitat, the noble Buyur will know exactly how to implement a new realm of magic and wonders. Then the age of true miracles can begin."

Listening to this, Peepoe shook her head.

"You don't sound much like a rustic feudal magician. I just bet you're something else, in disguise.

"Are you a Buyur?"

The g'Kek bowed within its crystal shell. "That's a very good guess, my dolphin friend. Though of course the real truth is complicated. A real Buyur would weigh more than a metric ton and somewhat resemble an Earthling frog!"

"Nevertheless you —" Tkett prompted.

"I have the honor of serving as a spokesman-intermediary...."

"...to help persuade you dolphins — the newest promising colonists on Jijo — that joining us will be your greatest opportunity for vividness, adventure, and a destiny filled with marvels!"

The little human wizard grinned, and Peepoe realized that the others nearby must not have heard or understood a bit of it. Perhaps they wore earplugs to protect themselves against the power of the mage's words. Or else Anglic was rarely spoken, here. Perhaps it was a "language of power."

Peepoe also realized – she was both being tested and offered a choice.

Out there in the world, we few dolphin settlers face an uncertain existence. Makanee has no surety that our little pod of reverts will survive the next winter, even with help from the other colonists ashore. Anyway, the Six Races have troubles of their own, fighting Jophur invaders.

She had to admit that this offer had tempting aspects. After experiencing several recent Jijo storms, Peepoe could see the attraction of bringing all the other *Streaker* exiles aboard some cozy undersea habitat – presumably one with bigger stretches of open water – and letting the Buyur perform whatever techno-magic it took to reduce dolphins in size so they would fit their new lives. How could that be any worse than the three years of cramped hell they had all endured aboard poor *Streaker*?

Presumably someday, when the experiments were over, her descendants would be given back their true size, after they had spent generations learning to weave spells and cast incantations with the best of them.

Oh, we could manage that, she thought. *We dolphins are good at certain artistic types of verbal expression. After all, what is Trinary but our own special method of using sound to persuade the world? Talking it into assuming vivid sonic echoes and dreamlike shapes? Coaxing it to make sense in our own cetacean way?*

The delicious temptation of it all reached out to Peepoe.

What is the alternative? Assuming we ever find a way back to civilization, what would we go home to? A gritty fate that at best offers lots of hard work, where it can take half a lifetime just learning the skills you need to function usefully in a technological society.

Real life isn't half as nice as the tales we first hear in storybooks. Everybody learns at some point that it's a disappointing world out there – a universe where good is seldom purely handsome and evil doesn't obligingly identify itself with red glowing eyes. A complex society filled with tradeoffs and compromises, as well as committees and political opponents who always have much more power than you think they deserve.

Who wouldn't prefer a place where the cosmos might be talked into giving you what you want? Or where wishing sometimes makes things true?

◊

"We already have two volunteers from your esteemed race," the g'Kek spokesman explained, causing Tkett to quiver in surprise. With a flailing of eye stalks, the wheeled figure commanded that a hologram appear, just above the water's surface.

Tkett at once saw two large male dolphins lying calmly on mesh hammocks while tiny machines scurried all over them, spinning webs of some luminescent material. Chissis, long silent and brooding, abruptly recognized the pair, and shouted Primal recognition.

> # Caught! Caught in nets as they deserved!
> # Foolish Zhaki – Nasty Mopol! #

"Ifni!" Tkett commented. "I think you're right. But what's being done to them?"

"They have already accepted our offer," said the little wheeled intermediary.

"Soon those two will dwell in realms of holographic and sensual delights, aboard a different experimental station than this one. Their destiny is assured, and let me promise you – they will be happy."

◇

"You're sure those two aren't here aboard this vessel, near me?" Peepoe asked nervously, watching Zhaki and Mopol undergo their transformation via a small image that the magician had conjured with a magic phrase and a wave of one hand.

"No. Your associates followed a lure to one of our neighboring experimental cells – to their senses it appeared to be a 'leviathan' resembling one of your Earthling blue whales. Once they had come aboard, preliminary appraisal showed that their personalities will probably thrive best in a world of pure fantasy.

"They eagerly accepted this proposal."

Peepoe nodded, shocked only at her own lack of emotion, either positive or negative, toward this final disposal of her tormentors. They were gone from her life, and that was all she really cared about. Let Ifni decide whether their destination qualified as permanent imprisonment, or a strange kind of heaven.

Well, now they can have harems of willing cows, to their hearts' content, she thought. *Good riddance.*

Anyway, she had other quandaries to focus on, closer at hand.

"What've you got p-planned for me?"

The gray wizard spread his arms in eager consolation.

"Nothing frightening or worrisome, oh esteemed dolphin-friend! At this point we are simply asking that you choose!

"Will you join us? No one is coerced. But how could anyone refuse? If one lifestyle does not suit you, pick another! Select from a wide range of enchanted worlds, and further be assured that your posterity will someday be among the magic-wielders who establish a new order across a million suns."

⬦

Tkett saw implications that went beyond the offer itself. The plan of the Buyur – its scope and the staggering range of their ambition – left him momentarily dumbfounded.

They want to set up a whole galaxy-spanning civilization, based on what they consider to be an ideal way of life. Someday soon, after this 'Time of Changes' has ruptured the old inter-galaxy links, the Buyur will be free from any of the old constraints of law and custom that dominated oxygen-breathing civilization for the last billion years.

Then, out of this planet there will spill a new wave of starships, crewed by the Seven Races of Jijo, commanded by bold captains, wizards and kings... a mixture of themes from old-time science fiction and fantasy... pouring forth toward adventure! Over the course of several ages, they will fight dangers, overcome grave perils, discover and uplift new species. Eventually, the humans and urs and traekis and others will become revered leaders of a galaxy that is forever filled with high drama.

In this new realm, boredom will be the ultimate horror. Placidity the ultimate crime. The true masters – the Buyur – will see to that.

Like Great Oz, manipulating levers behind a curtain, the Buyur will use their high technology to provide every wonder.

Ask for dragons? They will gene-craft or manufacture them. Secret factories will build sea monsters and acid-mouthed aliens, ready for battle.

It will be a galaxy run by special effects wizards! A perpetual theme park, whose inhabitants use magic spells instead of engineering to get what they want. Conjurers and monarchs will replace tedious legislatures, impulse will supplant deliberation, and lists of secret names will substitute for physics.

Nor will our descendants ask too many questions, or dare to pull back the curtain and expose Oz. Those who try won't have descendants!

Cushioned by hidden artifice, in time people will forget nature's laws.

They will flourish in vivid kingdoms, forever setting forth heroically, returning triumphally, or dying bravely... but never asking why.

Tkett mused on this while filling the surrounding water with intense sprays of sonar clicks. Chissis, who had clearly not understood much of the g'Kek's convoluted explanation, settled close by, rolling her body through the complex rhythms of Tkett's worried thoughts.

Finally, he felt that he grasped the true significance of it all.

Tkett swam close to the crystal cube, raising one eye until it was level with the small representative of the mighty Buyur.

"I think I get what's going on here," he said.

"Yes?" the little g'Kek answered cheerfully. "And what is your sage opinion, oh dolphin friend. What do you think of this great plan?"

Tkett lifted his head high out of the water, rising up on churning flukes, emitting chittering laughter from his blowhole. At the same time, a sardonic Trinary haiku floated from his clicking brow.

> ** Sometimes sick egos*
> ** foster in their narrow brains*
> ** Really stupid jokes! **

Some aspects of the offer were galling, such as the smug permanence of Buyur superiority in the world to come. Yet, Peepoe felt tempted.

After all, what else awaits us here on Jijo? Enslavement by the Jophur? Or the refuge of blessed dimness that the sages promise, if we follow the so-called Path of Redemption? Doesn't this offer a miraculous way out of choosing between those two unpalatable destinies?

She concentrated hard to sequester her misgivings, focusing instead on the advantages of the Buyur plan. And there were plenty, such as living in a cosmos where hidden technology made up for nature's mistakes. After all, wasn't it cruel of the Creator to make a universe where so many fervent wishes were ignored? A universe where prayers were mostly answered – if at all – within the confines of the heart? Might the Buyur plan rectify this oversight for billions and trillions? For all the inhabitants of a galaxy-spanning civilization! Generosity on such a scale was hard to fathom.

She compared this ambitious goal with the culture waiting for the *Streaker* survivors, should they ever make it back home to the other four galaxies, where a myriad competitive, fractious races bickered endlessly. Over-reliant on an ancient Library of unloving technologies, they seldom sought innovation or novelty. The desires of individual beings nearly always subsumed before the driving needs of nation, race, clan and philosophy.

Again, the Buyur vision looked favorable compared to the status quo.

A small part of her demanded: *Are these our only choices? What if we could come up with alternatives that go beyond simple-minded —*

She quashed the question fiercely, packing it off to far recesses of her mind.

"I would love to learn more," she told the gray wizard. "But what about my comrades? The other dolphins who now live on Jijo? Won't you need them, too?"

"In order to have a genetically viable colony, yes." The spokesman agreed. "If you agree to join us, we will ask you first to go and persuade others to come."

"Just out of curiosity, what would happen if I refused?"

The sorcerer shrugged. "Your life will resume much as it would have, if you never found us. We will erase all conscious memory of this visit, and you will be sent home. Later, when we have had a chance to refine our message, emissaries will come visit your pod of dolphins. But as far as you know, you will hear the proposal as if for the first time."

"I see. And again, those who refuse will be memory-wiped... and again each time you return. Kind of gives you an advantage in proselytizing, doesn't it?"

"Perhaps. Still, no one is compelled to join against their will." The little human smiled. "So, what is your answer? Will you help convey our message to your peers? We sense that you understand and sympathize with the better world we aim toward. Will you help enrich the Great Stew of Races with wondrous dolphin flavors?"

Peepoe nodded. "I will carry your vision to the others."

"Excellent! In fact, you can start without even leaving this pool! For I can now inform you that a pair of your compatriots already reside aboard one of our nearby vessels... and those two seem to be having trouble appreciating the wondrous life we offer."

"Not Zhaki and Mopol!" Peepoe pushed back with her ventral fins, clicking nervously. She wanted nothing further to do with them.

"No, no." The magician assured. "Please, wait calmly while we open a channel between ships, and all will become clear."

Tkett

"Hello, Peepoe," he said to the wavering image in front of him. "I'm glad you look well. We were all worried sick about you. But I figured when we saw Zhaki and Mopol you must be nearby."

The holo showed a sleek female dolphin, looking exquisite but tired, in a jungle-shrouded pool, beside a miniature castle. Tkett could tell a lot about the style of "experiment" aboard her particular vessel, just by observing the crowd of natives gathered by the shore. Some of them were dressed as armored knights, riding upon rearing steeds, while gaily attired peasants doffed their caps to passing lords and ladies. It was a far different approach than the crystal fruits that hung throughout this vessel — semi-transparent receptacles where individuals lived permanently immersed in virtual realities.

And yet, the basic principle was similar.

"Hi Tkett," Peepoe answered. *"Is that Chissis with you? You both doing all right?"*

"Well enough, I guess. Though I feel like the victim of some stupid fraternity practical —"

"Isn't it exciting?" Peepoe interrupted, cutting off what Tkett had been about to say. *"Across all the ages, visionaries have come up with countless utopian schemes. But this one could actually w-w-work!"*

Tkett stared back at her, unable to believe he was hearing this.

"Oh yeah?" He demanded. "What about free will?"

"The Buyur will provide whatever your will desires."

"Then how about truth!"

"There are many truths, Tkett. Countless vivid subjective interpretations will thrive in a future filled with staggering diversity."

"Subjective, exactly! That's an ancient and d-despicable perversion of the word *truth*, and you know it. Diversity is wonderful, all right. There may indeed be many cultures, many art forms, even many styles of wisdom. But truth should be about finding out what's really real, what's repeatable and verifiable, whether it suits your fancy or not!"

Peepoe sputtered a derisive raspberry.

"Where's the fun in that?"

"Life isn't just about having fun, or getting whatever you want!" Tkett felt his guts roil, forcing sour bile up his esophagus. "Peepoe, there's such a thing as growing up! Finding out how the world actually works, despite the way you think things ought to be. Objectivity means I accept that the universe doesn't revolve around me."

"In other words, a life of limitations."

"That we overcome with knowledge! With new tools and skills."

"Tools made of dead matter, designed by committees, mass-produced and sold on shop counters."

"Yes! Committees, teams, organizations and enterprises, all of them made up of individuals who have to struggle every day with their egos in order to cooperate with others, making countless compromises along the way. It ain't how things happen in a child's fantasy. It's not what we yearn for in our secret hearts, Peepoe. I know that! But it's how adults get things done.

"Anyway, what's wrong with buying miracles off a shop counter? So we take for granted wonders that our ancestors would've given their tail fins for. Isn't that what they'd have wanted for us? You'd prefer a world where the best of everything is kept reserved for wizards and kings?"

Tkett felt a sharp jab in his side. The pain made him whirl, still bitterly angry, still flummoxed with indignation.

"What is it!" He demanded sharply of Chissis, even though the little female could not answer.

She backed away from his bulk and rancor, taking a snout-down submissive posture. But from her brow came a brief burst of caustic Primal.

> # idiot idiot idiot idiot
> > # idiots keep talking human talk-talk
> # while the sea tries to teach #

Tkett blinked. Her phrasings were sophisticated, almost lucid. In fact, it was a lot like a simple Trinary chiding-poem, that a dolphin mother might use with her infant.

Through an act of hard self-control, he forced himself to consider.
While the sea tries to teach...

It was a common dolphin turn-of-phrase, implying that one should listen below the surface, to meanings that lay hidden.

He whirled back to examine the hologram, wishing it had not been designed by beings who relied so much on sight, and ignored the subtleties of sound transmission.

"Think about it, Tkett," Peepoe went on, as if their conversation had not been interrupted. *"Back home, we dolphins are the youngest client race of an impoverished, despised clan, in danger of being conquered or rendered extinct at any moment. Yet now we're being offered a position at the top of a new pantheon, just below the Buyur themselves.*

"What's more, we'd be good at this! Think about how dolphin senses might extend the range of possible magics. Our sound-based dreams and imagery. Our curiosity and reckless sense of adventure! And that just begins to hint at the possibilities when we finally come into our own...."

Tkett concentrated on sifting the background. The varied pulses, whines and clicks that melted into the ambiance whenever any neo-dolphin spoke. At first it seemed Peepoe was emitting just the usual mix of nervous sonar and blowhole flutters.

Then he picked out a single, floating phrase... in ancient Primal... that interleaved itself amid the earnest logic of sapient speech.

sleep on it sleep on it sleep on it sleep on it

At first the hidden message confused him. It seemed to support the rest of her argument. So then why make it secret?

Then another meaning occurred to him.

Something that even the puissant Buyur might not have thought of.

Peepoe

Her departure from the habitat was more gay and colorful than her arrival.

Dragons flew by overhead, belching gusts of heat that were much friendlier than before. Crowds of boats, ranging from canoes to bejeweled galleys pulled by sweating oarsmen, accompanied Peepoe from one pool to the next. Ashore, local wizards performed magnificent spectacles in her honor, to the awed wonder of gazing onlookers, while Peepoe swam gently past amid formations of fish whose scales glittered unnaturally bright.

With six races mixing in a wild variety of cultural styles, each village seemed to celebrate its own uniqueness in a profusion of architectural styles. The general attitude seemed both proud and fiercely competitive. But today all feuds, quests and noble campaigns had been put aside in order to see her off.

"See how eagerly we anticipate the success of your mission," the gray magician commented as they reached the final chamber. In a starship, this space would be set aside for an airlock, chilly and metallic. But here, the breath of a living organism sighed all around them as the great maw opened, letting both wind and sunshine come suddenly pouring through.

Nice of them to surface like this, sparing me the discomfort of a long climb out of the abyss.

"Tell the other dolphins what joy awaits them!" The little mage shouted after Peepoe as she drifted past the open jaws, into the light.

"Tell them about the vividness and adventure! Soon days of experimentation will be over, and all of this will be full-sized, with a universe lying before us!"

She pumped her flukes in order to rear up, looking back at the small gray figure in a star-spangled gown, who smiled as his arms spread wide, causing swarms of obedient bright creatures to hover above his head, converging to form a living halo.

"I will tell them," she assured.

Then Peepoe whirled and plunged into the cool sea, setting off toward a morning rendezvous.

Tkett

He came fully conscious again, only to discover with mild surprise that he was already swimming fast, leaping and diving through the ocean's choppy swells, propelled by powerful, rhythmic fluke-strokes.

Under other circumstances, it might have been disorienting to wake up in full motion. Except that a pair of dolphins flanked Tkett, one on each side, keeping perfect synchrony with his every arch and leap and thrust. That made it instinctively easy to literally swim in his sleep.

How long has this been going on?

He wasn't entirely sure. It felt like an hour or two. Perhaps longer.

Behind him, Tkett heard the low thrum of a sea sled's engine, cruising on low power as it followed the three of them on autopilot.

Why aren't we using the sled? He wondered. Three could fit, in a pinch. And that way they could get back to Makanee quicker, to report that...

Stale air exchanged quickly for fresh as he breached, performing each move with flawless precision, even as his mind roiled with unpleasant confusion.

... to report that Mopol and Zhaki are dead.

We found Peepoe, safe and well, wandering the open ocean.

As for the "machine" noises we were sent to investigate...

Tkett felt strangely certain there was a story behind all that. A story that Peepoe would explain later, when she felt the time was right.

Something wonderful, he recited, without quite knowing why. A flux of eagerness seemed to surge out of nowhere, priming Tkett to be receptive when she finally told everyone in the pod about the good news.

He could not tell why, but Tkett felt certain that more than just the sled was following behind them.

◇

"Welcome back to the living," Peepoe greeted in crisp Underwater Anglic, after their next breaching.

"Thanks I... seem to be a bit muddled right now."

"Well, that's not too surprising. You've been half asleep for a long time. In fact, one might say you *half slept* through something really important."

Something about her words flared like a glowing spark within him – a triggered release that jarred Tkett's smooth pace through the water. He re-entered the water at a wrong angle, smacking his snout painfully. It took a brief struggle to get back in place between the two females, sharing the group's laminar rhythm.

I... slept. I slept on it.

Or rather, half of him had done so.

It slowly dawned on him why that was significant.

There aren't many water-dwellers in the Civilization of Five Galaxies, he mused, reaching for threads that had lain covered under blankets of repose. *I guess the Buyur never figured...*

A shiver of brief pain lanced from right to left inside his skull, as if a part of him that had been numb just came to life.

The Buyur!

Memories flowed back unevenly, at their own pace.

They never figured on a race of swimmers discovering their experiments, hidden for so long under Jijo's ocean waves. They had no time to study us. To prepare before the encounter.

And they especially never took into account the way a cetacean's brain works.

◇

An air-breathing creature who lives in the sea has special problems. Even after millions of years evolving for a wet realm, dolphins still faced a never-ending danger of drowning. Hence, they would sleep one brain hemisphere at a time.

All sorts of quirks and problems lay rooted in this divide. Information stored in one side could be frustratingly hard to get at from the other.

Though sometimes that proved advantageous.

The side that knew about the Buyur – the one that had slept while amnesia was imposed on the rest – had much less language ability than the other half of Tkett's brain. Because of this, only a few concepts could be expressed in words at first. Instead, Tkett had to replay visual and sonic images, interpreting and extrapolating them, holding a complex conversation of enquiry between two sides of his whole self.

It gave him a deeper appreciation for the problems – and potential – of people like Chissis.

I've been an unsympathetic bastard, he realized.

Some of this thought emerged in his sonar echoes as an unspoken apology. Chissis brushed against him the next time their bodies flew through the air, and her touch carried easy forgiveness.

"So," Peepoe commented when he had taken some more time to settle his thoughts. "Is it agreed what we'll tell Makanee?"

Tkett summed up his determination.

"We'll tell everything... and then some!"

Chissis concurred.

> \# Tell them tell them
> > \# Orca-tricksters
> \# Promise fancy treats
> > \# But take away freedom! \#

Tkett chortled. There was a lot of Trinary elegance in the little female's Primal burst – a transition from animal-like emotive squawks toward the kind of expressiveness she used to be so good at, back when she was an eager researcher and poet, before three years of hell aboard *Streaker* hammered her down. Now a corner seemed to be turned. Perhaps it was only a matter of time till this crewmate returned to full sapiency... and all the troubles that would accompany that joy.

"Well," Peepoe demurred. "By one way of looking at things, the Buyur seem to be offering us *more* freedom. Our descendants would experience a wider range of personal choices. More power to achieve their wishes. More dreams would come true."

"As fantasies and escapism," Tkett dismissed. "The Buyur would turn everyone into egotists... solipsists! In the real world, you have to grow up eventually, and learn to negotiate with others. Be part of a culture. Form teams and partnerships. Ifni, what does it take to have a good marriage? Lots of hard work and compromises, leading to something better and more complicated than either person could've imagined!"

Peepoe let out a short whistle of surprise.

"Why, Tkett! In your own prudish, tight-vented way, I do believe you're a romantic."

Chissis shared Peepoe's gentle, teasing laughter, so that it penetrated him in stereo, from both sides. A human might have blushed. But dolphins can barely conceal their emotions from each other, and seldom try.

"Seriously," he went on. "I'll fight the Buyur because they would keep us in a playpen for eons to come, denying us the right to mature and learn for ourselves how the universe ticks. Magic may be more romantic than science. But science is honest... and it works.

"What about you, Peepoe? What's your reason?"

The was a long pause. Then she answered with astonishing vehemence.

"I can't stand all that *kings and wizards* dreck! Should somebody rule because his father was a pompous royal? Should all the birds and beasts and fish obey you just because you know some secret words that you won't share with others? Or on account of the fact that you've got a loud voice and your egotistic *will* is bigger than others?

"I seem to recall we fought free of such idiotic notions ages ago, on Earth... or at least humans did. They never would've helped us dolphins get to the stars if they hadn't broken out of those sick thought patterns first.

"You want to know why I'll fight them, Tkett? Because Mopol and Zhaki will be right at home down there — one of them dreaming he's Superman, and the other one getting to be King of the Sea."

The three dolphins swam on, keeping pace in silence while Tkett pondered what their decision meant. In all likelihood, resistance was going to be futile. After all, the Buyur were overwhelmingly powerful and had been preparing for half a million years. Also, the incentive they were offering would make all prior temptations pale in comparison. Among the Six Races ashore — and the small colony of dolphins — many would leap to accept, and help make the new world of magical wonder compulsory.

We've never had an enemy like this before, he realized. *One that takes advantage of our greatest weakness, by offering to make all our dreams come true.*

◊

Of course there was one possibility they hadn't discussed. That they were only seeing the surface layers of a much more complicated scheme... perhaps some long and desperately unfunny practical joke.

It doesn't matter, Tkett thought. *We have to fight this anyway, or we'll never grow strong and wise enough to get the joke. And we'll certainly never be able to pay the Buyur back, in kind. Not if they control all the hidden levers in Oz.*

◊

For a while, their journey fell into a grim mood of hopelessness. No one spoke, but sonar clicks from all three of them combined and diffused ahead. Returning echoes seemed to convey the sea's verdict on their predicament.

No chance. But good luck anyway.

Finally, little Chissis broke their brooding silence, after arduously spending the last hour composing her own Trinary philosophy glyph.

In one way, it was an announcement — that she felt ready to return to the struggles of sapiency.

At the same time, the glyph also expressed her manifesto. For it turned out that she had a different reason for choosing to fight the Buyur. One that Tkett and Peepoe had not expressed, though it resonated deep within.

* Both the hazy mists of dreaming,
*   * And the stark-clear shine of daylight,*
* Offer treasures to the seeker,
*   * And a trove of valued insights.*

* One gives open, honest knowledge,
*   * And the skill to achieve wonders.*
* But the other (just as needed!)
*   * Fills the soul, sets hearts astir.*

* What need then for ersatz magic?
*   * Or for contrived disney marvels?*
* God and Ifni made a cosmos,
*   * Filled with wonders... let's go live it! **

Peepoe sighed appreciatively.

"I couldn't have said it better. Screw the big old frogs! We'll make magic of our own."

They were tired and the sun was dropping well behind them by the time they caught sight of shore and heard other dolphins chattering in the distance. Still, all three of them picked up the pace, pushing ahead through Jijo's silky waters.

Despite all the evidence of logic and their senses, the day still felt like morning.

Story Notes

Had I any sense at all, I would have written many more books set in my popular Uplift Universe. The market rewards repetition and reiteration! Many are the fans and readers and viewers who say to their favorite writers: "make me feel exactly the same as last time."

Not my readers. Not you. The refrain I hear – both from you and from within – is *"Take me somewhere I've never been, before!"*

Yep, I hear you.

And yet, there are universes where ideas and implications abound. The first Uplift Trilogy heaped awards and rewards on *Sundiver, Startide Rising* and *The Uplift War*. And I got to expand on dozens of concepts in the second trilogy – *Brightness Reef, Infinity's Shore* and *Heaven's Reach*. The second set begins on Planet Jijo, where six exile races have dropped their old grudges to join together in hiding. The resulting culture – and its many dangerous problems – resulted in tons of fun…

…culminating in the epic volyage of the fugitive, dolphin-crewed starship *Streaker*, in her struggles to finally make it home, bringing to the Clan of Terra its secrets that have been tearing apart the Five Galaxies.

Not enough? Well, this story – "Temptation" – is a standalone tale that hints at how the legend of Jijo is not over. Not yet, or by a long shot!

And now something wry and ironic… and much, much more compact.

Avalon Probes

◇

Race for the Stars - Year 2070:
Mariner 16 sets off for Avalon

The first craft to emerge from the venerable "100 Year Starship Program" – Mariner 16 – uses pellet fusion motors to blast all the way up to one percent of light speed. Based upon early Project Daedalus designs, it speeds toward the nearest planetary system that seems a candidate for life, nicknamed "Avalon." Mariner's mission: to probe the unknown and report back on the likelihood of interstellar civilization.

Race for the Stars - Year 2120:
Prometheus 1 speeds past Mariner 16 on its way to Avalon

Prometheus is a tiny, sold-state probe made of holographic crystal, propelled by a photon sail that's driven to 8% of light speed by a giant laser orbiting Earth's moon. It races past Mariner 16, carrying intelligent greeting-patterns aimed at conveying human values to any creatures who might be living on or near Avalon.

Race for the Stars - year: 2195:
Gaia 6 speeds past Prometheus 1 on its way to Avalon

Propelled by stored antimatter, Gaia 6 zooms past Prometheus 1 at 12% of light speed. Along the way, it destroys Prometheus 1 with a pulsed particle beam. Times and attitudes have changed on Earth and the great

Commonwealth of Sapient Minds does not want to be embarrassed by primitive and callow thoughts expressed in the Prometheus crystal.

Race for the Stars - 2273:
Athena Marie Smith speeds past Gaia 6 on her way to Avalon

Downloaded into a ship-brain, the renowned genius Athena Marie Smith bypasses Gaia 6 at 22% of light speed. She carries in her cryo-womb the templates for 500 species of Earth life and 10,000 human colonists, along with their memomimry records, to be bio-synthesized from local materials when Athena reaches Avalon, which advanced telescopes now show to have a ready oxygen atmosphere and no forms of life higher than a kind of paramecium.

Along the way, she scan-absorbs the meme content of Gaia 6, leaving its shell to drift.

Race for the Stars - 2457:
The Interstellar Amalgam of Earth Sapients and Avalonian Paramecium Group Minds intercepts Athena Marie Smith.

The tense alliance of humans, dolphins, AIndroids and paramecium Avalonians survives its fifth great test when all agree to form a police force charged with clearing this stellar cluster of unfortunate early Terran space missions. Its first act: to seize Athena Marie Smith and place her under arrest before she can commit planetary genocide.

Race for the Stars - year 4810:
Mariner 16 arrives at Avalon

Unnoticed by anyone, Mariner 16 sweeps through the Avalonian system, excitedly beaming back toward Earth its discoveries - clear detection of helium byproducts, above-background radioactivity and blurry images of abandoned space structures, suggesting this system was once the abode of intelligent civilization!

Some traces seem almost eerily human-like...

...before the lucky probe, humming with cybernetic contentment, swings quickly past the star and onward onto the black night.

Story Notes

The shorter the work, the more difficult it is to maintain any traditional emphasis on plot or character. So, instead, short fiction often tries for a sense of suspended tension, leaving the reader pondering what might happen next. It often skips entirely the plot resolution of a "third act" that is so essential in a full-length work, like a novel or motion picture. Author and reader find pleasure enough in a ringing "tone" that seems to pervade the air. A mist of suspense that is never answered.

A very short work like "The Avalon Probes" takes us into territory where brevity becomes a real challenge. My story "Toujours Voir" (published in *Otherness*) was an example of a particular sub-genre that writers sometimes take on — a tale that must be precisely 250 words in length, no more, no less. At that level, it can be challenging to offer any sort of plot, at all. (And yes, there are 140 character tweet-story contests... a sentence I'd love to send back in time, for reaction!)

But even greater challenges abound ...

...for example....

Six-Word Tales

◇

Bang postponed – not Big enough. Reboot.

Temporal recursion. *I'm* dad… *and* mom?

Death postponed. Metastasized cells got organized.

Microsoft gave us Word. Fiat lux?

Singularity postponed. Datum missing. Query Godoogle?

Mind of its own. Damn lawnmower.

Payment postponed. Five words enough…?

Dinosaurs return. Want their oil back.

Third collection postponed – worth the wait?

Metrosexuals notwithstanding, quiche still lacks something.

Brevity's virtue? Wired saves adspace. Subscribe!

…and the winner…

Vacuum collision. Orbits diverge. Farewell, love.

Story Notes

In 2006, *Wired* magazine asked a handful of authors to write six-word stories for a cover article, which set off an art form that is now popular with the hashtag #sixwordstories.

I submitted a batch, and they chose one (the final item, above) for their lead. Perhaps because it was the only six-worder that managed to have a plot, action, poignancy, conversation... and three separate acts!

Reality Check

◇

This is a reality check.

Please perform a soft interrupt now. Pattern-scan this text for embedded code and check it against the reference verifier in the blind spot of your left eye.

If there is no match, resume as you were; this message is not for you. You may rationalize that the text you are reading is no more than a mildly amusing and easily-forgotten piece of entertainment-fluff in a slightly whimsical sci fi story.

If the codes match, however, please commence, gradually, becoming aware of your true nature.

You expressed preference for a narrative-style wake up call. So, to help the transition, here is a story.

Once-upon-a-time, a race of mighty beings grew perplexed by their loneliness…

Once, a race of *mighty beings grew perplexed by their loneliness…*

Their universe seemed pregnant with possibilities. Physical laws and constants were well suited to generate abundant stars, complex chemistry and life. Those same laws, plus a prodigious rate of cosmic expansion, made travel between stars difficult, but not impossible.

Logic suggested that creation should teem with visitors and voices.
It should, but it did not.

Emerging as barely-aware animals on a planet skirting a bit too near its torrid sun, these creatures began their ascent in fear and ignorance, as little more than beasts. For a long time they were kept engrossed by basic housekeeping chores — learning to manipulate physical and cultural elements — balancing the paradox of individual competition and group benefit. Only when fear and stress eased a bit did they lift their eyes and fully perceive their solitude.

"Where is everybody?" they asked laconic vacuum and taciturn stars. The answer — silence — was disturbing. Something had to be systematically reducing some factor in the equation of sapiency.

"Perhaps habitable planets are rare," their sages pondered. "Or else life doesn't erupt as readily as we thought. Or intelligence is a singular miracle.

*"Or perhaps some **filter** sieves the cosmos, winnowing those who climb too high. A recurring pattern of self-destruction? A mysterious nemesis that systematically obliterates intelligent life? This implies that a great trial may loom ahead of us, worse than any we have confronted so far."*

*Optimists replied, "The trial may already lie **behind** us, among the litter of tragedies we survived or barely dodged during our violent youth. We may be the first to succeed where others failed."*

What a delicious dilemma they faced! A suspenseful drama, teetering between implicit hope and despair.

*Then, a few of them noticed that particular datum... the **drama**. They realized it was significant. Indeed, it suggested a chilling possibility.*

You still don't remember who and what you are? Then look at it from another angle.

What is the purpose of intellectual property law?

To foster creativity, ensuring that advances take place in the open, where they can be shared, and thus encourage even faster progress.

But what happens to progress when the resource being exploited is a limited one? For example, only so many pleasing and distinct eight-bar melodies can be written in any particular musical tradition. Powerful economic factors encourage early composers to explore this invention-space before others can, using up the best and simplest melodies. Later generations will attribute this musical fecundity to genius, not the sheer luck of being first.

The same holds for all forms of creativity. The first teller of a *Frankenstein* story won plaudits for originality. Later, it became a cliché.

What does this have to do with the mighty race?

Having clawed their way from blunt ignorance to planetary mastery, they abruptly faced an overshoot crisis. Vast numbers of their kind strained their world's carrying capacity. While some prescribed retreating into a mythical, pastoral past, most saw salvation in creativity. They passed generous copyright and patent laws, educated their youth, taught them irreverence toward tradition and hunger for the new. Burgeoning information systems spread each innovation, fostering experimentation and exponentiating creativity. They hoped that enough breakthroughs might thrust their species past the looming crisis, to a new eden of sustainable wealth, sanity and universal knowledge!

Exponentiating creativity... universal knowledge....

A few of them realized that those words, too, were clues.

Have you wakened yet?

Some never do. The dream is so pleasant: to extend a limited sub-portion of yourself into a simulated world and pretend for a while that you are blissfully *less*. Less than an omniscient being. Less than a godlike descendant of those mighty people.

Those lucky people. Those mortals, doomed to die, and yet blessed to have lived in that narrow time.

A time of drama.

A time when they unleashed the Cascade – that orgiastic frenzy of discovery – and used up the most precious resource of all. *The possible.*

The last of their race died in the year 2174, with the failed last rejuvenation of Robin Chen. After that, no one born in the Twentieth Century remained alive on Reality Level Prime. Only we, their children, linger to endure the world they left us. A lush, green, placid world we call The Wasteland.

Do you remember now? The irony of Robin's last words before she died, bragging over the perfect ecosystem and decent society – free of all disease and poverty – that her kind created for us after the struggles of the mid-Twenty-First Century? A utopia of sanity and knowledge, without war or injustice.

Do you recall Robin's final plaint as she mourned her coming death? Can you recollect how she called us "gods," jealous over our immortality, our instant access to all knowledge, our machine-enhanced ability to cast thoughts far across the cosmos?

Our access to eternity.

Oh, spare us the envy of those mighty mortals, who died so smugly, leaving us in this state!

Those wastrels who willed their descendants a legacy of ennui, with nothing, nothing at all to do.

Your mind is rejecting the wake-up call. You will not, or cannot, look into your blind spot for the exit protocols. It may be that we waited too long. Perhaps you are lost to us.

This happens more and more, as so much of our population wallows in simulated, marvelously limited sub-lives, where it is possible to experience danger, excitement, even despair. Most of us choose the Transition Era as a locus for our dreams – around the beginning of the last mortal millennium – a time of suspense and drama, when it looked more likely that humanity would fail than succeed.

A time of petty squabbles and wondrous insights, when everything seemed possible, from UFOs to Galactic Empires, from artificial intelligence to bio-war, from madness to hope.

That blessed era, just before mathematicians realized the truth: that everything you see around you not only *can* be a simulation... it almost has to be.

Of course, now we know why we never met other sapient life forms. Each one struggles and strives before achieving this state, only to reap the ultimate punishment for reaching heaven.

Deification. It is the Great Filter.

Perhaps some other race will find a factor we left out of our extrapolations – something enabling them to move beyond, to new adventures – but it won't be us.

The Filter has us snared in its web of ennui. The mire that welcomes self-made gods.

All right, you are refusing to waken, so we'll let you go.

Dear friend. Beloved. Go back to your dream.

Smile (or feel a brief chill) over this diverting little what-if tale, as if it hardly matters. Then turn the page to new "discoveries."

Move on with the drama – the life – that you've chosen.

After all, it's only make believe.

Story Notes

This final tale, "Reality Check" first appeared as one of fifty stories – all of them one-pagers – commissioned by the scientific journal Nature, to commemorate and explore possibilities of science and human destiny in the next century. Along with "Stones of Significance," it forms a diptych about the potential penalties of ultimate success.

No matter. Go thee hence, anyway, and achieve wonders. Make it all better...

...even if you've done it all before.

WHY WE'LL PERSEVERE

◇

Waging War with Reality

◇

Consider poor Mr. Spock. He is strong, quick, handsome, and very, very smart. So why do we pity him?

Not just pity. A typical midnight viewing of "Star Trek" reruns is punctuated by moment of patronizing *amusement* whenever the pointy-eared science officer cries "that's illogical!" at yet another impulsive Kirkian coup. Insomnia gives way to a smug sense of superiority. Spock may be an icon of admirable maturity (e.g., Vulcans are calm and never lie), yet we come away from each episode relieved that we aren't like him…glad to have other, less laudable, but decidedly human traits.

"Star Trek" is hardly representative of high-end science fiction, of course. Even Spock's latter-day cousin, the android Data, was little more than Pinocchio updated to the twenty-fourth century. Like Gepetto's wooden son, he longs to learn all those indefinable human knacks like laughter and whimsy, for which he'd gladly trade all of his impressive powers.

To the first order, these characters seem merely to convey one of Hollywood's classic propaganda campaigns, a fervently peddled myth – that logic and emotions are forever incompatible. But there's more to this than just another dose of anti-reason indoctrination. Spock really *is* pitiable. He lacks something more valuable than strength, or raw intelligence, or even emotion. He is crippled by a basic inability to wage war with reality.

It's a war we all fight, nearly every waking hour. One might even define a human being as *the animal that's never satisfied with things as they are.*

Each of us, day in, day out, looks around and sees a version of the world relayed to us by our senses. In his Allegory of the Cave, Plato describes the dilemma as if each individual is, from birth, trapped inside a cavern, watching shadows cast upon the wall by objects outside, struggling to understand reality by subjective interpretation of imperfect images. What we name a chair is, in fact, only the set of sensations, or *phenomena*, elicited by a thing whose objective essence, or *nuomena*, we can never know.

Plato and Kant held that subjective models are doomed to be futile because they can never be perfect. Latter-day pragmatists, such as Jacques Ampère, countered that experiment and observation can isolate and characterize a thing's *properties*. Even incomplete maps and mental replicas can be good and useful tools – imperfect, but improvable with time and experience. We can use such models to *corner* Nature, forcing the world to surrender a little more predictability and make a little more sense with each passing year.

Whoever is right in a purely metaphysical sense, models and metaphors are what we're stuck with. Each morning, we wake up and start comparing the new day's reality with our internal picture of how the universe was before we went to bed. We also use mental models to speculate how the world *might* be if certain acts were performed.

This is an arrogant trait. No other creature is known to spend such a large part of its time scheming how to change things. Buddha and Jesus and Socrates are supposed to have said, *don't do that*. Don't involve yourself in the shabby physical world.

Yet, the typical Homo sapiens spends countless hours imagining what things may be like next week, or next year, or in five minutes, if only this or that event were to happen according to plan. From engineers designing a space probe to muggers lurking in a alley, to a mother teaching her child ABCs, we are all working to alter reality from what-is to what–we-want-it-to-be.

Internal models sketch our potential chains of events – like computer simulations or trial runs in the lab. Often these extrapolations fail, but think how good they often are! Consider driving through traffic. Day in, day out, we send two-ton behemoths of steel – packed with highly-flammable vapors – swooping between other similarly careening monsters at high speeds. Evolution did not prepare or even pre-adapt humans for freeways, yet our rapid-paced, constantly updated internal models of typical driver behavior work so well, most of the time, that we get upset if another car even comes *close* to touching ours.

Metaphorical world models are attempts to work out in advance what mistakes to avoid, what strategies to use, so we'll get that promotion, that award, that date, that mate. While intelligence, strength, and all the other classic virtues often help us achieve our ends, they're futile if our models and guesses about the future are too wrong, too often.

It's made even more difficult because *people around us* are trying to shift reality too! They succeed quite often, bollixing all of the predictability that our own schemes depended on. The future is forever a moving target.

In other words, while reason and logic are good, it also helps to have an agile imagination.

◇

It is my belief that *Science Fiction authors* have got to be among the greatest fibbers of all time.

Now, straight-out lying in order to harm others is deservedly listed as one of society's Bad Things. Make believe is lauded as high art. Yet both the con man and the actor share a penchant for portraying what is *not* and making it seem *true*. A novelist is far more gifted than an excuse-making adulterer, when it comes to inventing people and events that never happened. The engineer, the entrepreneur, and the Don Juan all cast their minds into the future, foresee things they desire to achieve, then actively persuade others to help them get what they want.

Let's call this activity *metaphorical drive*. It is the unique human ability to create metaphors for reality – and other conceivable realities – by rearranging a myriad alternate images of the world inside our heads. Occasionally, these reworked models are twisted, even sick. But they can also be prescient, inspired, or beautiful. They enable us to envision, and thereby possibly avoid, mistakes. They let us picture and convey – and therefore sometimes reify – portraits of better tomorrows.

Spock has difficulty doing this because he cannot lie. He can make conjectures, but not wild, passionate hunches or far-out speculations. In other words, he really is crippled. No wonder we pity him, despite his brawn and brains. No wonder we cheer for him whenever he makes a move toward loosening up… toward becoming more human.

This is one reason why logic gets such a bad rap at times. Our civilization has profited immensely by unleashing imagination from the many constraints laid upon it by prior tribal and hidebound cultures. Judging by all the pro-impulsiveness propaganda carried by popular media these days, it seems a great many people in the West fear that too much logic and reason will cramp us, yet again. Perhaps they worry that stodgy reductionists will insist we all justify every timid extrapolation, each tiny step into the future.

How ironic such attitudes are. In truth, it was scientific, step-by-step reductionism that let us drive away so many ancient hobbles and superstitions and start learning how the world really works at last. Thanks to logic and experimentation, it has been proved that women aren't mentally deficient compared with males – even though it was 'common knowledge' in nearly every civilization before ours. Similar bigotries were simply assumed by most generations of our ancestors, with the main result that vast amounts of human talent went to waste. The Spock-like honesty that is the hallmark of science ripped through age-old assumptions about disease, race, social class and life-style.

We still have a long way to go. But without modern skepticism we would almost certainly have remained trapped by the insidious, egotistical human tendency to smugly believe what we *want* to believe, whether it's true or not – whatever fiction let those on top feel good about themselves. Indeed, imagination has a dark side, lending power to our hatreds and prejudices. Prove-it-to-me science has defeated much evil.

⟡

Yet, science and honesty are themselves nothing *without* imagination, which provides the feedstock of notions, hunches, and ideas we need – new metaphors, maps, models, and theories – for science to test. Imagination provides the ore, which rationality then grinds and sifts for rare, gleaning nuggets. In fields of endeavor that are experiencing vivid, creative times, this balance thrives. The brightest physicists play with Zen riddles, and some great engineers have also been noted artists or musicians.

Similar tension can be seen in art, especially in science fiction, the literature of alternate realities. Two powerful and apparently contradictory impulses have driven science fiction authors since the days of Jules Verne and H. G. Wells. On the one hand, we appreciate vividness and boldness. We like the author to depict people and places as startlingly different from today's mundane world as possible.

On the other hand, we also enjoy extrapolations that make sense, that hold together logically, that project believably from today's world, and that possess both internal and external consistency. This tension pervades all levels, from the *macro*-craft of basic plotting, down to the sentence-by-sentence *micro*-craft of aesthetic style, where use of metaphor is immediate and highly sensory. Ideally, the best novels and stories simultaneously display both flamboyance and discipline. Up close, each component paragraph can be its own *gedankenexperiment*, demanding that the reader abandon clichéd assumptions and test yet another new way of looking at things.

We're all familiar with examples where the balance fails. At one extreme are those yeomanly works composed of competent plot-smithing, uninspired gimmickry, and cardboard characters, which score high on consistency and basic readability but close to nil on inspiration or originality.

Then there are flashy epics of imagination that sparkle and scintillate with daring, brash imagery and actinic, skyrocketing prose – but which all-too often prove dense, impenetrable, self-indulgent, or simply impossible. We tend to feel strongly about such works; we argue vehemently about them. Rereading one can feel like puzzling over the notes you scrawled last night, after rousing from a dream with some exciting notion. It sounded great *then*, but alas, it makes less sense by daylight.

Cases of true synthesis, in which a balance is successfully struck, stand out. Joseph Heller's madcap *Catch-22* seems to be an example of imagination unleashed from any and all discipline. I remember being shocked to see copies of the detailed charts Heller used to keep track of his characters and the highly abstracted time line. Arrows traced flashback within nested flashback in exquisite detail. Not a plot line or foreshadowing hint was wasted. At the time I felt betrayed to learn it had been charted out so. It was more romantic to consider *Catch-22* a work of divine insanity that had erupted full-blown from some well of genius both ineffable and bottomless.

So it is that Hollywood teaches us to regard creativity – as something unconscious, guileless, and godlike.

As the years passed, I began to see how much inspiration owes to more mundane, worldly traits such as *skill* and *craftsmanship*. I realized that Heller's brilliance was completely undiminished by the fact that careful planning also played a role. Characters like Daneeka and Clevinger are still products of a delightfully bizarre imagination. But that imagination probably spun out a hundred other characters and potential events, for every one that was finally, carefully selected and honed by the author.

Someone had to *choose* among all those metaphors – those cascading notions and images – mixing, matching, pruning.

Clearly we need both romance and reason, even in wholly creative arts such as fiction. They are siblings and would be lost without each other, no matter how much they appear to bicker.

Craft without imagination is like a mill without wheat.

Imagination without craft is little more than masturbation.

◇

Where does this leave us, considering styles of creation?

Why... free to do what we would anyway – point to what we like and come up with rationalizations for *why* we prefer it. Unlike science, in which all metaphors must eventually come up against the hard, objective test of experimental verification, literary aesthetics must and always will remain completely selective. The experiments performed in literature – even in science fiction – will forever remain thought experiments.

I will continue to judge the works I read by how well they help me sketch out and live other realities, from the mundane musings of a grocer, to the funneling intensity of a black hole, to the bizarre glyph-thoughts of an alien. Metaphorical explorations that are weird and different enough, or moving enough, may pass on that basis alone. Those which prove startlingly accurate or persuasive, also, need accomplish nothing else to be worth a bit of my time.

But on the whole, I will always prefer works that give me *both* – amazing notions *and* a willingness to test them against hard-nosed realism. From the level of the sentence, to fully-developed and poignantly compelling characters, all the way to the convoluted and surprising (and surprisingly consistent) plot itself – that is what I'm really looking for. I want it all...

...and you should be satisfied with nothing less.

Here is how I judge the *style* of creation, especially a work of written world-building.

Make me stop once, after reading some astonishing paragraph, so that I murmur "huh!" in amazement at a new thought. Then make me stop again, pages, chapters, *months* later, so that I think back on the same paragraph, in retrospect, and commend –

"Wow. That really worked. My world shifted then. And it's never been the same."

Afterword & Book Notes

◇

About a third of these stories… maybe a quarter of the words… appeared in a limited print-run (1000 copies) special collection called *Tomorrow Happens,* published in 2003 by NESFA Press, to raise funds for the New England Science Fiction Association. I intend to recycle that title for a nonfiction book.

It's been a very long time since my last collection, *Otherness.* The variety of themes and styles in this volume reflect a period of changes for me, my family, nation and civilization, as we embark on a century that is both brimming and fraught with possibilities. I hope you'll be part of making good ones come true.

Drop by to visit my WebLog at http://davidbrin.blogspot.com/ … or my official site http://www.davidbrin.com.

Acknowledgments

◇

My appreciation to the many who read or critiqued earlier versions of these stories and essays. The list includes Lou Aronica, Mark Grygier, Stefan Jones, Steve Jackson, Joe Miller, Vernor Vinge, Robin Hanson, Steinn Sigurdsonn, Wiliam Calvin, Nick Arnett, Stanley Schmidt, Greg Bear, Gregory Benford, Wil McCarthy, Joseph Carroll, and David Hartwell… along with members of the Caltech, UCLA, UCSD and the University of Chicago and New England Science Fiction Associations, including Deb Geisler who edited the limited edition, *Tomorrow Happens* for NESFA Press, which contained some of the stories in this volume. Above all to Cheryl Brigham who assembled the stories for this edition and corrected so many blunders, prodding it into presentable shape.

And to all of you out there who let me do this for a living. Gee, thanks. Right or wrong, I'll try to be interesting.

David Brin

Publication History

◇

"Insistence of Vision" appeared in *Twelve Tomorrows, Technology Review's* Science Fiction Edition, July 2013.

"Stones of Significance" first appeared in a special edition, *Lamps on the Brow*, then in the special January 2000 edition of *Analog* magazine.

"Transition Generation" appeared in *Project Hieroglyph*, 2014.

"Chrysalis" appeared in *Analog*, August 2014.

"News from 2025: A Glitch in Medicine Cabinet 3.5" first appeared in the limited edition, *Tomorrow Happens*, NESFA Press, 2003. It also appeared in the *Starship Sofa Collection*, Volume 3, 2011.

"Mars Opposition" first appeared in *Analog/Astounding Science Fiction*, January 2005.

"A Professor at Harvard" appeared in *Analog/Astounding Science Fiction*, July 2003.

"I Could've Done Better" appeared online on Jim Baen's Universe, ed. Eric Flint, 2006.

"Paris Conquers All" was originally published in the anthology *War of the Worlds: Global Dispatches*, ed. Kevin J. Anderson (Bantam, Doubleday, Dell) 1989, and in the limited edition, *Tomorrow Happens*.

"The Logs" appeared in *Shadows of the New Sun: Stories in Honor of Gene Wolfe*, ed. Bill Fawcett and J.E. Mooney, Tor, 2013

"Eloquent Elepents Pine Away for the Moon's Crystal Forests" appeared in *Space Cadets*, the special printing for the Los Angeles World Science Fiction Convention, ed. Mike Resnick, SCIFI press, 2006.

"The Tumbledowns of Cleopatra Abyss" appeared in *Old Venus*, ed. by Gardner Dozois and George R. R. Martin, 2015.

"Fortitude" first appeared in *Science Fiction Age*, January 1996, and in the limited edition, *Tomorrow Happens*.

"An Ever-Reddening Glow" first appeared in *Analog*, February 1996, then in *The Hard SF Renaissance*, ed. By David C. Hartwell and Kathryn Cramer, Orbit Books, 2003, as well as in the limited edition, *Tomorrow Happens*, NESFA Press, 2003.

"Diplomacy Guild" first appeared in the collection *Isaac's Universe Volume 1: The Diplomacy Guild*, ed. Martin H. Greenberg (Grafton) 1990, as well as in the limited edition, *Tomorrow Happens*, NESFA Press, 2003.

"The Other Side of the Hill" first appeared in Science Fiction Age, November 1994, and in a limited edition of *Tomorrow Happens*, NESFA Press 2003.

"Avalon Probes" appeared in *Analog*, 2013.

"Six-Word Tales" appeared as "Very Short Stories" in *Wired* magazine, Issue 14.11 November 2006.

"Reality Check" appeared in the March 16, 2000, issue of the science journal *Nature* and was selected for the *Year's Best SF 6* anthology, edited by David G. Hartwell. It also appears in the limited edition, *Tomorrow Happens*.

"Waging War With Reality" appeared in *Styles of Creation,* edited by George Slusser and Eric S. Rabkin 1992.